S

Amy Licence

First published 2017 by Endeavour Press Ltd.

For Tom, Rufus and Robin.

Now is the winter of our discontent
Made glorious summer by this sun of York

(*Richard III,* Shakespeare)

Table of Contents

Foreword

In 1455, England was languishing under the rule of a weak and unstable king. The Lancastrian Henry VI had inherited the throne as a baby on the death of his father but, unlike the martial Henry V, national hero and victor of Agincourt, the boy grew up to be peace-loving and pious, more suited to the monastery than the council chamber. By the age of thirty-three, King Henry was being manipulated by a powerful court faction, centred around his unpopular French wife, Queen Margaret.

Deep divisions opened in the realm, which descended into lawlessness and political infighting. Henry survived a large-scale uprising in the south-east under the rebel leader Jack Cade, but his own health was to prove a far more challenging obstacle. One hot summer day, he fell into a coma, unable to speak, move or feed himself, lying immobile in bed while the queen gave birth to a son. Surgeons, physicians, astronomers and astrologers were summoned to court but none could diagnose the cause or say whether Henry would recover. Nobody wanted a repeat of the long minority that came with an infant king, so the Protectorate was handed over to a senior nobleman, Richard, Duke of York, the king's capable and ambitious cousin, himself a great, great, great-grandson of Edward III.

After eighteen months of illness, the king recovered sufficiently to be able to recognise his young son, but the seeds of doubt had been planted. England began to fracture along family lines, torn between those who remained loyal to the Lancastrians and those who favoured York. In addition, while the king's marriage had only produced one child in a decade, the duke was already the father of a clutch of sons, headed by the thirteen-year-old Edward, Earl of March. Still professing his loyalty to the crown, York put aside his senior Plantagenet descent and swore that his only intent was to serve his king and protect him from divisive influences. For many in the queen's faction though, he was now too dangerous a figure to be allowed to live. The stage was set for civil war.

ONE: The Blade in the Darkness, May, 1455

A boy stood up from under the trees. He was nine or ten, stockily built. His jaw was still soft from childhood but his limbs were awkward with new growth. Narrowing his dark eyes, he strained to see through the falling darkness.

'Alan, get down.'

The voice from the weeds was harsh, unforgiving. The boy teetered briefly before a rough hand dragged him back down to earth, out of sight. He smelled fungus, rotting fruit, as the dark mass of his brother moved in and eclipsed all.

'They will see you,' he hissed. 'And you don't want that, do you?'

The grey face before him was all teeth and broken nose. Cruelty shone in its eyes.

The younger boy tried to reply with a laugh. 'Of course not.'

'Because that would spoil the fun. And if my fun was spoiled, I would get angry. And if I got angry, I might want to do something about it.'

The weeds around them trembled.

'But Rick…'

'And when you were asleep, I might take my knife and press it to your throat and make a little cut. You wouldn't feel it but your life would slowly drain away and…'

Something metallic glinted in the shade between them.

The younger boy's jaw trembled. 'What are you planning to do?'

His brother grinned: the terrible grin of a boy on the verge of manhood, dizzy with the new power he can wield and the stench of death on his hands.

'To them?' Rick's breath was hot, sickly. His mouth pressed close against his brother's ear and his voice was ominously low. 'Why, teach them a lesson, of course. I'm sick of their puny whining and their pretty-boy faces. Sick of the sons of York, sons of the traitor.' He ran his finger along the edge of the blade. 'I'd like to cut a slice off their fat cheeks and roast it over their own fire.'

And for the younger boy, that darkened spot of trees and weeds suddenly seemed hot with the fires of hell and all the avenging angels. He tried to stammer out some words of reservation but his brother's head snapped to one side.

'They're coming!'

At once the trees fell silent. The wind breathed through the leaves with a sort of pulse. They waited.

*

Edward glanced over his shoulder to check that his brother Edmund was still trailing behind him. They must hurry if they were to reach the castle before the fall of darkness, to cross this low green cradle of fields where the shadows seemed to pool and dim. Night was following closely upon their heels, snapping and urgent. They should not be out at this hour and they both knew it. Edward flinched at the thought of their father's almoner, with his lazy eyes and cruel mouth, praying he had not missed them. His new jerkin chafed his neck: his clothes were well made, cut from expensive fabric, he could not fault the man there, but Richard Croft's mind was too inflexible. And his sons were idiots.

Edmund came out from behind the bushes, his longbow slung across his boyish shoulders, its strings still warm from the pull of his fingertips. Like Edward, he wore a slim quiver of arrows across his back. His aim was definitely improving: just minutes ago they had been whooping in delight as he had hit the target again, two boys in the middle of the lane with the swallows swooping low overhead. The castle, Croft, lessons and dinner, even father, had all been forgotten in the moment. The early summer evening had slipped away from them while they were engrossed in their sport.

Edward paused to wait for his brother to catch up. He had walked at a swifter pace. His limbs were lean but powerful, a natural athlete, they moved with an easy rhythm that suggested speed and resilience, from long childhood summers spent running and riding, swinging from the branches of trees, swimming in rivers and laughing in delight at the cool water sliding over his skin. He was the sort of child who dives headlong into the water while his jealous friends dip in their toes, shivering in their fears and inhibitions. The weeds in the lane did not repress Edward, he did not see phantoms and assassins behind every tree like Edmund did. Edward was already tall for his age, coltish but well proportioned. His hazel eyes cast about from right to left, seeking the swiftest route or expecting to see it open up before them. It would seem perfectly natural to him, for the brambles to part at his approach.

For he was thirteen now. His birthday had fallen a week ago, long enough for him to wear his new age comfortably but still so fresh as to be a novelty. And thirteen years old, thought Edward Plantagenet, was so much more than the restraints of twelve, a definite remove from eleven and so far advanced from ten, that those childish years seemed as distant as winter on a hot summer's day. Thirteen would soon be fourteen: it was certainty, majesty, authority, with one foot in the arena of manhood. Thirteen was promise and pleasure. It was as good as near anything a boy might wish to be, hurrying back home to a hot dinner and a warm bed.

His brother was swept along with him, running every other pace to remain by his side. Edmund was shorter, slighter, at eleven years old; almost twelve, almost, almost. For the 'almost' infinitely mattered; he was almost as tall, almost as old, almost as strong; he proudly inhabited the space Edward had immediately vacated. His brother went before him like a God through the long twilight grass and Edmund planted his feet in those footsteps. He stepped over the furze before it sprang back up, his arms catching branches bent in their wake. Otherwise, they were physically similar. Both had thick, abundant sandy coloured hair, tousled from play fighting and adventures. Their faces were open, honest, with warm, sensitive eyes, quick to betray their emotions. The mouths were wide and generous, the lips full and finely modelled but they were still the faces of children. Something had yet to resolve in them before they took on the cast of men. And Edmund was perhaps a more ethereal character, his eyes given to contemplation, his expression suggestive of a thinker. While Edward battled his way through the physical world, Edmund was dreaming of knights and romances, jousting and chivalry, of the efforts of the tiny beetle to ascend the huge stalk or the trials of birds weaving twigs to build their nests. Yet suddenly, he was aware of the moment, bringing him back into the present. Something had shifted in his brother's gait.

'There's someone ahead, keep close.'

Edward's whisper scarcely rose above the rustle of the wind through the trees. For a second, all was still. The scene stretched out before them, with the irregular green and brown fields, the overgrown track and ahead, the stone bridge crossing the River Teme. Above, a sliver of cold moon had risen behind the castle battlements. A faint breeze blew the night into their faces, touched with the acrid tang of smoke rising from the town. They could almost hear the earth breathe.

Then came the sound of crashing; close, loud, violent, as a large creature burst through the undergrowth. Out of the darkness came violent hands, feet, claws, the rapid movement of limbs and a futile struggle. Edward was grabbed roughly on both sides and fell to his knees, arms pinned behind him amid shouts of triumph. The grass suddenly rose before his eyes, followed by a pair of dirty boots. He felt pain impact against his shoulder and his body folded in self-protection. His attacker glowered down, eyes bulging with advantage, mouth gasping wetly.

It was the Croft brothers, sons of the castle almoner. The idiots. Sometimes they were forced to train together in the field, at jousting, or ride in uncomfortable silence, after the hart. At fifteen, Rick should have moved on, into the adult world, yet he was simple and could make nothing but mistakes and his mind ran only on cruelty and pain. In disgust, Edward pulled away, turning to see Edmund being held by Alan, the lump-like child who had not yet learned to keep his balance in the saddle. The Crofts had the advantage of surprise, as an owl might bring down an unsuspecting falcon. Yet it was their only advantage.

'Walked right into our trap,' Rick leered, tall, solid and demonic. 'Right into our trap.'

'What do you want, Croft? Unhand us.'

The answering laugh was shrill with Rick's surprise at his own victory.

'Just a bit of sport. We all like a bit of sport, don't we?' He spotted Edward's bow, which had fallen onto the rutted track. 'Been playing at soldiers again?'

By now Edward was composed. The pain was fading. He caught Edmund's eye and some silent communication passed between them.

'I'll have you beaten for this.'

'Really?' The ugly mouth came back into focus, reeking and hot. 'They'll have to find you first, my Lords.'

The last was delivered with a biting sarcasm, unbearable to a proud boy with an innate sense of justice. Edward balled all his power into a fist and propelled it upwards, into his assailant's belly. Rick grunted and stumbled but if nothing else, he was strong and grabbed Edward's ankle as he turned, bringing him crashing down again.

'Wrong move. Silly little boy.'

But in that moment, Edmund broke free from Alan, whose arms were left waving windmills in the air, and launched himself against their larger assailant. For a moment, power hung in the balance. Edmund's fists flew quickly and Rick splayed open in defence but it was the battle of a fifteen-year-old against that of a child and, before Edward could turn and leap forward to intervene, Rick had raised his cruel fist and brought it down with brute force. The knuckles connected with Edmund's nose. He fell back, with a dark line of blood streaking his lips and chin. It was the spur his brother needed. Rising out of the foliage, Edward appeared taller, broader, older. A natural nobility sat in his brow.

'You will pay for this, Croft.'

Edward stepped forward, his face leaving no doubt of his impending triumph. They stood, eye to eye, an arched, thickset animal against an upright son of York. It was a test of audacity, of bravery, which Edward would always win. But then, Rick's arm moved slowly behind his back. His breath came in short bursts of ecstasy, as his fingers closed upon cold steel.

'Rick, no!'

Alan's cry shattered the moment. Edward understood at once, kicked out his booted foot and the concealed blade flew into the grass. Edmund reached over and claimed it, holding the dagger up to shine in the moonlight. It was an ugly, squat, cheap little weapon, previously used to gut fish and slit the throats of pigs at Martinmas. All eyes were drawn to it.

Slowly Edward turned back. 'A knife? Really?'

Stripped of his weapon, Rick's face became querulous. 'It was just to scare you.'

'I could have you dragged before my father's court for this. You'd be flogged until the blood flowed.'

He drew closer, filling the space around the bully, leaving him no hiding place. Edmund scrambled to his side, the dagger dancing keenly between his fingers. Their shoulders squared together. Authority spoke through them.

'But that won't be necessary, will it Rick? Because from this day, you will never cast your filthy gaze on us again. You will move out of the way when we pass by and, if we want to take a piss, you will offer us your boot. Do you understand?'

Rick bridled under the yoke. A kick to the shins sent him to his knees.

'Do you understand?'

'Yes!'

'Yes, my Lord. Say it.'

'Yes, my Lord.'

'We are the sons of the Duke of York. Never forget it.'

And Edward broke away, walking with a slow, deliberate dignity towards the path. Edmund was at his side, head held high as the blood on his lips congealed. The two figures left cowering in the grass made no move to follow them.

'Don't turn round,' Edward whispered to his brother.

'Won't they...'

'No. Just don't turn round, brazen it out. It's a show. Never turn round.'

They walked on, anticipating the blows to their vulnerable backs, past the trees to the river and across the bridge. The Crofts were out of sight. Then, the adrenaline rushed out of Edward's lungs and they were children again, exhilarated and triumphant, late for dinner.

'How is your nose? Anything broken?'

'I don't think so.'

'We'd better run the last bit, to make it to the hall in time. Don't mention this, it'll only cause a fuss. No one need know and all will be well.'

Edmund nodded. 'We fight our own battles.'

And they broke into a run, two darting figures scaling up the dark slopes towards the castle walls.

TWO: The Duke of York

A midday smokiness settled over Ludlow Castle. It was the hour of short shadows, of dogs dozing in the sun and the slow bubble of pots on stoves. Censers swung in the chapel, filling the lungs of those at prayer with the scent of Catholicism, while just outside, chickens strutted and clucked in search of grain. The river ran clear and green. Fish lay still in the dappled shallows, waiting until the women had finished pulping their laundry clean.

Within the thick castle walls, the time had come for Latin prayers to be translated, a time for concentration and for lazily tracing a finger down the window pane. Edmund's eyes were drawn outside, to the distant jumbled of roofs in the town, through their smoke rising to the clouds and into the flight path of a lone bird.

Edward looked up from his books. 'What is it? You're restless today.'

His brother sighed, drawing his knees up to his chest.

'You're not still worrying about the Crofts?' Edward darted a glance to the closet, where their tutor was writing letters. 'Because we won't have any more trouble from them.'

'No, not the Crofts.'

'What then?' He crossed the room and peered outside. 'Perhaps we should make a trip into town on market day, get out of here for a bit.'

'Will we go to court again?'

'Probably not. Father isn't needed now the king is better.'

'What was wrong with him?'

Edward shrugged. 'The physicians couldn't say. Some sort of fainting sickness or madness, so that he couldn't feed himself or recognise his friends, only lie on his back in bed. He was like that for months.'

'How terrible.' Edmund's mouth softened. 'A sort of death-in-life. Poor man.'

'Poor country! A country without a king, like a ship with no one at the helm. That's why they needed father to step in, and why they despise him now.'

'So we are not welcome there?'

'Father proved to be a better ruler than that feeble Henry and they know it.'

Edmund nodded at the family mantra. 'I know.'

The old man in the closet looked up from his writing and the boys pretended to bend their heads over their books. It was a long time before Edmund spoke again, his voice soft.

'I want to explore. To see the world, to visit the places we read about, the pope in Rome and the Holy Lands, even just to see spices growing on trees.'

Edward laughed, then saw his brother was serious. 'Spices and popes? What have you been reading? You're feeling hemmed in here, tied to one place?'

'I don't know, I love this place, perhaps it's just impatience with the slowness of things. Sometimes it feels as if we just sit out the days, waiting, learning these endless lessons. That we just eat and sleep. Do you never feel that?'

His brother thought of the pulse in his veins on waking, of the strength of his limbs and the sheer bodily delight of action and reaction, of meals to anticipate and hot fires, of warm refreshing sleep and the thrill of the hunt. For him, the present moment was everything. He was a child who lived physically, whose experiences were tactile and energising, of the five senses, bones, tongue and teeth. His eyes were drawn by girls with baskets, crossing the outer bailey.

'Why don't we plan a joust, invite some of the local families? That will give you something to think about.'

'Perhaps.'

'And we'll all be together again at Fotheringhay soon.'

From somewhere outside, a horn blasted. Pigeons rose in a cloud. The gatehouse ahead swarmed with movement and a man on horseback broke through. They recognised him at the same time and the world was suddenly transformed.

Edward was already heading for the staircase. 'It's father!'

'Wait. Should we tell him, about last night?'

The older boy shrugged, his lips already tempted to form the curve of a confession, to spill out the incident in the evening lane and see the wrath of justice descend. There was an undeniable attraction in the sharing of news. He pictured the warm fatherly hand on his shoulder, imparting the weight of government, legislation and a sense of the wider world, green and fertile, stacked up behind. It would be a comfort indeed, to slip back under the blanket of childhood and let father lift the weight of the memory. No doubt the hated Croft and his sons would be sent packing. But it was impossible.

Edward's young head teemed with the imprint of his ancestors, the boldness of John of Gaunt, the might of Edward III, of men steaming from the battlefield and fighting with words in the council chamber. Whatever the future might hold, he knew where he had come from.

'No, I've dealt with it. Father doesn't need our troubles added to his.'

Edmund accepted this, trusting that the right decision had been made. The sound of activity on the floor below sent them galloping down the spiral stairs as fast as they dared go.

*

In the centre of the room stood Richard Plantagenet, Duke of York. He was a wiry, dark-haired man in his mid-forties, his lean face and peppery beard seasoned by campaigns in France and Ireland. He was not a tall man but somehow his energy gave the impression of great height. In a state of perpetual readiness, his every muscle seemed alive and taut, ready to spring. His head was held high with an attractive blend of ease and control, of quiet entitlement but not arrogance, as though the rest of the world was simply a natural extension of himself, as much his own limbs as his arms and legs were. And those hands, powerful and broad, could command fleets and armies, loyalty and love, as well as instilling fear into his enemies.

His sons stumbled into the room but fell immediately on bended knee at the sight of him. He waited, pleased at their display of deference, a smile playing about his lips, knowing that they were bursting to speak. Anything might have happened in the weeks since they last saw each other. Edmund broke first.

'What has happened? Is all well?'

York let out a laugh. 'Come, boys, come to me, let me touch you, to see that these two fine young men are not phantoms.'

They ran to him, each one embraced under a strong arm. The familiar tang of leather and sweat stirred them to memories of other places, other people.

'Indeed, all's well with the world at this moment. And with you?'

'All's well here too, father,' replied Edward. 'We go about our books and our training, the days pass.'

York ruffled his sandy hair. 'As I knew you would, my boy, as I knew you would. I have ridden miles this morning and must eat, so let's sit and talk. Is this your dinner hour? Close enough, I should think.'

He called into the doorway. 'Bring food and wine, stoke the fire, bring linen and cloths, we'll dine here, at once.'

This energy broke the soporific spell and, at once, men in blue livery moved silently and swiftly to light more candles, replenish the fire and hurry down to the kitchens. They ate quickly out of habit, from the plates of baked meats and pies laid before them.

'So you've been to Fotheringhay?' Edmund finally asked, satisfying his appetite before the others.

'I left there on Monday. Your mother is tired, that's to be expected, but the younger ones are thriving and she has your sisters for company. The surgeon has bled her and she is content enough for one in her condition. The child has quickened and moves well; she believes it will be another son. She has sent me a letter for you both, here.'

York untucked a slim folded packet from inside his clothing; Edmund took it at once, snapped the seal and began to read.

Edward watched his father carefully. 'So why are you not at court?'

York smiled and drained his cup. 'Court is not a prison, not yet at least. A man may still come and go.'

'And the king, he is really restored to health?'

'His wits have returned so he no longer has need of me. For how long, I do not know. He has his wife and her lackey.'

'The Duke of Somerset?'

'The very same.' His face darkened.

Edward nodded, piecing together his limited knowledge of the Lancastrian royal family and their followers. Since Henry VI had recovered, his French wife and her favourite were in a position of strength again, their hatred of the house of York burning with a greater intensity.

'But why do they hate us so much?'

York laid a hand on his elder son's shoulder. 'The enmity goes back years, but of late, Somerset has mismanaged things in France. He did not

20

appreciate it when I tried to call him to account. He has the king's ear and he fills it with poison.'

'Is he dangerous?'

York's jaw tautened. 'As much as I am to him.'

'Oh! Mother writes that Richard has had his first taste in the saddle,' smiled Edmund, looking up from the letter he was reading. 'He hung onto old Fetlock all the way across the field to the butts, then slid off over his head, clinging to the reins until Georgie lifted him down.'

'So what now?' Edward asked his father softly. 'Will they send you back to Ireland?'

'No, I must be close to London. The situation is volatile. I do not know which way Somerset will jump next.'

'He plans to retaliate?'

York nodded. 'As Protector I could keep him out of the way, but now the king no longer needs me, he is after my blood. As soon as Henry recovered he released him from the tower but this time I have the support of the Earl of Warwick, so perhaps together, we might defeat him.'

'And the queen?'

'Loathes me.' He gave a small, wry laugh.

'And Exeter?'

Their father's face darkened again. The Duke of Exeter had been married to their eldest sister Anne when she was only a girl but that had not prevented him from rebelling against the family. York had managed to curb some of his violent excesses and place him under lock and key at Pontefract Castle.

'He has been freed.' York shook his head in disgust. 'And I have been relieved of my Captaincy of Calais, in favour of Somerset.'

'Not again! The man is the very devil!'

'He may well be, Edward, he may well be.'

'Oh, but Georgie has had a fever!' exclaimed Edmund, reading further down the page. 'Mother writes that he has been confined to bed with stomach pains and sweats these past three days and only now begins to recover. Did you see him father? It was a fever that took William, wasn't it?'

York turned to him. 'Don't be anxious over George, either of you. He has colour in his cheeks and is eating well; he'd eaten a little chicken and pudding when I left him and will soon be up and about again. In fact, he and Richard are probably already making mischief in the garden as we speak.'

'And mother writes that Elizabeth and Margaret have quarrelled again.'

'Now that I cannot remedy,' nodded York, leaning closer to his elder son and lowering his voice. 'I have more, for your ears, later.'

Wiping his mouth, he rose from his chair. 'Let's walk down to the stables, my men have brought new horses for you.'

*

Outside, Edmund ran ahead to see the pair of white stallions being rubbed down and watered after their journey. In the middle of the green bailey, with the crows circling above, York paused and looked about to check who was within earshot. A sense of urgency came into his brown eyes.

'I must speak to you only, Edward. The political situation has changed.'

At once the boy was all attention. 'How so?'

'The queen has summoned a meeting of the Great Council to Leicester.'

He looked over to where Edmund was running his hand gently over the mane of one of the powerful beasts.

'If we attend, we will almost certainly be arrested. Reliable sources tell me they are questioning my loyalty. There is no choice but to fight, so we have been assembling troops on the Welsh border; that is why I am in the area. We have three thousand men camped in the hills.'

Edward felt a thrill of excitement. 'A battle? A real battle?'

'It seems that it must be so, but listen, listen well. I have little time. If we raise our standard against the king and lose, we shall all suffer. You are my eldest son. If I am killed...'

'You will not be!'

'Listen. If I am killed, you will head the family. Trust no one, only put yourself into the Earl of Warwick's hands and he will guide you until you come of age. You may even have to flee, to Ireland or abroad, until the country settles or there is some other change. The horses I brought are strong and fast; handle them and get used to them but do not tire them out, so they are ready.'

The boy was silent, absorbing this.

'You understand?'

'Yes, father.'

'You must be prepared to go with Warwick at any moment; I will speak with your tutor so he may make the arrangements. Edmund need not know until necessary and your mother and the little ones will be safe at Fotheringhay. The king will be lenient with them and the queen will remember her former friendship with your mother.'

'Of course. What will happen?'

'If we win, I shall keep my life and liberty. I would not choose this path but the queen leaves me little choice.' He put his hand on Edward's hand. 'Don't worry; I shall appeal to the king. In spite of everything, he's not an unintelligent man; he's deeply devout and would prefer not to see bloodshed; this may still be settled with words, not blows.'

'Are you afraid?'

'It is mortal to doubt but only the weak man allows it to overcome him. Fear can lose battles. We must trust in the Lord.'

Edward nodded in recognition.

'Let's join Edmund. I must be on my way soon, as I plan to meet with Warwick before sunset. Remember what I have told you; be wise and secret in your counsel but when you act, be decisive and do not waver.'

'I shall never forget it.'

And York was again all smiles, crossing the yard in strides, catching the sunlight in his greying hair. He beckoned Edmund from the stables, where the boy was all admiration for the magnificent horses, measuring their height and strength, anticipating their speed and stamina. Edward hung back and watched them, stirred by the sense that he was moving from his brother's world into one of which he had previously only dreamed.

THREE: First Blood

England woke to a cold grey dawn. In the fields, colours slowly clarified as fingers of light moved in from the east. Rabbits lopped through hedgerows and birds sang. Cows lifted their heads into the mist, tongues lolling, as women's fingers searched for the soft fullness of their udders.

The routines and rhythms of life began again, of fire and water, death and life. As the sun climbed higher, it threw light onto the forms of men massing among the greenery, rising, assembling, moving in a single body. It caught the blade of an axe, the curve of a bow. Along the lanes echoed the earth-rumbling of marching feet.

In the little market town of St Albans, the first fires were being lit. Children yawned and stretched in bed and shutters were opened. A lone cart rumbled through the marketplace, carrying animal feed. The driver was sleepy, rubbing his eyes as he urged his horse forward. Someone called to him from a window and a hand waved down, a cheery voice called a greeting. He pulled on the reins to steer away from the deep verge ahead, tilting the cart, then swerving back to balance again. But the end of the street looked strange. He blinked. And then, a few hundred yards away, he became aware of a mass of life, hundreds of men, waiting quietly in the gloom, watching the road ahead. Suddenly he was awake. Snapping the reins down on his horse's back, he turned in a wide curve, cold with fear, bolting back along the road he had come.

'We are under attack,' he cried, softly at first. Then his voice grew louder as the image began to sink in; swords, axes, spears. 'Get out to the fields, lock your houses up, we are under attack.'

A woman spinning at her wheel heard him; a girl drawing water at the well looked up and dropped her bucket.

'We are under attack,' he repeated, before slipping from his cart and crashing to the cobbles. For there, under the overhanging eaves of the houses, another wall of men was creeping slowly into the heart of the town, a long chain of figures bent on death. And one among their number bore a flag, a stripe of green and white with the image of a red dragon. It was the standard of the king.

*

Geese were cackling below the window. Edward looked across to where his brother lay sleeping, hair tousled and one arm flung up behind his head. Once or twice in the night he had cried out, in the throes of some nightmare or wrestling with some demon. Now he looked at peace. It would be better to let him sleep.

Edward slipped out of bed and pulled on his shirt and braies. It had not been an easy night for him either, with the early morning hours bringing troublesome questions and fears. He knew of old that the dark hours before the dawn were the worst but, once the first bird had sung, hope had been born anew. Now, as he stretched his aching limbs, his father's words returned to him along with his familiar face; the dark eyes, and his warnings for the future. In the stillness of the rumpled bed sheets, it was hard to picture men locked together in battle, blood-drenched and gasping. Yet this might be the hour, this might be the moment. It might even be over already, with the day won or lost. A messenger could be riding this way right now, crossing the countryside with the fatal news. The realisation gripped Edward's stomach and he looked about with new eyes. Ludlow had been his home for so long; was he to leave these friendly walls behind forever?

He hurried outside, across the green space and into the chapel. The almoner, Croft was already there, his thin lips devoutly pursed. His two sons, Rick and Alan, stood on either side of him, watching Edward with sullen eyes. Croft nodded curtly to acknowledge his employer's son. Edward passed them and joined his old tutor, Peter, who was already at prayer, on bended knee before the shimmering altar. The carved silver cross and marble faces of the saints looked down benevolently, as they had each morning, noon and night for decades. The silence was so complete Edward could feel it pressing in on him on all sides, enfolding him in its safety. Not even the eyes of the Croft brothers could burn a hole in his back that day. Surely all would be well? Lifting his head, he met the carved eyes of the Virgin, cradling her child.

As Edward walked out into the daylight, Peter drew alongside him. He had served his charges since they were small boys, knew their moods and characters well. His kind grey eyes spoke of his knowledge and concern.

'You are thinking of your father?'

Edward winced. 'I am that transparent?'

'No, but it is a time of change, of great danger to the family. I would be surprised if you were not.'

'He has told you?'

'A little. Enough that I may be of use to you, if the time comes.'

The boy sighed. 'My mind runs on it incessantly. Not knowing is the worst. I wish I could be there with him, instead of here doing my lessons.'

'There is nothing you can do except wait and pray. You must trust in your father and in God.'

'I know.'

Croft and his sons emerged from the church, the almoner sweeping the courtyard with his acid stare. Then he gathered his sons close and appeared to be giving them instructions.

'No one else here knows?'

'No,' said Peter. 'No one else. Not Croft.'

Edward nodded. 'I don't trust him.'

'Forget him,' said Peter. 'He does not deserve your thoughts. Today, think of your duty and your family. I know you are afraid.'

Edward pursed his lips, refusing to acknowledge what Peter had intuited.

'Remember this is not the first time your father has fronted an army,' the old man went on. 'You were born in Rouen whilst your father was fighting the French. Do you remember anything of those days?'

The old family legends resurfaced, retold to the York children from an early age. To Edward it was a tale of wide, white skies, an old cathedral, leaning buildings. He had an image of his mother hurrying, looking worried; he heard the sound of a baby crying. 'Sometimes I think I remember.'

'You must have been three or four when you left. Edmund and Elizabeth had been born by then. It was soon after your return that the lieutenancy went to Somerset for the first time. Your father took it as a slight, part of this constant campaign to keep him from his rights; nor is it the first time he has marched against the king. You were only a boy at the time, you would not have known.'

Edward turned to him, his hazel eyes afire. 'Tell me.'

Peter's white head nodded. They reached the castle wall and he leaned against the step. The Crofts were heading off towards the stables. 'It was in the wake of the rebellion led by Jack Cade. Your father was in Ireland at the time but rumours flew about the country, blaming him for anything that went wrong. Some of the rebels even rose in his name, calling for the removal of Somerset but the king refused to listen.'

'So he marched against him? Did they fight?'

'London was in chaos and Somerset retreated to the tower for his own safety. Two years later your father tried again; he marched to Blackheath but the gates of the capital were locked against him and Somerset and the king tricked him into a false, shameful truce.'

'I remember it well, I was a boy of ten and all set to lead an army south myself to help father, before mother put a stop to it.'

'She was wise to do so; brave as you were, you would have ended up getting killed.'

But Edward's mind was already racing ahead. 'What has changed now?'

Peter frowned. The boy was quick. 'Now your father has Warwick at his side and the earl's father, Salisbury. Together they might accomplish much.'

'But if he loses?'

'How your mind runs on extremes! Do not think of it yet. Until we hear otherwise, we will assume he has won. Then, if the worst comes to pass, all is in readiness for the flight; we will go to Ireland, to the Mortimer estates in Dublin; your father has loyal friends there. But it will not happen so, I am certain.'

Richard Croft was heading towards the great gatehouse that gave out onto the town marketplace. Edward watched as he drew out his chain of keys.

'The gates are locked at this time of day?'

'Just a precaution. I have told him there are beggars in the town.'

Edward nodded, his mind running on battles of his own.

Peter clasped a hand on his shoulder. 'Let us go and breakfast now, there is no point pining away whilst we wait.'

The proud boy's eyes burned into the doorway where Croft had disappeared. If he could do nothing else, he would win his own victory today.

The Duke of York squinted into the sun. The narrow street ahead lay empty, with every house silent. The shutters were drawn across the windows and the doors were bolted fast. A mosaic of rooftops showed the direction of the main street, leading to the abbey and the marketplace. Somewhere below them was the king, Henry VI, his face drawn with displeasure as he tried to understand how events had brought him to this point. His pale eyes would be searching the skies in confusion, seeking answers that would do little to allay the political situation, whilst his advisers whispered into his ears. Despite everything, the duke could not help but pity him.

For Henry himself was hardly to blame. Fortune had placed him on the throne but not fashioned him to rule, filling him instead with a gentle nature and mildness more suited to the cloister than the court. It was hard not to measure him against the might of his father, the heroic Henry V, athlete, diplomat and victor of Agincourt. Such a man might have ruled England unchallenged for decades, stayed rebellion with his fearsome eye or a stern word of command. He would have bound east and west, north and south, straddling the country as a Lancastrian giant, making its green forests and mudded roads peaceful. But his early death had handed his throne to a nine-month baby. Young Henry had grown up being dominated by his uncles, his favourites and now, his French wife.

A movement further down the road caught the duke's keen eye. Someone was approaching under the house eaves, head bowed, walking in haste. With a quick gesture, he had archers training their bows at the form, ready to loosen their arrows in defence.

'Don't shoot! A message, a message!'

The bows lowered. A boy, panting and wide-eyed handed over a folded paper. York unravelled it at once, seeking the king's signature. He did not find it; instead there were threats, rebuttals, objections; Henry would not hand over the Duke of Somerset who threatened York's position, nor would he agree to name York as the king's heir. The final words stung: there would be no negotiations with traitors. The paper crumpled in his fist and with it, all hopes that the day would end peacefully.

The Duke of York turned to his waiting men, his eyes steeled in determination. They massed in the road behind him, ten or twelve deep.

'Our terms have been refused. Today, we must fight in order to protect our king from the influence of the ambitious and corrupt Somerset, who seeks to usurp the true line of succession and have me removed. We must defeat him or die in the attempt. The odds are on our side; the king's forces are but small and he awaits reinforcements that our scouts tell us are still many miles off. Warwick waits in the outlying fields with his forces, ready to act as soon as he receives word. They scarcely expect us to attack; our victory lies in the element of surprise. The moment is now, we must seize it. In the name of the king, of St George and for the true English line, the Mortimers, and for the honour of the house of York!'

He thrust his sword skyward and the blade glinted in the sun.

'For the honour of the house of York!' cried his men, their arms echoing his own.

*

It was quiet in the stables. Horses moved softly and gently in the half-light, drawing their hooves through straw with the grace of immense, controlled strength. Edward breathed in the stuffy air, acrid with the tang of dung. The world seemed different this morning, sharper and more real, as if childhood had already begun to recede. He could hear the rats scuffling in the corners.

An uneven shape appeared in the doorway. The air darkened. Concealed in the stalls, Edward watched Rick Croft approach, his face a snarl, thick throat pulsing with his short breath. It was almost too easy, knowing his daily routine, as simple as tempting a dog out of its kennel with a scrap of meat. He watched as Croft grappled with a bag of oats under his arm, dropped it so they spilled over the straw, kicked out in frustration.

'Pick them up.'

'Eh?' Still crouched, Croft swung round.

'I said, pick them all up.' Edward stepped out into the light. 'You dropped the oats, so pick them all up. Don't waste a single one or else you'll be sleeping out here tonight with no supper.'

Croft's squat head shuddered in his broad shoulders. He was clearly struggling with the desire to react but he could not refuse a direct order.

'What are you waiting for?' Edward urged, fuelled with the sense of battle. 'Get down on your knees and pick them up, every last oat.'

Grumbling, his enemy complied. Edward stood over him, recalling his taunting words and blows out in the field. The oats were tiny; they had scattered and mingled with the straw. Croft's clumsy thick fingers clawed in the dust but he was losing patience. Inching forward on his knees, he reached Edward's boots. One fist shot out and grabbed the boy's ankle, trying to tip him over but Edward was ready for him. He shook him off easily and sent Croft sprawling back.

'Nice try. You think I'm stupid? You can go to bed hungry for that.'

Croft snarled. 'Who the hell do you think you are, little boy? Now your father has gone, you're nothing.' He rose up to his full height, a tall, solid, imposing height, with the strength of an unthinking brute.

Edward came forward to meet him, his bravery registering as surprise in the cruel eyes. 'Who do I think I am? Who exactly? I am Edward Plantagenet, son of the Duke of York, recently Lord Protector, a descendant of Edward III and your lord and master.'

As soon as he had delivered the words, he followed them with his fist. His knuckles connected with Croft's cheekbone and sent him sprawling back into the muck.

*

It seemed as if they had been huddled inside the house forever. Father, mother, the children, grandparents and servants, crouching on the floor with the oak table pushed up against the door. They had been eating when it started, with fresh bread and jugs of ale set out on the table. Then there had been shouting outside, screaming and the dull thud of feet against the step but now it was quiet. Had the soldiers gone?

The man opened his eyes. In his arms, his youngest daughter was still trembling and gently, he handed her to his wife. The room was so still he could hear his own breath as he rose slowly, his eyes on the window. Beyond the pane, he could see a square of grey sky and the tops of trees. There was a path that ran from the back of the garden out to the fields.

He inched forward, daring himself to look. His back was hot with the eyes of his loved ones. The tops of the apple tree appeared, then the red brick wall and the point of the hen house. He felt his shoulders relax in relief and stepped closer, spotting the bucket that had been dropped as a child ran indoors and the white sheets his wife had draped over the bushes to dry. A green leaf fell from the skies, twisting and twirling its slow path to earth. He watched it with heart beating.

Then, as if out of some vision of hell, the wall shattered in the centre, sending bricks flying into the garden. A booted foot appeared, then another. As the dust cleared, there were suddenly dozens of men, armed and urgent, jostling their way through, stamping across the shrubs growing by the wall and trampling the sheets underfoot. For a moment they paused, and at their head, like the crest of a wave, appeared the Earl of Warwick, dark, swarthy and compact, bristling with energy. Then, as an unstoppable tide, they surged onwards, hacking their way into the fence of the next garden.

'À Warwick! À Warwick!'

If they saw the man at the window, they ignored him. They did not need him. The shaking figure heard their chant before he dived back down to the floor, lips mumbling in prayer.

*

In the marketplace, a basket of plums came crashing to the ground. The purple fruits rolled unnoticed across the cobbles, pulped under hurrying feet. The king's army was in chaos. Men spilled in each direction, fogged by confusion as arrows rained down from above. Some were still pulling on armour, balancing on one leg as the point of an arrowhead embedded itself in their vulnerable flesh. Bodies littered the ground, writhing and moaning whilst others limped to shelter, banging on doors that did not open. Amid them all, beside the market cross, the figure of the king remained motionless. Encased in armour, only his eyes flickered, betraying the terror and turmoil within.

Standing at the crossroads where the abbey's land met the town, Abbot Whethamstede saw the tide of men approaching. The little green lane had never before witnessed such a sight. Grasses blew in the breeze and a bird circled above, yet hell itself was coming this way on two legs. The sun shone on armour as one man hacked mercilessly at another, with blood pooling in sticky dark patches. He could hear the screams of the dying, the heart-rending screams of souls in torment that he would never be able to forget.

The news had reached him as he knelt at morning prayer. Terrifying, apocalyptic news for the little town, with its huddle of workshops, inns and homes around the market square, where women met to gossip and children played games. Sheltered inside the stone crypt, he had hardly been able to believe his ears, yet here it was, like one of the old

31

manuscript illustrations of the fires of damnation. He was no stranger to death and suffering; over the years he had sat at men's deathbeds and tended the sick and wounded, yet what he now saw turned his stomach. Some lay in the gutters, bleeding from wounds to the head, arm or throat. Others simply slumped where they had fallen, with their glazed eyes fixed on the heavens. The abbot knew he should rush in, offer them the last rites and the chance of salvation but he could be of little help if he was wounded or killed.

Hurrying back to the cool stone sanctuary of the cloister, he heard feet pounding after him. Cold fear prickled down his spine. Was this the moment God had chosen for him? Was he to become a victim in this senseless struggle? His chest pounded. He would embrace martyrdom if that was God's chosen path; if that was the destiny he was being offered.

He swung round. A handful of bedraggled knights were clattering down the path.

'For the love of God, let us in, let us in. They will kill us all, in the name of the king, let us have shelter inside.'

The abbot ran ahead and hammered on the door. It was thrown open at once and the figures staggered into the misty gloom of the nave.

*

Back at the market cross, Henry VI slowly dismounted. His pale eyes swept the scene. The low pitch of dying men's moans reached him from the surrounding lanes. Somerset was at his side, a tall, spare man, his cheek bleeding.

'You are wounded. Why did you take off your helmet?'

The king looked at him in surprise.

'Your neck, look.'

Henry felt the duke's fingers against his skin, then they came away red with blood. The sight of it curdled his stomach.

'I didn't notice, I didn't feel it. I suppose it must have been an arrow. I couldn't see with the helmet on. Is the day lost?'

'Never. Let us get you to safety. There is a tanner here who will shelter you, come with me, come. They will not think to look there. Warwick is about to burst through into the main street and meet York's troops. We cannot lose a moment, come.'

As they hurried away, the air behind them roared with the promised arrival and the clash of metal on metal.

Croft was not defeated yet. He sat up, hair full of straw, eyes blazing. He had guts, Edward admitted to himself.

'Just because your father happens to be a duke,' he spat, struggling to his feet, 'it doesn't mean I can't squash your snivelling face in the mud. You and your milksop brother.'

'No, you're right,' retorted Edward. 'He isn't here to stop you. But I am.'

Croft lunged forward but Edward was faster. His fist caught the thickset jaw and sent his enemy crashing back against the stable door. A second blow to the side doubled him over. Edward grabbed a fistful of his brittle hair, recalling Edmund's troubled night and moments when he had endured the bully's sneers and taunts, simply because he had been smaller and weaker.

'I've had enough of you. I've been lenient with your treachery but a man has his limits.'

With a huge shove, he projected Croft forward into the deep straw piled up with horse dung.

'Edward.'

The voice came from the stable door. He swung round to see Peter standing silhouetted by the sun. Shame seized him at once; Croft had had it coming, yet he knew such behaviour was beneath him.

Peter stepped oved the threshold. 'That's enough. You, get out.' He barely looked at Rick, sprawled across the floor, but the lout did not need another invitation to leave. He scrambled to his feet and disappeared.

'This isn't like you.'

'He's an animal,' breathed Edward heavily. 'He attacked Edmund, pulled a knife on us.'

'Then you should speak with his father.'

'But Croft...'

'I know, but it is the right thing to do. Let it go. Brawling like this is beneath you. We have more important battles to fight.'

Edward flushed. 'I'm sorry.'

'Let us forget it now. Come inside, back to your studies and we will try to divert your mind. Edmund is waiting. Show him the way.'

*

Warwick's men swarmed about the market cross. Their eyes were keen and their blades drenched in blood. The earl pushed back his visor as the Duke of York approached.

'He's inside?'

Warwick nodded. 'Holed up like a rat.'

York turned to survey the building, and a shadow drew back from the window.

'He's watching us, waiting for our next move. Is there no sign of the king's reinforcements?'

'Oxford's men are still a day's march away.'

York sighed, the inevitable dawning. 'Do we try and take him alive?'

Warwick stepped closer, conspiratorially. 'We've crossed a line. We can't go back. If he lives, we'll be attainted as traitors, perhaps worse. Blood has been shed on both sides, now it's him or us.'

'Then we must make it swift.'

York knew what Somerset would be thinking. He was a commander of the English army, a knight of the garter and Lieutenant of France: such men did not lurk in corners. He would step out into the daylight and face them, fighting to the last, even if it meant being cut down. A soothsayer had once warned him that he would meet his death in a castle. Now, the irony of the inn's sign, depicting the strong stone battlements of defence, was not lost on York.

He raised his gloved fist and gave the signal.

*

The afternoon shadows were long and lean as Edmund watched from the castle window. The archery butts were golden from the last sunlight as the day slipped towards evening; soon the bell for prayers would ring, followed by the dinner hour. Then, they might sit for a while before the fire, making plans or listening as Peter read stories of chivalry from one of the old French books.

Through the window, he could see Edward, bending to pick up a stray arrow from the ground. His brother had been restless, unable to keep his long limbs still so Peter had allowed him to go outside although he hadn't quite finished his reading. He was a far better archer than Edmund. Each time he practised, his balance improved, although his right arm and shoulder still hurt from the repeated exertion. One day he would be one of those men who could lift a cart singlehanded.

Then, as the sun slanted down upon Edward's head, Edmund saw his brother turn. His whole manner changed, his shoulders drawing up tall, his spine straightening. Edmund followed his gaze towards the castle gates, where a lone rider had been admitted. It was a man in the Yorkist livery of murrey and blue, his horse veering as he pulled up the reins. Edward hurried forward and received a message from the man's gloved hands. Edmund watched from a distance as his quick fingers broke the seal and scanned the contents. Even from the window, it was clear that the news was good.

FOUR: A Court Without a King, November, 1455

Edmund drew in his breath. London was busier than he remembered. The lines of the rolling Marcher countryside around Ludlow had been redrawn by steeples, towers and the evil claw of the gallows, by wine and song, by the tang of spices and the smoke of charnel houses. Merchants and pirates sailed up and down the Thames, unloading their bolts of dazzling Venetian cloth or bitter oranges from the Holy Lands. Pigs and dogs foraged in the ditches while nuns knelt in cool dark cloisters, their lips dry from prayer. At twelve years old, Edmund felt so temporary, so easily bruised, against the centuries embedded in the walls here, against the lives and deaths these streets had seen. And those they were yet to see.

Riding slightly ahead of him, Edward was soaking up the people's adoration. All eyes were hungry for the handsome eldest son of the Duke of York, with his finely chiselled features and the warm eyes that seemed to promise laughter. He wore his confidence like a cloak; casual, glittering, all-embracing. Edmund wished he could enjoy their adulation too but the crowd filled him with unease. He sensed the ripple of power that ran through them, the brute force of bodies packed in closely together, the animal spirits that could easily turn their good-natured welcome ugly.

'Wave, Edmund!'

It was Peter, at his side, urging him to play his part. He lifted a hand in response but the gesture felt awkward.

The procession moved on. Near the cross, sand and herbs had been strewn on the cobbles, making the horses tread more lightly. They paused briefly to be greeted by the mayor and aldermen, with their formulaic words and fickle smiles, flapping like moths around the latest flame. Their scarlet cloaks made a flash of colour against the drab house walls. Watching their faces, Edmund could not help but remember that not so long ago they had hurried to do homage to King Henry and his French queen.

Then, from amid the clamour of voices came music. Soft, sweet music. The boy lifted his chin to listen. For a moment he was stilled as the low, throaty notes of a pipe wafted down from an upstairs window. Slowly they ascended the scales, climbing higher and higher, then trilling in a little flourish of joy. Edmund was held fast by it. It spoke to him alone, above the heads of the crowd. Then, just as abruptly as it had begun, the piping stopped. The spell was broken.

'Edmund, wave to the people!'

The boy forced one hand into the air. It made a pathetic sort of flutter, falling as if there was no weight to it. He coloured at once.

And then the procession turned, blessedly, it turned. They had left behind St Paul's, Blackfriars and the crowds of Fleet Street and passed along the Strand to the village of Charing. Now, green fields were visible beyond the rooftops. Rising up ahead was the huge stone Eleanor Cross, carved with its figures and patterns, set in the middle of the thoroughfare. Relief filled his chest. It was almost over. There, in the distance, with the autumn sun gently warming its grey stones, lay the great gateway to Westminster Palace.

*

Inside the great hall, it was dark as the grave. The boys stood blinking in the doorway, as the bright day cast their faces into shadow. It was just possible to make out the vast vaulted cavern stretching before them. The lamps were not yet lit but, at the far end, came the gleam of flames, the hint of doors and corridors and a warren of rooms.

'This way.' Peter was at their side, steering them up towards the royal apartments.

'It's all right,' said Edward, stepping forward. 'I remember the way, I'll lead.'

And suddenly there was mother; all arms and folds of scarlet cloth as she wrapped them in her embrace. The softness of lace brushed their hot cheeks and, with it, the familiar warmth of her skin, overlaid with the smell of lye and roses. For a moment, Edmund was transported back to the world of the nursery, with the bustling of women and the creak of the rocking cradle. Edward pulled away first, cheeks red with excitement.

'They gave us a king's welcome in the city! Every citizen must have turned out to see us!'

Cecily, Duchess of York, smiled at her eldest boy. She was forty, still bearing the signs of the delicate blonde beauty of her youth, although her eyes were lined. She carried her proud Neville lineage in her expression, with her aristocratic profile and delicate features, yet in her generous mouth were the unmistakeable signs of pride and determination.

'And why would they not, given two such boys? Look at you both! Edward you are scarcely recognisable.'

He laughed. 'It hasn't been that long!'

'Long enough for a mother, long enough and far too long again, come,' she drew him back to her and pressed her lips on his forehead. 'A mother's blessing. How tall you are and how like my father you are growing.'

Edward endured her caresses before breaking away and heading to the window to scan the view.

'And my Edmund, my own comfort.' Cecily had a different voice for her second son. 'Did the journey trouble you?'

And although it had been a trouble, a trial and discomfort in the glow of all the faces, Edmund did not want to seem the baby, so he put on a show of bravery.

'It was no trouble to me, I've grown out of such childish fears!'

Perhaps the retort had been too brusque or too quick. Her gentle smile told him she understood; she saw through him but also recognised his need. She kissed the top of his head, his ear, his cheek.

'Of course, of course, for you are quite grown up now. But I am glad to have you safely at my side again. What a Christmas we will keep this year, what laughter and good times, with all of us here together, if it pleases God.'

'All of us?'

Cecily smiled. 'They will all come for Christmas, Elizabeth and Margaret, George and Richard, and we will be together again, every last one of us. The living in my arms and those already passed will be honoured in our thoughts.'

And just as he had been understood, Edmund knew the source of his mother's words. There had been other children, born before and after him, whom it had pleased God to claim in their infancy. The last had been little Ursula, who had only lived a few days after her birth, that summer. He knew it weighed heavily on her heart, no matter how stoic she professed to be.

Now she smiled and drew him closer to kiss him again and nibble at his rosy cheeks. He tolerated her and did not push her away as his brother had done, for Edward was a diplomat, a warrior, active, proud and independent, a man of action like their father, while he, Edmund, was his mother's son.

'We must explore the gardens!' called Edward, gesturing towards some unseen location outside. 'There is so much to do and we can take a boat from here up river to Windsor and hunt there.'

'Ah, but the king is at Windsor,' said his mother softly. 'Yes, he has taken to his bed again and, although the physicians are being cautious, it seems that he is in danger of losing his wits again.'

'Is he gravely ill?' Edmund spoke against her ear, remembering the fevered nights of childhood illnesses. At Middleham, it had always been the soft, scented form of his mother who had sat beside his bed through the long dark hours until dawn. Her white hands had moved like birds above his head, alternately mopping his brow and offering prayers.

'We cannot be certain,' she said to him. 'No one is certain of his illness. His body seems strong enough but his mind is frail.'

'Poor King,' said Edmund, as if he was speaking of a bird that had fallen from its nest. 'But what would happen if...'

'Ssh,' interrupted his mother. 'You must never speak of the king's mortality. Some people would see it as treason.'

'Treason?' The word left him cold with horrible imaginings.

'But remember King Henry has a son now to continue his line.'

'The prince is only three!' declared Edward, cutting in from across the room, 'and we cannot have another baby on the throne, so father should be king.'

'Should he?'

The voice, deep and echoing, came from an anteroom. For a moment the boys froze, wondering who had overheard their indiscretion, before the tapestries parted to reveal the Duke of York himself, his eyes burning with energy. He was dressed in splendid blue velvet, inlaid with silver tissue, while warm furs lay draped about his shoulders. The boys knelt, as protocol dictated.

The duke laughed, striding into the room, beaming across his tanned face. 'There is but one king in this kingdom and I would not exchange his poor lot for mine.' He drew them both to the window seat where the air was sweet with the scent of the rain-soaked meadow outside. 'Your mother is right, though, we must be cautious and wait. This new parliament will declare me Protector again and I have much support from among the nobles, yet the queen will seek to oust me in favour of her boy. We must be discreet.'

The fire crackled and burned behind them.

'Let no man overhear you speak of this, nor woman either. These things must remain between us until the situation resolves and there may be ears pressed to the door in the service of the queen.'

Edmund's eyes crept towards the wooden panelling.

'So in all outward things, let us be merry and celebrate the Nativity with divine service, feastings and disguisings. We will fill Westminster with music and laughter and show the whole of London just how a king should live. Let none have cause to criticise us or doubt our loyalty.'

As he spoke, there was a soft thud on the floor, like a footfall. They turned to see a log, fallen from the fire, blazing away on the stone flags.

York rose up immediately and hastened across the floor but Edward was already at his side. He reached for the cutters in the hearth and replaced the log, leaving only a scattering of grey ash. His hazel eyes beamed up at the Duke.

'You have us now father, whatever happens, you have us with you.'

*

A hum ran through the crowd as York cleared his throat and raised his goblet. Standing before them in green and brown silk, he looked every inch the king, with a dazzling ruby set into his cap and more gems sparkling on his fingers and chest.

'My Lords, Ladies, I bid you all give a hearty welcome to my eldest sons, Edward, Earl of March and Edmund, Earl of Rutland. They are newly arrived from Ludlow. I trust they will be welcomed at every turn and afforded their due respect and rank as sons of York, descendants of Edward III and as your cousins.'

He was answered by an array of cheering voices and clapping hands, some more enthusiastic than others.

It was late and the candles were burning low. The air was thick with smoke and the scent of roasted meat. The great hall had been transformed, with trestle tables draped in the finest cloth and set with the most exotic dishes that London's markets could offer. Musicians played softly and tumblers, dressed in particoloured hose, turned somersaults and walked on their hands to amuse the diners.

Edmund had no idea of the time. They had sat down at four, when the light was already fading outside and an endless succession of dishes seemed to flow from the kitchens. Even sharing his portions with Edward, there was yet another pie or pudding, more dressed poultry or baked fish set before them, coloured, gilded or scattered with herbs. After the humble fare of Ludlow, he had been amazed by the offerings of the Westminster kitchen and had eaten heartily; the tender haunches of meat in thickly spiced gravy, the soft white bread, a peacock dressed with almonds and violets, its rainbow tail spread wide in a dazzling fan. Then there were the puddings, the special favourites of the boys; quivering jellies dyed bright purple and red, golden tarts sprinkled with saffron, custards scattered with rose petals and cloves and sweet marchpane, painstakingly painted with geometric patterns.

Now the evening was drawing to a close. Servants in the Yorkist livery brought up the final dish from the kitchens and a hush descended on the assembly as it was set down on the high table. A huge sweet carving depicting St George and the dragon, it sparkled in gold leaf, glinting and shining in the light of the torches. Edmund's jaw fell open in awe as the dish was rotated to show it from all angles, before the pieces of sticky yellow marchpane were broken and distributed. He did not notice Edward lean in beside him.

'All our friends are here, and some of our enemies too. Before they leave, it would be good for you to know them, you must be wary as father says.'

Edmund nodded, urging himself awake.

'Why do we have so many enemies?'

Edward made an exasperated noise in his throat. 'Do you listen to nothing father tells us? Half of our guests tonight would rather be raising their glasses in a toast to the king, or perhaps bedding his French wife!'

Edmund looked at his brother with wide eyes.

'Just a rumour,' Edward faltered, his adolescent bravado briefly shaken. 'Forget it. But look, let me point them out to you.'

Edmund frowned and nodded, turning his attention to the long table flanked by men and women dressed in their best clothes.

'Look, there, our cousin, the Earl of Warwick, dressed in grey.'

Edmund peered at the hard-faced handsome man, his jaw square and firm as he surveyed the hall with astute eyes. His head was powerfully built and topped with a mop of dark curls. He ate quickly, mechanically, as if his mind was elsewhere. A diamond ring gleamed on his little finger.

'He fought for us at St Albans; together he and father are undefeatable. That ring was a present from father for his loyalty. And beside him is his father Salisbury, our uncle.'

Seated to Warwick's left, the Earl of Salisbury's hair was already white but his body was solid as a barrel. As their mother's eldest brother, he was fifteen years her senior, heir to the Neville title and had fought with their father in France. Edmund felt comforted to see him, recalling a spring day in the past, when the earl had held him in place in the saddle and led him on a pony around an orchard full of blossom.

'Oh yes, I remember...'

A servant brought a dish of spices. Edmund watched as his brother took a pinch of some rich red powder and sprinkled it into his wine glass.

'Beyond them, the three Bourchier brothers, our uncles by marriage. Henry is Lord High Treasurer, Thomas is Chancellor and the Archbishop of Canterbury and John, well, Uncle John is the youngest.'

Edmund nodded, taking in the three round grey heads with their family resemblance and modest but well-constructed features. Henry was married to their aunt Isabel, and had proved himself a capable reliable man, full of wisdom.

'And there, at the end, is Buckingham, Humphrey Stafford, another uncle to watch. He speaks of peace but he commanded the king's army in the battle; now he has lost favour with the queen but he will turn his coat again when it suits him.'

Edmund looked first at the long, lean man with gaunt cheeks, trying to commit his face to memory. As he gazed across the table, strewn with dishes, Buckingham turned and his brooding eyes met those of the two boys like a reprimand. A livid scar across one cheek marred the symmetry of his face, a legacy of his stand at St Albans. Edmund hurriedly reached for his goblet and buried his face in it.

'Beside him is mother's sister, the Duchess Anne and their two eldest sons, Humphrey and Henry,' his brother added, but Edmund dared not lift his eyes in fear of meeting the man's gaze again.

'And on the left,' Edward whispered, not noticing his discomfort, 'are the Tudor brothers, Edmund, Earl of Richmond and his younger brother Jasper, Earl of Pembroke; the products of a secret marriage between the king's mother and her squire!'

Edmund nodded at the scandal but he could not help admiring the two red-haired earls, tall, strong and handsome. The elder Tudor's face was softer and longer than his brother's more angular features. They seemed close, as he and Edward did, their heads bent together as they talked in soft voices. There was definitely something regal about them, these two sons of the beautiful Queen Catherine of Valois, but also something else, something that set them apart, which he could not quite put his finger on. After Henry V's death, she had made a secret marriage to her Welsh groom and these two tall young men had been the result. Of all those in the hall that night, they interested the boy the most.

'Then there is the Earl of Devon, who is Somerset's son-in-law and Lord Stanley and Lord Saye...'

Edward's voice trailed away as York rose to his feet again, addressing the hall. Edmund was relieved, his head spinning with all the new names and faces to remember.

The murmuring voices fell silent and all faces were turned in York's direction. The blazing light of torches glanced off their jewels and caught the whites of their eyes.

'My Lords, a final word of business before we part for the night. As you know, the council has appointed me lieutenant to open a new parliament. Tomorrow I go to visit the king and, after that, we will meet to discuss what action is to be taken.'

A low ripple rose from the floor. York waited until silence was resumed.

'I am sure I need not remind you of the importance of your attendance. Our country stands in need of guidance; it is for this purpose that you were issued with the summons to assemble. The last parliament granted a general pardon for the regrettable losses of St Albans, so let us forgive the conflicts that made us draw arms against our cousins and conclude a lasting peace in the name of King Henry and in the interests of England. I hope I can count on your support.'

There was a muted murmur again. Edmund noticed the Tudor brothers exchange a low glance.

'This parliament will set out the duties of the Protectorate. Then we will publish a new set of ordinances for the running of the royal household until such a time that the king may himself make his wishes plain. Each loyal man will have his place at the Protector's side and all those superfluous to the royal service will be removed. Until then, God be with you, my Lords, and good night.'

It was their cue to leave. York offered his hand to his wife, resplendent in a gown of yellow and gold, who swept out of the hall at his side. Edward and Edmund scrambled to follow, keeping their chins held high as they felt the weight of their enemies' eyes boring into their backs. Edmund wondered how long it would take for them to show their hands.

FIVE: The Riddle of the King

Birds circled in a dark cloud against the sky. They rose and fell in a graceful wave, high above the world of men. Winter was coming. A light drizzle was falling but rain could not entirely stamp out the tang of woodsmoke as four riders thundered through Windsor Forest towards the castle. A rabbit paused in the glades, then bolted from the approaching hooves, crouching, watching, until it was safe to emerge once more.

The riders passed under a wide stone arch, clattered into the inner courtyard and dismounted: the Duke of York with his eyes scanning the windows, the Earl of Warwick tall and alert, the white-haired Salisbury and a younger, slighter figure, scarcely into his teens, excited by the moment and what the world had to offer.

The boy was on the verge of manhood. He slid off his horse with ease and caught the reins in a gesture that stilled the animal. Since the summer, his limbs had lost their childishness and were lean with new growth. The new muscles on his forearms were soft, lacking the definition of experience and effort, but full of promise. He stood almost as tall as any of them, his neck losing its roundness to show the prominent Adam's apple and the sprinkling of light down that would soon require the edge of a blade. His lips were firm, determined, yet still trembled with excitement as he looked up at the towering grey walls.

Edward had been surprised when his father appeared in his Westminster chamber early that morning and told him to rise and dress. It had seemed like a dream, in the half-light, before the servants had even stacked the grate, the sort of dream he had frequently had at Ludlow, sleepy little Ludlow that seemed so far away. The scene of his youth was nothing but a green corner of the distant world now. While his brother slept on, he had pulled on his doublet and braies in the cold dawn and hurried down to the stables before the court was stirring.

Servants led them to the watching chamber. It seemed that they had been expected. It was a long room, low-lit with a high ceiling and thick stone walls. Tapestries depicted scenes of hunts and legends, mythological gods and goddesses with their bows drawn. Warming themselves by the wide stone hearth, stood two majestic figures, outlined in fire. The first was a woman of above average height, soft and well made, in her mid-twenties. Her dark hair was pulled up under a conical headdress, from which a gauzy veil flowed past her shoulders, concealing her features. Her figure was neat, youthful and slender. At her side was a tall youth, perhaps nineteen or twenty, with a melancholic cast to his brows, dressed in deep mourning.

York strode forth into the centre of the room and waited. The pair did not turn but steadily watched the logs being consumed by flames. When the duke dropped to one knee, Edward and the others followed suit. The minutes passed. It seemed that they remained there, bowed down to the tiled floor for an eternity. Edward's knees began to ache but his companions did not twitch so he gritted his teeth and waited.

Eventually the lady turned. Her skirts swung in a heavy circle as she came towards them, the weight of her stare boring into their heads.

'What is your request?'

Her voice was low and sweet. When Edward raised his head he saw her serene eyes, dark, slanting and almond shaped, her olive skin and the colour in her cheeks. She held her mouth a little pertly as she surveyed the men, her expression softening a little when her gaze fell upon him. Then her attention was drawn by his father's commanding voice.

'Most gracious Queen, I offer my humble thanks for this audience. I trust to God you are both well.'

He waited but no reply came. Margaret of Anjou's black eyes lifted coldly into the distance between them.

'The council have invested the authority in me to summon a parliament. It will meet at Westminster tomorrow but, today, we had hoped to see the king.'

'The king is indisposed.' Her answer was clipped. She lifted her chin and looked down at the men, awaiting their next move.

'We understand that, my Lady, this is the very reason we wished to see him and speak with his doctors.'

'So he must be disturbed because you have a whim to see him?'

'Not a whim, rather a necessity. If I am unable to see the person of the king, how might I convince the parliament of his ability to rule?'

She did not reply but worked her lips as if biting back a retort. The lean dark figure of her companion ranged up alongside her and let out a cough. He had only recently risen from his bed, suffering from wounds sustained at St Albans. Henry Beaufort might have lost his father but he had gained the Dukedom of Somerset.

'I hope you are well, cousin Henry, that your injuries are healing?'

York had gone too far. This comment seemed to unleash the young man's pent-up venom. His dark eyes flashed with hatred and his features contorted. 'They would have no need to heal had your lackey not tried to deprive me of my life while I was defending my father.'

The insult was directed at Warwick. He was not a man to accept such a blow, even in the presence of the queen.

'There were losses sustained on both sides.'

'But you targeted my father. It was murder.'

'The parliament of the summer issued pardons for all.'

'What good is that to me now? You may as well have killed him in cold blood.'

Warwick steeled himself. 'We would not have engaged, if our offers of peace had been accepted.'

'Offers of peace? You did not go there with peace on your mind.'

'We…'

'It was murder, nothing less…'

York raised his hand. 'Enough! This is not the place. The urgent matter is the king's health; we have come here with no other purpose today. We do not want to reopen the breach.'

Beaufort let out a sound of disgust and turned back to the fire.

Queen Margaret sighed. 'You may be admitted, for a minute only, just you and your boy, no one else.' She cast her eyes again on Edward, who bowed his head in recognition. 'The Nevilles may wait in the courtyard.'

'Thank you, my Lady, it is most gracious of you.'

'Now leave, I have no wish to see your faces any longer.'

*

A servant took them through corridors hewn from stone into the cold heart of the castle. The king's apartments were dark, as daylight had not been admitted and only a single lamp burned on the wall. The air smelt musty, with a mix of chemicals and sweat and the remains of an untouched meal sat on a table close by the door. Beside them, a phial of holy water stood beside a well-worn Bible. The curtains hung heavy at the sides of the bed. Propped up on a mountain of pillows, the king lay motionless, his careworn face pale, eyelids closed.

A boy seated on a stool in the corner jolted into life at the sign of visitors.

'He's been like this for weeks.'

'Fetch the doctors,' York ordered. 'Tell them the Protector would speak with them.'

As soon as they were alone, the duke lifted the lifeless arm and felt the pulse. Then he lifted the coverlet slightly and winced at the odour coming off the body.

'God's blood! Look at the state of him.'

Edward crept closer to the bedside and looked down at the face of the king. He looked serene, as if deep in slumber, a lined, worried face in repose, prematurely older than its thirty-three years. The mouth was mild, the nose bony and pronounced and the cheeks were dark with stubble. There was something both moving and grotesque about it; a living man so deep in a sleep from which nothing could rouse him, not even his kingdom.

'Why is he like this?' Edward whispered to his father.

York shook his head. 'No one knows. The first time his illness came on, two years ago, it may have been the loss of his French inheritance, or it may come from his grandfather, the mad King Charles. Perhaps it is just the will of God.'

'But why would God wish for the king not to be well?'

They both looked down at the silent form. Edward thought he saw the eyelids flicker.

'Do you think he can hear us?'

'Who knows what he hears, or thinks, wherever he might be.'

'Is it a form of punishment?'

'For his religious life? He may have been a weak king but his piety cannot be questioned. Ah, at last!'

Two men entered the room and eyed them with suspicion.

'Who enters the king's chamber in his debility?' asked one, a bearded man with a squint. 'On whose authority have you come here?'

'On that of parliament, with the blessing of the queen.'

'The blessing?'

'She gave her permission only moments ago. You must be new in attendance on the king, or else you would recognise your Protector of the Realm, the Duke of York.'

The bearded man shifted his gait. 'My humble apologies, it is my duty to protect the king's person at all costs, I had left his side merely to mix a poultice. My name is Doctor Keymer, Gilbert Keymer, and this is my assistant, John.'

'And what is your opinion of his condition?'

Keymer sighed and pulled at his beard. 'Well, there are things that can be ruled out, it's a difficult case, quite unusual, I don't want to commit myself to one diagnosis...'

'Have you tested his urine?'

'Of course, of course, that was one of the first things I did and it proved inconclusive.'

'And bled him? And his diet?'

'Yes, yes. He is bled often and his diet is strictly regulated. I am sorry but I can't give you the answers you hope for. It is just a question of waiting.'

York frowned. 'For how long?'

Keymer looked back helplessly.

'But you do see,' said York, balling his fist, 'that the future of the country depends upon this, that our lives and the lives of everyone in this realm are affected by the health of the king? Would you have us slip again into war?'

'I will pray but I cannot work miracles.'

The duke strode back to the bed and looked down at the pitiful figure who had not moved throughout the interview.

'You are sure he is still alive?'

'Of course he is still alive!'

'You will send word to me at court the second there is any change, any change in the least, the second it happens, you understand? And in the meantime, get these sheets changed and clean him up. Come, Edward.'

They hurried out of the room in silence and down to the stables where Warwick and Salisbury were waiting. A single nod from the duke gave them all the information they needed to know.

'Was it bad news then, father?' Edward asked, as he climbed into the saddle.

49

'Bad news?' answered York, with a sidelong smile. 'No, not bad news. The very best. The king cannot even flicker his eyelid and shows no sign at all of recovery. I shall be Protector, with God's will, for many years to come.'

And he spurred his horse on towards the forest, the river and the Palace of Westminster.

*

In the council chamber, grave faces lined both walls. Friends and foes alike stared across the table, contemplating York's news. Edward scanned them with his eyes, wishing he might read their thoughts. It was the first time he had been in the council chamber and here, the faces of those from the dinner table last night seemed less friendly.

'There is no doubt about his condition,' the duke repeated, his dark eyes flashing. 'I was a witness to it myself, with my son Edward. Henry is incapacitated, incapable of response, afflicted by some terrible humour. He is still not capable of rule. The queen and Beaufort are in attendance but there seems little hope for his improvement in the near future.'

Jasper Tudor rose to his feet, casting his pale eyes along the length of the hall. 'We should like to see the king and assess his condition for ourselves.' His brother nodded at his side.

'You are more than welcome to visit Windsor and ask the queen for an audience,' York offered. He had expected this. 'But you would save yourselves a journey if you put faith in my reports. My son, the Earl of March, can verify the facts.'

'It is true,' Edward nodded, addressing the men for the first time and feeling their collective gaze upon him. 'The king is unable to rule, a child could see it.'

Tudor lifted his square chin. 'What is being done for the king? Does he have new doctors, if the old ones cannot cure him?'

York spoke in low, reasoned tones. 'I spoke with the doctors myself. They have administered the usual poultices and cures; there is talk of alleviating the pressure on his skull but the queen is not in agreement. You are welcome to send your own physicians to Windsor for the sake of your peace of mind.'

Tudor frowned. 'There is talk of bringing in a surgeon?'

'A surgeon is already present, he visits the king hourly. There is a procedure by which an incision can be made in the skull and...'

The scar-faced Buckingham brought his fist down on the table, making Edward jump. 'Never! We cannot make the king undergo such a dramatic treatment. Think of the consequences if it should fail.'

'It is merely a suggested course of action, by no means the only one being considered. There could be worse consequences if he does not recover,' added York. 'Surely we are united in our desire to see the king return to full health. Can we afford to sit and wait for that to happen of its own accord? What if he is never well again, never capable of rule?'

'That is no reason to subject him to danger,' added Tudor. 'We may as well offer him the assassin's blade. This is our anointed king, the son of our revered Henry V, his life is not a plaything in the hands of those who wish to replace him!'

Edward was close enough to hear his father draw breath. 'That is not the case. We all wish for the king's recovery.'

'Perhaps some of us more than others?' Buckingham delivered his insult in hushed tones but, at that moment, the voices dropped, so it was clearly heard.

York turned roundly to face him. 'You are discontent, cousin. What would you suggest?'

The duke rose to the challenge. He looked around the room and his cheek that bore the scar seemed to twitch a little. 'Caution before action. None of us needs to take any rash steps. There is no imminent danger, no current foreign invasion, we should just bide our time.'

'I agree,' added Tudor. 'Allow the king another season, perhaps nature will run its course as it did before and all will be well again.'

'Aye, it is likely he will soon be back among us,' added his brother Edmund.

There was a murmuring among the lords of general assent.

A chair scraped in the corner. The Earl of Warwick had risen to his feet, his formidable presence commanding their attention. His voice was biting, cynical. 'Perhaps all will be well? Is this the ending of some tale of romance or chivalry? Even if the king does recover, what then? A country forever afraid of the future? An England that tremors whenever its king sneezes? Are we always to be in this state of guardianship over a leader who cannot lead? Isn't it time to face facts and stop pretending that the man can do any better at ruling even if he does get up off his backside?'

There was a horrified gasp in the room.

Tudor spoke first. 'My Lord! You forget yourself. You are speaking of the king.'

'Am I? Who is the real king of England? The man who lies in bed and does not know whether it is day or night, or my Lord of York, who runs the country better than Henry ever could?'

'This sails dangerously close to treason. Would you depose the king and step into the breach?'

Warwick opened his mouth but York got in first, shooting him a furious look, 'The earl has spoken hastily. He is a loyal subject of the king and means no treason.' Warwick turned away in frustration and York pushed on. 'You are right, my Lords. It is true that we should err on the side of caution when it comes to the king's health. There will be no more talk of such interventions. I will visit Windsor again in the new year and report back. Now let us turn to the ordinances for the household, if you are all in agreement?'

There was little movement; eyes were cast about sullenly and uncertainly.

'We have made a thorough assessment of the king's household and, at the last meeting, presented our findings for the alterations required. This will reduce the numbers of unnecessary servants and establish clear guidelines for the entitlements of rank. You have all had a chance to lodge any objections so, if you are all now in agreement, we will sign the document.'

He called for the manuscript and ink. Warwick sat back sullenly in his chair, surveying the hall. York frowned down at him.

'In God's name, Warwick, what would you do, depose the king? Such talk is unhelpful at best, treasonous at worst.'

'What good can come from him?'

'That is not the point. You are too hasty. Things must be done properly. See how you almost destroy our cause with your force!'

At the far end of the table, the bishops had begun to add their signatures to the yellow parchment. Edward watched the various factions regroup.

'I have seen thirty years of things being done properly and look where it has left us.'

'Curb your tongue now. Come and sign.'

York took the pen and dipped it in ink. He wrote his name large and high, in the centre of the paper. Passing the pen to Warwick, he looked on in satisfaction as the earl inscribed his signature below. As he turned to depart, a voice rang out through the hall.

'God save the king!'

Buckingham was standing at the head of the table, awaiting a response. His face shone with loyalty and defiance; his words were fitting but York could feel them as a reproach boring through him.

'Indeed,' he replied. 'God save the king. May it please Him to restore Him to his former good health for the relief of the country and the queen.'

He bowed his head and strode out of the hall.

SIX: The Italian Girl

Through the doors at the back of the hall, there came a line of dark figures. Six, seven or eight of them, creeping stealthily, like silhouettes out of the shadows, partly of this world and partly of another. Edward watched them, transfixed for a moment, forgetting himself.

The dark ones moved fluidly in front of the tapestries. A breathless hush descended on the crowd, which had so recently been animated by drink and talk, love and laughter. Each dark figure twisted and turned, contorting their bodies so that their limbs seemed to scarcely belong to them, thrown open wide like the wings of birds. One dancer moved close to the top table, caught in the light of the fire as he stretched out his hands, fingers entwined, face hidden behind a mask, having crept out of the world of dreams. His limbs were long and smooth, encased in silken sleeves, almost inviting a caress. Edward resisted the urge to reach out and touch them.

Then, just as the other dancers drew nearer, the doors at the back of the hall were thrown wide and a golden glow eclipsed the late-night torches and candles. The enchanted figures turned, circled and regrouped, pulling between them a low cart, mounted on unseen wheels; it was an entertainment, a pageant, dressed with silver bells that tinkled in the expectant hush. Set in the middle of it was a huge, bright sphere, taller than three men, with muslin stretched over its frame and lit from within by a multitude of candles. For a moment, it took Edward's breath away. This was what it must be like to be king, he realised, to conjure up such feats, to make fire burn bright like that inside those paper walls, to make the sun appear in splendour in the middle of the night.

The light inside the orb flickered and danced. Smoothly, it moved across the floor towards them like a ball of fire. The diners on either side put down their knives and watched as it approached, burning brightly, drawing the tables, dishes and guests into its glow. Delight shone on the faces of the children. Edward watched their expressions of rapture: his sisters, Elizabeth and Margaret, on the verge of womanhood, with their innocent eyes widening in surprise. His younger brothers seated at their feet, still round and resilient from the diet and routine of the nursery and even Edmund was transfixed by the pageant, scanning its shape to try and fathom its construction.

The giant orb came to rest before them and the dark figures melted away. Flickering shadows licked up the insides, hypnotic and captivating. The children could barely contain themselves. Six-year-old George, his body already tense with anticipation, could feel the emotion mounting in him. His little brow furrowed with concentration as he stood, hands on the hips of his little doublet. The tip of his tongue stuck out between his teeth as the wave of excitement threatened to engulf him.

Suddenly, one of the dark figures leapt up and the top of the sphere opened like a flower. There was a brief scuffle and beating of wings and a cloud of song birds flew up into the air, released from unseen cages within. George lost control. A shrill scream of delight escaped his lips. Feathers flapped and beat about them. Three-year-old Richard buried his dark head in his mother's skirts, overwhelmed by the enormity of it all.

Then the hall broke into laughter and applause. The dark figures took up their instruments and the sounds of violin and flute banished the silence forever.

'You enjoyed that then,' laughed York, laying his hand on George's shoulder. The boy's gaze was still fixed on the spectacle.

The two younger boys were quite different in looks. George had begun to grow out of the first chubbiness of his baby years and his green eyes were fiercely independent. He was a child who knew his mind, who had rolled on the nursery floor in a tantrum of tears when a favourite toy had been taken from him, who was happy to use his elbows, knees and teeth as weapons. Yet he had a winning smile, a charm and caressing way of laying his little brown head on his mother's arm that could soften hard hearts. Richard, his junior by three years, stood in his shadow a little, still finding his way in the world. He was the first of their sons to have inherited the dark curls and strong brows of their father. The eyes he lifted cautiously up to survey the room were black as coals.

'Can I go and touch it?' George asked, breathlessly.

And before York or his duchess could answer, their small son was already climbing down from the dais and heading across the floor into the orb of light.

'Be careful,' his father called. 'Be gentle, don't get burned.'

Edward was closest and followed his young brother protectively, just in case he should be too hasty. The tiny pink fingers, seeming so vulnerable, stretched out towards the light. Their tips brushed the muslin gingerly and recoiled, then touched again with confidence, as George's face split into a grin.

'It's not too hot after all!'

The doors at the back of the hall swung open again and all heads turned in anticipation.

This time the attraction was culinary. A new course was being brought up from the kitchens and the very air seemed to warm in anticipation of it: rich, salty and spicy. Dishes came out one by one, carried on silver or gold plate, by servants in livery. Fresh white cloths over their right shoulder, formal and courteous, their eyes never deviating from the top table as they passed the pageant by. Edward glimpsed knuckles of beef served with cloves and saffron, gleaming pink cuts of salmon roasted with ginger; crayfish, shrimps and eels stewed with lampreys. There were plates of delicious pies stuffed with venison and pork, baked until their cases were golden, bowls of pottage flavoured with rose petals and gosling roasted in pepper sauce. Alongside were placed moist custard tarts, fritters sharp with the tang of baked fruit, creamy blancmange and crispy gilded wafers. His mouth began to moisten in anticipation.

'Come on George, let's get back to our seats.'

Tonight they would feast and in the morning, Christmas morning, they would process solemnly to chapel and make their devotions.

Edward sat down beside his father, who was waiting patiently as the dishes were spread out for his approval. A servant held the water basin and York plunged his hands in, scattering the petals on the surface. Then he lifted them to one side, fingertips dripping, to be patted dry in the folds of crisp linen. The court waited, unable to touch the steaming food before them until the duke nodded his approval and the stillness broke. Edward was too hasty. He dipped his hands impatiently into the water bowl and wiped them dry on his braies, reaching for a cut of meat.

'Wait,' York commanded under his breath. Edward slid his hands into his lap, shamed by protocol, eyes low.

With an imperceptible nod, permission was granted and the table lapsed into movement. Edward pierced a thick slice of meat with the point of his knife and sank his teeth into it. It was hot, salty, soft. He chewed appreciatively and watched his family do the same.

Mother looked tired. She had little Richard beside her, whose dark eyes were dimmed by a mixture of childish emotions. Gently, she tried to coax him to eat, offering spoonfuls of sauces and pieces of white meat. He had grown fussy lately, his stomach upset by the rich ingredients and lavish Christmas celebrations. He was more used to the routine of the nursery at Fotheringhay, with its set hours, plain fare and quiet nights. Eventually, he accepted a bread roll and retreated to his seat, clasping it in his fist. At his side, George ate solidly, untroubled by the noise and the bustle. Edward had been something like that, at that age, he thought to himself. Determined, solid and unperturbed. He reached across and helped himself to a plate of baked larks.

It was then, as he relaxed back into his chair, that Edward saw her. Across the hall, on the edge of the glow from the great orb, she sat half in shadow, half in light. Her face was a pale ellipse in the shadows, framed by the dark train of her headdress. She could have been no more than thirteen or fourteen, her hooded eyes cast down demurely as she ate and her lips red and full. The actors passed between them and, for a moment, she was lost to him. There was a moment of dark impatience, filled with slow-moving forms. Then the view down the hall cleared again and he saw her long white neck, her exposed throat, somehow so narrow and vulnerable that it made his chest tighten a little. Her hands fluttered before her like two doves in the gloom. She was part child, part woman.

Edward cleared his throat, hot with a sudden flush of emotion. He had watched pretty girls before at Ludlow, serving at table, washing their clothes by the bridge, walking in the marketplace. He liked their soft skin, their supple forms and the way they moved. Something about this girl was different.

He rinsed out his mouth with wine and tried to sound casual.

'Anyone new here tonight?'

York stroked his peppery beard. 'A few new faces, no one important, mostly merchants, ambassadors from the city.'

Edward nodded. He watched the girl pick at her plate, pursing her lips slightly in a delicate gesture. The man beside her was dressed in the dark rich furred robes of a wealthy citizen; his beard was flecked with grey, his brow wary. On the other side sat an older girl, perhaps eighteen, with sallow, pocked cheeks. She was as different from the other, as chalk and cheese, but they had the look of a family unit.

'And them?' Edward asked his father, nodding in their direction. 'A merchant's family?'

York spooned out the content of a pie. 'Boratti. Italians. Merchants or money lenders. He came to ask for my help, there may be trouble brewing in their community.'

'Trouble?'

'A few attacks on their property, some horses stolen. Foreigners are often an easy target for malcontents. They resent their wealth and success.'

And as the boy gazed across the table, the girl lifted her gaze. Briefly, fleetingly, she met his eyes in the middle distance; dark, slanting, long-lashed eyes, that quickly darted away again once they sensed his. Edward's limbs burned with unexpected appetite. The hall receded, with its food and musicians, its rich orb of light and the family banter. His veins seemed to sing with life, almost like the moment in a hunt, before making the kill, or riding at top speed with the wind in his face, but even better. He had to speak with her, know her name, touch her skin. And then he flushed at the man's emotions coursing through the boy's body. These things belonged in the romances he had read at Ludlow; he did not have the words, nor the certainty to even hold her gaze.

'Can we help them?'

'Only so far. I've doubled the watch, imposed a curfew. Anyone who does attack them again will pay the full penalty.'

'And the family?' His voice broke and he coughed. 'The wife and daughters?'

'As I said,' repeated York. 'They need to stay inside, away from trouble. The city's streets can be a lawless place.'

The glowing orb was being wheeled slowly back down the hall. As it passed the place where she sat, Edward saw her face briefly bathed in golden light, setting her cheeks aflame before she was lost in the darkness again.

Now the space between the tables filled up with tumblers, turning, twisting and walking on their hands.

Duchess Cecily signalled to her women. 'Time to send the little ones up to bed.'

58

George did not want to go. He put his hands firmly on his hips and stuck out his belly in defiance but there was to be no argument. Richard was already rubbing his dark eyes when the nurse scooped him up in her arms and took his brother's hand.

'But I don't want to go to sleep.'

Cecily frowned. 'Christmas will not come if you don't go to sleep.'

But to George, Christmas meant prayers in the cold abbey, devotions, processions.

'And tomorrow night,' she added, full of maternal knowledge, 'the Goldsmiths are going to perform a play of the nativity, with sheep and pigs.'

'Real sheep and pigs, in here?'

And George allowed himself to be led off, chattering at speed about the problems of controlling livestock. Edward lifted his goblet to be refilled and looked back across the table, through the procession of acrobats walking on their hands.

She was still there. Her head was inclined gracefully towards the man beside her, who must be her father, he decided. The old merchant was nodding forcibly as he spoke; it seemed that he was in earnest but the girl was tired and made few responses. When the empty dishes were cleared away, the trio rose. Edward glimpsed her slender shape under her embroidered kirtle as she took the old man's arm and headed for the door.

He turned to York. 'Will they be all right?'

'Who?'

'The merchant and his family?'

'The Italians, again? So long as they keep their heads down and their gates locked. The successful will always arouse jealousy.'

When she had gone, he felt an almost overwhelming sense of disappointment. Yet he had done nothing to stop her, to detain her father, or to find out her name. An hour ago he had not even been aware of her existence. The tumblers spilled over the floor at his feet, contorting themselves into strange shapes. He applauded along with the others and raised his glass again to be refilled.

SEVEN: Disorderly City, January, 1456

The festival of Christmas came and went, amid incense, icons and prayers. The new year swept in with icy blasts down the Thames, freezing over the puddles and hanging long white fingers from the window ledges.

York shivered as he pulled his furs closer round him and looked out across the river. The rowers pulled heavily on both sides and, blessedly, the tide was with them, drawing them on smoothly over the grey waves. It was a wide river, a high river, a hungry river. This winter, it was swollen with the debris of the city, choked with waste and filth. York winced at the stinking odour coming off it.

'Faster,' he called to the oarsmen, whose blades bit more keenly through the water in response.

To their left, the fortified frontages of houses and castles spilled right down to the banks, forbidding and solid. From each a set of landing steps descended, allowing access to the river. The skyline was uneven, dotted with the spires of churches and the mosaic of sloping roofs. Streams of grey smoke rose from the chimneys, fading away into the murky clouds.

At York's feet, his two elder sons were wrapped up tightly. Edmund had sunk down into his collar, with his hat pulled low on his sandy locks and his hands clasped under his cloak for warmth. His eyes were drawn over to the greener south bank, where fields and trees filled most of the space. There, young men frequented the taverns and stews but Edmund's mind ran on the open spaces and religious houses, whose chanting sometimes reached them across the waves. Edward, however, had seated himself with a view of the city, eagerly searching its features for life, for colour and the landing place where they were to disembark. Both boys had been keen to attend the tournament and neither had been to Smithfield before: York had put aside business for a few hours to take them himself. He only hoped they wouldn't be disappointed.

They passed Bridewell and Blackfriars before landing at St Andrew's. Horses were saddled and waiting to take them the short distance north, past the Royal Wardrobe, up beyond Ludgate to the tournament field.

'Ready?' called York. 'Here we are.'

'Ready father!'

Admiration shone in Edward's eyes. Looking at him, York was reminded of a young colt, long-limbed, full of energy, clambering up to try to walk unaided.

Edmund hung a little way behind, trying to master a big grey steed. Both boys were accomplished riders but more used to chasing the hart through the woods of the Welsh Marches than these narrow colourful streets which provided much distraction. As they trotted into the city, dogs behind a gate barked fearsomely and Edmund's horse shied away.

'Rein him in,' called York, wondering if he should reach across and take hold of the animal himself.

The grey horse danced for a moment, hooves clattering on cobbles, head tossing before it became still again.

'Are you all right?'

Edmund took a deep breath and adjusted his position in the saddle. 'Fine. Only stupid dogs.'

'And remember you've never ridden him before, he's just getting used to you.'

'I'd have been fine,' repeated Edmund, 'if it hadn't been for the dogs!'

'Good man,' praised his father, pleased by the boy's resilience.

Ahead of them stretched the open space known as the Smooth Field. The outlines of colourful tents were visible, in red, blue and yellow, with their spangled pennants hanging limply in the January air. They caught the smell of smouldering braziers, sweet and musky from the burning pastilles placed on the coals. People had gathered despite the cold; citizens and visitors, numbering in their hundreds. The lists had been set up east–west and at either side, knights were donning armour and horses were draped in matching coloured cloth.

York headed for the tented pavilion, bright with its scarlet cloth, reserved for the mayor and his guests. There was no sign of the red-fisted butchers who generally used the field to sell their wares. The crowds parted to let them through and trumpeters in royal livery let out a burst of noise. They climbed the raised dais of the pavilion, striped in red and blue paint. Chairs with cushions stood in a row, where the beaming mayor was waiting to greet them.

'My Lords, I bid you humble welcome. Myself and my aldermen are most honoured at your attendance. Please, be seated. Men, bring refreshments. Stir the knights to action, let the joust begin.'

York nodded to his sons. They placed themselves on three carved chairs set before a velvet curtain, the duke in the centre. A brazier was dragged closer, so they could feel its warmth. Servants brought blankets, spiced wine and plates of venison pasties to take the edge off their hunger. They ate steadily, conscious of thousands of eyes turned upon them; the tall, fine-featured man with greying hair and steely eyes, his clothes proclaiming his status, and his two handsome sons, with their thick manes of hair ruffled by the wind; the noble jaws and clear hazel eyes. They held themselves aloof, regal, conscious of the press of faces in the crowd and the need for distance. York shot a surreptitious look at Edmund but the boy's chin was lifted, eyes confident. He had learned a lot since their arrival in the city last autumn.

Into the arena before them came armed knights, each bearing the colours of their house. Visors raised, they bowed low to the pavilion and awaited the duke's command. York raised his arm and for a moment they waited, suspended before action, on the verge of life or death. Then the duke gave the signal and they sprang to arms, writhing in a mêlée of flashing steel. At once Edward was transfixed. Two large figures, locked in combat, drew his eye for a while, then his gaze fell upon the other men, struggling to defend or attack. There was one knight in particular who caught his eye, dressed brightly in yellow and white, fighting manfully at the edge of the group. With sword in hand, the plucky little figure defended himself against a brute of an opponent, almost twice his size, without seeming to tire. To Edward, he seemed to embody the spirit of optimism.

'This is the best training for the battlefield,' said his father at his side. 'Watch them closely. See why they fail and where they succeed. Size and strength count for much but they are not everything.'

The small white and yellow figure lunged forward again, thrusting with his sword, driving his opponent back.

'See that?' noticed York. 'See how he holds the sword, hands apart for control, hands closer together for might.'

Edward nodded. 'He's the best of all the fighters, isn't he?'

'What makes him the best? The best can change. Is it speed, skill, strength?'

'Or simply fortune?' added Edmund from the other side, with a flash of insight.

They watched, rooting for his success, willing him strength and energy, as the little knight gained the upper hand. Once he stumbled and almost fell, before quickly righting himself again.

Edward broke out in applause, pleased to see the man's spirit. Momentarily, the figure paused and turned to the platform with a brief acknowledgement of the encouragement.

The throng of men broke apart and charged together again. The little knight braced himself for conflict, allowing the brunt of the impact to fall upon his flank before he began his counter-attack.

'You see his manoeuvre there?' asked York, leaning in closer to his elder son. 'It takes thought and cunning. You have to be three steps ahead of your enemy and predict where he will be. See, look, that lets him parry the blow without exposing his body, then he can turn and strike on the other side.'

Edward watched, seeing the brave knight move boldly through the mêlée.

'But he is vulnerable on the other side.'

'Yes,' York nodded. 'He has moved too far ahead. Watch though, see how he keeps turning so he is always the same distance from the enemy. But he had better watch his back!'

A large knight in black came bearing down on the jaunty figure from behind. Edward flinched as the smaller combatant went sprawling on the ground.

York tutted. 'He let down his guard. He looked scared for a moment and that's deadly. Once you're down, you're down.'

'But he'll get up!' insisted Edward.

'If he can. That armour is heavy. He made the mistake of being intimidated by the other man's size. Even if you're tiny, it is all about using your brains.'

'But it wasn't fair. The black knight came upon him from behind!'

York shook his head. 'Who ever said battles were fair?'

Edward gasped. The black knight had brought down his sword hard upon the yellow and white back, almost completely severing an arm. Blood appeared on the sawdust.

York rose to his feet at once and gestured, his voice carrying through the air. 'Enough, carry the man away.'

The fighters ceased for the moment to allow the injured knight to be borne aloft from the field. York turned to resume his seat and saw the conflicting emotion on his son's face.

'He will be well, never fear. A surgeon awaits him.'

But Edward was stilled by the brute victory of might over skill, contemplating its implications.

York turned to his second son. 'And you Edmund, how are you enjoying the tournament?'

Edmund had fallen silent but now he turned his attention to the field. 'I was watching the horses, they are restless. Is it their turn yet?'

York was surprised. Had the younger boy had not witnessed the bloodshed? 'Very soon, we will see them tilt at the ring. But look, here is Warwick.'

The swarthy and compact figure of the earl, wrapped in brown furs, appeared at the foot of the pavilion. With a leap, he pulled himself up beside them.

'I have asked cousin Warwick to undertake your training at Westminster, he will be continuing your preparation in the chivalric arts; I could think of no better tutor.'

Warwick nodded to Edward, then Edmund, before his eyes became focused.

'My Lord, there is trouble in the city, to the east. An attack has been made on the home of a merchant in Thames Street and it threatens to overspill the streets.'

The duke frowned. 'There are men in attendance?'

'Indeed but they lack direction. Shall I go to them? We must contain it before it escalates.'

York thought for a moment, stroking his beard. 'I will go. But there are my sons to consider. Warwick, you must get them back safely to Westminster, take the river route.'

'But I…'

'Those are my wishes. I must go to the scene and my sons must be safe. Let us act now.'

The duke spoke briefly to the mayor before turning back to Edward and Edmund. 'There is a disturbance in the city; it may prove nothing but I must go and put a stop to it in person; we cannot allow the lawlessness of the last year to return. Warwick will take you from here back to the river, to keep you away from the danger.'

'But perhaps we might help, if we came with you,' Edward offered eagerly.

'No, not this time. Your safety is paramount; you must return to Westminster and watch over your mother until I return.'

The boys exchanged glances, understanding their duty. 'Of course father.'

*

They headed off down past the church of St Sepulchre, the horses' nostrils flaring as if they could scent danger.

'Keep close,' urged Warwick, in his gravelly voice. 'We'll avoid the Blackfriars steps as an obvious flashpoint and pick up a boat a little further along.'

The streets seemed quiet enough but Edward had confidence in the earl's judgement; their father would not have trusted them to him otherwise. They headed towards Newgate, then down towards St Martin's where the bells were pealing out a warning, and on to Addle Hill. The houses on either side were tall and well built, their large glassed windows and shutters displaying the signs of wealth.

Edward turned to check that Edmund was at his side, his heart beating faster at the possibility of danger lying ahead. His brother was not far behind, clinging tightly to his mount, his eyes narrowed with concentration.

Warwick paused briefly, reining in his horse before a tavern bearing the sign of three bells. Chickens had broken loose from somewhere and were pecking about in the dirt.

'Ready? In a moment we will cross Thames Street; once we're across, we're almost at Paul's steps, so be swift and do not stop. Ready?'

The boys nodded.

But then the mood changed suddenly. The way ahead became misted over with people and voices. At the far end of the street, they saw shadows, swiftly moving forward, threatening to encroach upon their space.

'Damn,' cursed Warwick, seizing Edmund's bridle. 'They've moved west, we must double back and head for Blackfriars where we can shelter, do not delay.'

They wheeled round, clattering in the narrow space, their heads level with the upstairs windows of the houses. From afar they heard shouting. Edward spurred his horse onwards and it leapt ahead, with a jump, shaking him in his saddle. For a moment, he lost control, making him cold with fear. Then, as if his steed understood, it drew level with Warwick and the three of them galloped back up to the crossroads.

Turning into Carter Lane, they found their way blocked by the stands of a small market. Barrels of fish and loaves of bread were being sold, songbirds in crates and sacks of flour, but the people looked uneasy, as if the mood of discontent was spreading. Some were already packing up their wares, others seemed to be arguing. Beside them, a crate of turnips was upended and the vegetables rolled into the gutter. Their horses danced to avoid tripping.

Cautiously, they picked their way ahead. The street began to widen, although the press of people seemed suddenly to double.

'There!' called Warwick. 'The spire of St Andrew's. From there we can head to the river.'

He urged forward and Edward was about to follow. But then, a harsh, grating sound filled the air; Edmund's horse kicked up its hind legs and threw him from the saddle. He landed hard on the cobbles at the road's edge.

At once Warwick had dismounted and was bending over the boy, trying to raise him. Edmund tried to stand but his ankle was limp.

'Edward!' the earl shouted. 'Dismount and gather the horses.'

A man, sinister-eyed, moved to approach them.

'Keep your distance!' cried Warwick, drawing his sword. 'Here, Edward, follow me.'

'My apologies, my Lord,' the man muttered. 'I was sharpening knives, it was the grinding noise that made the horse turn.'

'Let us pass,' insisted Warwick. 'Sharpen your knives elsewhere, where they can do no harm. And clear out of this place, for trouble is brewing.'

He led them through the dark gateway of a large inn and into the courtyard. An ostler appeared in the doorway at once.

'Secure the gates. The riot is spreading! Secure the gates, man!'

The fellow did as he was bid and the threat was locked outside. Then he led them through wood panelled corridors into an inner room, where a low lantern was burning.

Warwick cast a critical eye around. 'It'll do. Get a fire going, bring blankets, wine. Move man, go. You will be rewarded. And call for a surgeon.'

'A surgeon?' Edmund's eyes widened as he eased himself into a chair.

'Just as a precaution, to check this ankle. Now sit and rest.'

He moved to the window, peered to see out of the tiny pane. 'The rioting must have spread east. Your father will soon contain it but it is better that we do not get drawn in; we'd be sitting targets here. When it quietens, we will head to the bridge and soon be back at Westminster. There is nothing to fear. We must just sit tight.'

He turned, forced a smile.

'Of course,' said Edward, trying to appear cheerful. 'Father will soon have it under control.'

A maid hurried in, clattering wood in a scuttle, and began to lay kindling in the grate. Soon there was a small bright spark of golden flame and a welcome warmth spread through the room.

*

The doctor bent his white head over Edmund's ankle. With careful but firm fingers, he felt the position of the bones and manipulated the joint. Edmund winced.

'Sorry my Lord, it was necessary.'

He straightened himself up and nodded at Warwick. 'Your diagnosis is correct. There is nothing broken but the ankle is swollen and should not have weight put on it; it must be rested and dressed in poultices of cabbage leaves and mint. I can prepare some and bring them over, all being quiet outside.'

Warwick nodded and handed over a small purse of coins. 'Thank you. We will wait here until the danger has passed and then venture down to the river. Edmund should be able to ride and once we find a boat, we will be straight back to Westminster. Send your poultices there.'

Edward frowned. 'So we will wait here until all is safe?'

'Indeed. The pot boy brought news of houses being looted near St Andrews. It would be wiser to remain.'

Edward bridled, his youthful manhood struggling with the idea of cowardice. 'But father is out there, should you and I not go and seek him?'

'And what good would your death achieve? I promised your father I would bring you back safely and I will do so; sometimes the wiser man waits while the fool rushes in.'

'Father is not a fool!'

Warwick grimaced. 'You misunderstand. It would be foolish to go outside now, into the unknown, for no certain gains or cause.'

Edward nodded. 'So it is I who am the fool.'

'No Edward, but you are young and inexperienced. You are being too sensitive.'

The youth's pride was piqued. Worse than that, he knew Warwick was right but he still burned with the desire to prove himself. 'I'll go through into the inn and take something to drink. You can find me there, when the danger has passed.'

It was dark in the next room. The torches burned low and Edward had the distinct impression that the inn was not open for business. A number of trestle tables and benches filled the space, some still set with the plates and tankards of last night and the sawdust on the floor smelt rank with urine and spillages. A dark doorway led to some back rooms but there did not seem to be anyone about. The fellow from earlier had disappeared.

'Hello?'

His voice echoed back to him from the bowels of the building. He stood for a moment, reluctant to go back to Warwick, and wandered to the window to kill some time. At first, there seemed to be little activity out in the street but, as he drew closer to the pane, a band of men armed with cudgels raced past, perhaps fifteen or twenty, shouting and cursing. Their angry glances and cruel mouths made him draw back again into the gloom. Warwick's caution had been justified. For now, this was the safest place to be.

He sat in the corner, unnoticed and unmoving. The minutes passed in silence. Light falling in through the window dimmed and ebbed as a brief shower of rain quenched the city. Finally, he could bear the inertia no more and got to his feet to explore. Through the doorway he found the other downstairs rooms; a dirty kitchen with large fireplace and spit, a storehouse with sacks and barrels and a tiny bedroom, dominated by a straw mattress with rumpled sheets left in the shape of the last sleeper.

'Hello?'

Again there was no response. He was about to return to Warwick and Edmund in the little room with the fire, when he spotted the staircase. It was solid, heavy, built of dark wood and seemed to form the heart of the house, almost as if the rooms had been added around it at a later date. Curiosity overcame him and he slowly climbed round its right-angled turns up towards the first floor. His skin prickled with the sense that he was entering private territory but he did not stop. Some sense of excitement, or the thrill of discovery, perhaps even of entitlement, sent him along the landing. At the end, the final door stood ajar. The dim light from a candle sent flickering tongues around its edges, like an invitation. There was movement within.

Some hidden sense awoke within him. He drew closer and put his ear to the wood. Like the faint constant beat of his heart in his chest, a low noise reached him, a lilting rise and fall, a soft, sweet drone, a revelation: a woman humming. It was intimate, encouraging. He felt acutely aware of his body, of the physicality of the space around him and his proximity to her. The strip of light revealed an expanse of floorboards and the side of a carved chest. She was some way off, possibly with her back to him. She probably wouldn't notice if he pushed the door open slightly. If he put his eye to the door, if he entered.

But Edward wasn't that bold. He was, after all, not quite fourteen years old, sure of his young strong body but aware of the attraction that women could hold. Without being taught, he had understood the promise in their eyes and the comfort they could offer but he had not yet reached out to accept it. Inexperience stayed him. At the door, he merely drew close and stared into the lit room, a tall, broad-shouldered boy, lips quivering at the thought of infinite possibilities.

She moved into his line of vision, a tune still resonant in her throat. Her fair hair was caught up on top of her head, as she undressed to wash herself, with loose strands hanging down the back of her long neck. She could have been fifteen, or twenty-five, her skin still plump and unspoiled by hard work or the bearing of children. The shoulders were rounded and pink, as she unbuttoned her dress and let it fall to the ground; he could imagine pressing his mouth against the skin at her throat and behind her ear. Swathed in her long white shift, he could trace the outline of her figure, of the fullness of breasts and hips. He lifted his fingers, almost involuntarily, but they fell just short of the door, of pushing it wide, stepping inside and claiming her.

Perhaps she sensed him. Her pert little chin lifted and she turned her head slightly, revealing the curve of her cheek. The bed beside her seemed like an invitation. Surely she would laugh, to discover a mere boy trembling at her bedroom door? As she turned, slowly, he held his breath. He saw the mould of her lips, the straight nose and generous chin, the wide blue eyes, the inquisitive cast to her expression. She was older than he had anticipated, maybe even twice his age, but she was at the height of her beauty. He gazed at her as a mortal may gaze at a goddess. Then her eyes slowly rested on him and he saw her give a tiny start, almost imperceptible, like the beat of her dark lashes. Her lips parted slightly. He saw small, white pearly teeth, the tip of her tongue, her interest. One arched brow raised in a question.

'Edward?'

The spell broke. Warwick was in the stairwell, calling up.

'Are you there? We must be on the move, hurry. Edward?'

Disappointment rushed over him, engulfed him, almost unbearably. Then there was the collapse of shame; of being a boy summoned away by a man at the exact moment of promise. She pouted slightly, bemused at this tall child whom she had transfixed.

'Sorry,' he mouthed and tore himself away, his body burning.

He half fell, half tumbled, down the stairs.

Warwick was in the doorway, helping Edmund out into the daylight. 'Where the devil did you go? I almost left you behind. Your father has sent an escort, let's get down to the river.'

Later, Edward did not remember the exact building, the dark deserted inn, or the little room, where he had seen the woman. Back at court, safely ensconced behind Westminster walls, the actual building faded into dust but he revisited the moment time and time again. Sometimes, in his imagination, she pitied him, embraced him like a mother. At other times, when he lay wakeful at night, listening to Edmund's gentle breath, he pictured her opening up her white body in the darkness and drawing him towards her.

EIGHT: Love and Duty

The rooks were circling over Westminster Palace. Its great sprawling complex crouched on the riverbank, a maze of red brick, arches, roofs and chimneys, of blazing fires and scurrying feet, of clerks writing letters and seals imprinted in wax. In the kitchens, cooks sliced the flesh of roast meat and kneaded pastry with their fingertips; inside the royal wardrobe, white linen was scrubbed with lye and scented with lavender. Wood was chopped, water poured and, somewhere, a lackey sat on a step, polishing the Duke of York's boots.

Edward threw open the window. Cool air raced inside, sharp with the tang of grass and water. The royal apartments looked out across the gardens and down to the river, grey and unpredictable, lapping against the palace steps. Below, he could see boatmen on the wooden jetty, winding in long coils of ropes and the keeper of the hounds exercising the dogs in the orchard.

He had left the others in the bedchamber, where the walls were hung with scarlet cloth and tapestries of saints and knights, locked in prayer and battle forever by the warp and weft of woven thread. Edmund still needed a few more days' rest before his ankle was strong enough to walk on and he had been amusing himself with ancient stories of romance and chivalry. The book lay on the seat in the alcove. Edward took it up and paused. From outside, he heard the first, faint patter of rain drops striking the glass. As he pulled the window shut, a pair of riders made their way through the gates and into the courtyard below.

He was crossing the floor when he heard voices approaching. Some instinct made him pause and draw back behind the heavy curtain, as his mother and father entered the chamber. The door closed behind them before they started to speak.

'So the rioters have been caught and punished?' His mother asked softly.

York's voice was strained. 'The ringleaders. It should show the rest that we mean business.'

'So why are there still whisperings about it?'

'It is an easy weapon against me. No doubt there will be those who wish to read something into it and say that I am unable to keep the peace.'

Cecily sighed. 'But you did, you restored order the same night.'

'That fact is less important to some than the outbreak of violence itself.'

'Beaufort?'

'Perhaps,' York mused. 'He has little reason to love me. Or the Tudor brothers, I don't know for sure.'

'But the tensions in the city have been there for months; it is always the way when foreigners meet with success. Someone will resent their hard work and use it as a chance to settle scores. It was the same under the king, if not worse.'

York paused. 'The truth never hinders those with malice in their hearts.'

'My poor love,' The duchess's voice was low and soothing. Edward imagined her laying her hand gently on the back of York's neck, which was her habitual gesture of comfort. 'Is there anything else to be done?'

'I will make a statement in the council but, beyond that, we know what these Lancastrians are capable of. It is probably their intention to poison the queen and young Beaufort against me, if it was possible that they could dislike me further.'

'Would it help if I write to the queen again? I could enquire after the king's health and send some comfits for the prince.'

'It cannot hurt. Perhaps she will take more notice of you.'

Edward dared to peep out between the curtains but his parents stood by the roaring hearth, intent on their troubles and did not notice the movement.

York was pouring wine from a jug on the table. 'And then there is the star. People in the city are buzzing with the news of a great gleaming star which appeared in the sky the other night.'

Cecily raised her arched eyebrows, prone to belief in the superstitious and unexplained. 'A star?'

'I know. In the north, apparently. The timing is not good, I cannot think what it means but there are already whispers that it will mark some sort of change.'

'Then let it be a good one,' Cecily placed her hand on his arm. 'Why would it not be a bringer of good news for us, a sign of our success? I will offer my prayers again and ask for guidance.'

York nodded and drained his glass.

There was a knock at the door. Edward stepped back again into the shadow and heard his father's reply, followed by a scraping as the handle turned.

'My Lord, there is a merchant downstairs who would speak with you; he has letters of introduction from my Lord of Warwick.'

'Then show him in. His arrival is timely as we were just speaking of the recent rioting.'

Edward shifted his position slightly and parted the heavy curtains an inch, to allow him a glimpse of the new arrival. A man shuffled humbly into the room, warm in his rich furs although his brows were knit with concern. Edward recognised him at once as the Italian merchant Boratti he had seen dining in the great hall a few weeks before, with his daughters. That graceful pale face and slanting eyes flashed inside his mind again.

The merchant bowed low.

'Please, rise, you are welcome. You have letters of introduction?'

The man handed over a paper which York took and scrutinised.

'But of course, I remember you. When you came here last we discussed the damage to your property. Will you sit, take some wine?'

'Thank you my Lord, I have no need.'

'Then tell me how I may be of assistance. How did you fare in the recent rioting?'

'Not too badly, in comparison with others. Our horses were turned loose but we recovered them and shut the gates before the worst of it.'

'Were your family at home?' asked Cecily gently.

'Yes. We were unfortunate in that respect, my Lady, thank you for your concern. My wife and daughters were alarmed but they suffered no other injury, thanks be to God.'

'Indeed, He is merciful.'

Boratti turned again to York. 'I have come to ask, my Lord, for your blessing regarding my daughter Alasia's marriage. I would have asked her godfather, but he passed away in the riots and the rest of our family is in Milan still.'

Edward's attention was caught. He watched the merchant tugging at his grey beard as he spoke. 'She has been betrothed to a neighbour since she was a child but now we have the chance of a far better match, a leading guildsman, a cousin of the mayor, recently widowed. We do not wish for any trouble if we break the original terms of the betrothal.'

'Have promises been exchanged?'

'Only when she was seven years of age and now she is fourteen.'

'And there has been no consummation?'

Edward tensed.

'Indeed there has not! I have guarded her most zealously.'

'Then rest assured, you have my backing. I will answer that you are acting legally and justly. The first contract is easy to dissolve; your daughter may wed without any concern.'

Boratti bowed low. 'Thank you for your kindness, thank you, my good Lord.'

With characteristic generosity, the duchess added, 'Why not bring her to court and she can pass a few days with my ladies and acquire a little courtly polish?'

The merchant was visibly moved. 'Your goodness overwhelms me, I cannot thank you enough. In fact, my child awaits me downstairs.'

'Then I shall come down and meet her,' smiled the duchess.

As they left the room, Edward breathed out deeply. He could scarcely conceal the smile from his face as he hurried through into the adjoining bedchamber, his fingers wrapped tightly around the book of romances.

Edmund was sitting in the chair where he had left him, his ankle stretched out on a cushion. He did not mind the enforced stillness, in fact it almost suited him, as a period of contemplation, of observation and deep thought. At his feet, his younger brothers were being taught their letters. Margaret's dark head was bent over her primer, her finger reverently tracing the line of the words. Behind them, Elizabeth was sitting on their mother's bed, unpicking a knot in a pair of gold laces.

It was a peaceful scene, a safe, comfortable place, but Edward's heart rebelled against it. In Elizabeth's dutiful fingers and in Margaret's low tones; in the unfinished game of chess on the table and the half-drunk cups of watered wine; in the small boys' bent heads and in the wooden toy soldiers in their painted box, Edward was reminded of everything to do with his childhood.

He dropped the book into Edmund's lap. The hazel eyes warmed in a brief smile, then into comprehension.

'You're not staying to read?'

'I will be back shortly, I promise, but there is something I must... I have to... I'll be back.'

He darted from the room, leaving childhood behind, and headed down the corridor in the wake of his parents.

*

Edward reached the bottom of the staircase in time to see his parents enter one of the council rooms and the heavy carved doors closing behind. He stopped in the corridor to catch his breath, hesitating whether or not to knock against the solid wood. Inside, there would be Warwick, Salisbury and his Bourchier uncles, gathered to discuss the war with France with the likes of the Tudors and Buckingham, drawing a silent line between the life of the court and the world of men, of business and statutes and acts of law. Yet, if his mother had gone in there, if the merchant was with them, it meant that the formal meeting had not yet got underway. A faint ray of sunshine spilled down at his feet from a high, unseen window. It seemed to be a sign of encouragement. He stepped up to the door and listened. One hand rose gently and he grazed the wood with his fingertips.

Then, as if he had knocked, the door pulled back, enough to allow a single figure to leave. Instinct drew Edward towards the shadows but it was too late, he had been seen. And yet, this slight figure, dressed in grey cloth edged with dyed fur, seemed as hesitant as him. She closed the door softly and stepped into the light. The sun caught her modest headdress, with its graceful folds of white linen, the pale curve of her cheek and throat. Slanting bright eyes lifted to meet his.

She dropped into a curtsey at once.

'I was, I was just about to...' he stammered.

She inclined her head and stepped aside to let him pass.

'I mean, no, I won't go in now. What are you doing here?'

The girl looked up, surprised, as if she had broken some rule.

'No, I don't mean that.' He coloured at his clumsiness, he must pull himself together and act according to his rank. He stiffened his shoulders. 'What brings you here, my Lady?'

The formality made her feel safer. 'I came here with my father; he is attending upon the Duke of York.' She dropped her eyes again and added, more softly, 'your father.'

'So you know who I am then?'

'Of course, my Lord. They sent me to wait outside while they arrange my future.' He could not help but notice the sting in her voice as she spoke those words.

And that might have been it: he could have nodded, given her his blessing, passed on by, entered the chamber and seen her no more, this delightful girl who was expected to better her family's fortunes. Instead, in spite of himself, a little voice in his head urged him to stay.

'What is your name?'

He knew the answer, but it seemed the easiest way to get her to speak.

'Alasia Boratti, my Lord. My father is Giotto Boratti, a merchant of Gold Lane. Off Thames Street.'

'I know it. What does he deal in, your father?'

'Spices, my Lord.'

'And is that his business here today, selling spices?'

He watched the blush spread through her cheeks, the discomfort that seemed to crumple her paleness. It ignited something like pleasure in him.

'No, my Lord.'

He waited, slowly taking her in, detail by detail. Her mouth was wide and generous, covering small, well-shaped teeth. The dress she wore was modest enough for her station, with a few tasteful adornments at the neck and hem. It fitted her closely at the waist and he could not help his eyes from noting the swell where the material strained across her young chest. He swiftly darted his eyes away, embarrassed by his interest.

'My father seeks to give my hand in marriage. They asked me to wait outside while…'

'Ah. You are of age to wed, then?'

'I will be fifteen this winter.'

'You are fortunate to have a father who makes good provision for your future.'

'I am fortunate indeed.' Her lower lip quivered a little. She looked away.

'Here,' he led her towards an alcove.

'My Lord, I…'

'Don't worry, you will come to no harm, you are under my father's protection. We can talk here.'

'But I…'

'You can fear nothing from me, nor in such a place like this, which is so open and busy. I mean only to aid your advancement.'

'Forgive me, my Lord, I meant nothing by it.'

'You do not wish to be married?'

She let out a deep sigh. 'It is not that. Please don't think me ungrateful.'

'Then what is it? You dislike the man they have chosen?'

'That would be simple.' She replied softly. 'He is honourable, and a good man. But…'

'But what?'

'I do not feel ready. He is old, almost as old as my father.'

Edward winced.

They stood, side by side, as servants carried trays of spices and jugs of wine past them towards the Council Hall. As the door opened to admit them, Edward heard the sound of raised voices within and frowned.

Alasia had heard them too. 'Is there trouble?'

'Not for you to worry about. My father debates the peace with Normandy, but it comes at a cost.'

'Then my father will be leaving soon, to take me home.'

Edward recalled his mother's words. 'Perhaps you might stay at court for a while; how would you like that?'

The dark eyes were curious. 'Me? At court?'

'Why not? I would like that.'

She shifted her position and Edward caught the faint scent of her clothes, of the musky fragrance caught in the folds of the linen. He found he could not take his eyes from her lips, wondering if he dared lean forward and brush them with his own. Something in her trusting manner made him bolder.

'Come, let me show you around. They will not come out yet.'

She did not refuse.

He led her to the little chapel. It was the only quiet place. She followed him with slight reluctance and gazed up at the panelled walls and painted faces of the saints. The eyes of the saints looked back blankly from on high, picked out in gold or blue.

'It's beautiful!'

He wanted to repay her comment with a compliment but inexperience made him awkward. Instead, he lay his hand lightly upon her small white one, as it rested on the back of a pew. Her skin was cool and smooth; he felt the contact for only a second before she withdrew it. Her face clouded in confusion.

Suddenly his courage returned. 'I saw you once, at dinner in the great hall, before Christmas. I've been hoping to see you again since then.'

She inclined her head slightly. 'I saw you too.'

'Did you, really?' He felt the warm spread of confirmation through his stomach.

'Yes, I saw you at the high table, but I didn't think I might speak with you.'

He smiled. 'I wish you had.'

'We had to leave, and you looked so…'

'What? I looked so what?'

She blushed and shrugged her shoulders. 'I don't know, so, perhaps so grand?'

It was all the invitation he needed. Leaning forward, he planted a kiss on her soft lips; the brief, fleeting brush of one mouth against another, which left him trembling. She shook her head a little and breathed a word of protest but she did not move away. He kissed her again, this time more slowly and deliberately, and felt her relaxing under the pressure, her lithe body bending towards his. Wrapping an arm about her waist, he pulled her close to him, as she began to respond. Her head tipped back, her eyes closed. She was small and slender; he could easily have picked her up in his arms and carried her away. He could hardly conceal the mounting excitement in the pit of his stomach; the blurring of his senses, the feeling of melting together as they stood in the gloom of the painted chapel.

Suddenly, she drew back, one hand raised to her mouth.

'What? Sorry, did I hurt you?'

'No, no, but I shouldn't.'

'But no one will know. I won't tell.'

'My father?'

'He won't know.'

'And I am to be married.'

'You will have my protection, my word, my silence. I promise. It's only a kiss.'

She allowed him to enfold her in his arms again, trembling with his new-found passion, and rain kisses down on her pale, upturned face.

The crash of the chapel door broke them apart. The Earl of Warwick looked impatiently at Edward, his brows darkening.

'Yes,' he called to someone outside, his tone scathing. 'I have found the Boratti girl. God's blood Edward, get yourself into the council chamber; a message has come from the queen.'

Alasia scuttled out ahead of him, head bowed. Burning with desire and shame, Edward followed, caught in Warwick's disapproving gaze.

York was standing in the council doorway, hands on hips. Edward glimpsed the forms of his mother and Boratti close behind, waiting to spirit the girl away.

'Edward, there you are! A message has come from Windsor. The king is well again. The queen has closed up their household and they are on their way here.'

'God be praised.' Edward knew the formula, his mind still afire with the exchange of kisses. He watched as Alasia was led away.

'He will be able to take over the reins of government again.'

'That is indeed a blessing.'

'So,' said York pointedly, 'we will be leaving Westminster. It is time to return to Ludlow. We must pack up our affairs and head north again. I want to be out of here before they arrive.'

Edward snapped back to reality. That was when he realised it was over: London, power, colour, life and love. They were to return to the quiet of Ludlow, with its wide open fields and endless roads, miles from here, miles from the king and queen and Alasia, and he was powerless to object. He dropped his head in duty. A door had been opened and quickly slammed shut.

*

They were heading back into the hall when the sound of trumpets reached them.

'So soon?' questioned Cecily. 'It cannot be.'

Edward saw his parents exchange glances. But before they had time to think, the silence broke. The castle suddenly flooded with noise.

'What,' exclaimed Warwick, 'can it be, so hot on the heels of the messenger?'

'Oh yes,' York nodded cynically. 'They chose to give us no warning, to surprise us before we could leave. Margaret wants to turn us out in person.'

Warwick hastened to a window. 'There, on the road, men in royal livery. By God, Henry is almost here. You're right, this is some trick of the queen's, to catch us unawares.'

'The king!' announced York, to the waiting attendants. 'The king approaches, go quickly to your positions, make his chambers ready.'

The court wheels began to spin into life. Footsteps echoed through the corridors and voices called out instructions and warnings. The Borattis were swept away amid the movement.

Cecily was wringing her hands. 'But the children are still in our chambers, the king's chambers.' She thought of the bed she had slept in that night, the large, bright rooms with their views across the river.

York came back and whispered hotly in her ear. 'Then they must leave. We must find other lodgings at once, before we depart for Ludlow.'

'But...'

'There cannot be two kings in Westminster, you understand?'

She nodded, drawing herself up to her full height to face the task ahead. 'Let's head outside, we must wear our smiles of welcome.'

Edward followed his parents towards the distant doors. The guards threw them open at their approach and faint sunlight streamed in. On the cobbles of the yard, people were gathering nervously, blinking in the light as the castle emptied out. Alasia and her father were hovering by the kitchen steps, unsure of where to stand, but he could not concern himself with them now. Horses were being led away and a pile of hay in one corner was being hastily swept to one side. Over at the entrance gate, he saw the red heads of the Tudor brothers, as they peered eagerly down the road, hoping to be the first to confirm the news.

A second messenger galloped in: Jasper grabbed the reins and pulled the man towards him at once. A few seconds were enough to confirm the first report; he nodded to the assembled crowd with satisfaction.

York stepped forward to take charge at once. 'Make way for the king. Assemble. All waiting people inside, stable hands at the ready, the king comes here this moment.'

'So it is really true,' said Cecily softly. 'Is it just to score a point against us?'

'I don't know,' York replied. 'Unless, of course, Henry does not trust us.'

But it was not Henry who rode through the gates. A gold-covered litter decorated with a fleur-de-lys trundled into view, its occupant hidden by thick curtains.

'The queen,' whispered Cecily. 'You were right, Margaret has come alone. No wait, let me be the one to welcome her, woman to woman.'

Drawing in a deep breath and smoothing down her skirts, Cecily advanced to meet the carriage, standing tall and regal, her spine a straight sweep. The golden coach drew to a halt and busy hands moved to pull the drapes aside. From the dark depths inside there appeared a figure wrapped in powdered furs, heavy Italian brocade and cloth of gold. Margaret of Anjou pushed back her hood and coolly surveyed the assembled court with her dark intelligent eyes. Then she looked down at the kneeling figure of the duchess before her.

'My Lady of York.' Her voice was cool, clipped.

'Most honourable Queen, you are welcome back to court, we all rejoice to see your return. I trust you had a safe journey. Please come and take some refreshment whilst your rooms are made ready.'

'Thank you, Duchess,' Margaret replied in her low tones. 'I shall do so, but before I do,' and she turned to the courtyard, running her eyes across the assembled figures before fixing her gaze on York, 'let it be known that by the will of almighty God, King Henry has risen from his bed and will be arriving amongst us tomorrow, to call a new parliament. The king is king again.'

York bowed his head, biting back the bitter taste in his mouth. 'Amen to that.'

A cheer ran through the yard, initiated by the loyal Tudors.

York caught his wife's eye as she led the queen inside. The pale winter sun disappeared behind the clouds and the courtyard was cast suddenly into shade. The last thing Edward saw of Alasia was her father hurrying her out of the gates.

NINE: Faces in the Dark, January, 1458

It was not yet light. The sky was still full of stars as the sun began to spread across from the east, through the darkest of blue winter mornings. Slowly, the city came to life, with braziers lit at crossroads and the glow of lamps and fires flickering behind locked doors and shutters. The air was mild for the season, clean and cold, with the promise of later warmth.

A man yawned in firelight, a woman called upstairs to wake her child. Traders were hawking wares, carts heading for market and girls with bleary eyes carried buckets in search of water. Along the Thames rose the towers and chimneys of great men's houses, hidden away behind thick walls that enclosed courtyards and scent-filled gardens. In a quiet street, a massive pair of gates swung open and a small group of riders clattered purposefully out into the dawn.

The leader grasped the reins in his powerful hands. His eyes scanned the street with experience and a sense of ownership; they were set in a lean, tanned face, with a peppery beard that had become more white than black in recent years. His hair was dark but thinning a little through care and age: three more summers would bring him to the age of fifty. Richard, Duke of York, was a powerful figure in the saddle, an extension of the horse's speed and strength, as he guided his mount with careful, exact commands. He was still a neat, compact man, at ease in his limbs, who moved with a natural sense of nobility. The past three years of stress and cares had not detracted from his bearing: with Henry VI re-established and Queen Margaret pulling the strings, he knew he was treading a fine line. Now, he narrowed his eyes and checked up and down the street outside his London home.

On his left rode the Earl of Warwick, his dark curls tucked under his fur-lined hood. He was York's cousin and ally, but he was his physical opposite in many ways: the earl's powerful head was squat and round as a cannonball, ending in a square jaw and cleft chin. He sat heavily in the saddle, leaning forward and the cold morning air had already brought a high colour to his ruddy cheeks. He exchanged glances with York and nodded as they headed north, past the Royal Wardrobe, then west past the monastery of the Blackfriars.

On York's right rode a tall young man in green velvet. The last couple of years had transformed Edward, Earl of March, from a long-limbed youth into a lean and imposing figure. His chest had broadened and endless hours in the field and tilt yard at Ludlow had given his muscles a lean definition. The hazel eyes and close-cropped sandy hair served as reminders of the boy he had been but his face had lost its air of childishness and resolved itself into the handsome angles of high broad cheekbones and wide forehead. His nose was straight, with aristocratic nostrils and his lips formed a sensuous curve. Nearly sixteen, he had shot up in recent months and now sat higher than his father, with his shoulders square to the front and his chin held nobly high. His eyes conveyed a sense of promise, while his mouth betrayed a certain impatience. Flanked by their guards, the three crossed the Fleet River then rode on to Temple Bar, through Blackfriars and into the Strand.

Recent years in the city had seen an uneasy truce. The Lancastrian king and queen had lost any popularity they had enjoyed in the city, with constant whispers about their private life and the extent of Margaret's ambition. It had been a relief when they had left and ridden north, to establish themselves at Tutbury Castle, leaving London under the free hand of York and his allies. At first, the distance had helped. Without King Henry's wan face in Westminster, business was conducted more swiftly but the queen was another matter entirely. Her supporters continued to stir up trouble both in and out of the chamber. Now, two years since York had reluctantly stepped down from the position of Protector, an uneasy stasis held the country in its grip: one king ruled in the north whilst York did his job in the south. Soon enough one of them would have to make way for the other.

In silence, the riders passed by the turning to Little Drury Lane, leading up to the wide open fields of the Convent Garden. Their thoughts were elsewhere; on last night's revels or their dawn prayers. Edward was closest to the darkness, his senses sharp and alert despite the early hour. Suddenly, a feeling of unease gripped him. The morning seemed to change colour slightly as something in the shadows disturbed him; an unexpected movement perhaps, or a shape. He raised his hand and the others at once drew in their reins, their horses rearing up at the sharpness of the command.

'What is it?' asked York in low, precise tones.

'I'm not sure.' Edward's voice had broken, deepened. 'Something isn't right.'

'What did you see?' Warwick was quick to draw his sword, wary after decades of conflict.

'Nothing yet. It was more of a sense of it.' Edward's lips hardened into a concentrated line. He just knew.

In recent years, York had come to trust his eldest son's judgement. Edward's skill at riding and bearing arms, along with his youth, had often given him the edge over his father's experience. On this occasion, he was not wrong.

The shadows of the passageway began to teem with men and a motley collection of armed figures launched themselves out of the darkness towards York's party. Edward's awareness had forced their hand, putting them on the back foot.

'An ambush!' cried Warwick at once, his sword bearing down upon the first unfortunates to cross his path.

Edward kicked out his boot and felt his foot connect with a man's shoulder. The attacker stumbled but came back at once, a long knife glinting in his hand. York's guard fell upon him before he could reach the duke's party and Edward turned his sword instead to parry blows coming from behind.

'Who are you? Who sent you?' York shouted.

The dark figures fought with a sort of desperation, as if to be slain in the scuffle was preferable to survival. For a few minutes they made a valiant effort to dismount the riders but were soon beaten back and while some fell, wounded, others continued to stand their ground in spite of being overpowered. When Warwick's sword sliced through the torso of the ringleader, spraying the cobbles with his blood, those still able to run took it as their cue to flee.

Warwick dismounted and pulled aside the cloak of the dying man. He let out a cynical laugh. 'Beaufort's livery.'

'Of course,' York grimaced, shaking his head. 'Retribution for the death of his father at St Albans.'

'Who sent you? Who ordered our deaths, admit it, was it the Duke of Beaufort?' Warwick shook the blanching face, making a wave of dark blood ebb from the gaping mouth. The man was incapable of speech, so the earl let him fall back against the kerb.

'It's Beaufort's men all right,' Warwick agreed. 'He would have known we were to ride this way, on our way to the council, so he set this trap. It is not the first time. Last year he tried a similar trick when I was in Coventry.'

'He will answer for it!'

'He will deny it.'

'Let's away,' urged Edward, ever practical, 'in case any more appear. Our men can finish the job.'

He spurred his horse onwards and the three galloped side by side down the narrow street to Charing Cross, into King's Street and on to Westminster.

As they entered the palace gates, where the torches flickered and dimmed, Edward caught sight of his father's expression. Resolution and dismay fought for mastery across his grave features, as he struggled to come to terms with the attack.

For Edward, it was natural that they should attract enemies. Their position provoked antagonism and there would always be those who resented their positions. But York, for all his wisdom and experience, could never seem to shake off the sense of injustice. He was royal by blood, with as good a claim to the English throne as King Henry. In many ways, he and the ineffectual king were as different as chalk and cheese, but their common bond showed, thought Edward, as he slipped from his horse. They were both too trusting.

*

Inevitably, they were late. The council chamber was already full by the time they strode in through the carved double doors and took their places. Wine and spices had been laid out, drawing the men into a knot around the table. Edward assessed them rapidly: the clergymen gathered in their familiar group, with Thomas Bourchier, Archbishop of Canterbury, at their head, along with the Archbishop of York and eight or ten bishops. Then the Earls of Worcester and Devon, loyal to the Lancastrian cause, the Stanley brothers deep in conversation with Baron Audley and the more friendly faces of John de Vere, Earl of Oxford and

Warwick's father, the white-haired Salisbury. At the end of the table, Jasper Tudor sat alone, his angular face glowering at them all. Since the plague had claimed his brother Edmund, in the damp autumn of 1456, his features had always worn a sullen cast as if he was stewing some terrible revenge for those he believed responsible. There was a resolution in him, a burning intelligence and resourcefulness that might make him their most formidable opponent yet. Edward's eyes moved on, disliking the cast of Tudor's features. Beside him, bowed over some papers, was the smooth head of Baron Rivers, the Lancastrian knight who had married the king's widowed aunt.

York's indignation had resolved into anger. He stood at the head of the table, one arm smarting with a blow from his attackers. At the far side of the chamber, the lean, black-clad Beaufort rose to his feet, alongside the scar-faced Duke of Buckingham. The pair exchanged a silent glance that told York all he needed to know.

'You are tardy, my Lords,' Beaufort began. 'We have already begun our discussions on the...'

York cut him dead. 'We would have been here sooner, except we were set upon by a band of men on the road, intent on our destruction.'

'You were ambushed?' asked the ruddy-faced Bourchier, genuinely aghast.

'Indeed we were. It was only due to the presence of mind of my son Edward, and the bravery of our men, that we escaped serious harm.'

'There is no question,' added Edward at his side. 'It was a deliberate attack. They must have known we were to pass that way and lain in wait for our appearance.'

'God's blood!' exclaimed Salisbury. 'Are any of you injured?'

Warwick answered his father. 'Just bruises. We were fortunate this time.'

'And next time?' York asked. 'What then? This is not the first time that I have been attacked in this way; it seems that my enemies conspire to send me to a better place.'

There was a murmur in the hall.

'Do be seated and rest,' spoke Beaufort, his oily voice cutting through the noise. 'You are in need of some medical attention perhaps; should I call the surgeon?'

'You would do better to call off your men.' Warwick snapped.

His retort hung in the air.

'My men?' asked Beaufort with elaborate formality.

Warwick was still angry. 'Before they do any further harm.'

York lifted his hand slightly in warning but a confrontation could not now be avoided.

'Call off my men?' Beaufort repeated calmly. 'Whatever can you mean by that?'

'Do you think this was an attempt on your lives?' asked the archbishop. 'Not merely a group of criminals?'

'Criminals in livery perhaps,' added Edward.

Beaufort coloured. 'Are you making an accusation? Do you wish to offer a challenge?' His hand crept inside his clothing, as if seeking a concealed weapon there. 'I will gladly accept any challenge any of you wish to extend.'

'Now, Beaufort,' cautioned Buckingham at his side. 'You go too far.'

'We make no challenge,' York replied in controlled terms. 'Although there is reason enough for such a challenge to be made, given the cowardly circumstances of the attack this morning. Yet we make no formal accusation at this time. However, if we are met again in similar circumstances, we shall not be so restrained.'

'Restrained?' Beaufort sneered. 'Are we really to see the house of York exercising some restraint?'

'Enough!' said Salisbury decisively. As one of the oldest council members, he commanded a certain respect, regardless of his Yorkist affinities. 'This is not a battlefield, we are here to debate the law in the king's name.'

'May I then suggest,' added the archbishop. 'If York and his men are quite well, that we partake briefly of some refreshment and then resume business.'

'It has always been our intention,' complied York, 'to attend this council session for the sake of business and business alone, in the interest of national peace and the name of the king.'

'Then that is agreed,' stated Bourchier. 'A moment to recollect yourselves, my Lords.'

Noise broke out in the hall.

'So he tries to kill us and gets away with it!' exclaimed Warwick, almost spitting in rage as he turned away to a corner of the chamber.

York's forehead was lined. 'Be calm, this is not the way. He will get what he deserves when the time is right; he will show his hand again but next time we will be ready for him.'

'I wish I had your patience!'

'Do not let him see that he has angered you. Nod and smile, play the game. Keep your powder dry.'

'You are unhurt?' asked Salisbury, approaching with concern. He was still strong but recent years had seen the old pain in his legs return.

York nodded.

'No thanks to that dog,' Warwick snarled.

Salisbury levelled at his son. 'You are angry, justifiably, but it does your cause no good to show it in this way. You give Beaufort what he wants. Bite your tongue and bide your time, his day will come.'

'Hush,' Edward urged, seeing Archbishop Bourchier leave his place at the table and head in their direction.

As York's brother-in-law, Bourchier trod a fine line in the council chamber, his office requiring impartiality and fairness. Yet his face was full of concern. 'I am sorry to hear of the attack made upon you. If you have your suspicions, there are ways you can lodge them, officially. Do you wish to make an accusation against Beaufort?'

'Not today,' said York. 'There is no doubt he was behind the attack; probably as vengeance for his father.'

Bourchier twitched. 'Perhaps, perhaps not. He may have been acting on other orders, or on his own account, in an attempt to find favour.'

York's dark eyes narrowed. 'You think this may have come from the king?'

Bourchier shrugged diplomatically.

'Henry would not wish me harm. I am his close kin, next in line, until such time as his son is grown to be a man.'

Warwick snorted. 'I cannot believe it of Henry, he is too interested in his mortal soul to sanction violence.'

The archbishop's voice dropped. 'Not the king, no.'

York nodded, a light dawning. 'The queen. Thank you for your warning. She and Beaufort are as close as ever and neither of them has any love for me.'

'Just my suspicion. You did not hear it from me. Take some refreshment and consider your position for the moment. We will resume shortly.'

York accepted the wine. He sipped it slowly, tasting its fermented sourness on the tip of his tongue, while his eyes gazed coolly back at the council. Soon, the political wheels were turning again and the fine details of the law were being applied to the ownership of properties and land disputes.

Yet Edward could not keep his hazel eyes from turning to the figure of young Henry Beaufort, his distant cousin, where he sat back, smugly in his black robes. They were related on his mother's side, from the line of John of Gaunt: Cecily's mother had borne the name. There were perhaps five or six years between them, but Beaufort's superiority meant he was now of age, in possession of his titles and lands, a powerful magnate in his own right while Edward waited on the cusp of adulthood. Henry's face had fleshed out in recent years, since his recovery after St Albans and although he was strikingly handsome, his dark eyes seemed shifty and malicious. Yet Edward could not help a tinge of envy creeping in, that this young man had fought and proved himself in battle. There were rumours too, about the mistress he kept on his country estates, unrivalled in her beauty: some even dared to whisper about his influence over the queen. He might be the enemy, but there was a restlessness and force about him, that drew Edward's attention: the fact that Beaufort wanted him dead drew him compulsively to watch the man's face. In its mouldings and shadows, he memorised the lines of his nemesis.

*

They came back along the Thames for safety, letting their guard ride the horses back through the streets and taking a boat from the Westminster steps. Behind them the sun was setting, casting a warm glow over the rooftops and red brick walls that fronted onto the river. As Salisbury had urged them, it was better to be back behind their own locked gates before darkness fell. There was no knowing what steps Beaufort might take, if he thought they might be planning some retaliation.

Edward's stomach was still in knots from that morning's attack. Not even the prospect of food and wine could shake off the memory of Beaufort's hypocrisy as he had sat in the chamber and nodded and debated along with the rest of them. No doubt the young duke would sleep soundly on his feather bed that night, or expend his energy entwined in the arms of his mistress. The man's dark eyes had imprinted themselves in Edward's mind.

Eventually, the walls of Baynard's Castle came into view. The king had granted it to York as a London base the year before and, with its four solid wings enclosing an inner courtyard, it was almost impenetrable, a bastion in the middle of the city. A garden lay along its western side and, against the river, the limestone walls rose up out of the water, flanked with octagonal towers. A little wooden pier allowed them to disembark and enter the castle through the river gateway. Edward paused a moment to give thanks at their safe arrival, aware that, had things gone differently that morning, they would never have been coming back. Together with his father, and their guests Warwick and Salisbury, they headed for the safety of family.

Flickering tapers lit their way inside, and the smell of roasted meat drew them on. Servants were dressing the table in clean white linen and a fire burned in the grate. In the great hall, Duchess Cecily was supervising her carver, who was holding out his knives for inspection. She looked up in surprise to see them all appear looking so grave, her beautiful features marred by concern. York nodded to dismiss the man.

'You are back,' she smiled. 'I did not hear the horses.'

She was dressed in a simple but elegant gown of silver tissue and white satin. A string of pearls and amber beads was draped about her neck, complementing her pale colouring.

York threw off his cloak. 'We came back by the river. Who is that man? How long has he been in our employ?'

'His name is Griffiths. He was hired at Michaelmas.'

'Only since then? Does he do his job well?'

'Indifferently well.'

'Then let him go. We must only take on trusted staff, known to us or our people.'

'But who will carve your meat?'

'I will carve it myself if need be. No strangers in the house.'

'Why so? What has happened?' Her eyes ran to her nephew Warwick and to her brother Salisbury, standing behind him. 'You are all welcome, sit and rest.'

The white-haired man kissed her cool cheek. 'Good even, sister.'

'Something has happened, has it not?' With the same sensitivity as her son, she could read their mood and the extent of what they were hiding.

York seemed reluctant to answer, so Edward explained to his mother. 'We met with a few men on the road this morning, who were bent on our destruction. A cowardly attack, but we saw them off, it is over now.'

'An attack? Another one! What began it?'

'Nothing, they lay in wait, knowing we would pass that way. It was planned.'

He saw his mother's face darken.

'Who was behind it? Just tell me who it was.' She spoke through gritted teeth.

York sat down at the high table. 'I am starving. Call in the servers.'

Edward obeyed, but chose a seat close to where his mother stood, clutching her hands together. He bent closer to her, to continue their conversation. 'It was Beaufort, perhaps acting for the queen.'

'The queen? The very queen whom I nursed as a sick child in France? To whom I have written with kind words when she was heavy with child?'

'The very same. She has Beaufort eating out of her hand, with Tudor, Worcester, Clifford and others. My uncle Buckingham may still be turned.'

'If Anne can help, she will, I shall write to her too.' For all the portents of his scarred face, Buckingham was still married to Cecily's sister Anne.

'It is time to eat,' called York, frowning. 'We have had enough talk for today.'

Edward raised his eyebrows, his look conveying to his mother a mix of emotions. She read the message well, of her husband's anger and frustration, his disbelief and outraged justice and the shred of hope he preserved, that he had been mistaken, that all would still be well. York saw it too.

'Enough of this! Bring the food out at once! Call for the minstrels to play.'

Edward watched his father fill his plate but, once the notes of the lute filled the hall, very little food passed his dry lips.

*

Edmund hovered in the stairwell as the men dined. Something prevented him from joining them, some invisible line between their world and his. They carried the air of government with them, of importance worn lightly about their shoulders; they had been into the very heart of England, where laws were made, where men's words and choices set in motion peace and conflict: the beating heart of business, of power, of life. Even his brother, only a year his senior, had been striding along with them, shoulder to shoulder, a man to be counted among other men. As Earl of March, Edward represented the ancient royal line of the Mortimers, with confidence and ease. Men listened as he spoke. But Edmund, Earl of Rutland, had been reading sermons that afternoon, while his mother and sister Elizabeth darned stockings and discussed jewels for her wedding.

He jumped up as Edward strode across the hall, having spotted him on the stairs. 'You're back, then.'

'This past hour, why didn't you come and eat with us?'

'I wasn't hungry.' Edmund followed his brother up to the first floor. The truth was, he had already eaten a nursery supper with the younger children, but was reluctant to admit it.

Edward pushed open the door to the chamber they shared, kicked off his boots and sprawled on the bed.

'So, what news from court?' Edmund sat down opposite him, crossing his slim legs nonchalantly.

'Nothing new except that Beaufort has an eye asking to be blackened.'

'But what was debated in the chamber today?'

'How the king of France has fallen out with his son, who cowers under the skirts of Burgundy.'

Edmund nodded. 'What else, what of the business of the country?'

Edward sighed. 'Debts and payments, shipments of wine from Winchelsea, pirates in the North Sea that makes Philip the Good refuse to come to terms over trade. Who should own which parcels of land and why. You have done much better here, Edmund, being devoted to your books than listening to such tedious matters.'

'But I would like the chance to know, or else how am I to know to stay out of it?'

'Be kind to your stomach, refrain from such a bitter dish. Study the politics of France, your future may still lie there. I am sick of business and all the men who make it.'

Like his brother, Edmund had been born in Rouen, in the massive solid castle overlooking the town. Edward arrived in a chilly spring, when the buds were late in coming and the land still barren of crops. He had been a large baby, born late and struggling for hours to emerge into the light. Concern for him had shaken the castle. In haste, a priest had splashed his forehead with holy water as the midwife slapped his blue back to make him draw breath.

Edmund, by contrast, had slipped into the world the next summer with his mother barely so much as crying out. Pink and healthy, he had been carried to the cathedral and baptised to the sounds of trumpets by the font. From then, his father had cherished some plan that he would be a great landholder in Normandy one day. It had always been an accepted part of the family story, that Edward would inherit in England while Edmund would cross the Channel and establish himself there.

'And the king and Queen Margaret?' he asked.

Edward shook his head. 'They remain in the north, knowing they do not have support in the city. We can only tread water, waiting for their next step. You must remain in the castle until we know more.'

Edmund flushed hotly. 'Why? Remain here like a prisoner? What have I done?'

'Nothing, it is not about you. We may all be in danger.'

'Then let me go with you, out into the world to confront it. If you go into the council, why can't I? There is barely a year between us.'

Edward folded his arms behind his head. 'Thirteen months.'

'Am I a fool, or slow-witted or a baby, that I am not trusted, that I must remain here among the women and not take my proper place?' Edmund turned his head away to conceal the tears threatening to sting his eyes.

But Edward had understood. 'All right, I will speak with father about it. Now get some sleep.'

*

The church bells pealed out their chord; long, deep and sonorous. Behind the steeple of the little Suffolk church, the spring sky had remained obligingly blue and the threat of rain was kept at bay. Through the doors, into the porch, the young couple appeared, swathed in their cloth of gold and red velvet. Sparkling with rubies and pearls, Cecily was beaming at her daughter, the tall, fair-haired Elizabeth Plantagenet, who had followed her own example by becoming a wife at the age of fourteen.

The bridegroom was short for his age, but the sixteen-year-old John de la Pole would grow taller in time and his eyes were kindly and full of understanding. As they watched, he took Elizabeth's hand and a smile lit his gentle face.

'A better son-in-law than our first,' breathed York cynically at her side.

Cecily winced. The wedding of their eldest child Anne had brought little joy to anyone concerned. The poor girl had been just eight years old, dressed up like a child's doll in her furs and diamonds. Her husband Exeter had been an arrogant, callow youth of seventeen, bursting with pride at his royal descent, although his heart was already filled with hidden cruelty and treachery. He had bridled against his new family, taking all their kindness amiss and fighting against them at St Albans.

'There could hardly have been worse,' she admitted. 'We did not know at the time that we were making a mistake. Yet this new match will bring loyal and lasting connections, I am sure of it. Perhaps even some personal happiness for Elizabeth.'

'Time will tell,' her husband added, watching as the pair processed towards the pavilion.

After them came the younger children, Margaret with pious eyes and milk-white skin, wearing her eleven years with a degree of seriousness; eight-year-old George bearing a ceremonial cup and little Richard, aged five, his chin held high as his dark curls blew in the breeze. It would be their turn soon, their mother thought, watching Richard take an uncertain step then right himself again.

York and Cecily waited until the children had passed, then brought up the rear of the procession. People from the village had turned out to see them and some came forward now from the road, bearing gifts of flowers and fruit, eggs and herbs; one shepherd offered a newborn lamb wrapped in cloth. York received these with smiles and kind words, as they were gathered up by his servants and carried away. It was good to see the esteem in which the common people held him.

'Thank you my dear, most kind,' said York, as he accepted a basket from a young woman waiting on the corner. Then he spoke quietly to Cecily at his side: 'The king and queen are returning to the capital.'

'Are they? To what end?' his wife asked, smiling down into a bunch of flowers.

'She summons us to another council, in the hopes of making a public gesture of peace.'

Cecily turned to him, her arms filled with sprays of spring blossom. With a smile for the crowd, she handed him a sprig of tiny pink flowers. He held it up to his nose but the scent was faint.

'A peace gesture? If only we could believe in it.'

'We must. We must hope that they will act for the best.'

'And if it is a trap?'

York tucked the flowers behind the clasp of his cloak. 'This has the flavour of a truce, as Henry is involved. We cannot refuse to attend, think of the consequences.'

'Think of the consequences if you do. It may be the difference between life and death.'

'I know it.' York nodded as they headed into the pavilion. Ahead, Edward and Edmund were laughing together, their heads bent close.

'Edmund is restless,' York stated baldly. 'He talks constantly of being out in the world and chafes at the bit of his confinement. He has been speaking to Edward, asking if he can accompany us. I am of a mind to take him to the next council meeting.'

'But he is still so young.'

'He is fifteen in May. Old enough to be married. Edward was already out in the world long before then.'

'It is still too dangerous for him, I fear for Edward but he will not be governed by me and remain at home. At least Edmund still follows my will.'

'Edward is already a man, with a man's awareness. Edmund is not; he is a dreamer, a thinker, a scholar, he must learn to be patient. He is too soft, too gentle, too inexperienced for the dangers of this world.'

As if to underline their point, Edmund bent to caress the ears of one of the dogs.

'Yet it is the world he lives in, the world he was born to,' said York. 'He must face it one day.'

'Not today,' said his mother softly, 'and not tomorrow.'

TEN: The Loveday, March 25, 1458

'Pray kneel for the king!'

The hall of the Bishop's Palace hummed with anticipation. On bended knee, between his father and brother, Edward kept his eyes on the double doors, where heralds stood with trumpets and guards with swords held back the crowds. Forming an aisle inside, men shifted their weight cautiously, ill at ease despite their velvet and furs, conscious of a wind of change blowing through the court.

'Can he really be well enough to rule?' he whispered to his father. 'Can Henry really be trusted?'

'It matters little, he is our anointed king,' York insisted, 'so we must bow down.'

'You have already seen him?'

'When he opened parliament. Since then, he has been hidden away at Berkhamsted.'

'And the queen?'

Across the hall, a man tried to stifle a cough. Edward's hazel eyes flickered across the gathering and caught the gaze of Jasper Tudor, his angular face cast in shadow. He inclined his head slightly in formal greeting, sensing the forms of Buckingham and Beaufort beyond. For all he knew, these men might be plotting his own death in some darkened city alley but, today of all days, appearances had to be maintained.

Warwick spoke from behind. 'This is it. He's coming.'

From within the bowels of the palace came a mighty rumbling; the approach of feet and voices, the scraping of doors and the alarums of trumpeters, heralding the progress of the king through the corridors of power. Edward felt a tingle run along his spine. He remembered Henry prostrate and senseless on his bed at Windsor three years earlier. How easy it would have been then, to pay his surgeon to open his veins and let the deep red lifeblood throb out of the lean, pale body. At that moment, the power of life had lain in their hands, that precious, tenuous grip on the world that seemed so permanent in the bright light of day. How easy to have made it seem an accident; for father to assume the role of

98

Protector again, in the long years until the little prince came of age. Such thinking was a sin, a terrible sin. He knew it, but sometimes he could not stop himself.

At his back, Warwick was still growling. 'Any minute, then we can get up from this damned cold floor. Will the bishops be issuing us with hair shirts next?'

A ripple of applause washed in from the corridor outside and silenced him.

Edward turned at the outbreak of noise. Then the daylight darkened and the space disgorged a collection of figures, centred round a tall, regal man in the cloth of gold and purple velvet that marked out his rank. For a moment, there was stillness.

Henry stood tall, taller than most, wearing a heavy, jewel-crusted circlet of gold. He surveyed the hall with heavy-lidded sleepy eyes, a long, narrow face and dark, close-cropped hair. People said that in looks, he took after his father, the warlike Henry V, hero of Agincourt: some still recalled his triumphant return to the city, with blood dried on his skin and his helmet dinted by French blows. But if his son had inherited the curve of his cheek or the line of his brow, the resemblance stopped there. Cecily had always said there was something of his manner, his soft-spokenness and way of looking up to the heavens that reminded her of his mother, the late Catherine of Valois.

Now Edward felt the weight of the king's gaze. It made his head hang heavy, almost as if his guilty thoughts had been detected. From the corner of his eye, he saw the soft leather of Henry's boots, cleaned and polished, with the buckles shining bright. As they paused before him, he heard the thin, reedy voice address his father in tones more suited to that of prayer.

'You are here, cousin, to welcome my return?'

'My family and I sincerely welcome your return to Westminster; you are always in our prayers.'

'And this is your son?'

'This is my eldest boy, Edward, Earl of March.'

For a moment, Edward was swept up in the wave of majesty. He found himself looking up into Henry's wide eyes, murmuring a few words of respect and feeling something like a genuine sense of awe. And yet, there was a curious blankness about them, as if they were the eyes of a portrait, somehow disengaged from life.

'Ah, the Earl of March; you bear the old Mortimer title and something of their looks perhaps? I remember you as a child but I see you are a child no longer. You are welcome at my court on this Loveday, young cousin.' And briefly, a warm palm was placed on the top of his head.

Edward blushed at the unexpected kindness, but the king had soon moved on to where Beaufort was rising up from the floor in an effusion of warmth. As he fell in line behind his father, Edward could just make out his syrupy words of greeting and flattery. But it was time to move and he got to his feet, straightening his doublet and cloak. The plan was for them to process outside, across the yard and into the cathedral, in a show of unity and peace before the assembled people. Perhaps it really would herald a new start after all.

'So wonderful to see the king so strong and in such good health; we can rest assured that the kingdom will again be run according to God's law.'

Edward turned sharply. Behind him, Tudor's face was a picture of serenity. One look at the smug, fixed grin was the spur that Edward needed but he would not rise to the bait today. Instead, he smiled: 'God moves in mysterious ways, my Lord, beyond the comprehension of his sheep.'

Edward had the satisfaction of seeing Tudor's brows furrow in confusion as he turned away.

In the doorway, the queen was waiting. Her proud chin was tipped up and her long, almond eyes surveyed the men as they approached in line, as if she could cut into the very marrow of their bones. Her lithe, winsome form was swathed in red velvet and gold tissue, embroidered with fleur-de-lys and spangles, with a great string of rubies sparkling about her slender throat. She already knew the part she had to play. Without casting a glance at her husband, she pursed her lips and held out her hand to York as he approached. He accepted it graciously, with a bow. Her fingers were warm.

Next came the dark figure of Beaufort, with his quick smile and fox-like cunning. He paired up with the white-haired Salisbury, bowing low in an elaborate gesture of reconciliation and leading the old man onwards. Edward watched him, sensing the tension behind his suavity.

The assembled Londoners outside were already cheering and calling as the spectacle unfolded before them; such a strange mix of the familiar and unfamiliar. Then another man, fair-haired and tall, resplendent in green and tawny, appeared haloed by the daylight.

Edward paused. He had not seen his brother-in-law Exeter in a while. He recalled the image of his elder sister Anne in tears, her head bent over a letter: there had been no way of knowing that her headstrong teenage husband would rebel against the family. Now, freed by the queen from his confinement in Wallingford Castle, he stood proudly, shoulders squared, looking Edward in the eye. Rumour had it that he had been enraged when his position as Lord High Admiral had been awarded to Warwick last month. Edward's stomach turned at the sight of him.

'Brother?' Exeter said lightly, with a laugh in his tone.

'It's all right, I'll take this one,' said Warwick with a glint in his eye, stepping between the pair and leading the surprised duke swiftly outside.

Edward followed on, accepting the arm of his uncle Buckingham, to the roar of the assembled crowds. The man kept his scarred face turned away, unwilling to soften for the occasion. And thus Lancaster and York walked, side by side in a show of love, who had so lately borne arms against each other.

The trumpeters sounded their chorus and the procession headed out of the double doors at the far end, into the dazzling daylight. The spire of St Paul's Cathedral loomed above them and, as the sunlight fell on their faces, the tolling of its great bells seemed to spread across the world, for the feast of the Annunciation of the Blessed Virgin Mary and the Loveday.

On the steps outside, the king paused and turned to the crowd, surveying lords and commoners alike with an even gaze. A hush fell upon them all. The mad king was about to speak. Edward carefully extricated his hand from that of Buckingham.

'Friends, this day will mark a new beginning, a new brotherhood among us,' Henry said softly, with his eyes fixed on the stained glass gleaming in the sunlight. 'Past wrongs will be forgiven in the true sense of Christian kindness. From this point forth, we shall go with our hands joined and love in our hearts, for the good of the commonweal.'

Henry held out his hand to his wife. 'And Margaret my queen, with York, my closest cousin, shall be at my side, united in love, as my dearest and most trusted counsellors.'

Margaret inclined her gracious head.

'There shall be no more bloodshed in this kingdom,' the king continued. 'Only the true Christian virtues of peace and goodwill. In this holy place, beloved of St Edward, we embrace this new mood of love and, on this Loveday, the truth will shine in all men's hearts.'

Edward listened to the applause. Henry might be sincere enough but it was the queen's black eyes that drew him, with their promise of passion and defiance.

'Amen!' cried the crowd, as the musicians began to play.

*

While wine and spices were being served, Edward made for a side chapel. He had seen his father and Warwick heading away from the crowd when they entered the cathedral and he guessed them to be deep in conversation somewhere. As he approached, candles flickered and precious gems glinted through the wooden lattice that gave the chapel some privacy from the main body of the nave.

'So, once again we must pay,' the earl was saying, 'while our wrongs remain unrighted. We cannot be safe whilst Beaufort maintains this smug pretence, and now you have to line his pockets. It is an insult, by Our Lady, an insult to the house of York.'

Edward stepped through the open door. York and Warwick were standing before the altar, watched over by the eyes of carved birds and beasts. Behind them lay the tomb of St Erkenwald, the Saxon Bishop of London, a reminder of an older, more savage time. They looked round in surprise.

'What insult do you speak of?'

'I told you to be quiet,' York berated Warwick. 'You see how easily you have been overheard? Lucky it was Edward, not the king himself! Or worse!'

Edward looked from one to the other. 'Of what do you speak, I heard you talk of payment?'

'Not here,' York frowned. 'The cathedral has ears. Now we must put on our smiles again and dine with our enemies. We must try to make this peace work. There are grievances on both sides, but we must try and overcome them, truly and lovingly, for the sake of all.'

Warwick snorted.

Edward caught his father's arm as he tried to pass. 'Don't exclude me, do let me share in the family, for better or worse.'

York nodded. 'Later, away from here. Put this aside for now, there is nothing so important right now as keeping this peace.'

*

They dined in the Bishop of London's palace. The king and queen at the head table, York and Edward seated with Exeter and Buckingham; Warwick and Salisbury with Beaufort and Tudor. Oaths were made and goblets drained dry in pledges of loyalty. Yet the meat seemed to stick in Edward's throat along with the protestations of new-found friendship. From the corner of his eye, he could see the fluttering of hand over dishes, with Exeter helping himself to the spread of plates. Something about the man's haste, and his sense of acquisition, filled Edward with annoyance. As soon as the minstrels started playing, he made an excuse and left his place, heading further down the hall to where his uncle, Thomas Bourchier, Archbishop of Canterbury, had stretched out his legs.

'Please, don't get up,' he urged Bourchier, as the older man began to stir. 'Stay as you are. I simply had no stomach for Exeter.'

Bourchier raised a hand of greeting, already sated by meat and wine. It was then that Edward noticed the woman sitting in the shadows behind him, a young woman in a plain dress, hidden from the crowds by the curtain of an alcove, her fingers entwined in the back of the old man's hair.

Bourchier shot him a guilty look. 'You may have my seat. I am done here for the night.'

Edward nodded as the old man took the girl upon his arm and allowed her to lead him out to the doorway. As they disappeared together, her soft laugh stirred something in him, and a sort of wistfulness arose in his chest. He took the archbishop's position on the bench and called for more wine.

At that distance, he could see his father and Warwick on one side of the king, and the queen and Beaufort on the other. As he watched, the vulpine features of the handsome young duke resolved into a smile, he touched Margaret's sleeves, almost imperceptibly, and she inclined her head to hear his whispered words. It all looked so simple; a mathematical or geometric division, like pieces on a chessboard, waiting for their players to commence action. Here, he was among the citizens and aldermen, admitted to the hall on special occasions, their bejewelled wives gawping at the spectacle of the feast. He could hear none of their words, the minstrels made certain of that, with their low, melodic tones pulsing below the high trill of the flute. And now the king's fool was dancing, with bells on his hat and toes, tumbling in circles and pretending to fall. Yet only Henry was laughing.

Edward felt dissatisfied. The whole day had the ring of discontent that sat uneasily with him; he had no stomach for these protestations of friendship that masked such desperate acts of desire, these falsehoods that allowed enemies to wear their painted smiles while their hearts curdled in hatred. And he hated that he had been a part of it; that his father and Warwick still sat at table with Henry and Margaret, as if there had been no concealed knives in the darkness. Yet, as ever, his father had taken the path of the pragmatist, the optimist: was there really any other way, when they must submit to the reign of such a man? He emptied his glass and raised it again for more.

He felt her gaze before he saw her. Looking further down the hall, where the merchants and minor churchmen shared dishes of plain fare, his eyes found her face among a sombre group who seemed to be measuring the evening with invisible scales. She had changed very little in the intervening years. If anything, her face was paler, her eyes larger and darker, the curve of her long throat exaggerated where it met the swell of her breasts, firm against the low neckline of her dress. He had thought of Alasia Boratti many times after they had been forced to leave Westminster; in the quiet evenings at Ludlow, in the winter, when the snow drifts piled high against the castle wall and the Crofts were sent out to sweep them clear. The memory of her soft lips on his had lingered far longer than the duration of their real kiss, but yet, with the arrival of that spring, he had forced himself to discipline his mind, turning it to his work, to matters of local business, knowing that she was likely to have been married and bedded long before then. The girls in the Ludlow market were pretty; he was drawn by their colourful skirts and the long looks they cast him over their shoulder, but there had been no one else.

She knew at once that he had seen her and, despite the distance, something was communicated between them. Her dark hair was covered with a sheer white veil, overlaid with silver and her throat shone with jewels, glowing in the firelight, but she sat motionless as those around her ate with appetite. She gave no sign of acknowledgement, no smile, no wave, just the meeting of their eyes across the table, across the floor which divided them. Edward's stomach contracted. To her right sat a man in his thirties, a reedy, hollow-looking man wearing too much fur, who moved slowly and deliberately. Edward knew at once that this was Alasia's husband, the influential match her father had hoped for, and had appealed to York to help achieve. He disliked the man upon sight.

As he watched, Alasia rose softly to her feet, spoke a few words to her husband, and started to make her way carefully past the benches and tables, past the minstrels and fireplaces, towards the door at the far end of the hall. All of Edward's senses seemed to heighten as he watched the graceful movement of her lithe body, the drape of her skirt, the fall of her veil down her back. When she reached the door, she paused and looked back to catch his eye. It was an invitation he could not refuse. Leaving his place at the table, he hurried after her, out into the corridor beyond, where she had led.

She was standing, silhouetted in the far gateway. He covered the distance between them quickly and she turned, with a graceful gesture, to meet him. Just yards away, he faltered and stopped, not knowing how to greet her.

'It is you, then.'

She nodded. 'I wasn't sure if you would follow me. I needed some air.'

'I did. I have.'

They both smiled.

'It has been a long time,' she said.

'Yes. How are you?' he asked, feeling as bashful as a boy again. 'How have you been? I have been much in Ludlow, too little in London.'

'You have changed,' she said softly.

He nodded, watching the rise and fall of her throat. 'So have you.'

Forces seemed to be drawing him towards her, dizzying his senses, closing the gap between them.

She straightened her shoulders, as if feeling the same pull and struggling to resist. 'It is good to see you, my Lord. You may know that I am married now.'

'As I thought.'

She nodded, meeting his eyes straight on. She seemed bolder than when they had first met, as blushing children.

'My husband is the treasurer of the Guild of Merchant Taylors; we have a house in Thames Street, near Queenhithe.'

'And your father is well?'

'Sadly he was taken from us, last winter, after a short illness.'

'I am very sorry to hear that. God rest his soul.'

'Thank you, my Lord. I trust God has kept you well.'

He paused. Her deliberate formality caused a rush of emotion in him, a desire to sweep all barriers away.

'I have thought of you,' he admitted. 'I have thought of that day often.'

She did not reply, but he saw her lips part.

Behind them, the door opened. She saw the figure appear at once and her demeanour shifted. Her husband approached them slowly, before making a low bow before them.

'Please, rise,' Edward insisted, without looking down at the man's head.

'My Lord.'

He was gaunt-faced, with skin tanned deep by the sun and tiny eyes set brightly below heavy brows. The effect was not as unpleasant as Edward had feared, but he could not help thinking of that thin mouth, those crude fingers, touching Alasia's skin.

'May I present my husband, Antonio Salucci.'

Edward forced himself to say the man's name. 'Salucci. You are a merchant, I understand?'

'Your Lordship is most gracious. I trade with Italy and Turkey, in spices, furs and carpets.'

'And you are based in Thames Street?'

'I have a large warehouse; if there is something in particular that you desire, I could send my apprentice to you, with samples.'

'No, no, I desire no such service. Here is your wife, I believe she required some air, but she is quite well again now.'

106

The Saluccis bowed as he began to make his retreat. But something made him pause and turn.

'You are coming to watch the joust tomorrow?'

'Oh, well, my business,' began the merchant, before meeting Edward's steely gaze. 'Business must wait, we are most honoured, my Lord, thank you for your kind attention.'

Having secured their attendance, Edward turned on his heel and strode away.

ELEVEN: The Lists, March 26, 1458

Flags fluttered in the breeze along the top of the stage. Draped in azure blue silk, the roof bore the design of the silver fleur-de-lys, a reminder of the French descent shared by the king's mother and wife. Henry sat enthroned in the middle, his crown still perched high on his brow, his hands gripping tightly to the arms of his padded chair. On one side stood his small son, Prince Edward, a stubborn-faced five-year-old, with rosebud lips. Slightly further back, amid the many folds of fabric, the queen sheltered from the harsh wind, wrapping herself about with furs and calling for the braziers to be stoked up. The English winters had never seemed to agree with her, not in the thirteen years since she had arrived in the country, nor the springs or summers either. At her side, the attentive Beaufort plied her with sweetmeats.

York turned away from them in disgust. His own family group, seated along carved benches, included his wife, Edward and the excited Edmund, Earl of Rutland. He had bowed to the young man's insistence and allowed him to accompany them to the joust, to Edmund's restrained delight. Now he sat on the edge of his seat, watching as the tilt yard was cleared and fresh sand and sawdust scattered along the lists. Beside him, Cecily's pale beauty and regal, well-defined profile were the perfect complement to Queen Margaret's dark European looks; today she had chosen a delicate tissue of gold and white velvet, appearing clean and spotless beside the mud of the field, every inch a woman fit to occupy the throne. They had been married young: she had just passed her fourteenth birthday, but there had never been any alteration in his feeling for her. With her beauty, determination and sense of family, he could not have chosen a better wife. Flanked by her two eldest sons, she fixed the jousters with an air of interested detachment and waited for the tournament to begin.

At the far end of the yard, the horse kicked up a cloud of dust. Knights waited, arms outstretched as their armour was tightened and their colours tied to their lances. The first competitors were riding a solemn parade along the lists, basking in the encouragement of the crowds before they took their places at each end. Their visors were lowered, yet neither moved.

'They await the queen's word,' said York, turning back to the king.

He could not see Margaret of Anjou now, from where he sat, but he could hear her low tones.

'The queen?' he repeated, directing his words at Henry.

Slowly, the king rose to his feet and, in sight of all, gave the signal to begin the joust. It was unusual, a departure from the traditional form that favoured the queen's hand, but it was what the moment demanded.

At each end of the lists, the knights sprang into action. At first their progress was slow, the sound of the hooves distant, then they became louder, scattering sawdust as the distance between them narrowed. York held his breath. The platform was positioned in the middle of the lists, where the impending clash would soon take place. His eyes ran from one horse to the other, watching as they thundered ever closer. The distance closed in a blur of speed. The crack of wood against wood marked a shattering first encounter. Around the king, the crowd breathed a collective sigh of relief.

Unhurt, the riders parted, rode on to the end, and circled in a cloud of dust. Without waiting, they galloped on again, faster and harder, making the platform reverberate beneath York's feet. The sensation travelled up through his limbs, into his belly, something like the thunder of horses in battle. Something about this second charge was more determined, more focused. This time, the blow of the long, solid lances struck home. Wood impacted on wood again but, now, there was a duller sound too. The closer rider was unseated, toppled and fell to the ground. A gasp rushed through the crowd, drawing some to their feet. Squires hurried forward and helped him to his feet while his competitor prepared to meet his next opponent.

York looked briefly back at his family. Edmund was perched beside his mother, keenly watching the action but, for once, Edward was the one who seemed withdrawn.

'You are quiet?'

His son turned his handsome profile, newly grown into his manly features.

He shrugged.

'What is it? You don't enjoy the entertainment?'

Edward shook his sandy curls. 'Yesterday, in the chapel?'

'What you overheard? It was nothing, just money, nothing to worry about.'

'Whom are you paying?'

York lowered his voice. 'It is nothing for you to be concerned about, just parliamentary business, compensation to Beaufort for his father's loss. I cannot speak freely here, you understand?'

Edward's sense of pride and justice could not endure this. 'Compensation to Beaufort? Why, in God's name?'

'For St Albans.'

'God's blood!'

'Edward!' Cecily had heard his exclamation.

'Sorry mother.' He lowered his voice, turned back to York. 'I am sick of us being held to account for St Albans, when you fought to clear your name. It was a fair fight. Why must we pay still?'

'You would have me shout it out for all to hear, to criticise our enemies openly on this day of reconciliation? Don't you think I am sick of it too?'

'You really believe they will abide by these new oaths of friendship?'

'I have to believe it. As they must believe we will keep ours. As we will.'

Edward shook his head cynically.

'What?' asked York angrily. 'So you know better? Would you like to see a war in England?'

Cecily turned again, her pale brow furrowed. 'Hold your tongues. If I can hear you, others will too.'

'If I hold my tongue much more it will begin to bleed!' Angry and impatient, Edward was prepared to rise but the approaching bulk of Warwick blocked his way.

'Stay,' he urged, holding up his gloved hand. 'There are people I wish you to meet.'

The man at his side, perhaps in his late twenties, had a round, good-natured face, with close-cropped fair hair. The blue eyes were intelligent but the wide mouth seemed built for laughter and, against the fashion of the time, he wore a neat beard, quite golden in colour. He bowed in respectful greeting but his demeanour was relaxed.

'I found him lurking in the crowd,' Warwick told York. 'You recognise him? This is William, son of old Sir Leonard Hastings.'

'Ah! Old Hastings' son? Cecily, this is Hastings' son, descended from the Mortimers, on his mother's side.'

Cecily turned and inclined her head in greeting. 'Of course, I see the likeness. Another distant cousin. We knew your father during our service in Normandy. He showed us great kindness in our youth.'

'My Lady,' the youth took her hand with a gesture that was both graceful and charming.

'Do join us to watch the jousting,' invited York, seeing that his wife was taken with the young man. 'We need a little good humour amid all this cordiality.'

'You do me a great honour.' Hastings accepted the invitation and took his place on the bench just as the next jousters thundered past. They watched as the pair clashed and one man fell to the ground.

'Do you joust?'

Edward looked into their guest's blue eyes, unsure yet whether or not to like the affable young man. 'Do you?'

'When I need to impress someone.'

'Indeed?' Edward smiled noncommittally and turned back to the lists. On the far side, he spotted the figures of the Saluccis, the merchant shivering in his foreign furs and Alasia dressed in satin of emerald green.

'It's dangerous, of course.'

'It is.'

'That's why I only do it when there is someone worth impressing.'

Edward did not feel the need to reply but that did not stop his companion.

'And when I do, I always win.' He paused for a moment, then repeated. 'I always win.'

The tone rankled. Edward cast him a long look, still chewing over his anger. 'Is that so?'

Hastings grinned. 'You should try me. I could not fail to win today.'

Edward feigned interest. 'And why is that?'

'Because the most beautiful woman in the world is here.'

Edward gave a wry grin. 'Is she indeed?'

'You have not noticed? Your eyes are perhaps bewitched?'

'I see as plain as day.'

'Then feast them upon Earl Rivers' daughter, whom Warwick brings this way.'

As he spoke, Hastings rose to his feet and Edward saw that his cousin was approaching the dais, with a small party. Leading them was the Lancastrian Baron Rivers, with his smooth head and the neat features that Edward recognised from the council chamber; he had an air of elegance but it seemed a shallow, shifting thing, rooted in the man's clothing and his studied smile. On his arm was a tall, majestic woman, draped in gems, with a long thin face and large dramatic eyes. Behind her came a younger couple, a solid, plain man who barely merited a second glance and a fair-haired woman in blue, whom Edward saw at once was the one Hastings described as being without equal. There was no denying her beauty. Edward estimated that she must be five years his elder, perhaps more, and there was a stillness and composure about her face that made her seem inscrutable. Her bone structure was exquisite, finely modelled around the temples and chin to give the impression of both strength and fragility; her skin was clear and fresh, her lips a bow of pink, her nose straight and, as for her eyes... Her pale hooded eyes were the seat of her beauty. She lifted her chin and looked at York and his family on the dais, but her gaze seemed remote, as if fixed in the middle distance, as if not really seeing them at all.

'Baron Rivers, my Lady Jacquetta,' York inclined his head coolly.

The pair bowed low. 'My Lord, my Lady Duchess, we are thankful to see you in such good health,' said Rivers in his smooth voice. 'May I present my son-in-law Sir John Grey and my eldest daughter Elizabeth.'

The young people inclined their heads; Grey made an effort to catch Edward's eye but he could not tear his gaze away from the fascinating creature at the man's side. He had hoped for a smile from her, but Elizabeth did not meet his eyes. Once the formalities had been exchanged, the party passed along to take their seats without so much as a backward glance.

'Upstarts,' hissed Warwick. 'Who the hell do they think they are? Why are they so damned pleased with themselves?'

'Don't show them they have riled you,' warned York. 'Their time will come.'

Edward watched the upstarts passing down the field; a tight little unit which seemed inviolable, unwilling to engage with anyone else, secure in a world of their own creation. He was interested and repelled by them in equal measure.

Trumpets sounded. The lead jouster rode past the platform in a lap of honour, resplendent in scarlet and people rose to their feet to applaud him. Across the lists, the figure of Alasia caught his attention again. Beside her on the bench, Salucci appeared to be asleep, his fur collar pulled up to his ears. Edward drew a silk favour from his pocket, called to a servant and whispered instructions in his ear. Sitting back, he watched the man scurry down the steps and head around the back of the tents. He reappeared on the other side of the crowd, squeezing his way along the ranks of the crowd, before reaching Alasia in her green dress. It was accomplished admirably. He was able to see the exact moment when the piece of silk was pressed into her palm: her look of surprise, followed by her smile, then her eyes sought him out on the royal stand. Holding her gaze, he dipped his head in greeting. With a little planning, they might meet in the York family tent.

'Can't I leave now?' he leaned forward and asked his father. 'I've shown my face, done my duty.'

York frowned. 'It would be a breach to depart before the king; we must take our cue from him.'

'Then let me joust. I cannot bear to sit here any longer.'

'Joust, you? A boy against these trained champions? Are you mad?'

'I am strong for my age and well-practised in the tilt yard, I can hold my own.'

York shook his head. 'It would be taking an unnecessary risk.'

'But I can do it, I know I can and I will be careful.'

'You had my answer, I said no. Now let that be an end to it.'

'But I am a man now, I can joust!'

York stared back at his son incredulously, his eyes blazing with anger at the defiance.

'What did I hear?' The reedy voice reached them from the throne behind. 'The young Earl of March wishes to joust?'

His father swung round quickly, containing his fury. 'Indeed, your majesty, the young earl does, but the old duke has advised him against it on account of his youth and inexperience.'

'I don't see that it can do much harm,' spoke the king slowly. 'Particularly if he was matched against one of our squires, why not let him joust?'

'Yes,' said the queen archly, appearing at her husband's side. 'Do let the young Earl of March joust.'

'But he has no clothes,' York protested.

'He will soon be equipped and ready,' promised Henry with a wave of the hand.

Edward rose to his feet, coursing with mixed emotions, not daring to meet his parents' eyes. He was conscious of Edmund, watching agog, as his brother bowed low to the throne.

'Don't do it, I absolutely forbid it!' York muttered between clenched teeth but it was too late.

Henry beckoned to one of the squires, standing on the straw below the royal platform. 'The earl is to joust. See that he is fully prepared and match him against someone suitable.'

Edward felt his mother's anxious hand upon his arm and, for a moment, he paused.

'Am I suitable enough?'

Hastings had spoken. Now he stepped up alongside Edward. 'I would be honoured to ride against the earl, should it please my Lords.'

'It would please us very much,' Cecily whispered, with tears in her voice. 'Thank you.'

Edward was relieved but determined not to show it; he shot a look over towards Alasia and followed Hastings' broad back down the steps towards the yellow tents.

*

'So,' smiled Hastings broadly, as he pulled on his gloves, 'you're really going to do this?'

Edward raised his chin as he was laced into his breastplate. The tent billowed above them.

'So young and so fearless,' the older man laughed. 'I hear Beaufort was keen to challenge you. No wonder, when your father killed his.'

Edward refused to so much as twitch an eyelid. He strode out onto the sawdust, where a squire was waiting to help him climb up into the saddle of a black stallion, clad in blue and white livery. He fumbled with the heavy lance at first, before finding a way to tuck it under his arm. The lists lay ahead, seeming very long and close, in comparison with the view from the benches. He must have watched this a dozen times; how hard could it be?

'Are you coming or not?' he called back to Hastings, and spurred his horse abruptly into a walk, without waiting to hear the answer.

By the time he had reached the far end, he had a sense of the horse's strength, a huge, dumb brute that would speed him across the intervening distance so long as he did not take fright. Circling and raising his lance, he stared back at his distant opponent, dressed in red, already ready for the off. He nodded over to the anxious figures on the edge of their seats under the fluttering flags, then snapped his visor down into place.

Perhaps he missed the signal, for someone to the side dealt his horse a blow in the hindquarters and the creature sprang ahead like lightening. Edward was thrown forward but quickly righted himself and locked his arm against his body tight, bracing himself for the oncoming impact. The distant figure came closer and closer. The horse hooves pounded in rhythm, like the beating of his heart, almost fit to burst. Clouds of sawdust whirled about them. Then there was a rush and he was clear. Blessedly, incredibly, he rode clear. He spun round, checking the lists: they had passed without making contact. Feeling the sweat beading on his forehead, he breathed a sigh of relief and continued to the end.

Slowly, he turned his horse round in a circuit. They would ride again and surely, this time, Hastings would not be so merciful. Before he had a chance to catch breath, the red figure had begun to ride again, without waiting for his signal, intent on the attack. Edward grappled with his lance, feeling himself unready. His mount had other ideas. They clashed again. A blinding pain caught him on the shoulder, unseating him briefly. He gasped, feeling the shock travel right through his body but some instinct made him clamp his knees fast against the horse's flanks and, by some miracle, he remained in the saddle. Galloping to the end of the list, adrenaline and anger spurred him on, forcing him to square up to his opponent and begin a third charge.

This time he had Hastings in his sight. He would not go into the lists unprepared again. The years of tilting at the ring in the green fields around Ludlow had served him well: he squinted, recalled the boy he had been and the man he was becoming, his parents' pride and the sly eyes of the queen watching from the sidelines. Lowering his lance, he lined it up carefully, as the red figure drew closer again. Closer, closer. He urged forward. The red figure of Hastings loomed large. There was a huge impact. Edward was shaken but rode on, with his lance reverberating in his hand, sending a powerful jolt up his arm and into his painful shoulder. As he reached the far tent, he circled, searching the field for his opponent.

The red horse was running loose, galloping along the side of the lists with its saddle empty. On the ground, a crumpled figure was being helped to his feet by the squires, amid the sawdust. Edward flicked up his visor. The crowds were cheering. It took him a moment to realise they were applauding him. Over on the platform, he could see the white and gold figure of his mother waving. He had won. He had been challenged and won, proved himself to his father, the king and queen and the whole court.

Relief washed over him. Then the pain of his shoulder kicked in again. He would have a powerful bruise there but it didn't feel as if anything was broken.

'Well done, well done, that was magnificent! You did it!'

It was Edmund. He had been waiting by the tents for his brother's return, his young face flushed with pride.

'I did, didn't I? I really did it!'

'Father was furious! You should have heard him.'

'I showed him I could do it though!'

'And I thought mother was going to faint.'

The armour felt stiff and heavy now. He could not wait to dismount but the squire was making no moves to assist him.

'Hey you, get me off here.'

'You have a second challenger, my Lord.'

Edward turned slowly. At the far end of the lists, a figure in black was already seated on the back of a huge brown stallion. He felt himself go cold.

'It's Beaufort,' breathed Edmund. 'The snake!'

Edward made no reply. They both watched as the limping figure of Hastings was helped from the scene.

'For God's sake,' said Edmund. 'That's enough, come off, say you're wounded. Call a surgeon. You're not seriously going to ride against him? It would be foolish!'

'I can't refuse.'

'Yes you can. It is an unfair match.'

A steely resolve settled across Edward's face. 'I must ride against him, stand aside.'

'He will kill you!'

'Then it will be an honourable death.'

Edward's knuckles whitened around his lance. Not daring to look at his parents, he spurred his horse forward and felt the rush of air as he realised his visor was still up. It was too late now, too late for anything but a sort of foolish desperate bravery, a mad God-like rashness that would lead either to death or glory. The thundering black figure descended. Automatically, Edward's lips began to move in prayer. He thought of the quiet grey walls at Ludlow, the deep surrounding woods, the window in his nursery with the wide sill where the birds used to nest. His mother had used to sit in the window there and sew, while they sang songs. He thought back to the softness of Alasia's lips, then the hooded eyes of Elizabeth Grey flashed into his mind. A conviction came over him that this was not his day to die.

For a split second he saw Beaufort's eyes, narrowed in menace. Then, with a rush, they had passed each other. There was no pain; there had been no contact. Edward breathed heavily in relief as he reached the far end of the lists. He circled, slammed down his visor and rode at his enemy again.

The glory was short lived. As they drew close, the point of Beaufort's lance reared up against him. He heard it first, that smack of wood on metal, then he felt it ricochet all through his body. A massive blow to the chest had knocked the wind out of him. He felt himself sliding backwards, saw the hooves of his horse and fell with a thud to the ground. Noise seemed to break out on all sides but he was drifting and it grew dimmer and dimmer.

*

There was a billowing whiteness all around him. The tent was blowing in the breeze, filled with sunlight like sails on a boat, as he opened his eyes. His armour had been removed and a surgeon was applying an ointment to his shoulder. For a second, all was calm and he felt wonderfully still, as if he were floating. Then a searing pain racked his chest and he groaned.

'Thank God,' he heard his mother saying. 'He has woken, thanks be to God.'

'He has woken?'

The voice came from behind them. Cecily knew it at once and turned, with a gracious curtsey, to face the queen.

Margaret of Anjou stood just inside the entrance to the tent, flanked on both sides by guards. She held her thin shoulders erect and her dark, slanting eyes were difficult to read. From the bed, Edward squinted at her form, thrown into silhouette by the sunlight spilling in from behind.

The queen stepped forward, bypassing his kneeling parents and cast an eye over his reclining form. He felt her scrutiny, exposed and vulnerable as he lay stripped to the waist, her eyes running over him like a caress. She was looking at the extent of his injuries, but there was something more in her gaze, as if she was assessing his strength.

She nodded slowly. 'You put up a brave fight.'

'Thank you, my Lady.' The words hurt.

'You could have refused to joust against Beaufort, but you didn't. I remember you as a child, in Rouen, when I was only a girl. You were stubborn then, too.'

He looked at her sidelong, at the long embroidered gown of blue and gold, at the diamonds on her fingers and throat. She must be in her late twenties now, although her skin was still bright and warm across her cheekbones and her lashes were dark and long as she blinked down at him. She might cherish a loathing for him in her heart, but Edward could suddenly see her as a woman: not just the enemy, a beautiful woman whose presence stirred something in his chest. There was a subtle change in the mood between them, barely perceptible but he definitely felt it: the awareness between a man and woman. He felt himself colouring.

The queen stepped closer then; as she turned, she allowed her hand to brush against his arm, from elbow to shoulder. Her cool fingertips sent a shiver through him.

Then it was over, she had already turned away, nodding to his kneeling parents.

'You have raised a son to be proud of.'

And she swept out of the tent.

*

Edward was just pulling himself upright when Hastings appeared in the doorway, wearing his shift and braes.

'You survived then?'

118

'As did you. Put some clothes on.'

'There's a woman out here, asking to speak with you.'

He knew who it was at once and pulled his shirt on. 'Show her in.'

Alasia looked nervous. She fiddled with the sleeves of her green dress and started towards him, then stopped. 'I thought you had been killed.'

'Not today.'

'I'm glad.' She looked over her shoulder, nervously. 'I only have a minute.'

'What is it, are you all right?' He wanted to reach across and touch her, but he wasn't sure.

'Yes, I am now. I wanted to tell you that Antonio sails for Italy tomorrow, on the first tide.'

Edward laughed. 'And he will bring me back some spices?'

He saw at once that he had misjudged the moment.

'No, not that.'

'No,' he echoed, suddenly serious. His hazel eyes locked with her dark ones.

'My house stands to the east of Queenhithe, on the corner of Thames Street and Trinitie Lane.'

He nodded. 'I will come after dark.'

'Around the back, there is a door with a low gable. I will set a lantern burning there.' She paused. 'Please don't think that this, that I usually…'

He leaned forward and planted a quick kiss on her warm cheek. 'I understand. Until then.'

She smiled, and was gone.

TWELVE: The Encircling Net, May, 1459

Edmund drew in his breath and squared his shoulders. He was almost as tall as Edward now, his eyes reaching up to his brother's solid chin, modelled along similar lines. They had both had their sandy hair cut shorter: it had been Edward's idea, so Edmund had submitted to the barber's knives at once, watching the soft golden clumps falling at his feet, feeling that he was cutting ties with his infancy. And Edmund had been practising with the sword and lance. Warwick had set him new challenges of strength and endurance on the Westminster fields, so that he could almost feel his heart burst as he pushed his body to its limits. Yet he was still not quite as broad, not quite as strong as Edward. And while Edward's hazel eyes radiated confidence, the cast of Edmund's features portrayed a mixture of pride and doubt. He was the son of York, their legacy carved in stone, but Edmund felt the passage of time, the fragility of the human heart, the beauty in heavy skies and fallen leaves pressing upon him.

Yet, seeing the three of them, arriving at the great door of Westminster Palace, anyone might think them inviolable. With York in the centre; splendid in his maturity, his descent from the Mortimers and his Plantagenet blood, his noble brow marked by wisdom and experience, his manner regal and full of authority; they appeared the personification of strength, of power. Justice sat squarely on his shoulders and defined his noble brow. Dressed in magnificent black and purple velvet, hung with jewels and his chains of office, York was the lynchpin of the family. His sons flanked him on either side, like the wings of a triptych. Edward was a head taller, swathed in russet silk and fur, his cheeks smooth from the barber's blades, his neck solid and his fiery eyes sweeping the whole palace, taking everything in, reading the reactions of the crowd almost before they made them. For one still so young, he carried an enviable sense of knowledge with him, as if he could read men's hearts, and yet those who feared him were also drawn to him. When his face softened, it wore smile of such charisma, such ease and warmth, that even his enemies softened.

On the other side stood Edmund. The three of them together like this seemed right, natural, like a sort of completion; they made a unit, as if about to raise their weapons and charge into battle. He was proud of his new tunic, made from emerald green and tawny, proud of the jewels he wore on his cloak and the rings on his fingers, proud of the new boots commissioned from the softest red leather; proudest of all of his family. Today, he would make his first attendance in the council chamber, among the lords and bishops, the friends and enemies, the king's servants and the makers of the laws of the land. Today, as he turned sixteen, he was joining the world of men.

*

They stood in the open doorway, shoulder to shoulder. The bright spring morning lit them from behind and blew their cloaks, billowing around their calves. The hall before them was full. It stretched ahead towards the dais and the doors to the chambers, overlooked by wooden statues of kings in red and green crowns, by Richard II's ceiling decorated with fleur-de-lys and angels, flanked by pillars. Fixing their eyes ahead, they began the walk. Perhaps a hundred people were milling about, turning quiet as the three York men passed, some bowing from respect, some out of fear, some barely able to contain their hostility. Edmund felt their eyes. He knew of the time that his brother and father had been attacked one chilly dawn on their way into the city, and of the other times their lives had been threatened, or their journey home dogged by footsteps. A year ago they might have intimidated him but now there was no emotion that was stronger than the pride and strength he felt at standing beside his father. He had learned this walk, learned this swagger; it was all a performance, an act. He only hoped that he looked as convincing as Edward. Fixing his eyes on the royal canopy ahead, he strode along, not letting the people's gaze touch him. Together, they passed the dais and the empty seats at table, and headed through the doorway into the dark corridor.

York seized the moment to whisper to him. 'Well done.'

Then they were out into the light again, at the broad wooden doorway where the council was meeting. Edmund took another deep breath and then they were inside. They were ranged around the table; his relations Salisbury, the Bourchiers and Buckingham; the Earls of Worcester,

121

Oxford and Devon, Lords Stanley and Clifford, Baron Rivers and the hostile faces of Beaufort and Tudor.

The doors closed firmly behind them. York approached the table, with his sons alongside.

Thomas Bourchier rose to his feet. 'I call this meeting to order.'

And Edward took his place among them, listening as the petitions were put forward and the objections made. He saw Bourchier speak for the church, for the souls of the people; he saw Beaufort narrow his eyes and argue about the divisions in the nation and the queen's hopes for reconciliation; he heard the titles of Lord Stanley's late father being conferred upon him and Buckingham requesting the settlement of land upon his new daughter-in-law, Lady Margaret Beaufort. And he could not help but think of all the people represented here; those praying in far-flung churches in the land, kneeling devoutly on stone, those counting out the portion of their income they were due to yield to the tax collectors, those waiting to hear news of decisions made by those men, in that room, on that day. And then he thought of the past, of the men who had spoken of such matters with such passion, arguing for lives to be saved or sacrificed, who now lay under marble tombs, their souls having been called to be with God. His eyes came to rest upon the carved wooden device of the white hart, above the fireplace, which was the symbol of Richard II. That king had sat in this chamber, anointed by holy oil in the abbey, wearing the robe of state; he by whom their Mortimer claim had been granted, he who died an ignominious death, stripped of his crown.

'Are you quite well?'

It was Edward, leaning across in his seat.

'Quite well,' Edmund replied, watching as Jasper Tudor got to his feet.

Almost thirty, Tudor's features had taken on a determined cast since the loss of his brother. As the half-brother of the king, he occupied a unique position in proximity to the king. Behind him, Edmund spotted a handsome, shifting figure; a man past his prime but still remarkable in looks, wearing a silver collar and jewelled cap.

'Who is that?' he whispered to his brother. 'The man behind.'

'Owen Tudor, the king's step-father.'

Edmund had heard the romantic tales of the secret marriage that the king's mother had made for love. Catherine de Valois had still been young and beautiful upon the death of Henry V. She had fallen in love with her squire and borne him children, before dying in the humble quietness of Bermondsey Abbey. The rights or wrongs of it had never mattered to Edmund, just the connection of two hearts, and he looked at this new figure with renewed interest.

Jasper looked pointedly down the table towards York and his sons. 'The king continues to wish for peace and reconciliation in his realm. He sends his best wishes for the good health of all his loyal servants and his thanks for their continuing dedicated work in his service.'

There was a ripple of muted applause.

'When will the king return to London?' York asked.

Tudor turned, with a controlled smile. 'The king's realm is a diverse one. At the present it suits him to remain in the north.'

'The king's support is already strong in the north,' York pressed. 'I am sure his southern subjects would benefit from his presence.'

'No doubt they shall soon enjoy that benefit.'

Tudor bent to sit, but York pressed him again. 'Does that mean the king has definite plans to return? Perhaps for his next parliament?'

'I would not presume to speak for the king,' smiled Tudor in mock surprise, spreading his open palms. Behind him, his father's handsome face creased with mirth.

'And yet you have,' York pointed out. 'My only concern is for the king's welfare. It is so long since we have seen him in the capital, it must be, since the Loveday, that his presence is greatly missed. It would be good for the king to return and show himself, in order to reassure his subjects that he remains in good health.'

'Oh, his health is excellent, and...' retorted Tudor.

But York cut him off. 'And that he is fully capable of making his own decisions, for which we continue to pray.'

'And the king proved such a loving friend at the Loveday,' added Edward, with his tongue in his cheek, 'that the city sorely misses his amorous benevolence.'

Glances were exchanged about the chamber but Tudor rose to the occasion. 'I will pass on your best wishes to the king and queen; I am sure they will be received most lovingly.'

'And our desire to serve him at his next parliament,' added York. 'We shall await his instructions.'

'Very good, my Lord,' Tudor bowed and turned away.

'And now the question of the household expenditure of the Prince of Wales,' interjected Bourchier, rising to his feet.

Edmund sat back in his seat with a mixture of emotions and listened as the prince's chamberlain put forward the balance of his income and expenditure. While the figures were being amended on a document, the Earl of Salisbury got to his feet, a little stiffly.

'I hear that, in the north, the queen has been distributing badges in the name of her son.'

'I have heard nothing about that,' said Bourchier. 'Tudor?'

For a moment, Jasper looked uncertain but the lithe, dark form of Beaufort rose to his feet. 'If I may, my Lords, I believe the queen has resurrected the symbol of the king's de Bohun legacies, simply as a mean to reward loyalty.'

'And the expenses are to come out of the boy's household budget, or the queen's own?' Salisbury asked.

'Whichever you wish, my Lords.'

'It seems,' interjected York, 'a little undignified, perhaps even disrespectful, for the queen's affairs to be settled in her absence. If she were present in the capital, we would have ample opportunities to display our loyalty, without the need and expense of these badges.'

'I think that matter has already been addressed,' Bourchier stated firmly, 'so we may progress to other matters.'

*

When the meeting finally drew to a close, they spilled out of the room, stretching cramped limbs. Edmund was relieved to be out of the glare of their enemies, of the minutiae of land debates and accounts.

'Your first taste of council business,' smiled Edward over his shoulder at his brother. 'Thrilling and deadening in one.'

'And still the king cowers in the north under the queen's skirts, while his country is being run from miles away.'

Both young men looked in surprise at their father.

'It is unlike you to be so outspoken,' ventured Edward. 'What has become of your usual diplomacy?'

York shook his grey head. 'It is buried, along with Tudor's wit and Beaufort's diplomacy. I am tired of this constant game, of always watching our backs. The king is calling a parliament imminently and yet he will not name the place or the day. What am I to think of it? God's blood, I am sick of it all.'

'Hush,' said Edward quickly, as he spotted Bouchier coming up behind them.

The archbishop clapped the duke on the shoulder. 'Are you dining in hall tonight, my friend?'

'I think not. You are most kind, but we must return home.'

'Then God be with you. Good Even.'

They watched the archbishop disappear.

York turned to his sons. 'I am resolved, I am for the country. The king knows where he can find me. We depart tomorrow for Fotheringhay.'

*

As Edward opened his eyes, he sensed the sun would soon be rising. The simple room, with its draped bed and tall cupboards, was bathed in a sort of grey light; enough to see by, but not sufficient to make the world's soft edges sharpen yet. He knew the creak of the wood at night, the glow of the fireplace while the embers died, the contours of the mattress beneath his shoulders. He knew the number of steps up from the hallway downstairs and he could find his way into this chamber in the dark, by running his hand along the panelled wall. He knew the warmth of the welcome that awaited him between the sheets of Italian silk, the softness of an encircling arm, the press of limb upon limb and the urgency of the mouth awaiting his. Alasia's home had come to feel like his own in the past year.

He pulled the covers up and turned onto his side. She lay with her back to him, still deeply asleep, and he buried his face in the fan of dark hair spread across the pillow. It was such fine hair, thin and silky, smelling of musk. She stirred slightly and he slipped a hand across her waist to draw her body close to his. She nestled her warmth against him, lacing her fingers into his. He had arrived late last night, after York had talked about his plans at length and given instructions for the house to be closed up. It was almost midnight when Edward finally slipped out to the stables, followed by his brother's rueful gaze. Lately Edmund had taken to asking him where he crept away to through the city streets after dark but Alasia was his secret and he would not share it. Only Hastings knew of their liaison, in case of emergency, otherwise his lips were sealed. Alasia had already been in bed when Edward turned his key in the back door last night, where the lantern burned on a low gable, and slipped up the stairs. They had made love with an intensity and urgency, before falling asleep in each other's arms.

Slowly, she rolled over to face him. He kissed her lips once or twice, then buried his head in the heat of her full breasts.

'Hello,' she whispered into his sandy curls.

'Mmm, hello,' he replied, in appreciation.

He ran his fingers lightly down her spine, feeling her back arch in response. Their lips met and she swung herself up to sit astride him. Her long dark hair fell down on either side, tickling his face as she leant forward. She pressed herself teasingly against him, as her mouth sought his chest, feeling the texture of his skin, of the wiry hair, the swell of his muscles. He was so familiar to her, and yet she could never be sated of him. Edward groaned in anticipation as her hand slid down to his groin and began to coax him with her fingers. Her grip was gentle but firm, and she knew the amount of pressure he enjoyed, verging on the threshold of pain, until he felt himself growing hard. Then she rocked her hips backwards and eased him inside her. They moved together, gently at first, enjoying the slow build of passion. He saw her face soften in passion and thought he had never seen a woman so beautiful.

Afterwards she was pulling on her shift, silhouetted by the morning light.

'Antonio is expected back next week.'

Edward nodded, still lying supine on the bed. 'I remember.'

She shook out her hair. 'I have something to tell you.'

'So do I.'

'Oh,' she looked surprised. 'Then you go first.'

'No, you must.'

'I insist. I want to know what it is.'

He propped himself up on one elbow to study her face. Every time he saw her she seemed to grow more beautiful, with her dark cat-like eyes and the winsome little smile in the corner of her mouth, which he had come to love. And yet, he had never told her that he loved her, not in all this time. He did not fully understand the reason for his silence: she was in his mind's eye, his first waking thought, his last image at night, the throb in his veins, the feeling deep down in the pit of his stomach, his best friend and lover. Surely she knew; surely she could feel his love, and that words were not necessary.

'I have to go away,' he said simply. 'Father requires me to go to Fotheringhay with him and we leave at once.'

'So soon? Without warning?'

'The decision was only made yesterday after council, I must follow his ruling.'

She nodded but he could feel her folding inwards, like a flower when clouds pass before the sun.

'I hope we will not be long, a month perhaps, three at most, but I don't know what is going to happen. Something is brewing between him and the queen and he has not shared it with me fully.'

She nodded.

'But I will write to you, I will return as soon as I can. It might be that I will be able to ride back to London for a few days at the end of the month, to collect the rents.'

'That would be good.'

'But at any rate, the king's next parliament is due to meet in September, and we must attend.'

'September,' she sighed.

'But it is probably good timing, with Antonio's return. We would not have been able to be together again properly until his next absence.'

He thought of the snatched moments they managed to share when her husband was home, in the dark little room with the hard bed that Hastings had rented in an inn on London Bridge. Once or twice they had managed to spend an afternoon together there, before she had to return home to sit at the head of Salucci's table.

Her pale face seemed to tremble. He sat up and took her hand.

'What is it? What's the matter? You know that I won't forget you, there will be no others. I shall live chastely until I return to you.'

'It's not that.'

'I know it is a long time. I will write to you, I give you my word.'

'I'm going to have a child.'

He had not been expecting this, but at once it struck him as surprising that it had not happened before.

'You are sure?'

'Not completely, it is still early, but I believe so.'

Edward paused, taking the enormity of this in.

'It doesn't please you?'

'But of course.' He stood up and took her in his arms, where they were both bathed in the morning sunlight. 'It's wonderful. I am sorry that I am going away, but there is nothing to worry about at the moment, is there? I mean, you are quite well?'

'Yes, quite well.'

'And your belly will not start to grow for months.'

'No. Antonio will assume...'

'Quite.'

He kissed the top of her head. 'A child, our child!'

'Yes,' she laughed. 'Our child.'

'I will write to you from Fotheringhay and you must write to tell me how you fare. You shall want for nothing; clothing or medicines, or if certain foods take your fancy, you must write and let me know. I will take care of it all.'

'And you will be back soon.'

'Indeed, sooner than you think.'

She lifted her chin, to look into his hazel eyes. 'I love you.'

Edward kissed the tip of her nose. 'I know.'

THIRTEEN: Fotheringhay, June, 1459

They galloped across country, through woodland and fields bright with the promise of crops. The air rushed past them, clean and crisp. Overhead, blue skies stretched to the horizon and seemed to go on forever. London was far behind, with its smoking chimneys and stinking ditches, so far behind that it seemed to belong to another world. Ahead, the whole of England lay before them, rising and falling in gentle squares of green and yellow, cut across by the pulsing routes of rivers and the rutted tracks of roads.

Presently, the road mounted a ridge. At the summit, York reined in his horse and gazed down across the landscape beyond. There, in a bend of the winding River Nene, sat a magnificent castle. Ringed by a deep moat, its grey turrets rose strong and boxy against the bright sky. Fotheringhay had been the main family home for decades, Cecily's favourite castle among all the family possessions, more picturesque even than Ludlow. Somehow, the sky behind the towers seemed bluer here than anywhere else.

'They're not expecting us,' York grinned. 'Let's surprise them.'

Edward flashed his smile. He was two months past his seventeenth birthday but still appeared to be growing, now considerably taller than his father. Edmund, just sixteen, was rapidly catching up. When he looked upon these tall, handsome young man, York could not help but swell with pride.

'Let's go and greet your mother.'

They thundered down the bank, through a sunlit patch of wild flowers. Red, white and yellow petals dotted the rippling grasses. As they drew closer, the familiar lines of the outhouses could be seen, with their uneven tile roofs, the gable end of the kitchens and stable block. Smoke pumped out of the castle's many chimneys. Beyond was the little walled garden with its sun-blown roses and fragrant herbs and further, through the gate, the apple trees were unfolding into bud, scattering their pink blossoms to the wind.

*

Richard lay on his back in the tall grass. The long stems grew right up past him, almost covering him completely. He watched their tips waving gently. The earth was dry and hard beneath his shoulder blades and the sun was warm on his skin. Somewhere behind him in the orchard, his brother George had swarmed up into the apple tree, clasping its gnarly trunk as he ventured higher and higher to the thin branches. He was nine and fearless, convinced of his own perfect right to conquer the tree and impose his will on nature. Richard was no less brave, but he could somehow see the dangers that George overlooked; the sharp sticks, the distance to the ground.

An insect buzzed close to Richard's head and he waved it away. They had escaped their lessons by hiding behind the curtain in the alcove. Peter, their white-haired tutor, had called for them, but his voice had echoed wanly through the room and, shaking his head in despair, he had gone off to seek his rebellious young charges elsewhere. Giggling, with the scent of freedom in their nostrils, they had tumbled down the back stairs and out into the orchard, tasting the sharp green air of early summer. No doubt their delicious stolen moment in the sunshine would soon come to an end: mother knew all their best hiding places. She was supervising the dairy but it would not take long before Peter, panting from his efforts, would find her.

Richard watched a cloud pass slowly behind the tree. Its shape was fluid, changing, like a spot of blood in water, making one shape then another. The wind must be strong up there. It caught birds travelling across land and blew them off course. And he was such a small part of it all, lying awash with grass while his brother scraped his shins on the branches overhead.

'Wheee!' George let out a triumphant cry.

He was perched right at the top, scanning the horizon, with his hand as a shield against the sun. Richard propped himself up on one elbow.

'Can you see inside the nest?'

George inched a little further along the branch. 'Looks empty to me.'

'It's too early then. What can you see?'

'Everything. I can see London from here.'

'No you can't!'

'Can too! How do you know?'

Richard shredded grass casually, secure in his knowledge. 'We're too far away.'

'We're not, I can see that far, all the way to London, the spire of St Paul's and down to the Channel and over to Calais.'

Richard jumped up. 'Liar!'

'Am not! I can see Westminster and the windows of the royal apartments. They've changed the curtains.'

'I don't believe you, you're making it up.'

'I can see the king, he's waving at me out of the window. Come up here and see for yourself then!'

'No, I don't need to. I know you're lying.'

The thunder of horse hooves on cobbles beyond the garden wall made them both spin round.

'It's father!' cried George, beginning to scramble down as quickly as he could. His hair was a tangle of sticks and leaves. 'And Edward and Edmund, come on!'

*

Their approach had been spotted. As York clattered into the courtyard and swung himself down from the saddle, the household was already turning out in greeting. Margaret appeared from the south wing, dressed in a simple kirtle and from the garden door, George and Richard came scrambling and tumbling, panting with exertion, with leaves in their hair. Then from the dairy came Duchess Cecily, with a kerchief thrown over her fair hair and her sleeves rolled up to the elbow.

'We did not expect you until next week,' she laughed, coming forward to greet her husband and sons.

'We were of a mind to leave early,' York explained. 'We thought we'd surprise you and here we are!'

'Then come, take off your boots and have some wine, tell us how it goes at court.'

'You are all well here? You and the children?'

'We are indeed well and the estates have been running smoothly, there is nothing to worry about, come and take off your boots.'

The duke smiled. It was something of a personal tradition between them that, upon his return from court, his wife would remove his boots herself. Now she led him inside, where the hall was cool and scented of rushes. He sat on a bench in the sunlight of the oriel window while she knelt before him.

'You don't need to. I'm all dusty from the road.'

'But I want to.'

Her face lit up as she unlaced first one boot then the other and drew them from his tired feet. Her beautiful smile had been one of the first things he had noticed about her, all those years ago, how it spread slowly from cheek to cheek and seemed to send a warmth up into her blue eyes. He knew there were men who envied him such a beautiful wife, yet they little knew the reserves of her character: her strength, resolve and loyalty. Had they known the full extent of her nature, they would have envied him more.

Then she moved to sit beside him. Through the glass they could see their children; Edward with Richard in his arms and Edmund placing George upon the back of one of the horses as Margaret looked on. The duke enfolded his wife in his arms, pressing kisses into the soft curve between her ear and shoulder.

'I have missed you, it has been too long.'

She turned her face to his so their lips could meet.

'Welcome home, I hope your stay will be a long one.'

She sensed the slight change in him at once.

'What? What is it?'

'Nothing, nothing at all, nothing to worry about.'

He moved back to kiss her again.

'You can't hide anything from me, not after all these years.'

York sighed.

'Not more trouble at court?'

'I'm sorry, I don't want to bring this back with us, into the peace and quiet here.'

Cecily took both his hands in hers. 'Nonsense, we are in this together: what troubles you must be shared so I can take some of the burden of it.'

He kissed her forehead and sighed. 'If only we had our fair share of troubles; they seem to go on and on. You recall last year, there were plots laid against us, attempts on our lives?'

She nodded, warily.

'And last autumn, when Warwick's men were set upon at Westminster and he had to fight to defend himself.'

She recalled it well, particularly the moment she had been nursing Richard, who had lain ill in bed with a fever, when the messenger brought word to Baynard's Castle.

'And he had to flee to Calais that same night.'

York nodded, his grey eyes creasing with concern. 'Where he remains. Now the queen has issued a warrant for his arrest; she will stop at nothing to remove the threat she believes we pose to the throne.'

'But I thought this quarrel had been put away with the Loveday. Otherwise what was the point of it?'

'That was a show. It has never gone away.'

'But you have done nothing except support the king and rule his kingdom effectively in his absence.'

'And that is the problem. There are those who say I would make a better ruler than Henry.'

'Forgive me if I number myself among them.'

'Ah, you are always my greatest supporter.' He moved to kiss her again but she put a hand gently in the middle of his chest.

'Tell me.'

'The queen is planning a parliament at Coventry. The rumour goes that we will not be invited. She is gathering troops. It is happening again as it did four years ago. I fear another battle.'

'To what end?'

'To remove me, perhaps, as we removed Somerset,' his eyes strayed to the scene outside the window. 'I don't trust her, I believe this parliament has been located away from London in order to exclude us.'

'What will you do?'

'It is early days but, if I have to, I will seek an audience with the king.'

Cecily was silent.

York signalled to a servant to bring wine and watched while two glasses were filled.

'We are heading for a crisis. Warwick will return this summer with an army of French mercenaries.'

She nodded. 'But you fought before and what did that achieve?'

Her husband looked grave. 'At the time, we hoped to rid the king of his evil councillors but one Beaufort simply replaced another and the grudges and compensation have long outlasted the day. But if Margaret pushes us into a corner, she gives us no choice. I will always be a threat to Henry, simply because of my descent. I fear she will not rest until she defeats us.'

'What will Henry say?'

'Nothing new, I expect. I tried to see him before we left but was told he was not receiving visitors.'

'That does not bode well.'

A clamouring in the doorway warned them of their children's approach.

'Now, let us not speak of it again until we are in private. I don't want the younger children worried.'

Cecily nodded as little Richard came running into the room and straight into his father's arms.

'Father, we found a nest, high up in the apple tree. George climbed up but there were no eggs in it. He said he could see all the way to London but he couldn't, could he? Tell him he couldn't.'

York smiled at his other son, lurking in the doorway. 'Perhaps George climbed so high he could see London in his dreams.'

Richard thought about this for a minute, then turned to his brother.

'George, did you see London in your dreams?'

George's face contorted. 'No, I saw London, all of it. I saw the king and queen and they were laughing.'

York frowned. 'George? I'll ask you again, think carefully before you answer. Did you see London from the tree?'

And George let out a laugh. 'Of course not, it is miles and miles away. I wanted to see if Richard would believe me.'

He ran towards his father, to share in the embrace. Richard shot him a satisfied glance but George just grinned in response.

'I didn't see London,' he whispered, 'I was looking the wrong way but I did see Scotland!'

*

Edward lingered outside after the others had gone in, breathing in Fotheringhay's air. Each window, each corner, was filled with the memories of happy summers as a child, running in the fields and swimming in the river, content with the warmth of the sun and the knowledge that all his family were safe and close. As the stable hands led the horses round to the stable, he trailed after them, keen to see the haunts of his childhood again. Behind the castle stood the little courtyard

134

flanked by low-roofed domestic buildings; the bakery and dairy, the wash house and larders and the gates to the gardens.

He followed the horses to the stable door. It had been here that he had learned to ride, making his first little trips around the orchard, clutching tight to the reins. The old master of the stable, a freckled Dutchman named Cloet, looked up from his work inside and a broad smile split across his face.

'Master Edward?'

'Yes. We're here for the summer, just arrived.'

'All of you? My Lord and Master Edmund too?'

'All of us, safe and well.'

'You've grown, let me look at you.' The man rose to his feet, still wiry and strong from outdoor work, despite his years.

'Indeed, it must be a year or more since I saw you last. How are you? How is your wife?'

'Still troubled by her legs but we're well; happy to see you back, my Lord.'

'I'll make sure mother sends round some cordials for her.'

'My Lady Duchess is always most attentive to our needs, thank you.'

'I'll call in to see you both soon,' smiled Edward. 'Are the horses all well?'

'All as well as could be.'

'You take such good care of them, you always have.'

He turned and headed along his favourite walk, through the grounds and down to the riverbank, where he used to sit patiently as a boy with a fishing line. As he passed through the outer courtyard, the kitchen door swung open and the sound of raised voices could be heard.

'We could get two pence more at the market,' a woman was saying, 'but we came here first to offer you the freshest bird. And there's no reason to turn us away like this, all we were doing was having a little joke, we didn't mean any disrespect!'

A tall, fair-haired girl stood in the doorway, clasping a dead goose in her arms. She was well built, statuesque yet graceful in her simple dress. Beside her, a second figure, slighter and darker, hovered nervously, twisting her arms about in distress.

'Go on, take the goose,' the woman persisted. 'You won't find a finer one, fed on the best scraps from the table and killed only this morning. It'll be a fine feast for your duchess.'

Someone from within repeated a blunt negative.

'See how plump it is,' she offered, holding the beast forward. 'Go on, don't turn away a good goose just because you don't like our manners! That's cutting off your nose to spite your face, or your duke's face! I bet he'd like a nice plump goose on his table tonight. Call him out here, I'm sure he'd give me a different answer.'

Edward was curious. The girls looked too well dressed to have come up from the village but they were clearly keen to sell the bird; he guessed that perhaps they were the daughters of a local farmer fallen on lean times.

'I do find myself feeling rather partial to a good goose,' he said, strolling towards them. 'What's the asking price?'

'Who's asking?'

The woman turned, squinting in the sunlight. She must have been nineteen or twenty, with a broad face that had something vibrant about the eyes and a defiant cast to the mouth. The skin of her face, throat and exposed forearms was tanned a deep golden brown and the end of her little nose turned up pertly.

When she saw Edward approaching, dressed in velvet and silk, she dropped a curtsey.

'Forgive me, my Lord, I did not hear you approach.'

'So how much is this goose?'

'Six pence,' she replied quickly before the castle cook could contradict her.

'Six pence!' repeated Edward. 'That sounds like London prices. Cook, what are you offering?'

'I said I'd give her four, my Lord,' the Cook confirmed.

'So why not make it five, as it does seem like a fresh bird?'

He flashed a smile over to the young woman. 'And you are?'

'My name is Mary Denny, my Lord, and I'm not to take anything but six for the goose.'

Edward laughed; he was in a mind to humour her. There was something about her bold eyes that appealed to him. Even the stains of mud and grass on her skirts drew his interest.

'Is that so, Mary Denny?'

'That's what my mother says.'

'Well, I dare not thwart your mother's desires. Here.' He reached for the purse hanging from his belt and counted out six coins of his own. 'Lucky for you, I have a taste for goose tonight, hand the bird over.'

Mary nodded to her companion to take the coins before she dumped the creature in the outstretched arms of the cook.

'But think yourself lucky that I am in a forgiving mood, I should have sent you packing.'

The girl turned her nose up pertly and flashed her eyes. She was certainly pretty and bold, but Edward thought of Alasia back in London, of their last lingering kiss and the child she was carrying.

Mary took a step back and looked him up and down. 'Well that would have been a shame, as I can be very friendly when I choose.'

He laughed. 'I am sure you can. Now be on your way and thank you for the goose.'

*

There was a full moon that night. It seemed to hang heavy and full right over Fotheringhay Castle whilst they all slept. All except York, who had dozed off and then woken, to find the bright moonlight peeping in round the corners of the curtains.

At his side, Cecily lay sleeping. She had rolled away from him and her form in the half-light was one long, smooth silvered curve, rising at hip, breast and shoulder, then tapering away under the sheets. During their earlier lovemaking, he had pulled her long fair hair loose and now it lay across her shoulders. They were unusual in their choice to share a bed, through until morning. Both had their own apartments within the castle, as custom dictated, but from the very start of their marriage, they had enjoyed each other's company and warmth.

Softly tracing along a golden lock with his finger, he saw the threads of grey that had appeared in recent years. There would be no more children now. Four years had passed since she had borne her last child; little Ursula, whom they had lost. He recalled Cecily's brave public front, her insistence that it was God's will and her devoted prayers for the souls of her lost children, for the little girl and her five lost brothers. Yet it was only with her husband, late at night, that she had allowed herself the release of a mother's tears.

He sighed and rolled onto his back. Here at Fotheringhay, the world seemed an idyllic place, as his children grew up and the summer days stretched out long and warm. If only the outside world might be shut out forever, they might live the contented lives of dumb beasts, oblivious to the existence of king and court, of foreign and civil wars, of jealousy and petty rivalries. For all the estate's charm he knew that, on the horizon, danger was lurking. In a matter of weeks, he must decide whether or not to face the king. If the Coventry parliament met as planned, without his presence, it was tantamount to a declaration of war. What would happen then, to his wife and family, to this precious haven?

Somewhere outside, a fox barked. The world seemed too peaceful to disturb with such dangerous thoughts. Tomorrow, he would pray for guidance. Tonight, he would try to get the rest he needed to face these problems.

Cecily stirred and resettled herself on her pillow. York leaned across and placed a gentle kiss upon her cheek. Her skin was both cool and warm. He saw her lips curve slightly before he closed his own eyes.

*

In the flickering light of the candle, Edward pressed his seal to the hot wax. Almost two months had passed since he had parted from Alasia, riding away from her house into the coolness of a London dawn, leaving her with his child growing in her belly. It felt like longer. They had been parted before, on the occasions that Antonio Salucci's feet were on dry land, but they had always been able to contrive to see each other, at the cross of St Paul's or in the little dark inn chamber on the bridge, rented by William Hastings. Since their affair began, they had never been apart this long, his final memory imprinted on his brain, of her standing in the doorway, wrapped in a white robe, her dark hair loose about her shoulders.

He had received one letter from her only, brought by a trader who supplied the castle with spices from the London warehouses; it was folded and sealed, smelling of saffron and powdered ginger, bearing a small, dense hand in weak ink. He had tucked it inside his doublet and fled into the garden for privacy. Alasia's words tumbled out under the unfolding green leaves on the apple tree. She was well, but missing him. Her health was good, she had not been suffering from sickness, just an increase in appetite; she had all she needed, save for him. *Save for him,* he repeated to himself, with a rush of longing for her. She wrote that Antonio was set to depart again in a month, sailing across the Mediterranean to Cyprus and then on to Lebanon, where he knew a trader who dealt in perfumes. It should be a very lucrative trip. In his absence, her sister would move into the house in Thames Street to keep her company. The child was due early in the new year.

In the still of the summer night, Edward could think of little to say beyond the conventions. He could only write that he had thought of her often, and solicit her to take care of her health. She should rest and not tire herself, and not go walking in the heat of the midday sun or eat foods that were too rich. He smiled as he wrote those lines, smiled at the novelty and incongruity of it; who was he, after all, to be giving advice to an expectant mother? Yet he knew it was what she would be hoping to hear from him, to feel from his words that he cared about her, that this little new life she was nurturing, mattered to him. It was their secret, his and hers. He pressed his signet ring onto the page and watched the wax dry. Tomorrow, York's clerk was heading back to London to collect the quarterly rents owing. No doubt Edward could pay him a little extra to carry the letter and find the house on the corner of Trinitie Lane. By the evening, his words would be in her hands. He turned it over and pressed his lips to her name.

FOURTEEN: Traitors at Play

Edmund heard the birds calling. Their piercing cries drew him away from his dreams, from some distant place of memory that he associated with happiness. For a moment, the real world eluded him; where was he? Daylight penetrated his closed eyelids: white, harsh, unyielding. Then came the realisation; it was Fotheringhay, home of daydreams and the long warm summers of babyhood, of blossom falling into long grass and the braying of donkeys in the meadow. Of mother's stillness and safeness, of father's action and solidity.

He sat up and blinked at the window. Outside, the birds made a dark foreboding knot against the clouds but it seemed as if it would be a fine day. Someone had already been in and opened the latch, so the fresh air of the morning swept in, bringing with it the scent of mown grass. A soft movement nearby made him aware of her presence.

'Edmund,' called his mother softly, 'are you awake?'

He nodded, swinging his legs round so they dangled above the floor. She extended her hand, smiling.

'Come and pray with me. It's the feast day of St Mary Magdalene.'

Edmund pulled his shift straight and stretched. His muscles eased into life.

Through the window, he could see the dark triangle of his brother. Edward was standing on the grass, swinging his arms as if practising with an invisible sword, thinking himself unobserved. One arm pointed up towards the sky then sliced down, with precision and power. He seemed to be working out an immense store of energy.

Edmund padded across the floor with bare feet. Cecily was kneeling before an ivory and gold triptych, adorned with jewelled white roses and the portrait of the Virgin Mary. It was her favourite icon; he had seen it many times in his youth as it travelled wherever she did, wrapped and bound carefully in cloth, and packed in straw. They had knelt side by side and prayed many times in this fashion, in the early morning light, before breaking their fast. The boy dropped to his knees and began to recite his devotions. She leaned across to kiss the top of his tousled head.

In tune, they murmured their prayers, their lips hung with the names of saints and loved ones, with Latin phrases and the age-old rhymes of humility and hope.

Eventually she crossed herself and rose slowly to her feet.

'Edward has not prayed this morning?'

Edmund shrugged, pulling on his clothes. He knew that his mother's love for her eldest son was fierce; she could forgive him many things, because of his strength and beauty, because he was her eldest son. It was a love that cherished from a distance, that admired and contemplated, as if it was part of her religion. Yet, he also knew that although he might not be as tall or handsome as his brother, it was his company that she sought most often: Edward might be her warrior but he, Edmund, was her comfort.

'Come.' She linked her arm through his and they passed out of the chamber, down the stairs towards Fotheringhay's great hall.

'Father has gone to hear the court sessions in Peterborough,' she told Edmund, 'but he'll be back tonight. I thought we might sit by the brook when the day warms up. You boys could fish or swim.'

He knew the spot she meant; her favourite place at the end of the meadows, where the white willows cast dappled shade on the bank.

One of her hands alighted on his arm.

'So long as you have nothing else planned? You could tell me about London. Did you go to the council meetings with father?'

Edmund swelled with pride at the memory. 'Just before we left, I did attend the council, I can tell you all about it. Of course we'll go to the river. I think Edward said something about riding in the woods so I won't repeat the story to him. Perhaps Margaret will come too, while the others are having their lessons.'

'Shall we let them off their lessons today, so they can come with us? It can't hurt, just for one day.'

He nodded, thinking she was too indulgent with the little ones, but saying nothing.

She looked into the sky, stretching wide and pale above them. 'We'll wait for the sun to rise higher. These mornings have been so cold but by noon it is always warm and dry.'

Edmund's stomach growled, making his mother laugh.

'Come, let's go and eat something. We'll call for the others on the way.'

They sat in the hall, on the corner of the table closest to the oriel window. Cecily was in the centre, her pale cheeks flushed with the presence of her children: Margaret and Edmund on one side, George and Richard on the other with their eyes still sleepy. Edward sat at the head, in his father's usual seat, brooding about something, although his brother could not imagine what. Outside, the courtyard was bathed in light and full of the yapping of the hounds, being led out for exercise. The servants brought cold cuts of meat, white rolls and jugs of small beer.

'And I completed the whole of the flower on the sleeve and part of the vine this morning,' Margaret was explaining to her mother. 'But the light blue yarn is almost used up and I shall need more of the pink and green soon if I am to finish it.'

'I shall send to Peterborough for some,' Cecily reassured her. 'If father goes again to the assizes tomorrow, he can deliver the message in the morning and collect the package before he leaves, so you will have your thread tomorrow night. Have you thought what you will do with the edging? I have some of the silver lace left from my green dress, if you think it will suit.'

Margaret nodded enthusiastically, her mouth filled with bread. Before she had a chance to answer, a messenger approached the table.

Cecily took the letter from the salver and broke the seal.

'It is from my sister, Anne.'

'Buckingham's wife' said Edward, coming round from his reverie.

'Yes, wait a moment.'

There was a pause as she read. George took advantage of it to reach across and claim another slice of meat. Edmund did not stop him, but watched his mother's face. Midway through, her mood seemed to change.

Edward noticed the change too. 'What does she say?'

'Mostly about her boys,' Cecily answered quickly.

'What about them?'

Anne, Duchess of Buckingham, was four years Cecily's senior. Her marriage to the scar-faced duke had put them on opposing sides and their letters and meetings were intermittent.

'Oh! Poor Anne, her eldest boy has succumbed to the plague. They have lost Humphrey.'

Edmund recalled meeting their elder cousin once or twice; most recently at Elizabeth's wedding. At almost twenty years his senior, Humphrey had already been a married man with an infant son; he had kept away from the court and council, preferring the quiet of the countryside.

Cecily reached across to him, her closest child, and seized his hand.

'How terrible, I must write to her, poor Anne.'

Edmund saw her eyes moisten as she struggled to control her emotions.

'I am sure she would be comforted to hear from you.'

'I wonder where she is; perhaps Maxstoke or Tonbridge, she does not say. I might send the letter to court except I would not be certain that Buckingham would pass it on to her.'

'Send two letters. I will copy out the second if you like.'

She squeezed his hand. 'You are so thoughtful. I can hardly bear to think of her loss. All this time and we did not know. God have mercy on her.'

'It is terrible, God rest his soul,' declared Edward. 'Is there any more news?'

Cecily read on. The children ate, watched and whispered to one another, until their mother abruptly folded the paper and slid it inside her dress.

'Nothing more, now eat and we will go and enjoy the sunshine.'

*

The evening light was golden across the Nene valley as York approached home. Coming from the east, with the setting sun behind him, the castle was bathed in warm light and the glass gleamed in the windows. There had been a number of difficult cases to be dealt with that day: as he sat in the guildhall at Peterborough, a stream of the poorest of humanity had been brought before him; debtors and thieves, abandoned women and murderers. His natural inclination was towards clemency but that was not the way of the law: justice must be seen to be done to deter those others who might be mindful of crime. He shuddered as he thought of the pale faces of the sinners. At least he had been able to save one woman from the gallows.

As he rode into the courtyard, Cecily was waiting for him. She must have been at the tower window, watching for him on the road. The sun blazed behind her, ringing her head with a bright fiery halo.

'I am back, at last. All is well here?'

'All is well.'

'And the children?'

'Listening to the minstrels in the hall. All is well with you?'

'Well enough. A long day, but a productive one.'

She came towards him closely, confidentially. 'I have had a letter from my sister Anne.'

'What does she say?'

His wife spoke softly but her voice was controlled and careful. 'She writes of the next parliament. It is being convened at Coventry by Bishop Morton, at the request of the queen, to pass acts of attainder against you. Anne writes that you must not attend.'

York was at once grave. 'So it is as we suspected. Margaret tried to bring an earlier parliament together this spring but nothing came of it; now she has decided to act once and for all. I knew they would exclude us. I could get no answer at the last council meeting.'

He thought for a moment.

'We must leave here. The king is in Cheshire, so we should gather our allies at Ludlow to plan our next move; I will seek an audience with Henry but, if that fails, we will strike at them before they have the chance to injure us.'

'Is there no other option?'

York shook his head. 'We always knew it would come to this. We must fight or be killed.'

'But the king? Surely the king does not agree with this?'

'It depends how much he has been told; if he believes we pose a danger to him and his son, then he will act as he sees fit.'

'You are speaking folly. Kill the king?'

'Of course not!' York's voice rose. 'Remove those who would harm us, as with Somerset, so we can better serve the king. We must reason with him, otherwise they will attaint us. Forgive me.'

'But are we traitors?'

'We have served Henry loyally, so far as we have been able,' York replied. 'Only he has not always made that easy. We must trust that it is all part of the Lord's plan.'

The mention of a higher authority brought Cecily some reassurance.

'It was good of Anne to write,' she added softly.

York nodded. 'She does not quite forget her blood. It is the spur we needed. If there is really no doubt about the queen's intentions, we cannot carry on playing this elaborate game of cat and mouse. Tomorrow we will leave here; the servants can pack up the house and follow us to Ludlow.'

'You will write to Warwick?'

'Yes. If he can land in Wales, he might reach Ludlow before the queen realises. Where is your brother?'

'Salisbury wrote from London that he was leaving for Middleham. That was five days ago.'

He stepped closer and took his wife's upturned face in his hands. 'Then I will write to him there. We must prepare ourselves for a fight.'

She nodded, holding back her tears.

'I know, I know.' He kissed the top of her head and she flung her arms about his waist and held him tight.

'We have done all we can,' said Cecily, 'you have done all you can. Now let us enjoy our last evening here, then we must all get some rest, we have a long ride ahead of us.'

*

The mood in the hall that night was sombre. A knot of minstrels was playing in the gallery but even their jaunty tune could not lift the quiet heaviness that had settled on the castle. Trestle tables had been set out and covered in fine cloth, the braziers burned bright and the food was plentiful enough but even the villagers admitted for the feast sat and ate in a subdued manner. Some had heard rumours of their lord's departure, when they had been counting on supplying his table for a good few months. Edward was seated with his father and sister, while Edmund and his mother had George and Richard between them. Only the two small boys were unaffected and chattered excitedly about removing to Ludlow.

'Try and lift your spirits,' said York under his breath, as he took his portion from a plate they shared.

'I can't stop my mind running on it.'

'Nor me. But you must show a mask to all these people watching you.'

Edward lifted his eyes and faced the hall. There were perhaps a hundred people seated at table, some known to him from the estate, others from the church, the hospital or the village. Men and women, old and young; reeves, farmers, butchers, weavers.

'What you feel matters less than what you show,' York continued. 'Never forget that. People will choose whether or not to follow you on the outward face you present, on whether they can believe in your authority.'

'But they are bound to us, bound to follow. They pay us rents.'

York inclined his head. 'The ties that bind must be based on confidence and loyalty. Those things cannot be bought. Let them see a leader that they would choose to follow.'

Edward nodded. 'Yes father.'

'And later we will have dancing and laughter.'

'Yes, let's.'

'In the morning we will pray and depart, but tonight we will be merry. It is all part of the act, and the act is an important part of securing the victory. The people must believe in you: everything depends upon it. Battles can be lost or won before the armies engage.'

*

As the plates were being cleared, York and Cecily led the dancing. Edward called for more wine and watched them, moving in time together, touching first their hands and their feet, stepping close together then apart again in perfect rhythm, as if they were able to communicate without words. He could see that mother was looking tired, but she kept a smile on her face and her delicate beauty still eclipsed that of any woman in the room. She was the perfect foil for York's strength and breadth, her eyes fixed on him adoringly, listening to his every word, approving his every action. In turn, he reverenced her as his lady, the epitome of grace and virtue, the ideal woman and wife. He watched their heads bend together, intimate in spite of the formality of the dance. They had been married for thirty years and were still as close as ever. It had been an arranged match too, made by her father, although it had proved to their liking from the moment they first met.

Edward sighed. He might be seventeen but the question of his marriage still hung in the air. Years ago, York had hoped to marry him to a French

146

princess, writing letters of sweet persuasion to Charles VII, but the world had changed since then. After the loss of Rouen, father had told him not to think of Princess Madeleine anymore. Edward had never even met the girl, but sometimes his curiosity conjured up a pair of soft eyes, a skein of glossy dark hair, a winsome figure, who might be sitting in the window of a French chateau overlooking the green valley of the Loire, thinking about him. It would have been a good match; a match to rival that of the king, with the girl's Valois blood and his Plantagenet descent: perhaps that was why it had come to nothing.

Yet no other names had been suggested. As the highest family in the land, after that of the king, the York men had to choose their wives carefully; they had to be sure of loyalty, of fertility, of virtue. Edward knew his parents would never approve of Alasia as his wife, even if she was widowed at some future time. She was beautiful enough, clever and discreet and witty, but she was the daughter of a merchant, already touched by man. Even if he told them about the child, she would always be unsuitable in their eyes. Would he ever be blessed with a match as strong as his parents? After thirty years, would he still want to take his wife in his arms and look at her the way his father looked at his mother? He was surprised by the emotion rising in him, in the lump in his throat. He called for more wine to wash it away.

*

The evening wore on, the shadows growing dim in the corners of the hall as the fire began to die. Edward partnered his sister Margaret, whose dancing was so much better than his and easily put him to shame.

'You've been practising,' he grumbled.

'It's the wine bewitching your feet,' she laughed and twirled away to extend her hand to Edmund, who proved to be far more elegant and sure-footed. Edward leaned against the doorframe, bidding his parents goodnight as they headed away to a quieter corner of the castle, where George and Richard were already asleep, tucked into their little cribs by the soothing hands of their nurse. The night was drawing to a close and Edward's head felt heavy with wine; no doubt he would sleep heavily tonight and the long ride tomorrow would give him a chance to recover.

'You need a partner who can teach you a thing or two.'

He turned. Mary Denny was standing behind him.

'Ah, the girl with the goose. And what would you know about it?'

He tried not to notice the way her scarlet dress clung to her breasts and hips, or the flush in her cheeks, or the blonde curls that clustered around her temples.

'Clearly a lot more than you do,' she laughed. 'I would have thought you could dance better than that, coming from court and all.'

He was annoyed, but he wasn't going to show it. 'There are far more important things to do at court than dance.'

'Oh, I am sure,' she replied with inscrutable innocence and he could not be sure if she was being deferential or mocking.

'I didn't think you would be here tonight.'

'You had thought about me, then?'

She was clever. He frowned. 'I mean I am surprised to see you here.'

'Where should I be?' she asked, quick as lightening.

'Chasing a goose somewhere?'

'Not good enough to be at your table?'

Edward looked away. 'You are bold.'

She knew the social code. 'Forgive me, my Lord.'

He waited a little, then turned and shot a sly look at her. She was indeed very pretty, with her upturned nose and expressive eyes.

'Come on then, if you're such a skilled dancer, show me how it is done.'

She arched her brows and flung back her head pertly. For a moment he thought she was about to refuse him, but then she pursed her lips and swept past him, her feet already finding the rhythm of the music. There were few pairs dancing now, following the motions of mirroring and double-stepping with varying degrees of success. He stood face to face with her, the space of a hand between them. He could see the texture of her skin, white and smooth, with the spread of very pale summertime freckles. Her little chin had a dimple in the middle. She began to move, confidently, as if dancing was second nature to her; fluidly, as if she was moving through water; supply, as if her limbs needed little guidance. He followed, as she led. His body filled the spaces she had just occupied, his feet in the spaces hers had marked, his hands almost copies of hers. Then, as the dance required, they came together and touched: hand upon hand, hand upon shoulder, then he had his hands around her waist. She was firm and warm. Her soft hair brushed against his cheek and longing stirred in his chest.

He found and held her eyes.

'You dance well.'

'It's too easy.'

She turned away from him with a flourish, then they passed down the row and came together again at the bottom. He could glimpse her sturdy body moving along behind the other dancers, a smile fixed on her lips. He couldn't shake the feeling that despite his superiority in rank, she was playing with him. They came together again at the bottom of the row and touched fingers.

'Who are you?'

She merely smiled.

'You live with your mother, in the village?'

'That is what I told you before, my Lord.'

'And you have no husband?'

Her eyes dropped coyly, secure in his interest.

The dance came to an end and the partners began to disperse. The hall was emptying and servants began to clear away the trestles and lay down their pallet beds for the night.

She inclined her head. 'Thank you, my Lord, for the dance.'

He could not take his eyes from her face. 'It was my pleasure.'

'I bid you goodnight.'

Something made him follow her towards the door. The night was beckoning, sweet and warm across the fields. As she turned to leave, he reached out and grabbed her bare wrist. She spun round to meet him, but not in surprise.

He pressed the palm of her hand to his lips. 'Do you have to go so soon?'

'That all depends,' she whispered, her body straining towards his.

'On what?'

'On whether or not you can catch me.'

And she gave him a swift push in the centre of his chest, so that he took a few steps backwards, giving her the moment she needed to wriggle free and dart out into the darkness.

His interest was piqued at once. Without hesitation, he plunged out into the night after her, where the fields led to the orchards, and stables, beyond which stretched the woods, dark and silent in expectation. There was something of a moon that night, but at that moment it was masked

149

by clouds and he could only just make out the shape of her bright dress as she headed for the path. She was already a good distance away, holding up her skirts so as to run all the faster, but he could not resist a challenge.

He sprinted across the garden, round the corner and onto the path. She was heading into the orchard, but he knew he would have the advantage there, with its long grass and bumpy ground. Beside the clump of trees in the middle, she was beginning to stumble, her fair hair flying about her face.

'I've got you,' he called, picking his way between the gnarled branches.

But Mary was strong and determined. He was almost within reach when she picked up speed again, finding a clear stretch of grass and pulling away from him. And as he tried to follow, his foot caught on a root and he stumbled. She heard him fall, turned and laughed.

But her laughter was only brief, as he launched himself towards her and his fingers caught her ankle. At once, she was down on the grass ahead of him, wriggling and kicking.

'Now I have you.'

'I think not, my Lord,' and he felt the leather of her shoe come into contact with his shoulder: once again she was off, heading for the dark shadows of the woods.

By the time Edward reached the road, she was nowhere to be seen. The pale moonlight barely penetrated the thick canopy here but he could see that the long line of the road was empty. He stopped, waited, listened to the sounds of the night and of his own heavy breathing. She was hiding behind one of the trees. But which one?

He crept forward, stepping off the road onto the grass, so that the tread of his feet would not be heard. He passed the first tree, then the second, but she was nowhere to be seen. Ahead, the broad trunk of an ancient oak spread over his way and behind it, the shadows seemed to be darker. He almost thought he saw movement between the arms of knotted wood. As he drew closer, his breath short in anticipation, then there it was: the flutter of her red dress.

Burning with passion, he launched himself around the tree, only for his fingers to grasp at the empty material. The red dress hung there from a branch, dancing before his eyes, but Mary was nowhere to be seen. He clasped the material to his face, smelling the musky warmth of her still upon it.

And then he saw her, in the clearing, lying on her back in the moonlight. She wore only her shift, thin and white as it clung to her. Her limbs were pale and stretched out under the stars, her hair shaken loose, her mouth open to invite him. As he reached her, his fingers closing about her thighs, he could not tell if she was shivering from the cold, or from her passion. She was responsive to his touch, her back arching up to allow her body to meet his as he lowered himself softly down. They did not need words. He crushed his lips down onto hers and felt her shudder in surrender.

FIFTEEN: The Road to War, September, 1459

The Earl of Salisbury surveyed the men massing before him. He estimated there to be several thousand, perhaps a little more, spread across the field and into the lane beyond. They had been marching most of the morning, on their way across the autumnal countryside from Middleham to Ludlow, passing along the hollow ways and stubble fields as workers gathered in the harvest. Once or twice, a tousled head had lifted from its work to watch the men pass; mostly they carried on the gleaning, the threshing and sorting that were part of the ritual year.

For a moment, he had brought them to a halt on the heath between a tall hedge and the River Tern. They were tired and needed to rest. Most of them could do with a good meal too, but they would have to content themselves with cold fare, as this was not the place to be building fires and cooking meat. The air hung heavy with the scent of leaves and the gentle mist that spread across the valley but there was something else that did not quite sit right, something he couldn't quite put his finger on. He scanned the horizon, as far as he could see, picking out the distant chimneys of a village, a church spire, the tall points of trees tapering away against the clouds.

A moving speck caught his eye. The scouts were on their way back and the first of them had reached the clump of bushes along the distant ridge. Soon he would know how the land lay. Salisbury had served with York in Normandy and as a warden of the West Marches; over the decades his long, hooked nose had become well tuned to danger. Yesterday, he had narrowly avoided the king's army as it marched forward to meet him from Coventry. Now, a little over fifty miles separate him from York and Warwick at Ludlow, but he sensed he would not make it without a fight.

Since he had first received York's letter, at Middleham that summer, he had known this moment was coming. His wife Alice had remained behind on their estate, with their two little granddaughters; they would be sitting down to eat about now, with servants lying out clean white linen cloths. He wiped the sweat from his brow and peered down the road. A figure was hastening towards him and he sensed that its urgency was a portent of serious news.

The messenger leaped off his horse and fell before him, panting on his knees.

'Come, what news?'

'The Lancastrians, a huge army, twice our size...'

'The king's army?'

'No, another one, under the command of Baron Audley, they lie not half a mile away, across the brook.'

'That close? You are certain?'

'We saw the banners first, through the woods. When we got nearer, there were the men, ranks of them, waiting for the signal to advance.'

'And where might I see them?'

The man pointed. 'Along the ridge. They can't be aware of quite how close we are.'

'Good work, thank you. Spread the word among the men to keep quiet.'

Salisbury turned away, his face grim. With the king's army close upon their heels, this new force stood between him and Ludlow: there was no choice but to fight. He was more than a match for any king's army but now, as he approached the age of sixty and his hip kept giving him the old trouble, he had hoped these days would be passed in peace and contemplation. It seemed it was not to be.

A little way off, the generals awaited his command. At his signal, they rode over; three trusted and loyal men who had been in the service of his family for years. He had been fortunate to inspire loyalty among good men.

'A Lancastrian army awaits us half a mile to the south. We have the advantage of being forewarned and we have the brook which lies between us, as well as the incline on our side. They outnumber us, perhaps as much as two to one, but we will be prepared for them and use the terrain to our advantage.'

'Yes, my Lord,' agreed one.

Salisbury turned to him, his heart racing. It was time to think quickly.

'John, you will lead the left flank with the woodland to your rear. Hide your archers among the trees, to pick off the Lancastrian advance. Robert, gather the supply wagons together to the right, to provide cover for your men there and block their approach on that side. Stack up the cannons along the ridge, pointing down the valley. Jack, you will take the centre. We will let the arrows do their work and then see how willing they are to cross the brook.'

'It runs high with the autumn rains,' added the first.

'It may serve us well. We shall need to outwit this force and draw them towards us; do not let your men take fear at the size of the enemy, encourage them to be in good heart and all may still be well. God be with you.'

'And with you, my Lord,' they chorused.

He pulled on the reins of his horse and galloped away up to the ridge. Reaching the top, he advanced slowly, until the plain came into sight. For a moment it seemed misty, shifting, then the scene resolved before his eyes. What he saw there sent a shiver down his spine, in spite of all his experience. The whole field was alive with men, standing quietly en masse, awaiting instructions. Brightly coloured flags betrayed the arms of the king and queen and those of their Lancastrian commanders. The sun glinted on one sword, then another. So it had come to this: York had been right.

It seemed that the old certainties of right and wrong, peace and war, were being redrawn. Somewhere, further than these men could see, perhaps ten miles down the road, the queen sat in her tent, swathed in French silks and English jewels, listening to the reports of her messengers. In all his years of service, Salisbury had fought against men in close combat, been able to look them in the eye as he struggled for his life. The image of the queen, a woman, whispering in the ear of the king, was quite another matter. He could do his best on a battlefield but this was an enemy he lacked the weaponry to defeat.

He turned his horse around. There were prayers to be said before the opposing armies clashed.

*

In the gatehouse of Ludlow Castle, York shaded his eyes against the noonday sun. With each passing hour, he had expected to see Salisbury approaching with his men, but the streets of Ludlow and the distant hills lay quiet. The last information he had received was a brief note written from The Sun Inn at Stoke, where the earl had been recruiting more men.

That had been two days ago; two days of cold early dawns and long sunsets. Since then, nothing.

He knew the king was on the move with a sizeable army. Now it was a tactical game; waiting, planning and choosing a route carefully to avoid meeting the royal forces before the three armies came together.

'No sign?'

Warwick had climbed up the tower steps behind him. He had arrived the previous night, marching up from the coast with a group of Calais soldiers. The line of his square jaw betrayed his concern for his father.

York shook his head. 'Nothing yet. Perhaps they have been forced to take a longer route; I had hoped to hear of their arrival in Shrewsbury by now.'

'Then we can do nothing but wait. There is no point wondering, until we hear news. Come down, we are about to eat.'

'In a moment. You go down, I want to watch for a little more.'

'All right,' Warwick conceded with a shrug, 'but your boys will put away the best cuts of meat.'

York laughed, 'So be it. I will join you presently.'

He turned back to the road, the long mud and stone track that stretched north through the woods and ran on through Shrewsbury, Crewe and on to York. What secrets were concealed among those blue distant hills?

*

The wind was blowing from the east. As the archers loosed their arrows, Salisbury's grey eyes watched them rise on the breeze, turn and fall in a rain on the distant men. A number of figures crumpled and fell; he estimated perhaps thirty or forty. The archers stretched and drew back their long bows a second time. With a terrifying rush, almost deafening to those in their midst, the arrows flew from their hands again. They soared high into the sky, a flight of thin, deadly sticks mocking the path of birds, then paused, curved down and built up momentum as they fell. This time, they hit the central and left flank, causing a silent, distant panic as man piled upon man.

Salisbury nodded. 'One more.'

All attempts at parley had failed. Reading between the lines, it seemed the queen's commander, Lord Audley, was bent on destroying his force before it merged with the Yorkists.

The third round of arrows flew up and arched back down towards the enemy lines. This time, the wind had dropped slightly, letting them fall right into the centre of the men, spreading them out across the ground like flies. Would this force them to advance, or would they fall back?

The answer came from a new body of soldiers, rising up behind the pile of bodies, drawing out their long bows and waiting for the command.

'Be ready. Draw another round!' Salisbury commanded.

The archers acted at the same moment. He saw the exchange of arrows mid-air, crossing in a hail of sticks, like some strange omen, rising and falling. In a second, they had struck home. A man beside him fell, and three more in front. One arrow lodged by his foot and another grazed the armour of his flank. Looking around, he quickly surveyed that they had lost several dozen men.

There was a terrible moment of waiting. He knew the men were shaking in their boots, their hearts pumping, as the dying lay groaning at their feet. One man with his face covered in blood writhed about on the earth, calling out to God.

'Stand firm!' Salisbury shouted. 'We still have the advantage of them.'

'They seem ready to advance,' his commander called from behind.

'Right! Men in the centre, we will fool them. Fall back, fall back towards the road, quickly but do not go too far, stay close and wait for the call to return.'

'Fall back!' his man repeated. 'Fall back but wait to return, spread the news.'

The earl watched as the enemy regathered. The archery volleys had shaken them but they still outnumbered his troops so that hand-to-hand fighting would likely go against them. The only way now was to outwit them.

'Fall back,' he called again. 'Fall back to the road.'

Salisbury pulled his horse around and galloped back a little way, keeping the figure of his opponent in view, mounted in full armour in the glare of the sun.

His men began to turn from the scene, as if under retreat. They came in a wave, some hobbling, others defiant, towards the place where he waited. Surely Audley would take the bait?

'Slower,' he called in a low voice. 'Make it seem definite but move more slowly, pretend to be wounded.'

There was a moment while the enemy considered their position. Then, just as Salisbury had hoped, he saw Audley lift his arm in the signal to charge. Thinking themselves victorious, the larger army thundered forward, heading for the brook, intent on cutting down their fleeing opponents.

'Wait! Wait!' Salisbury counselled his men. 'Wait until they are mired in the mud, then we attack with all haste.'

As the Lancastrians pushed forward, a sense of secret camaraderie ignited his men; he could see it in their eyes, their glances to each other, the cast of their heads. Their earlier fears were turning to confidence.

'A little longer,' he urged. 'Then we will have them.'

And then, the opposite ranks broke and a few men came tentatively forward. They seemed unsure. Salisbury watched them with sidelong caution. Suddenly they were followed by a rush and the enemy were charging. Audley's men pitched headlong into the waters of the brook, still swollen with recent rain and began to scramble up the other side.

'At the ready!' Salisbury shouted. 'We have them! Cut them down as they struggle up the bank! Now, fast as you can!'

With glorious speed and determination, he rode forward and his men kept apace. As they drew closer, the faces of the enemy loomed large; it was going to be a fight to the death and Salisbury knew that confidence counted: he must look them in the eye as he cut them down. He picked his focus. A group of three men was slightly ahead of the others, urging them on, their leader was tall and broad, a fighting man, but he was floundering in the mud.

Salisbury's pollaxe cut into the man's stomach before he had a chance to react. Blood spilled down his side as the earl lifted his arm and brought the deadly blade down into his skull. It embedded with a sickening crunch. The figure crumpled, first onto its knees, and then down onto his side, groaning as the fires of life made their last flicker. Salisbury turned, swinging into the torso of the next and the hip of the third, leaving them prostrate in the mud, bodies convulsing in death. His army was engaging around him. Already the chorus of metal on bone was ringing out on all sides.

Now the men struggled together, locked in a deadly combat. Fingers scrabbled for bare flesh, chinks in the armour, for targets in which to press a weapon. Bodies thundered together, bruised and bloodied with impact. The hot sting of fear and pain made men fast but it also made them vulnerable. One man fell, rolling in terror, before the thud of an axe blade severed his head. Blood pooled in the footsteps, printed in the mud. Others clawed desperately at their opponents, shrieking in agony as metal sliced through their skin, striking against bone. The familiar stench of death was already rising from the earth.

Suddenly, from the left, a man hurled himself at Salisbury. He saw him just a fraction too late, caught the movement and turned to feel the weight of a blow to the shoulder. Luckily, his reaction had lessened the effect of the attack and the blow glanced off him. His attacker was briefly off balance. Quickly, he swung back his weapon and buried the blade deep in the man's back. The figure sank to his knees. A second strike against the back of the head sent him face down into the mud.

Now, the next wave of men was clambering up the bank. Salisbury prepared himself. Charging forward, he brought the axe head down with force on the shoulder of a slow-moving man in old armour. A bubble of thick, dark blood appeared under his helmet and ran down his chest. Salisbury pushed him aside: there were dozens more after him, who would lie caked in their life's forces before the day was up. With God's blessing, the earl hoped he would not be among them.

*

The day had long since faded and the lamps were burning low around the castle. Outside, the sky was deepening from violet into grey. Warwick scanned the map that was spread out on the table. York was at his side, whilst Edward and Edmund were seated on the opposite end, lit by the dying hearth.

'The messenger said they'd been intercepted here,' York pointed, 'just south of Drayton, on the River Tern.'

'So they were probably taking the Shrewsbury Road,' Warwick nodded, 'and on to Ludlow, through the hills.'

'How long do we wait,' asked Edward, 'before we send out scouts to look?'

The older men were silent.

158

Cecily appeared in the doorway, her eyes drawn and tired. 'The young ones are asleep now, is there any more news?''

York shook his head and extended his arm to her. 'Your brother knows how best to guard himself, we must have a little faith.'

She nodded and went to him, taking his hand.

'If, as the message suggests, there has been some sort of skirmish, what next? We will have taken arms against royal forces. Where does this leave us when the king arrives?' asked Edward, rising from his chair to his full height, head and shoulders over the others.

There was an awkward silence. All that could be heard was the crackling of the logs. Edmund shifted his position in his seat uncomfortably.

'It depends upon the outcome of today,' said Warwick slowly, preparing to face the question head-on. 'We have been under attack too often, it is only a matter of time before one of us is killed.'

'Don't worry yet,' reassured Cecily. 'The worst may not have happened, Salisbury won't...'

Her voice trailed away and Edward hurried to fill the gap.

'There was an attack on you at court last year, and the men awaiting us in an alley as we rode from Baynard's to the council.'

'And I was set upon in Coventry too,' added York. 'Had it not been for the mayor, who opened his home to me, I would have been overcome.'

Warwick struck the table with his fist, making the candles jump. 'It must end.'

'But how?' snapped York. 'We know all this. We do need to list these moments again. Edward's question remains unanswered. We may have to face the king, having been defeated by his forces. But even if Henry grants us an audience, he will not listen, or else it will not matter, because of the she-devil who rules this country in his place. And if we stand against him, even to defend ourselves, we are guilty of treason. If I would, I'd go back to Normandy. Things were clearer then, in the days when we still held Rouen.'

In the flickering light, York's face was lean and troubled, his eyes clouded. Such action went against his better nature but he knew that they had finally reached an impasse, that there must be some dramatic change and the next few weeks would be decisive.

'Where is the king?' asked Edward.

'I believe he is in, or near, Worcester. We must go to him, it is the only right thing to do.'

'Damn your obsession with the right thing to do,' raged Warwick. 'No one else is doing the right thing and we may well die in the attempt to walk the noble path. We must do the only thing, not the right thing: we must fight and win.'

York returned his fire. 'And fight as traitors? What if we are killed, what happens to our wives and children then?'

'Exactly the same as what will happen to them anyway, as the she-devil is set on this course! But at least if we fight, there is a chance we might win.'

'But to fight against an anointed king?'

'Which we have already done!' Warwick cried in exasperation.

There was a pause, whilst each of them thought.

Edward spoke first, in measured tones. 'But who exactly is our king? Who really rules England?'

'The boy's right,' nodded Warwick. 'Henry has proved he is not to be trusted and his rule does the country more harm than good. We have fought to free him from his evil councillors, been damned in the council for doing away with old Beaufort, and yet Henry remains unmoved. He may be corrupt, but he is allowing himself to be corrupted. It is an intolerable situation for us, and for the common good. We have a duty to fight.'

'We do!' Edward echoed in triumph. 'It is no less than our duty. Edmund?'

His younger brother nodded, 'I know less about this but you speak sense, I can only agree.'

Cecily placed her hand on York's arm.

The duke nodded. 'Then we must take to arms, if all else has failed and our very lives are threatened. We must reclaim England.'

The lights flickered from the hearth as they each contemplated this irrevocable step.

'Wait!' said Cecily. 'What was that?'

They listened and York turned towards the door. A gate banged in the courtyard.

'Is it news?'

They waited again, listening to the darkness outside.

Night had fallen across the field. A faint glow of light came from the bonfire lit on the hill, bathing all in a grisly orange light when the moon passed behind the clouds. The friar crouched among the brambles, hugging the cold metal of the cannon.

From the hedge to the brook, the earth seemed to lie still, but then, after a moment, a faint rippling was visible; a rippling of the rise and fall of dying men. An arm, a leg, the final exhalation of breath. They lay where they had fallen, men in liveries of all colours, some still clutching wounds while the hands of others had become still. It was hard to distinguish any one man amid the mass, with limbs entwined in fatal embraces, a landscape that rose to the peaks of shoulders and hips and descended to those choked in the wet river mud. The air reeked with death.

His fingers numb, the friar struggled with his charge. Then, the light took and he hurried away into the darkness, to clamp his hands over his ears. The thundering boom came again, as the cannon discharged into the death-field, shaking him to the core. He thought he would never rid that deep shock from his body; he had heard it so many times, it had imprinted itself in his flesh. Slowly, he crept back towards the gun and curled up again by the wheel. They had made him promise to remain in place, half hidden in the bushes, until the first fingers of dawn appeared on the horizon.

'Discharge it at intervals through the night,' the earl had said. 'As much as you can but not so much that your position will be discovered. The enemy must believe that troops are still in the area.'

He had nodded and accepted the money. The old earl was streaked in blood and sweat, his armour dinted and a wound to his right hand had been loosely bound with cloth. That had been hours ago and the friar had heard fresh fighting break our near the bridge soon after. Where was he now? Dead or alive? At least his gold could pay for masses to be said for his soul.

A movement caught his eye, just beyond the edge of the trees. The lake of bodies was shakily resolving itself into an upright figure. He watched as a man rose to his knees, then pushed himself up to his feet and stood for a moment, swaying in the orange light. His body was strangely broken, out of kilter and, as he watched, the friar's stomach contracted with the sense of inevitability. The man staggered, outstretching one arm, as if to reach for someone who was not there, then pitched face-forward to the ground. He lay still.

That made forty-three. He had been counting their death-blows since dusk. Every so often, a man made an attempt to escape, but the claims of the next world hung too heavy on him and his final moments came. Friar Paul was no stranger to death; he had sat beside the beds of rich and poor alike, administering the last rites. He had gone bravely among lepers and those taken with the plague, to men crushed under carts and women in childbed. He had seen their hollow, sunken faces, looked into their eyes as the blue pallor spread across their skin, but never so many in one night. Nor had he ever felt so helpless. Lips murmuring in prayer, he reached for another cannonball; it was time to fire again.

*

Footsteps were approaching. No one dared breathe. The room was still as York looked to Cecily, then to Warwick, Edward and Edmund.

In that moment, the future seemed to hang in the balance. In the crackling of the fire, which broke the complete silence, and in the shadows that gathered in the corners of the castle, the duke knew anything might be possible. This messenger might bring a warrant for his arrest or the hope of reconciliation. Imperceptibly to the others, he squeezed Cecily's hand, which lay under his.

The footsteps stopped. There was a pause.

Something in Edward snapped. 'I can't stand this waiting!' He darted forward and threw open the door. The castle steward stood there, holding a letter. He handed it to York and withdrew.

The seal was quickly broken. As the others watched, York scanned the note, hastily written and smudged in one place. Halfway down came the reassurance they were all waiting for.

'Thanks be to God, Salisbury is well!'

His relief was echoed by his family.

'Just south of Drayton, the queen's forces were waiting for them. They parleyed, to no avail,' he read on, scanning for news. 'They engaged in the morning and losses were sustained on both sides but, here it is, Salisbury feigned retreat and drew them into the brook, where he was able to effect a victory.'

'Thanks be to God indeed,' added Cecily, visibly moved.

'He will lie tonight at Shrewsbury and then ride on to join us on the morrow.'

'Good news, good news,' repeated Warwick, his voice betraying unexpected emotion.

'Perhaps it will make the queen think twice,' said Edward. 'We have won a victory against her, yet again; surely she will now concede defeat, or allow you an audience with the king?'

'I will write to him at once, stressing our loyalty and suggesting that we meet at Worcester. Then we shall see what the queen has to say.'

'Be wary, not too hasty,' counselled Cecily. 'This victory is like to harden her resolve against you. If she cannot defeat you on the battlefield, she may return to underhand methods.'

York's expression hardened. 'She may indeed. But I cannot let her stop me from trying. We have the upper hand now and the time has come to use it. I will no longer be content to be the man-in-waiting, constantly under threat, looking over my shoulder and fearing for my family.'

He turned to face them all.

'I am the king's true heir. My Mortimer blood, my descent from Lionel, Duke of Clarence, should have placed me on the throne but for the actions of the Lancastrians, generations ago. Richard II himself named the Mortimers as his heir and their position was usurped by Henry Bolingbroke, who deposed our ancestor by force. I will be loyal to Henry so far as I am able but he, in turn, must keep faith with me. He has proven his judgement to be faulty. Illness aside, he has placed his trust in those whose intentions for the country and its true heirs may be harmful.'

York looked across to his eldest son.

'The king's wife is our sworn enemy. She will stop at nothing to prevent us from receiving our rightful inheritance. The Prince of Wales is only a child and many years will pass before he is capable of ruling for himself. Between then and now, England may be ruined and the Mortimer bloodline destroyed. We cannot let this happen. I have tried to serve my king as best I can. Now the time has come to serve my country.'

There was a pause, then the sound of applause rang through the chamber.

'And I stand with you!' cried Warwick. 'And father too.'

'And so do I!' Edward declared.

'And me!' echoed Edmund, rising to his feet, stirred by the glory of the moment. 'Me too, me too.'

SIXTEEN: The King in the Field, October, 1459

There was a wind blowing in from the west. Cecily looked to the horizon where the clouds were darkening over the Welsh hills. Servants were clearing away the remains of their meal and replenishing the jugs of wine. Ludlow was quiet. Beside the fire, Margaret looked up from her embroidery.

'It is getting late, too dark to see, I think I might go to bed.'

Cecily nodded. 'Be sure to say your prayers.'

'I always do. You need not remind me.'

'Well, a good night to you then.' Cecily turned back to the window again.

But the girl did not move. She pushed back the kerchief that covered her dark hair and fixed her eyes on her mother. 'You are not retiring?'

'No, not yet. I will watch a little longer.'

'There will be no more news tonight, it is too late.'

Cecily shrugged.

'Mother, no messenger will ride through this storm, the news will come in the morning.'

But the figure at the latch did not move. 'It is better than doing nothing.'

Margaret put her sewing down and crossed the floor to stand by her mother. The moon hung heavy, mottled by clouds and the fields around the castle were a dark sea of waving branches and grasses.

'What is it?'

'We have been happy, haven't we?'

'Yes, of course we have. It may not be Fotheringhay but it is a good place.'

'I didn't just mean here but yes, it is a good place, we have been happy.'

'Don't speak like that, as if we are at the end of something. We will all be happy again.'

Cecily thought of the men, riding away along the east road to Worcester; York and Edward in front, followed by Warwick and

Salisbury, with Edmund between them. In their wake marched an army of a thousand. It was a week since she had waved them goodbye and three days since she had received news.

'I should not have let Edmund go.'

Margaret smiled. 'I don't think he would have given you the choice. Father will meet with the king and they will talk. All will be resolved without more bloodshed. Henry does not want war.'

'Come,' she took her daughter's arm and led her through the chamber to the adjoining bedroom. 'We'll keep each other company a little longer, I don't think I could sleep.'

At her signal, the servants pulled the thick crimson drapes across the window and around the bed. The wind howled outside, whipping against the castle walls.

Cecily unlaced her kirtle and unpinned the hennin headdress. Her fair hair tumbled down her back, still long but streaked with grey.

'Will you help me, save me from calling the women?'

Margaret lifted off her mother's kirtle, gently removing the embroidered garment and until she stood in her loose white shift. Then she turned, to allow Cecily to perform the same office for her.

'You remember, when you were a little girl, I used to come in and undress you every night, and tuck you up in bed?'

'I do.'

'Times move so fast. You have all grown up so quickly, all my babies.' She untied her daughter's long day hair and combed it out with her fingers. 'You will be wanting a husband soon. I was married when I was only months older than you.'

'But you were betrothed before. Who would you betroth me to?'

Cecily sighed. 'Your father's troubles with the queen have not helped us provide for your future, I'm afraid.'

'Father will work it out, you know he always does,' replied Margaret confidently, kneeling at the foot of the bed.

'Of course he will,' Cecily reassured her. 'Of course, let us pray for his guidance and the benevolence of the king.'

But the stone flags were hard beneath her knees and the wind was gathering apace outside.

*

York gazed up at the face of the Madonna and child. Carved from wood and painted in bright blue, white and gold, she was the fixed point at the centre of the altar, with candles burning on either side. Around her neck were hung great ropes of pearls and precious gems: rubies and emeralds glinted at her throat, while at her feet, gifts of gold caskets from the rich sat beside the eggs, herbs and flowers brought as offerings by the poor. Incense burned and low music came from a choir concealed behind the screen.

York crossed himself and placed his gift of gold coins on a silver salver. Rising to his feet, he turned to his two elder sons, their sandy heads bent low in prayer. Placing a hand silently on each, he gave them his blessing. He left them where they knelt and crossed the east transept down to the dazzling golden tomb of St Wulfstan. The figure of the saint returned his gaze benevolently, wearing his mitre and carrying in his hand the crozier of his office. They had come to Worcester in the hope of meeting with the king, in the belief that words, exchanged in this holy place, might still avoid bloodshed.

York knelt. 'Beloved Saint, I beg you to hear the humble plea of your devoted servant, Richard Plantagenet, look upon me and my lineage in your mercy and guard us from all earthly evils that seek to prevail against us in this hour of need.'

He cleared his throat.

'I have served Our Lord with the honesty and devotion of a true subject and a truly devout disciple. I have striven to serve His anointed king, though it has led me into perils of my life. Beloved Saint, once a man of flesh and blood, who knew the temptations of the living and the fears and terrors too, guide me now. You are known for your all-seeing eyes: the future holds no secrets for you. Tell me what I should do. I humbly pray for you to direct me according to the will of Our Lord.'

Warwick and Salisbury were waiting in the choir. With the vast perpendicular arches stretching above them in stone, and the soft low light, the place had a sense of majesty and intimacy. When York emerged, his expression was serene and there was a sense of acceptance, a resignation in his eyes.

'The hour draws on,' snapped Warwick. 'The king does not intend to respond to our pleas. He will not come.'

'Patience a little longer,' his father counselled. 'We can afford to wait.'

A sudden shaft of white light beyond the font told them that the distant doors had been opened. A tall figure stepped into the cathedral, followed by five or six others, dark against the sunlight. Their leader walked quickly down the nave, then signalled to his men to wait as he strode up the steps into the central transept, under the tower. There he stood, proudly, with chin lifted, waiting for them to advance to meet him. His dark, handsome eyes already wore an air of victory.

'So the king sends Beaufort,' Warwick sneered.

'We had better go and see what news he brings,' replied York, leading the way.

The young man did not flinch as they approached. At a distance, his men-at-arms stood ready, nerves attuned to any slight signal.

'You have brought your men armed into a place of God?' asked Salisbury softly.

'After the losses you inflicted on the king's army, we must be ready for any eventuality,' Beaufort replied.

'But we are honourable men, there would be no fighting in a church.'

'You did not hesitate to send Baron Audley to his death.'

'The men were set upon,' Warwick interjected. 'They were travelling peacefully, from Middleham to Ludlow, when the queen's army lay in wait for their approach. What would you have them do, bend down and meekly offer up their necks?'

'You fought against the king's army, that makes you traitors.'

'No,' said York, stepping forward. 'He defended himself against the queen's army, sent to remove the king's loyal subjects through her misguided counsel.'

Beaufort opened his mouth to respond but York had not yet finished.

'We have requested an audience with our king. I represent the senior line of the Mortimer family, loyal to the true crown of England and I will speak with our king and none of his minions; I will know his mind, so that we can act in accordance with his wishes. Do you bring an answer to our letter?'

Beaufort's lean face was red with suppressed rage.

'I said,' repeated York, his grey eyes full of steel, 'do you bring an answer to our letter?'

'The king of England is beholden to no man!'

'Nor to any woman,' retorted Warwick.

'He does not grant audiences to traitors.'

'Yet he has your constant company.'

Beaufort's hand twitched, as if it would move to draw his sword.

At this point, Edward and Edmund appeared in the choir, hearing the voices.

'What is this?' asked Edward, hurrying down the steps as he spotted Beaufort's dark form. 'Have you come to unseat us from our saddles, my Lord?'

Beaufort blazed. 'You may consider these negotiations to be over unless you submit to the king's will in everything.'

York's curiosity was piqued. 'In everything? What might those things, those terms be? The surrender of our claims, our lives?'

'The king will no longer tolerate the bearing of arms in his person. You are to submit, in his presence, without your weapons.'

Each of them knew the dangers this would entail. York thought of the assassins waiting in the London lanes, Warwick of the attempts on his life at court.

'We would gladly appear before the king without our weapons if he can guarantee our safety. Yet, while we trust that the king's intentions are always honourable, we fear that there may be those around him who would take the opportunity to destroy us.'

'Then you disobey the king?'

'No, we seek to obey him in safety.'

Beaufort shook his head. 'I speak directly to you now, York; the king will receive you as his kinsman and loyal subject if you present yourself to him in the next six days. You must cut all ties with the traitors who fought against Audley and throw yourself on the king's mercy. There is to be no forgiveness for those who return to arms against the king, as you swore not to do after St Albans.'

'So my line is to be dispossessed because I sought my own defence?' asked Salisbury.

'Your line is to be dispossessed because you took up arms against the king.'

'This is taking us nowhere,' interrupted York. 'Is there any more to your message?'

'The king awaits his cousin,' said Beaufort, turning on his heel. 'But for the rest of you, the gates of hell are opening.'

He walked smartly out, followed by his shadow of guards.

'You should go,' said Salisbury at once. 'You should go to Henry. There is still a chance for you and your family.'

'And abandon you, after all your loyalty?'

'Warwick and I will go to Calais, we will be safe there until the wind changes.'

York shook his head. He looked to his sons and saw the answer in their eyes. 'We stand together on this. We cannot live in permanent fear of our lives.'

'Then what do we do next?' asked Edward.

'We shall return to Ludlow and say our farewells. Then we shall face the king's army. His pardons are no true pardons and those about him do not observe his commands. We must remove those evil influences and guide the king to understand our concerns.'

'Is this wise?' asked Salisbury. 'How can you strike at the heart of government and not seek to remove the queen?'

York frowned. 'It is a riddle too difficult to resolve. We will seek guidance in prayer.'

Warwick and his father exchanged glances.

Edward saw their scepticism. 'To Ludlow then. We will observe the feast day of St Denis and then let us see what we can resolve between us.'

*

The fires in the castle kitchen had been burning since before dawn. Spits had turned, almonds were ground and pastry rolled, in preparation of the duke's return. As he and his sons had galloped along the Shrewsbury road, crossed the river and headed through the market square, Cecily was watching from the chamber window. They clattered into the outer courtyard with heavy hearts, while spices were being weighed in silver scales and puddings decorated with rose petals. The sun was sinking low against the horizon, and the castle blazed with light, as the musicians assembled in the gallery. The day had been filled with the scents and textures of luxury and now they bled into the evening: in fingers strumming the lute, in flagons of wine and the softness of fresh scented rushes underfoot.

Their mother's greeting had been as warm as ever. She listened to their news with a determined cast to her face, then urged them all down to the hall in order to eat. Edward smoothed his sandy curls and followed her down the staircase. He could feel the shadow of war hanging over him, like a heavy cloak on a hot day. It would not be shaken off as he hurried through the corridors, thinking of the hours to come, slowly slipping away like the flickering of the candle flames. And the spectre of Alasia had returned to haunt him, her dark eyes full of reproach and her hands folded across the curve of her full belly. He had hoped to find a letter waiting for him at Ludlow but, so far, there had been nothing.

Tumblers were turning somersaults in the hall, flipping over and over in giddy circles. Edward paused at the foot of the staircase to watch them. Their bodies were a mass of limbs, linked then uncoupled, whirling and curving as they performed for the delight of the audience. Around their wrists and ankles, bells tinkled and bright spangles on their clothes caught the light. Between the tables, George danced with his sister Margaret, a small, restrained dance, but gleeful in the child's enjoyment of the moment. His face was solemn in concentration but his eyes were afire with smiles. Richard, who had been suffering from an upset stomach, sat quietly in his mother's lap, his cheeks still plump and rounded with babyhood. York was eating solemnly at the head of the table.

'Come, sit here,' Edmund beckoned to his older brother.

Edward strode across the floor to join them.

'So we will march south to meet the king?' Edmund was asking, full of enthusiasm. 'If we take the initiative, I suppose we might engage in a week, or even less. Will it be enough time to prepare? What formation shall we use; I suppose it depends upon the lie of the land? What do you think will happen?'

York continued to eat.

'We'll want a good flat plain, I think, with perhaps some boundaries: a river or ditch, perhaps hedges and a wood, where we can conceal our archers. If you, Warwick and Salisbury command the three bodies, where will Edward and I be deployed?'

'Slow down,' York urged gently, wiping his mouth. 'These are not questions you need to concern yourself with tonight.'

'But I must be prepared. I must know what to expect, so I can sleep easy. It is not so much the battle that concerns me, but the not knowing. When do these questions get answered?'

'Not at dinner.'

'Then when?'

'You are impatient. Trust that we have had years of experience and you will be informed of developments at the right time, now eat and rest. That is the best preparation you can make.'

Edmund scowled as York reached for a plate of mutton and prunes.

'I'd like to know, I'd rather know. I've not fought before.'

His father ate steadily on.

'And I will be fighting, won't I?'

York turned to the bowl bearer and dipped his fingers in the rose water.

'Father? I will be fighting! I'm ready, I know I am. I'll be fighting beside you and Edward.'

But York was frowning. 'I don't know.'

'But you must let me fight, I am sixteen years old and you can't stop me.'

'It doesn't sit easy with me.'

'But Edward will fight, won't he?'

York looked across to his eldest son, who sat devouring his meat. 'Edward is a full year older than you. He has lived in the world more.'

'But I am not a child. Many men fight at sixteen. Father, come on, please do not exclude me.'

'I don't know if your mother would ever forgive me.'

'But I won't stay here with the children. You took me to Worcester with you!'

'Let me think on it.'

'No.' Edmund jumped up, his eyes blazing. 'I have been treated like a child for too long, I will not be kept back like this. I will be fighting with you.'

'Sit down, don't make a scene.'

But Edmund was firm. 'Not unless you let me fight.'

York shook his head. 'This is not the way. If you wish to fight like a man you must conduct yourself like one.'

The words stung. Edmund's face flickered before he hurried away from the table.

*

York folded his wife in his arms and pressed his lips against her soft hair. Ludlow was ringing with the sound of preparations; weapons being

172

gathered and horses saddled. Grey, early morning light crowned the windows.

'So it must be,' she murmured. 'I will commence my prayers the moment that you leave.'

'We will return soon enough, never fear. And remember, you are to wait here until you hear word from us; on no account must you leave the castle.'

She nodded.

A mere half hour earlier she had been sleeping. He had woken early though, listening to the birds calling as the day struggled to dawn and envying her ability to lose herself in dreams.

'Here,' he slipped a ring from his finger, a gold band set with a ruby. 'Wear this as a remembrance of me, keep it safe until I return to claim it.'

Cecily could not reply, her mouth was wet with tears. He slipped the ring on to her right hand.

'It suits you, red always suits you.'

She turned the ring between finger and thumb as the tears spilled down her cheeks.

'Come now, there is no need for this. It is the Lord's will and we must accept it. Do not fear for me, I have good men at my side.'

'When do you depart?'

'The men are camped out on Ludford Field, just beyond the river. According to our scouts, the king's army lies just north of Worcester. It is likely that we will not engage for a few days but we must be prepared.'

The door of the chamber opened. Edmund appeared first, dressed proudly in a silver breastplate, swollen with the sense of being trusted, of being a man amongst older men, seasoned with experience.

'Mother, I come for your blessing.'

She flew to her son's side. Yet the words would not come; the rush of emotion was such that it rendered her almost speechless. She drew his head down to hers, for he was taller than her now by a finger or two, and kissed his forehead, his cheeks, the crown of his head.

But Edmund's eyes shone with excitement. 'Never fear. This is just the start. I am a man like any other and can bear arms, remember all my training here, with Edward, as a boy. We ruled these fields with our bows and swords; I have tilted at the ring a thousand times and handled an axe against invisible warriors in this very room.'

Cecily could not help but smile.

'You have indeed, you could not be better prepared, but these warriors will be real enough.'

'I will watch him,' added Edward, stepping up alongside them. 'Together we are strong enough to defeat this. We will make the king see who his true loyal subjects are.'

Edward wrapped his arm about his mother's shoulders and gently kissed her white brow.

'See what fine men you have made,' York whispered beside them.

She laughed through her tears.

'And you will be safe here, with the little ones. We will march south but our army will lie between you and the king.'

Cecily nodded. 'Just come home safely.'

There was a rap at the door, then it burst open and Warwick hurried in. He gasped for breath before delivering his message.

'The king is on the move. He has been spotted mobilising just five miles to the south.'

'Only five miles away?'

'They must have marched through the day yesterday. This is it! We must go at once! Never fear, we are ready.'

York pressed his forehead against that of his wife.

'God be with you.'

'And with you, always.'

He kissed her lips, drawing out the seconds. Then, she turned and buried her head against Edmund's side.

'God be with you mother, we will see you soon.'

And then the room was silent. She heard their footsteps clattering down the steps and the raised voices of men outside, urgent in their movements.

The window overlooked the south road. It gave a view across the rooftops of the little town towards the river and the woods. Cecily hurried across the room and lifted the catch. Moments later, the procession clattered out, with York and Warwick at the head, followed by Edward, Edmund and Salisbury, then the array of liveried men and the ammunition train. She shivered at the sight of the cold steel of cannon, dragged along on the back of carts. Her eyes did not leave them until they were out of sight.

SEVENTEEN: Shame

They were approaching a ridge of trees when York raised his hand to halt the men. Edward pulled up his reins sharply and nodded to Edmund to do the same. Half the army were still trailing behind them across the bridge, making a blue and silver snake across the solid stone crossing while the grey waters of the River Teme rushed beneath. Edward shaded his eyes from the sun and tried to make out what his father had seen.

Ahead, the road curved to the right before stretching out to the south. A few buildings were dotted along the route, with smoke rising in one or two curls from their red brick chimney pieces. The land began to rise slowly, obscured by the dark masses of trees, before racing up the curve of the distant hills. Overhead, the October sky stretched away grey and clear and, as his eyes followed a dark cloud of birds rising, Edward saw it. They had been disturbed by a single rider, travelling at speed, heading directly towards them. Edward and York exchanged glances. They waited as the man approached, hoping to recognise the colours of the Yorkist livery.

'It's all right,' said Edward, his young hazel eyes sharper than the rest. 'One of ours.'

The rider approached then slowed his horse to a walk. He dismounted in a single, easy move and it was then that Edward recognised him: the broad shoulders and unmistakeable low brow of Rick Croft. He hadn't set eyes on the man for a couple of years, yet here he was, a grown man dressed in Yorkist livery, as the bearer of news.

Croft hurried forward to kneel before York. Edward was able to take in the familiar thickset brows, the cruel eyes and mouth. He recalled the way the boy had taunted him and Edmund in the field, mocking their father and threatening them with a knife.

York was impatient. 'Come, what news?'

'The king's army approaches from the south. They lie just beyond the hill.'

'What? Here already, so soon? You are certain?'

Croft nodded. 'I've just come from the ridge; I saw them myself.'

'How many?'

'Three thousand, perhaps four. They're flying the king's flag.'

Croft must have felt Edward's eyes burning into him. For a second, his gaze left the duke's face and flickered across to his son. Scars to his cheek and chin suggested the brutal life he had lived since they last met.

'Good work,' York admitted, drawing Croft back. 'They have taken us by surprise but it does not guarantee them a victory. We must prepare ourselves to face them.'

He looked around, judging the lie of the land: the top of Ludlow Castle was still visible and he winced at the thought of engaging within its sights.

'Forgive me, my Lord,' added Croft, 'there is little time and less space. You must prepare your defences here.'

York dismissed him with a nod, a sinking sensation in his gut.

Salisbury, though, was not prepared to be disheartened. 'So it must be. At least we have advanced warning and the choice of where to deploy the men. I'll scout out the fields to the east and see if there is any chance of pushing in that direction.'

'We have the river too,' added Warwick, grimly. 'I'll base my Calais troops along the bank to the west.'

As they rode away, Edward shot Edmund a glance. The boy looked worried but he was trying to put on a brave face.

'Do you trust this messenger?' Edward asked, drawing close to his father, and watching Croft's disappearing back. 'Shall I ride up to the ridge and take a look?'

York shook his head. 'Unfortunately I think he speaks the truth. We must make the most of this ground and quickly, too. Let's ride along the river and see the terrain.'

*

With a beating heart, Edward climbed to the high point of the hill, screened by the trees. Below, across the long sweep of fields, lay the king's camp. It clung in a hollow, a cluster of tents and the rising lines of smoking fires. Thousands of men were waiting in that green space, for the clash of steel on steel, the crunch of bones and the spilling of traitors' blood. Even the rumble of voices could be heard at that distance, as the wind was blowing towards them.

York was behind him, assessing them with narrowed eyes.

'They outnumber us, significantly.'

His son nodded. There was no point pretending otherwise. 'They do.'

'That need not matter, recall Salisbury's victory. We can make use of these woods too, position our archers here to pick them off as they advance.'

'Yes, that could work. And our right flank could be waiting over by that barn.'

'With the left positioned further along the road.'

Edward nodded. They would be taking a chance, but if they attacked at an unusual time, before sunrise perhaps, the element of surprise was worth a battalion alone. His eyes were drawn to a movement in the centre of the camp.

'Father, look, there!'

Edward pointed out a blue and red flag flying above the tent roofs. 'The king's standard.'

'By God!' York's face blanched. 'The king is actually with them. I thought he would sit it out at Worcester.'

'Does it change anything?'

'Of course, of course it does. I had not seen this coming. How very clever of them.'

Edward watched the distant flag. 'But Henry himself wouldn't fight, would he?'

'It makes little difference, if he is actually there, in the camp. Fighting against an army is one thing: our men can imagine it under the command of the queen or Beaufort, but to bear arms against the king himself...'

'Is treason,' completed Edward. 'And if we lose, the price is too high.'

York wiped his brow. 'This news cannot reach our camp. It will destroy morale. I must think, I have to think about this. I must pray and ask for guidance.'

Edward bridled at this passivity. 'But we've come this far. We're going to be openly declared traitors anyway, we lose nothing now anyway, but we might gain everything!'

'What can we gain now? The removal of Beaufort and a new set of promises? That takes us right back to St Albans. We cannot ask for the removal of the queen. God's blood this is a dilemma. If we take arms against the king, I cannot think that this will end well for us.'

Edward's blood boiled. 'But we have an army sitting waiting. We have refused his terms. We must stand our ground.'

'And all be slaughtered?'

'And all fight honourably. The best we can hope for is to take the king into custody, as you did after St Albans; then we can carry him with us to Westminster and make him put his signature to an act nominating you as Protector.' The idea began to seize hold of Edward. 'We must make him sign his rights over to you, or at least a joint Protectorate. He must acknowledge you as his heir, instead of that half-French brat; God even knows if the boy is his child!'

'Edward!'

'Well!' Edward threw up his arms. 'It would serve us better if he were the spawn of old Somerset or some other royal favourite.'

'The queen would strangle you with her bare hands if she heard you speak such words.'

'I stand facing her army right now, so I may as well say them.' He pictured the queen standing over his bruised body at the jousting, her eyes narrowing.

York was silent.

'What?'

His father shielded his eyes and scanned the enemy.

'What, why don't you reply?'

'A woman's good fame is something brittle and pure. Once it is destroyed, it is gone forever.'

Edward tried to put aside the image of Alasia that flashed into his mind. This was no time for romance. 'But this woman has tried to kill us!'

'Even so.'

'But father!'

'Whatever happens, never forget the respect that is due to women, all women. We might loathe the queen but we cannot touch her. That's how it is and how it should be.'

'Too honourable by half,' Edward muttered under his breath.

'What was that?'

'I hope your enemies will stick to these ideals of honour for as long as you do.'

York frowned, turning to his eldest son. 'Yes, I know you think me an idealist. And this is something frustrating to you. But let me tell you, there is no other way in this life than to stick to your ideals and defend them to the death, then you can depart this life with a quiet soul.'

Edward was subdued. 'Yes father.'

'Now, let's go and gather the men. We must try to keep up morale, prepare them for the fight. There must be no talk of Henry's presence.'

He set off back down the hill with an air of forced confidence. Edward watched him go. Between York's single-mindedness and the king's standard, flying defiantly in the breeze, the trees cast a dark shadow.

*

The leaders had gathered around York's tent, a mix of loyal Yorkists, local men and the mercenaries brought by Warwick from Calais. Beyond them milled the men under their command. Some were dressed in full armour, while others wore single pieces, perhaps just a breastplate, dented from a previous battle. Those without armour had done their best to find warm clothing and arm themselves with whatever lay to hand. Edward surveyed them from his horse, trying to get a sense of their number but no matter how many times he counted, he could not make the force larger than that of the king.

'They have dug in,' York was saying. 'They are preparing for a fight but it will not come until the morrow. The sun is too low in the sky now and nightfall is only a few hours off. Now is the time to rest and pray. We will send for provisions to be brought down from the town, so you will have a decent meal in your bellies. We will wake you early, before the dawn, so try to get some sleep. God bless you all.'

'Amen,' the leaders chorused.

A handful added, 'Thank you, my Lord.'

Then, just before they began to disperse, a lone voice spoke. 'But where is the king?'

York flushed. 'The king?'

'Aye, the king. His standard is flying over the hill.'

A ripple ran through the crowd.

Edward scanned the men to find the speaker. It was Rick Croft, leaning against a wagon, with his eyes full of darkness. Edward's stomach contracted at the sight of him.

'The king is there?' asked another. 'We fight against the king?'

'No, not the king. It is only his standard,' York reassured them quickly. 'Our enemy flies his standard in an attempt to disarm us, do not let them. It is Beaufort's trick; he will stop at nothing. We would never fight against the king, only to rid him of such evil Councillors.'

Edward was relieved to see one or two of the men nodding at each other.

'I saw the king.'

Croft's voice cut across the heads of the crowd. 'Oh yes, I saw the king myself this afternoon, riding up and down along the ridge, larger than life.'

Edward's blood seethed. He shot a look at York, whose face spoke thunder, then at Warwick. The earl was already in action: four men were approaching Croft from behind.

'You were mistaken, it was not the king.' York's voice did not waver but his heart quaked. It was a necessary lie, to preserve them all. If the men took fright now, the battle was already lost and all their lives were forfeit.

But the leader of the Calais men, Lord Trollope, was looking doubtful.

'But they are flying the standard?'

'Yes,' said York earnestly, 'it is a trick, I tell you, a trick. See how cleverly they planned it. They mean the king harm and it is our duty to fight in his defence. We are the king's loyal supporters, never forget that. We are fighting in the name of the king and this is merely a way to unsettle us. It reveals their fear. Trust in me, trust in God and all will be well. Let us all join together now in prayer. With the conviction of our hearts and our Lord, we will stand strong and defeat this threat to our realm. Bow your heads, one and all, bow your heads.'

As York began to speak the Lord's prayer, Edward saw Croft being dragged away, Warwick's stout hand over his mouth.

The men muttered their words in unison but there was still an air of unease. Trollope was shaking his grey head as he walked away. Now the idea had been planted, it hovered like a ghost among them, inescapable and persistent: each man went away with the image of the king lying in his tent just over the hill. York's heart was heavy with vexation.

Edward clapped a hand on his father's shoulder. 'You did what had to be done. There was nothing else to be said. All will be well.'

*

The sun had set behind the hills and the stars had spread themselves overhead. Edward had lain down on the pallet along with the others but it was hard under his bones and, after turning this way and that, he realised that sleep would not come. He pulled on his cloak and headed out of the tent. The camp was quiet, defined by the smoke of quenched fires and the silent vigilance of the sentries, posted at north, south, east and west. Over the crest of the hill, he knew that the enemy was waiting, in a camp just like this, where men like him tried to sleep, or whiled away the hours with talk or morbid thoughts, knowing what the dawn would bring. A great white moon hung over them all, watching both sides alike, shining on both with equal light.

A figure moved behind the wagon and made him start.

'Edward?'

He recognised the voice. Edmund stepped out of the shadows.

'You're awake! I couldn't sleep either. I keep thinking.'

Edward frowned. Even allowing for the moonlight, his brother was drained of colour. 'You will be tired in the morning, you need your rest.'

'I can't rest. You may as well tell the moon not to shine.'

'You're tormenting yourself with thoughts of the battle, aren't you? You've let your imagination get the better of you.'

Edmund sighed. 'Actually, I was thinking about Mother. I was picturing her...'

His voice broke.

'Don't think too much, it will do you more harm than good tonight. Can't you try and sleep some more?'

'No, I can't. I wanted so much to fight, to stand with you and father. But now, when the moment has arrived, I... I...'

Edward put his hand on his brother's arm.

'There's no shame in being afraid. Everyone is afraid, even me and father, we all feel doubts but we pray and trust that all will turn out well.'

'I wish I had your confidence. It's less fear of the battle than... I don't fear death, I know that the Kingdom of Heaven awaits, that salvation is for eternity and any pain we suffer now will be brief. I think what I fear more is letting you down.'

'Never! You could never let us down.'

'But I don't know. Until that moment comes, I just don't know.'

182

'There is nothing you could do, nothing that would make us doubt you. You are here among us, a man like any other, in our eyes and in the eyes of God. We place our faith in you until the end, in the hope of resurrection, when we will all stand together again in God's Grace.' He looked out over the sea of tents. 'You think there isn't a single man here tonight who isn't having similar thoughts?'

'Really?'

'Of course. But you,' Edward smiled at his brother's sensitive face. 'You are a son of York, never forget that.'

Edmund nodded. 'Don't tell father about this.'

'Of course not.'

'What do you think it is like? I mean, to die?' Edmund shivered as he spoke.

'Death is only the beginning.'

'Yes, yes, I know.'

'And we will live long, happy lives, devoted to the service of God, the king and the Yorkist cause.'

'I'm not the same as you.' Edmund studied his brother's eyes. 'You're so certain, so confident, in everything you do. You just live without question, it's all like a gift to you.'

It was true. Edward sought for an answer, a denial of the obvious truth, but Edmund went on.

'I don't feel that I've lived anything of life. I've been a child until now. I've never fought, or argued in council, I've never been tested.' He gave a wry laugh. 'And I've never lain with a woman.'

Edward smiled. 'Well that's easily remedied.'

'No, I mean I don't want to, not like that. I just want a chance to live a little.'

'And you will, I promise, you will! But hush, who is that?'

A man was approaching them from the road. Edward recognised him first.

'It's father. Another one who thinks so much that he cannot sleep!'

York strode towards them, throwing his cloak to the side.

'Good, you're awake.' His grey eyes scanned the camp and the starry skies. 'Have you seen any movement?'

'Nothing. Not a mouse.'

'Then it is done.' York's face was stony.

'What is done?'

'Trollope has gone, taking his men. They were camped over to the east, but while I was watching up on the ridge, I saw them stir. They've deserted, gone over to the king's side, perhaps several hundred men or more, I can't be sure.'

'What?' cried Edward. 'It can't be. The traitor!'

'I wish I could refute it.'

Edward's stomach twisted into a knot. 'Then what is to be done?'

York found it hard to contain his rage. 'Once the men wake and hear the news, doubts will spread. It is all because of that damned fool speaking up at prayers.'

'It was Rick Croft,' said Edward, watching the effect of the name upon Edmund. 'Son of our old almoner. Where is he now?'

'I thought Warwick dealt with him; had him in chains among the camp baggage but the deserters appear to have taken him with them.'

'Damn, damn him, damn them! What now?'

An owl hooted in the trees. York sighed.

'An ill omen. I fear the morning now. Here comes Warwick.'

The earl came hurrying towards them, his face furrowed. 'It is as you feared. I went up to the ridge and saw Trollope arrive in the king's camp. He has taken six hundred men.'

York's jaw dropped. 'Six hundred? You are sure?'

'At a rough guess, it might be more.'

York seemed to step away from them, as if crushed under the weight of the news. For a moment there was silence as they awaited his next words. For once though, he did not speak, his eyes wandered aimlessly and for the first time, their leader was lost.

'Well, you know what we need to do,' said Warwick, seizing the initiative. 'We cannot win, so we cannot fight.'

'Cannot fight? What then?' asked Edward. 'Submit to the king and be attainted as traitors?'

'No. We may as well go and lay our heads upon the block.'

Edward nodded. 'Better to die honourably fighting in battle.'

'That is a young man's way. It is better not to die at all, but to return and fight another day, and to win!'

'But how?'

'We must leave now, under cover of darkness, flee this place. York, you know we must! We must go into exile and gather ourselves before we come back with a greater force. It might take two months or six months but then we get to control when we fight. We give ourselves a chance. It is the only way.'

'Run away?' Edward exclaimed, the earl's words sinking in with horror. 'And bring dishonour on ourselves?'

'Better dishonour than death. What purpose would our deaths serve? While we live, there is still hope, still a chance to restore our honour. York, you are silent, what say you?'

York looked up slowly, with the weight of the situation heavy upon him. 'It is true, we cannot fight.'

'You, father? You agree with this?'

York turned to his eldest son. 'You would have me lead all these men to a certain death? To make their wives widows and their children orphans, to let their fields lie fallow?'

'You would prefer us to run away instead, under cover of night, while our loyal men sleep?'

'The king will be merciful to them,' said Warwick. 'They will be back on their estates and farms in a day or two.'

Edward could not believe what they were suggesting. 'Father, surely? Edmund, what do you think?'

But Edmund would not meet his eyes.

'Edward,' said York softly, 'it is not a solution any of us would choose. Sometimes the wise man must decide it is nobler not to fight, than to fight a losing battle. He must know when the time comes to retreat, in order to fight another day.'

Edward kicked out against the wagon in frustration. 'Well, I see no nobility in it!'

'Nevertheless, you will see the wisdom of it. We will head into Ludlow now, in no great hurry, as if there is nothing wrong. We will have it given out that we intend to purchase more supplies for the morning and will be back before dawn. From there, we will ride west into Wales. On the coast we can take boats, myself and my boys to Ireland and Warwick with Salisbury to Calais. There, we will bide our time.'

Warwick nodded. 'It is the only way. I will wake my father.'

*

Edward's guts were still knotted as they rode back across Ludford Bridge towards the town. On either side of the street, the shutters of the houses were drawn across their windows, the doors locked and bolted. The castle loomed darkly ahead, where his mother, sister and young brothers slept, unaware of the dishonour in the hearts of the men approaching. In the marketplace, straw covered the cobbles, littered with the debris of the day's trade, softening the tread of their horses.

Edmund's eyes were cast hopefully upward at his childhood home. 'Shall we wake mother?'

York cast a glance at the gates. 'No, we have said our goodbyes. If we rouse the castle now, we will create a stir, we might put them in danger.'

'Will they be safe?'

'Of course. Mother will go to her sister Anne until it is safe for us to return.'

Edward could not contain himself. 'So we are to sneak off like thieves into the night?'

'Yes,' York rounded angrily. 'We are. What else would you have us do? What is your solution? Do you want us to ride to our deaths when it could be prevented? Fighting is always the last resort: think about the reality of this, think about your mother.'

Edward blushed furiously.

'Now we will part,' York went on. 'That way we will be more difficult to trace. I will go north to the coast, where I can make for Dublin. We will be welcome there.'

'And we will ride south,' said Warwick, nodding to Salisbury at his side. 'We can find a boat at Milford or somewhere nearby. They cannot touch us once we get to Calais. We will write to you at Dublin Castle once we have arrived.'

'Then it is farewell, gentlemen, and God's Grace go with you.'

'And also with you.'

York reined in his horse and began to turn.

In that moment, Edward's heart made a sudden rebellion. 'Wait. I will go to Calais too.'

'What? Come on, don't be a fool, we need to go, now!'

'No, I will go to Calais with Warwick.'

'Stop this stubborn idiocy! You are putting us in danger.'

'Listen! It is better for Edmund and I to be parted. We are both the sons of York, both your heirs. If we sink on the same ship, or meet with the same assassin, or if we are both taken by the king's men, just a mile down the road, there will be no one but children left to fight our claim.'

The truth of his words cut through them like pain.

'But Edward?' Edmund struggled to conceal the emotion in his voice.

He turned to his brother. 'This is it, this is our moment to prove ourselves. You will be safe with father; we are the two sons of York, remember; the two boys Croft could not defeat in the field just over there, that summer when we were just boys. All will be well.'

Edmund nodded, his mouth trembling.

'Then, Edward, you are to come south with us,' said Warwick, 'and you are as welcome as if you were my own son.'

'So be it,' said York, his eyes inscrutable. 'I believe there is a danger that we may be taken. They might already have noticed our absence. It must be done but parting my sons tears me in two.'

'There will come a time when we repair this damage,' said Salisbury, kindly. 'But let us make haste now, before we are caught.'

'Keep in mind the time to come,' added York. With a last look at Edward, he spurred his horse and galloped away, with Edmund in his wake.

Edward watched them go, until they reached the corner. Briefly, his father turned and looked back up to the square. Their eyes met across the distance. Then he was gone.

'That was a brave choice,' said Warwick at his side. 'Now, here lies our way. We must put as much distance between us and this place before the sun rises.'

EIGHTEEN: Wind and Waves, January, 1460

Calais was cold that winter. The town was a jumble of roofs and spires, packed behind salt-spattered walls, a bulwark between land and sea. All through the hours of the day and night, the waves battered against its jetties and the Rysbank Tower, dominating the entrance to the harbour. The hulls of great ships groaned and creaked, wood on wood, lying low in the water with cargo they dared not set sail to deliver. Sometimes a mist blew in from the channel, a fine, grey-green cloud that left a wet film on every surface and clung about the tower so that only its crenelated top was visible from the town, rising up like a castle in the air. Along the town's tight knot of narrow streets, the merchants' houses seemed to strain forward, their tallest storeys bending over the cobbles below, as if seeking to keep out the harsh wind. In his room in the castle, protruding into the waves, Edward felt as if he was surviving on the very edge of the world.

'We will be more comfortable at the Exchequer.'

He turned at the sound of the voice, to see Warwick standing in the doorway behind him. After two months' residence in the castle, they were moving a short distance into the town, to the larger, better appointed rooms of the inn. Servants were carrying across chests of linen and books, pots and pans, bumping on the winding stairs.

'Yes, I'm sure.'

Warwick stepped into the room, his dark curls tousled. 'This is the last of it, I've sent father ahead to supervise the unpacking.'

Edward nodded.

'The change will be good for him, I know he's been feeling the cold in his bones.'

Salisbury was never one to complain: he would sit up all night telling stories about his campaigns in Scotland and Wales, or march at the head of an army from dawn to dusk but, at almost sixty, his body was starting to feel the strain.

'Yes,' Edward agreed, looking round the room, 'it will be good for us all.'

There was nothing else to pack; the four thick walls with their faded hangings, the cold fireplace and draughty bed with its thin hangings, were left over from former days of glory. A single candle flickered on the table which Edward had used to write his letters. He had lain awake here these past weeks, thinking and planning; he knew every crack in the walls, every dimple in the ceiling, but he would not miss the place. He turned back to Warwick.

'Any more word from Ireland?'

'Nothing new. At least we know they are settled safely. I'll write and let them know about our move.'

'It's all right, I'll write to Edmund tonight. There's a merchant from Cork waiting at the Staple for the wind to change, who has promised to carry it.'

'Ask what York's plans are, whether he will sit tight in Dublin Castle or move south.'

'I will.'

He cast a last look around and stepped forward to blow out the candle. The little window behind it showed him the vast stretch of water that lay beyond: the immense greyness that hung between him and England. But there, moving through the mist, he caught sight of the top of an unfurled sail, billowing wide, and another behind it.

'Look, ships, approaching the harbour.'

Warwick stepped up beside him. 'It's Dynham; he set out early this morning for Sandwich.'

The loyal Yorkist John Dynham had helped them escape from the south coast after the disaster at Ludlow, loaning them his small fleet of ships based in a blue Devon bay and sharing their exile.

Edward was confused. 'Sandwich?'

'To see the fleet Henry Beaufort has been building there. He whom the queen appointed Captain of Calais as my replacement.'

'Ah, the new Captain of Calais himself!' Edward recalled the young man in black, with the flashing eyes, and the blow he had received from him at the Smithfield joust.

'Yes,' Warwick laughed, 'except my men refused him admission to the harbour and turned him back to England. He thinks that a few new ships should do the job for him. I heard tell that he got the sickness as soon as he set eyes on them. Let's go down to the harbour and hear Dynham's news.'

*

They had barely reached the Watergate when they spotted the long-legged figure of Sir John Dynham striding towards them. With his cloak thrown over his shoulder and a smile spread across his broad face, he had the appearance of a man who was very pleased with himself.

'Warwick,' he clapped the earl on the shoulder. 'I have brought you back an unexpected prize!'

'Good, we could do with a stroke of good fortune.'

'More than good fortune,' laughed Dynham, with a nod to Edward. 'The tide turned at midnight and the sea was calm as a glass. You wouldn't believe it now, to look at it, but we sailed across smoothly as if we were being pulled by horses. I was in Sandwich bay before dawn and the whole town was asleep.'

'And Beaufort's fleet?'

'Made an excellent blaze. A light breeze carried the flames from one ship to the next before the alarm could be raised. He won't be putting to sea any time soon. I half wish I was still in England to see his face.'

Warwick let out a hearty laugh. 'And I, it would almost be worth risking my neck in order to hear him curse this morning.'

'But wait,' said Dynham with a grin, 'there's more. The best is still to come. Follow me.'

He beckoned them through the gate onto the breezy harbour walk, where the hulk of his ship bobbed on the waves. The deck was piled with barrels and a group of sailors on board were busy unloading the cargo down planks onto the shore, where carts waited to carry it away.

'Supplies?'

'Oh, this? I happened to run into a Hanseatic carrack on the way back, so we have Burgundian wine, sugar and spices. But better still, we have prisoners.'

He gestured to the men, who disappeared below deck and returned with three figures, two men and a woman, blinking in the grey daylight after their long confinement. Edward recognised two of them as the smooth-headed Lancastrian Baron Rivers and his wife, the beautiful Jacquetta, accompanied by a tall young man whose sensitive mouth wore an angry cast: from his appearance, Edward guessed it must be their son.

'I found them asleep in their beds. The queen sent them down to defend the town but they made a pretty poor show of it. I thought our pompous friends could do with a little reminder about precedence.'

A dishevelled Rivers stepped onto the quay, brushing down his tabard. He pulled a face of annoyance at the group watching him.

'Warwick, this is quite unacceptable. My wife and I were almost dragged from our beds in the darkness, without even a chance to dress ourselves as befits. What do you mean by this grave insult?'

The earl did not reply. Instead he turned to Dynham. 'We're relocating to the Exchequer. Take them there; keep the gentlemen fast but the countess must be restored to her liberty.'

'Indeed I will. And there is this. One of York's men found me on the dock, I've saved him a trip.' He held out a letter to Edward, who turned it over and recognised that it was stamped with his mother's seal.

'Thank you.' He paused, then tucked it inside his clothes. 'I'll follow you to the Exchequer once I've had a chance to read this.'

Warwick nodded and strode off through the gate, soon to be lost among the maze of staggered roofs.

'The king will hear of it,' Rivers called after him. 'Never doubt that the king will hear of this!'

Edward watched as Dynham led his captives away, then he hurried along towards the Lantern Gate, where the sign of the Dove swung above a low, three-storied building washed in brown paint.

The place was fairly busy, with men sitting along the benches and round the two tables, with tankards and pewter plates spread before them. A bright fire burned in each of the grates, most welcome after the cloying dampness in the air outside. The odour in the air told him that mutton stew was on the menu again. His usual spot in the alcove was free, partly hidden from the rest of the room by a curtain.

She came out of the kitchen almost as soon as he had sat down, as if she had been expecting him. Mother Jacobs had been running the place for a dozen years or more and she knew how to cater to all her customers, as Edward had discovered when Warwick first took him there. In spite of her fifty years, she wore the traces of her former beauty well, with her grey hair pulled back from a delicate forehead and her green eyes still alert and warm.

She set down a tankard and a plate of pies on the table before him. 'Hot from the oven.'

'Thank you,' he nodded, and she melted away discreetly as he took out his letter to read.

The news was brief. Cecily had focused on the facts, as if she feared that her letter might be intercepted and fall into the wrong hands. She had travelled east from Ludlow to Coventry, leaving their home to the mercy of the royal army, who were looting and pillaging the town. Edward winced as he imagined uncouth hands overturning their childhood beds, rifling through their cupboards, tearing the pages of books. Cecily had little choice but to submit to the king, waiting in the council chamber while oaths of loyalty were sworn to the Lancastrian dynasty. She spoke simply of her gratitude for Henry's mercy, but Edward could read her pride and fury between the lines. Now she was under the care of her sister Anne, Duchess of Buckingham, with a small royal allowance to pay for the needs of Margaret, George and Richard, who were with her at Tonbridge Castle. They were all well and hoped that Edward was also in good health and fortune.

He winced as he put the letter aside. The hardest part of this situation was the suffering of the women and children. Something inside him had hoped that the letter would contain news of Alasia and her baby, which was due that month; that somehow his mother had discovered their existence and helped them, that a son had arrived and both were thriving. He knew it was a childish hope.

Mother Jacobs appeared behind him and put a hand on his shoulder.

'We have Anne and Janette upstairs at the moment and Melisende will be arriving later. I could put her in the back room for you, if you like, my Lord.'

Edward rose. 'Not today, I am not here for that today.'

The grey head bowed. 'Another time my Lord.'

*

The light was already fading when Edward left St Nicholas' Church and crossed the High Street to enter the gates of the Exchequer. Braziers had been lit in the main courtyard, showing him the way through the passageways to a private dining room overlooking the Green Yard. He heard Warwick before he pushed open the door; the earl's voice raised in laughter, fuelled by wine. They were seated around a table before a

192

blazing hearth; Warwick, Salisbury, Dynham and one or two others, and the half-empty plates showed they had already feasted well.

'Edward!' cried Warwick as he entered, 'I was about to send out the watch to seek you.'

'My apologies, my Lord.'

'There is news from home?'

'Nothing significant. Mother and the younger children are safe and well with the Buckinghams.'

Warwick winced. 'There are worse places for them to be. But see, my uncle William is here, with Thomas.'

Edward nodded at the two men at the end of the table: both with their shock of dark hair. He had met the lean and spare Lord Fauconberg before in Calais and marvelled at the differences between him and his elder brother, Salisbury, but this was the first time he had met Fauconberg's son, born to a serving woman on the Lord's estates. Thomas's features had a pinched, hungry expression and his shoulders stooped a little; he must have been a good ten years older than Edward.

He pulled out a chair. 'You are welcome, my Lords. I see we have become a veritable hotbed of Nevilles.'

Warwick looked up sharply.

'But that is most welcome,' Edward added diplomatically, calling for wine.

'Where have you been?'

'Just walking, thinking, praying for guidance.'

'Whoring again?'

'No, not this time.'

'Well, eat then, before it all goes.'

Warwick gestured to a groom of the table. 'Take some of these plates down to our guests, and tell them their host is feeling generous tonight.'

'Generous?' laughed Thomas Neville, 'I have seen you more so; I recall a single day when you fed four thousand upon fatted oxen at the Erber.'

Warwick nodded, remembering his beautiful London home, with its wide hall and flourishing gardens. 'Those were good days indeed.'

'The like of which we will see again soon.'

'Amen to that, Thomas, amen to that. Go, man, take the plates. Order the lighting of the torches.'

'Our guests?' Edward enquired.

'Rivers and his son.'

'They are here?'

'Where else? Perhaps we can use the loyal Lancastrians as bargaining points with the king.'

Edward ate although, unusually for him, he had little appetite.

'Salisbury has an idea,' said Warwick at length. 'We have been talking over the manner of our return.'

Edward looked over at the old man with the snowy head. 'Return to England, already?'

'Aye, indeed, unless you want to sit out your years in exile. Tell him, father.'

Salisbury sat forward and wiped his mouth. 'It should be this spring, early summer at the latest. The longer we are absent, the more ground the queen can gain. For some reason, she remains in the north and that is our chance, our way back in. The men of the south will support us and, if we can land safely at Sandwich and gain enough support in Kent, we can take London.'

'But there's more,' said Warwick, impatiently. 'Tell him your idea about the rebels.'

'You may not remember the uprising in London under Jack Cade ten years ago,' Salisbury began. 'You were only a boy then, Edward, of seven or eight.'

'Oh I remember, father talked to me of it.'

'Most of the rebels came from Kent and Sussex, and made their protest against the corruption of those surrounding the king. Then it was Somerset and Suffolk. Your father was in Ireland at the time.'

'Yes, I was at Ludlow.'

'There were calls among the rebels, even then, for York to replace Henry. Your father had to walk a fine line, to write to the king insistent of his loyalty. He knew nothing of the rebels.'

'Who were they?'

'No one of any stature, and poorly organised, but this is the thing,' Salisbury leaned forward. 'We can use their complaints for our cause. The losses in France, the unjustness of the law, the greed of the king's favourites.'

Warwick nodded. 'We will issue our own manifesto and distribute it from Sandwich; we will appeal directly to the men of Kent and champion their cause, and they will back us against the queen.'

'So we fight directly against the queen?' Edward said slowly.

'Her council attainted us as traitors. There is no point pretending any more. If we are to return, if we are to do this, and force our way back through conquest, we must look our enemies in the face.'

'But how?'

'We take control of the king and capital and pray that we defeat the queen's army. Either that or we kick our heels here in Calais until we turn to dust.'

There was a scraping of the door and the groom returned, still bearing dishes.

'What's this?' exclaimed Warwick.

'My Lord, Baron Rivers and his son return your food with the message that they refuse to eat the meat of traitors.'

Warwick's chair went crashing to the floor. 'What? I'll give them traitors!'

Edward followed, along with Salisbury, as the earl strode out of the door.

*

Rivers and his son were standing by the window in one of the small back chambers, their faces defiant. Two guards were stationed either side of the door, drawing back the bolts as Warwick approached.

'Too grand to eat our food?' steamed the earl drawing level with Rivers. 'So you prefer to starve instead?'

The older man kept his composure. 'You have no reason to keep us locked away here. You have abducted us from our beds and detain us here against our will. I demand that you release us at once.'

'You demand?'

'On the authority of the king,' added the younger man, with an air of composure.

His tone enraged Warwick. 'You, Anthony Woodville, you dare to speak to me like this. I, who am of the royal blood; my father a descendant of John of Gaunt? You talk to me of wielding the king's authority?'

The younger man held his eyes with certain confidence. 'This is unlawful. You know it.'

'And you dare to call us traitors,' added Salisbury, appearing at Warwick's side. 'We shall be found to be the true liegemen of the king, while you and your families are the traitors, supporting those who scheme to disinherit us, taking arms against us. And who are you?' He turned to Rivers. 'I remember your father. You are nothing but the son of a knave.'

'A mere squire,' added Warwick. 'A royal hanger-on who had the fortune to make a good marriage. An upstart who took advantage of a widow.'

'Take that back at once,' Rivers squared his shoulders. 'I took advantage of no one. My marriage is lawful and has the blessing of the king.'

'Only after he fined you a thousand pounds for making it in secret.'

'He gave us his blessing, who are you to say otherwise,' retorted Rivers. 'And where is my wife?'

'Comfortably lodged on a ship back to England, where it might be hoped she realises that she deserves better.'

'Take that back. My honour demands it.'

'Or else what? What will you do? You talk of honour, but you do not know the meaning of it.'

'God's blood,' spat Rivers. 'You are all scoundrels. You have all been attainted by the king's council and your lands and titles are forfeit. You have nothing; even the lowliest English peasant has more than you.'

Edward felt the rage rising in Warwick and put a steadying hand on the earl's shoulder.

Equally, Anthony Woodville recognised the danger of their situation. 'Father, we are not at liberty; there will be time enough to redress these wrongs when we return home.'

'Listen to your son,' added Salisbury tersely. 'He is wiser than you.'

'And as for your liberty,' said Warwick softly and dangerously, 'it lies in the hands of traitors and outcasts, so you had better say your prayers. Tonight you will go to bed without supper, and,' he said with a flourish, 'without light.'

Leaning forward, the earl blew out the candle that had been burning on the table beside them.

'Now come away,' said Edward, leading him out of the room, with Salisbury following. 'Forget them. We will plan for our return to England in the summer and then every squire in the land will bend his knee out of respect or fear.'

'Damned upstarts!'

The bolts of the door grated sharply against the stone as they strode away, leaving that part of the world in darkness.

NINETEEN: The Blood of Others, June, 1460

The sky stretched wide and blue before them, wider and bluer than in any other place in England. Edward stood at the bow, steadfast despite the swell of the sea beneath him that caused the boat to roll, despite the waves smacking against the side and spraying him with showers of droplets and despite the hot sun bearing down mercilessly. For this was England: that distant line was the white cliffs of Dover and beyond them, the green rolling hills of Kent and the road that snaked its way through The Downs to London. And England's blood flowed in his veins, and he would fight for it, or die in the attempt: he was part of it and it was part of him. From the corridors of Westminster and the Smithfield tilt yard, to the meadows of Fotheringhay and the ravished towers of Ludlow, this was where he belonged. Here, he had grown to be a man, had laughed, wept, fought and loved, and here he would lay his bones. Edward was coming home.

For a while there was a lull in the wind. They waited off the coast like wild creatures nervously sniffing a baited trap; waited for the current to pull them in, to draw them close alongside the stretch of shingle beach with the dangerous sandbanks close to the surface. From the deck, they could see church spires and house roofs. Edward tried to scent the air, to catch the taste of greenness and the mulch of the earth, the blossom and the crops in the fields. Along a ridge above the beach, a line of men began to wave their arms wildly.

'Friends or foe?' Edward asked dubiously.

'Never fear,' grinned Warwick, slapping his shoulder. 'Dynham went ahead. They're expecting us.'

And when they turned into the sound that led windingly down to Sandwich harbour, the whole town had spilled out onto the quayside and the air was alive with cheers and offers of welcome. Edward felt himself flush with something like pride and shame together as he leapt out of the boat and looked up at the solid gateway. The narrow streets were packed as they strode across the cobbles, feeling the world still lilting underfoot, towards the grey stone church with the square tower.

'Let us give thanks for our safe arrival,' urged Warwick, 'then after prayers and food, we will begin the march to Canterbury. Fauconberg is waiting just outside the town with troops and arms.'

And a surge of hope rose again in Edward's chest: the people, the sunshine, the sweet air of England. On the stone floor of St Clements' he clasped his hands together and closed his eyes to contain his emotion.

*

They rode at a good pace, with around two thousand men in their wake. The crops were high in the fields on either side of the straight road and at each village, more men came out to join their cause. In Ash and Wingham and Bramling, Warwick addressed the crowds, calling upon them for their good wishes and proclaiming their intent to defend the king and protect him from evil counsel, to restore him and the country to glory.

'They didn't listen to us ten years ago,' cried a man in reply, on the steps of Wingham Church, 'pray God with the help of these lords they might listen to us now!'

'Aye,' said another, 'for our country is run by a Frenchwoman and her bastard.'

Warwick glanced from Salisbury to Edward.

From Bramling to Littlebourne, they passed through the peaceful meadows, with horse hooves and marching feet stirring up the summer dust. Most men walked together, spurred by the company of others, armed with pitchforks and spears and whatever came to hand; hardy country folk who knew how to light a fire and wrap themselves for warmth against the chill of a night passed under the stars. The next morning dawned crisp and bright and, before long, they had reached the crest of a green hill and were staring down into a valley, touched by a hazy mist, out of which rose the triple spires of Canterbury Cathedral, buoyed like a boat above the red and grey mass of the town. As they approached the walls, Warwick raised a warning hand. Edward reined in his horse and followed the earl's gaze to where three men were waiting in the graveyard of a little church, watching them advance along the road. Seeing them halt, the men stepped out into the road. The lead figure, a wide, spare figure of some sixty years spoke directly to Warwick.

'The Earls of Warwick, March and Salisbury?'

'Aye, the same,' Warwick replied. 'At the head of an army in the name of the king. Who are you and what is your business?'

'I am John Scot,' he replied, 'and this is Horne and Fogge; we have been dispatched hither by King Henry with a commission of array to prevent your entry to the city.'

Edward laughed, 'All three of you?'

'However, my Lords,' Scot continued, 'we intend no such action, but merely to welcome you to the city and to join your cause.'

'Then you are indeed welcome!' stated Warwick and turned to Edward. 'See, we will have our day. There is so much support for our cause.'

*

As the sun climbed higher, they knelt in the acrid clouds of incense before the shrine of St Thomas. The polished flagstones were cold beneath Edward's knees and the candles danced before his eyes.

'Draw strength from this place,' said Salisbury, quietly at his shoulder. 'It was here that the martyrdom took place, on this very spot, before the doors. The saint was not afraid to defy the misrule of an anointed king, and he will be generous in his help if we ask him.'

Edward nodded and crossed himself. Rising, he followed Salisbury and Warwick in solemn procession up the flight of steps and into the shadowy apse where the daylight filtered down through stained glass miracles depicted far above their heads. There, fashioned in stone, lay the bones of Henry IV and the Black Prince, quiet and still after their labours; Edward's eyes lingered upon them with the realisation of how briefly their candles had burned. Then, beyond them, sparkling in the gloom so that it almost took his breath away, was the golden bejewelled shrine of St Thomas. An effigy of the man lay beneath the ornament, surrounded by flickering tapers and the many gifts left by pilgrims; simple piles of coins, wilting flowers, baskets of eggs and flasks of milk, through to rubies, pearls and emeralds, guarded by the monks.

'Here,' said Scot, still at their side, holding an ornate silver cross. 'This is Becket's sacred cross, you must take it with you, the archbishop sent word that he wishes it.'

Warwick nodded and folded his hands around the silver, before pressing his lips to the feet of Christ. 'A sign of support from Thomas Bourchier.'

'It's dazzling,' Edward breathed. And again, on bended knee, he felt a sort of strength flowing through him, and a quiet certainty about his destiny.

By the time of their departure, wending their way along the old northern pilgrim's route, Edward put their number at around ten thousand. Word spread ahead of them, passed in taverns and marketplaces, stirring memories of those who had rebelled a decade before, and now turned out in the streets as they rode though Rochester and Dartford. At Blackheath, their support had increased fourfold.

'And now,' said Warwick, turning his horse round to address them, on a warm afternoon, 'now we head for London. The king is still at Coventry but the mayor remains loyal to him, yet the common council would make us welcome; let us make our way into Southwark and see how the city lies.'

*

The fields and marshes lay quiet as they made their way towards the city. Edward felt his stomach contract when he first caught sight of the distant spire of St Paul's Cathedral, rising high on the opposite bank, only a short ride from Baynard's Castle, from Thames Street, from Queenhithe and the Salucci house. Had Alasia heard of his return? Once he set foot inside the city, he would dispatch a message to her at once; the child must be four or five months old by now.

'By our Lord!' Warwick stood in his stirrups, shielding his eyes from the sun. 'It's George.'

Edward's attention snapped back to the moment, to the men milling in the distance and the rider heading towards them. He recognised George Neville, Bishop of Exeter, from council meetings, to whose clever eyes and swift tongue he had never quite warmed, although they were welcome enough now at the head of a troop of men.

'Brother!'

Warwick dismounted to meet him and the two men met in a hearty embrace. Neville then turned to his father, Salisbury, who remained in his saddle.

'I bid you a good welcome, my Lord, your exile is over.'

'And we are home at last,' added Salisbury.

Warwick laughed, 'And spoiling for a fight.'

Neville looked over to Edward. 'You are well, my Lord of March? I see you have grown into a man since your departure.'

Edward inclined his head graciously and urged his ride forward.

'Your armies can rest at Smithfield,' Neville added. 'There are tents erected and we will send over provisions; we have prepared lodgings for you all at the Greyfriars of Newgate.'

'And I thought we might have to fight our way in,' said Warwick, grateful for the reception, spurring on his horse. 'To London, Edward, to London and victory.'

*

Edward pressed his seal against the hot wax of one letter, then another. The chamber was quiet and cool; the monastery of the Greyfriars was tucked away in the north-west top of the city, snugly enclosed by the thick wall and ditch, between Newgate and Aldersgate. Neville had housed them with Friar John Kyrye, a slight, red-haired man whose warm and open manner led Edward to trust him at once.

'We are most humbled by the opportunity to be of service to your Lordships,' Kyrye had said graciously, as he led them through the great cloister. 'And the library of Mayor Whittington is entirely at your service during your stay.' But once he had led Edward through to his chamber, his tone had become more confidential. 'You are safe here, my Lord, you may rely upon me for my discretion, I was once afforded help by your father in an estate matter and I am much beholden to his kindness. Your mother is in the city, lodging at the property once owned by Sir John Fastolf; I shall send word to her at once.'

Edward had been warmed by the man's loyalty. 'Thank you, I shall not forget it.'

Now the wax seal had set. He strode to the doorway, called to the boy waiting outside.

'This letter is for Ireland, for the Duke of York in Dublin. Take it to the docks and enquire among the merchants for someone trustworthy to ensure its passage. This second letter is for the city, for the house of the merchant Salucci in Thames Street; you are to take it there yourself, to wait for a chance to speak to the mistress in private and put it no one's hands but her own. You understand?'

The boy nodded.

'Good lad; return with those charges complete and I will see you rewarded.'

As the boy sped away, Edward saw Kyrye approaching along the corridor.

'See who I have found, my Lord.'

He stepped aside and dropped a low bow to let Cecily pass. She rushed towards Edward out of the gloom and pressed her cheek against his. She was well wrapped in furs despite the summer day, but felt somehow smaller and frailer than before. A lump rose in his throat at her familiar scent. When she stepped back, he dropped to one knee on the stone.

'Mother, I must beg your forgiveness. I left you alone and friendless, unprotected in Ludlow. It was not...'

'It was not avoidable,' she interrupted, raising him to his feet. 'There is nothing to forgive. Had you remained, your lives would have been forfeit, I have no doubt of that. I prayed for you every day, I knew that you would return when you were able.'

'And the king was lenient?'

'To a deserted woman and children? Of course, there was never any risk of otherwise. I have been living with my sister Anne.'

'Yes, I received your letter, months ago. Did you get mine?'

She shook her head. 'None got through, but that matters little now. We shall all be reunited soon.'

'The children?'

'They are at Fastolf's; you can come and see them later. All safe and well, and you will not believe how they are grown.'

'God be thanked for that. I have just sent word to father, to speed his return.'

'But listen,' she said, looking around, 'this is your chamber? We will not be overheard? Come inside with me a moment.'

'What is it?' Edward pushed the door shut behind them.

'Your father is already planning his return, but he will not be back in time. Anne's husband, your uncle Buckingham is with the king's army: she tells me they plan to march south from Coventry any day now. He has Lord Egremont, the Percies, the Greys and Exeter with him.'

'That turncoat.' Edward winced at his brother-in-law's name. 'Then there is no time to be lost. We must meet them.'

She nodded.

'Neville tells us the bishops are assembling at St Paul's. We will go before them and put our case.'

There was a loud rap at the door and Warwick entered, bearing a sheet of paper.

'Aunt Cecily!' The earl kissed her hand. 'It is good to see you safe and well.'

'And you too, my Lord.'

'Mother brings news of the king's army, led by Buckingham.'

'I have just heard of it myself, but we also have this.' He brandished the paper. 'The papal legate himself has just issued a warning to the king to prevent bloodshed, and to insist that we mean him no harm.'

Edward scanned the paper then read aloud: '...*out of the pity and compassion you should have for your people and citizens and your duty, to prevent so much bloodshed, now imminent. You can prevent this if you will, and if you do not you will be guilty in the sight of God in that awful day of judgement in which I also shall stand and require of your hand the English blood, if it be spilt.*'

'A copy has been sent to Henry, another posted up on St Paul's cross and more distributed in the city. We have our validation; we can approach the king with this and plead our case. The legate has also written that we mean him no personal harm.'

'Will he listen?'

Warwick shrugged. 'Probably not, if his advisors even allow him to see it. But we have the word of the pope behind us and that cannot be lightly dismissed.'

'Surely he risks excommunication if he disregards this?' questioned Cecily.

'Perhaps,' Warwick stated. 'Unless he dismisses us as traitors. Although I do not intend it to be our blood that is spilt. Edward, let us go to the bishops in the cathedral and make a vow of our allegiance to the king. Then we will rouse our armies and head north.'

'Amen,' said Cecily, crossing herself with fervour.

*

Edward turned and gazed across the field, where the king's army was massing. He had come upon them just outside the town of Northampton, marching into the grounds of the abbey, where the women had gathered up their habits and raced, wide-eyed, for sanctuary. So it would be here, in these usually peaceful gardens, where the hourly tolling of the bell would take on a new significance. It would be here.

Now the rain beat against him, warm summer rain, that made the air humid and the skies both bright and dark. Normally he enjoyed days like these. But today his surcoat was unpleasantly damp and heavy with moisture; even his linen shirt and leggings below his armour felt wet. Yet it must be. All attempts at negotiation had failed; Buckingham had sent back the message that they were merely anticipating their own deaths by choosing to face the king. Warwick had shrugged it off. Now he signalled the papal legate, Coppini, who was standing before the Yorkist forces. It was time.

At Warwick's sign, Coppini stood tall, squaring his shoulders and raising the standard of the Catholic church alongside Archbishop Bourchier, who held the cross of St Thomas. The two emblems pierced the summer sky, somehow out of place amid these fields. Edward listened as the legate's words travelled across the men, extending the pope's blessing to them all and offering remission of sins for the deeds they would carry out that day. It was a stroke of brilliance; none of them could forget that the presence of the king outside Ludlow had been their undoing. That morning, their scouts had brought word that Henry was lodged in a tent, in a field beyond the main camp, but Coppini's blessing should stouten even the most tremulous of hearts. With a controlled gesture, Bourchier censed the men, sending an acrid cloud of burning spices up to disperse among the rain.

Salisbury came riding up, cheeks flushed. 'The divisions are as we thought; Egremont and Shrewsbury to the right, Grey to the left, Buckingham in the centre.'

'Grey alone?' mused Edward. 'That's an interesting choice.'

'Why so?'

'I suspect he may be vulnerable to suggestion. It might work well for us.'

'How so?'

'I recall that he is locked in a land dispute with Lord Fanhope; it has been running for years. My father may be in a position to assist him, if we are victorious; bring me a messenger.'

Warwick signalled to a boy in livery. 'You think he will take the bait?'

'We can but try. His heirs might be more important to him than his king. Boy, go to my Lord Grey of Ruthin,' Edward instructed, quietly but firmly. 'Tell him you have been sent by the Earl of March, who is willing to help him gain Ampthill if he will lay down his weapons. Bid him send me a token if he is in agreement, and all his men will go home safely to their families this night. God speed you.'

Bourchier had finished his business. 'We will withdraw.' His eyes sought a cross that stood on a distant ridge. 'Coppini and I will observe proceedings from up there and offer our prayers. God be with you all. With his blessing, we shall all meet again in Westminster.'

'I shall roast twelve oxen and feast you all at the Erber,' laughed Warwick as he waved away the men of the cloth.

'You are confident,' Edward observed.

Warwick looked at him in surprise. 'You are not? What would your father say?'

'Father is not here.'

The earl considered for a moment. 'Maybe not in person. Not just yet. We cannot wait for his return; we cannot hold back this moment, it must be faced here, now, today. But never forget you are fighting under his banner. You are fighting as a son of York.'

Edward turned to the men. In the central flank, their massed heads stretched thirty or forty deep and a hundred wide; their eyes were turned to him in expectation, their hands clasped about their weapons. They were already muted by the archbishop's blessing, waiting for leadership. Some were grey-haired, old enough to have been his father, perhaps his grandfather, taken after a lifetime of service in the fields or halls.

'Men!'

Expectation hung over them.

'Today, I call upon you to do a great thing. We fight in the name of the Duke of York, loyal servant and Protector of our true anointed king. We fight to free him from tyranny that he may better serve God and lead us to the true path of service and faith. God sees each and every one of you men; he sees your journey here and the sacrifices you have made. He watches over you as a father and he will be with you in battle. I speak for my own father, the Duke of York, in extending our blessing to you. What you do here today will not be forgotten by us.'

He bowed his head and the men let up a cheer.

Then Edward raised his sword. 'For the king, the duke and the house of York!'

The feet of hundreds of men thundered after him.

*

All he could hear was his own breathing. It even drowned out the pumping of his heart that was making his head and chest throb, powering him forward. They came at him, one after the other, as he swung his great sword from right to left, then back again from left to right. He had a vision of the harvesters cutting their way through the summer fields at Ludlow, swinging their scythes through the corn as they advanced in a line, like a ripple over the horizon, seen from the tower window. But it was not the golden stalks of corn left on the ground as he advanced. As he raised his sword again, he saw that his hands were spattered in blood. Still they kept coming but his army was pushing forward, undaunted.

'My Lord of March!'

A messenger was approaching from behind. Edward signalled to his men to continue then dropped back out of the front line.

The boy handed over a letter. 'From Lord Grey.'

It was a short but simple reply. Unambiguous. Grey had bowed to his suggestion, just as he had hoped. Their way to the king lay clear.

Edward signalled to Faunconberg to continue and hastened back to the command line, where Warwick awaited him.

'We have it, we have our way in.' He brandished the letter. 'You are facing Grey, he will let you pass without conflict. We will keep up a show of resistance here and as soon as I see you have broken through, I will divert half my troops to follow you in.'

'We aim for the king's tent?'

'Aye, we do. The person of the king is everything. Once we have control of him, the fight is over.'

'They will fight like cats to protect him.'

'That they will. I shall try to press through here and meet you on the other side.'

'So be it. God be with you.'

'And with you, cousin.'

*

The royal flag still fluttered above the white tent, as if there were birds singing sweetly in the hedgerows and lovers idling in the high summer

207

lane. As if the field was not awash with blood and the souls of the dead not ascending above their heads, stained by the violence that had torn them from their earthly forms. All was still as Edward approached. Two Yorkist soldiers standing guard outside put down their swords to let him pass.

Inside, there was no source of light but for the harsh day that penetrated the canvas walls. Edward cast a quick glance about; there was a bed, table and chair, chests and a cupboard bearing plate and holy relics. King Henry was on his knees before a portable altar, which stood open to reveal the benign features of the Virgin.

Warwick, Salisbury and three or four others stood in the centre.

'Edward!' The earls clapped him by the hand. 'How goes it with you?'

'We have destroyed the centre and put them to flight, all in the space of a half hour. And you, here already?'

'Thanks to Lord Grey,' said Warwick. 'He laid down his arms as promised, so we met with little resistance. I have sent him on his way. He will wait upon you at Westminster.'

'And the casualties?'

'We had to fight our way through Egremont, Shrewsbury and Buckingham to gain access to the tent.'

'Buckingham?' Edward thought of his uncle with the scarred face, the husband of his mother's sister. Cecily would celebrate the battle but grieve his loss.

'But the king is unharmed and the day is ours.'

Edward nodded, letting his eyes rest upon the back of Henry's head, encircled in a gold coronet. He had not opened his eyes or ceased moving his lips in prayer.

'Here is George,' added Warwick, turning to his brother. The dark-haired man approached, his hands cradling something precious and heavy. Edward stared down at the heavy silver disc, engraved with the image of a seated king.

'The great seal?'

'His Highness has surrendered it to my keeping.'

Edward felt a surge of emotion in his chest. 'We will take his majesty to the abbey and say masses for the souls of the dead. Then we head back to Westminster. With the blessing of our Lord, our work today is done.'

TWENTY: To be a King, October, 1460

Edward followed King Henry out of Westminster Abbey into the sunlight. Birds rose up at their appearance and a fresh salty air was blowing in off the river. Somewhere over on the Lambeth side, bells were being rung.

The palace stood out against the sky before them, its doors open wide, soldiers in a row and braziers glowing bright. Yet halfway down the path, Henry paused. And when Henry paused, his confessor paused at his side, Edward paused behind them and after him, Warwick, Fauconberg and Salisbury, Cecily and her children, followed by the Bourchier brothers, Lords Stanley and Saye, the bishops, then the officials of the court in royal livery. Each paused and waited, still as the stones, awaiting the king's word. The world seemed to wait with them.

Henry half turned, preoccupied by thoughts of another realm. Thirty pairs of eyes fixed upon his profile with the narrow bony nose, the thin ascetic lips and the scanty, dark hair. Jewels sparkled on his hat and at his throat, meaning he had not resisted the advisors Edward had sent to help him dress. Otherwise the king was likely to appear at chapel with his hair shirt visible under his gown. He was becoming unpredictable enough, insisting on fasting even on feast days when plates of roast meat were being served in his hall.

'Your Grace?'

Henry heard Edward but did not turn. 'The council meets today?'

'Yes, your Grace. At noon.'

'I shall dine in my chamber, with my confessor.'

'Very good, your grace.' Edward bowed as the king passed by and the rest of the court followed suit.

*

They took their seats in the hall, on either side of the empty throne. Warwick rubbed his hands as the servers brought out the wine, watching the seats along the trestles fill up. Salisbury took the place on his left and Fauconberg on the right. A figure in blue with sandy hair and beard slipped in beside Edward, flashing them with his piercing eyes.

'Forgive me for missing the mass,' winked Hastings. 'A heavy night in the stews so I woke late. Wasn't quite in the mood for my Ave Marias.'

'Hold your tongue,' frowned Salisbury. 'Keep your private business to yourself.'

Hastings raised his hands in mock surprise but he was still smiling. Since their return to Westminster, he had been something of a familiar face, but Edward still did not feel he understood the man: he sensed there were serious depths beneath the light-hearted exterior, but Hastings had not yet chosen to reveal them.

'Perhaps one day you'll come with me,' the lord smiled, leaning in close to Edward.

Edward broke his bread. 'Perhaps, and perhaps not.'

'Too busy to play the bawd?'

He was too clumsy. Edward grimaced. 'Or too selective. Too discreet.'

'Indeed!' laughed the older man raising his eyebrows.

'You will be at the meeting this afternoon?'

'I don't know, I'm tired.'

'Then you won't be requiring Westminster lodgings, if you're not engaged in Westminster business.'

'All right, all right, you make your point.'

Plates of pies and stew were placed before them. Edward found himself in the uncomfortable position of sharing portions with Hastings, whose appetite appeared to be prodigious.

'You have heard any more from your father?' Warwick asked.

'Not in the last few days. They had landed safely and mother was planning to meet them near Hereford. They will be on the road, I am sure.'

'Edmund too.'

'Yes, with Edmund.'

'They will be most welcome.'

'Yes,' Edward smiled, thinking of the brother he had not seen in over a year. 'There will be much to share.'

Warwick nodded. 'The king seemed distracted this morning.'

'Indeed. His mind is elsewhere.'

'In Coventry?' added Hastings, with his mouth full of pie.

'He is very devout. He prepares himself for the feast day of the Confessor.'

'Which is also the birthday of his son.'

Edward turned to Hastings. 'Yes, it is. Well remembered.'

'Will the queen return to London?'

Warwick and Salisbury exchanged glances. The younger earl wiped his mouth. 'Would you have her return?'

'I would have her do as she wishes,' added Hastings with a flourish. 'With whom she wishes.'

They all knew he was speaking of Henry Beaufort. It was impossible to avoid the whispers in the London taverns about the handsome pair. Edward recalled the last time he had seen Margaret, when she had run her almond eyes over his wounded body.

'You speak of our anointed queen,' he said quietly.

'I do speak of her, and she bears you no love.'

'She is still our queen. Put your foolery away, it does not serve you well.' Edward rose to his feet. 'Excuse me, my Lords. I have no appetite.'

He headed out into the sunlight. The courtyard was quiet now, but for the line of petitioners waiting to be granted an audience with the king. Nothing could stop them: they came carrying piglets and chickens, bowls of nuts and apples, quarts of milk and bottles of small beer. Often they wanted little more than the gentle pressure of the king's hand, laid on top of their heads. Their faith was simple but powerful. After all, royalty still counted for something.

He was in a mind to visit his young brothers, George and Richard, who were lodged near the river during their mother's absence. When she had ridden out of the city in her blue velvet chair three weeks ago, Cecily had entrusted Edward with the two boys and he had been to see them every day. In fact, they had just celebrated Richard's eighth birthday; he was still very much a child, delighted at trinkets and sweet treats, but George, at eleven, was about to begin his chivalric training, verging on the threshold of early manhood.

But as he headed along the path towards the gate, a man and woman came into view. She was short and dark haired, wrapped in a cloak, her eyes nervous as she received directions from a herald in livery. It was evident from their faces that it was Edward himself they had been seeking. As they spotted him, both began to hasten in his direction.

'Forgive me, my Lord,' began the herald, 'this woman would speak with you.'

Edward looked into her dark eyes, trying to fathom her business. She was not expensively dressed but her clothes were of good quality and she still had a little of the freshness of youth. He put her age in her late twenties.

'Is this a matter of urgency? Something that cannot be dealt with by petition? You see the long queues for audience.'

She spoke softly, with an accent. 'It is of a personal nature, my Lord.'

She was not attractive to his eyes, but something in her features or her demeanour resonated with him.

'You have a moment.'

She looked relieved. 'Might we go somewhere we will not be overheard?'

Edward led her towards the walled garden. Located on the river bank, it was overlooked by the palace but there would be opportunities for private discourse among the dying flowers of summer. As they passed through the archway, he saw he was right. The sweepers were raking their brooms along the paths and two kitchen maids were trimming herbs inside the box hedge but otherwise they were alone. They walked along one of the railed paths, where the sun was filling the late-blooming roses with light. After a little, he paused and turned to her.

'Now, what is so important to bring you here?'

'Thank you for your kindness in granting me an audience. I was not sure whether I should come, I have been meaning to for weeks. Ever since I heard of your return.'

'Please, tell me who you are.'

'My name is Lucrezia Boratti.'

At once the world seemed to become still around him. He had twice been to Alasia's house in Thames Street, only to find it had been taken over by a Venetian family importing carpets from Turkey. At once a terrible presentiment struck him.

'Where is she?'

'I'm sorry, I couldn't…'

'Where is she? I wrote, I went to seek her, to the house.'

The woman nodded.

'I had to move away. I am living outside the walls, near Newgate.'

'She is with you? And the child?'

Lucrezia shook her head.

'She, they, did not survive.'

He heard the terrible words but could not absorb them.

'My Lord?'

'Tell me.'

'The child came late. He was large.'

'It was a boy?'

'Yes. I was with her. Salucci was at sea. She spent weeks in confinement but the child did not come. In the end he was too big. There was nothing to be done.'

'You sent for doctors?'

'Of course. They could do nothing.'

Edward took a deep breath. 'When?'

'It was around Candlemas. A priest was present at the end. I made sure the child was baptised.'

'Thank you.'

'They buried her at St Mary Botolph, they could not take her at St Laurence's.'

'Did she get my letters?'

'She got these.' Lucrezia drew a packet from her coat, of three or four folded letters tied with thread. 'It was how I knew to find you. She never told. I thought it was Salucci's child until I was putting her effects in order.'

Edward took the letters. They felt so thin between his fingers, such lightness to represent such love. And yet, he had never said so. He had never told her that he loved her. She had died without the words being spoken. Something inside him seemed to break.

'I am sorry to bring you such bad tidings.'

He nodded, not trusting himself to speak.

'Shall I leave you now?'

'Wait.' He reached for his purse, pressed some coins into her hand. 'For your trouble.'

And she was gone, passing between the flower beds and out of the gate, out of sight. And the sun still cupped in the roses and the river still flowed past the palace but Edward could hardly bear to see them, could hardly bear the choking sensation in his throat. The thought of returning to the palace, with all the people, was too much. Anger and grief rose in his chest. If only he could get to his horse and ride out of the city, and just keep riding until he was alone.

'Edward?'

It was Hastings. He turned away, hoping the man would disappear.

'Edward? Are you coming to the meeting?'

'By and by.'

'They're going in now. They want you to open.'

'I said I will.'

'But they're...'

'For God's sake, man, leave me alone!'

Hastings paused, his face a puzzle. Edward turned away to the river and closed his eyes. Time seemed to flow past him. The noises of the court receded. He had lost Alasia and their child: a son who did not have the chance to grow into a man. He had not even been in the country when it happened. He had not been there to hold her, to comfort her, to see their child born, or to close her eyes. She had gone to her grave while he remained in ignorance, perhaps asleep, or in the arms of another woman. It was more than he could bear.

'What is it?'

He did not realise he had fallen to his knees until Hastings was kneeling beside him.

'Are you unwell?'

'Yes, yes I am. Some bad news.'

'Not your father? Your mother?'

'No, nothing.'

'The woman? The woman I passed on the path?'

'No, I am unwell. You must tell no one.'

'May I call for assistance, or help you inside?'

'I cannot... Yes, I need to go to my chamber. I must wait until this passes.'

'Then let me assist you.'

Hastings helped him stand and pulled his arm across his shoulders. 'Lean on me, we will soon be there.'

Fortunately, most people were still in the hall, so their journey was not interrupted. The darkness and quiet were welcome. With promises that he would soon be well, Edward insisted that Hastings leave him. Then he turned the key in the door.

*

He must have slept. The next thing he knew was the hammering upon the door and Warwick's insistent voice. Edward buried his head and tried to shut the noise out but the earl was not going away. Then the remembrance hit him again: Lucrezia, Alasia, the sun in the roses, their child. He stumbled to the door.

'What is it?'

Warwick peered at him. 'What in God's name? There is no time. It's your father, he has entered London.'

'Father? He's back?'

'With Edmund and your mother.'

'But this was not planned. I have had no letter from him.'

'Letter or not, they are in London. But wait, there is more. Reports say he is riding with a drawn sword before his horse.'

'A drawn sword? But that is the privilege of the king?'

Warwick held up his hands. 'Come, he will be here soon enough.'

They hastened down to the hall, where people were assembling. Salisbury and Archbishop Bourchier hurried across to meet them. 'The king was here, asking questions. I thought it best that he retired to his chambers.'

'Yes,' agreed Warwick, 'then he can grant York an audience once he has arrived. What is the man playing at?'

'I am sure he comes for reconciliation,' said Bourchier optimistically.

'With a gesture such as a drawn sword?'

'To protect himself? Until such time as he has heard in person that his attainder has been reversed.'

'Of course,' said Edward at once. 'It must be. They are uncertain of their reception here.'

'Not with your mother at his side,' added Warwick quietly. 'She will have told him how the land lies.'

Salisbury shook his head. 'I am at a loss.'

The heralds had barely lifted their trumpets to their lips when the doors to the hall swung open. Sunlight streamed inside, making them blink. There was movement and figures outside, horses being led away. Then, in the doorway, the forms of three people; a man in a long cloak striding

215

in confidently, with two others in his wake. There was no doubting his shape, from the cast of his limbs to the shape of his head. Even though he was bathed in the shadows, York's movements proclaimed his arrival, the easy, long step by which he travelled and the sense of innate energy that seemed to ignite the hall.

Warwick took the lead, bowing his head in greeting. The others followed suit but Edward could not take his eyes from his father. York was both the same and different after his year in Ireland. His head was held high, hair perhaps a little more grey, but jaw and temples bearing a noble air. His grey eyes swept the scene and his mouth was resolutely fixed. Edward could see at once that he had come with a purpose and he seemed to fill the entire hall to the rafters with his authority. To his left stood Cecily, her proud chin lifted, her fair hair piled up under a jewelled headdress, to his right, a composed youth in furs, with sandy hair brushed back from his pale brow and eyes that seemed to have darkened and grown wiser. There was something about the set of his lips that spoke of experience along with sensitivity. Edmund, Earl of Rutland, had grown as tall and broad as his brother.

'Father!'

York clasped his eldest son by the hand and looked searchingly into his eyes. 'You have achieved wonderful things while I was away. You and Warwick together.' He clapped the earl on the shoulder. 'Your mother has told me all.'

'Edward!' It was Edmund, stepping forward, his eyes level.

For a moment they could only laugh at one another, in remembrance of summers drawing their bows in the fields, of winters by the Ludlow hearth, of the curve of the land they both knew and the pull of rivers where they had swum side by side.

'You are most welcome back.'

'It is good to be here.'

'Ireland agreed with you?'

'More than agreed. And Calais?'

'Not so much as here.'

Edward clasped his brother about the shoulders. 'I am glad to see you safe and well. And mother too.'

Cecily stepped forward to allow him to press his lips to her cheek, then to her hand. 'Welcome back, mother. The young ones are well. We are all together again.'

'And so soon,' added Warwick. 'We scarce had warning of your arrival.'

'You shall hear more at present,' said York, lifting his head, 'but for now I must enter the council chamber.'

'Right now?'

'At once. They are in session?'

'Indeed they are.'

'Is Henry Plantagenet in the chamber?'

Warwick and Edward exchanged glances.

'Not at this moment.'

'Then follow me. I am resolute. This day will be the change I have long awaited. A great victory will come out of the work of my son. Edward, walk with me.'

His mind full of questions, Edward could only obey, falling into line shoulder to shoulder beside Edmund.

The heralds threw open the doors ahead of them. Inside, the council chamber was packed with lords and bishops, ranged around the table according to their affinities. Empty chairs stood on either side, which Warwick and Salisbury had left vacant moments before, and the rolls of office lay on the table, beneath the scribe's quill, to record the day's business. York had his audience. Edward hesitated, unsure of what his father was about to say, but one glance showed him that Edmund had complete confidence in what was about to happen.

But York did not speak. Instead, he strode past them all with his long, confident step, past the long table and the rows of men, right up to the distant dais and the carved chair reserved for the king. Turning to face them, with all eyes fixed upon him, and perfect stillness in the room, he paused. Then, with one clean movement, he drew his sword from its sheath and held it aloft. With slow deliberation, he placed his other hand firmly upon the back of the throne in a gesture of possession.

A gasp of surprise ran through the room. Edward looked to Warwick who stood agog, then to Edmund whose face was set in pride.

It was Salisbury who recovered first. 'What means this my Lord?'

York looked at them all with a level gaze. 'I assert my right to the throne of England, France and Ireland through my descent from Edward III, through the inheritance of the Mortimers whom King Richard II named to be his heirs before the line of Lancaster usurped his position.'

Warwick was blushing furiously. 'Do you wish for an audience with the king, my Lord? I can conduct you to him, providing he is disposed to...'

'No, I am not here to seek an audience with Henry Plantagenet' York thundered. 'I know of no one in the realm who would not more fitly come to me than I to him.'

A gasp ran through the room.

Edward took Edmund by the elbow. 'What madness is this?'

'No madness,' said Edmund coolly, 'just father asserting his inherited right.'

'But what would he do? Depose the king?'

'He is king by rights.'

'You should have warned us. This is grossly misjudged, look about you.'

Some of the lords were trying to creep away unnoticed. York simply stood proudly, in anticipation, waiting to be acclaimed by his subjects. It created a pang of agony in Edward to watch him.

'Come down, father,' he offered, approaching the dais. 'This is too much of a shock, too unexpected. Give the council time to deliberate.'

'What is there to deliberate over? I am the rightful king, the only man who can run this country. I am declaring myself king by rights and my coronation will take place in three days.'

Edward stepped up and took York by the arm. 'Come down, father. Let us go and talk through the details, there is much to arrange.'

'Yes in truth, there is much to arrange. I will occupy the queen's chambers.' His hand fell from the chair.

Edward shot a look at his mother as he led York from the room. Cecily's face was blanched white, her eyes dark and huge in surprise. Warwick was behind them at once, dragging Edmund along.

'Has he lost his mind?' barked the earl.

Edmund shrugged. 'Lost his mind? How?'

'You saw the reaction? What was he thinking?' They stared after York's disappearing back.

Edward rounded on his brother. 'Does this seem right to you? We have done everything in the king's name, proclaimed our loyalty, fought for his freedom. It has been our badge of honour, our motivation and our salvation. This act makes it all seem like nothing but gross ambition.'

'But father is king by rights. You know it. The line was usurped.'

'Perhaps. But we have an anointed king already, whom we have sworn to protect. What would you have us do? Put him aside? Send him to France, or north to his wife?'

'It is father's right. And ours.'

Warwick rounded on Edmund in a rage. 'You have lost your minds. This makes it all count for nothing.'

'Hold back,' Edward urged the earl, sharing his frustration but seeking to curb it, turning to his brother. 'How long has he been planning this?'

'I don't know,' said Edmund. 'He started to speak of it first about a month before our return.'

'Was he ill in Ireland? Did he have a fever?'

Edmund's brows knit. 'Not at all. It was the decision of a sane man. Think about it. Things could not go on forever with us bowing and scraping before an idiot while his wife planned our deaths. The only way to end it was to strike first and take what is owed to us.'

His words stunned them into silence.

'Come on,' said Edmund, pushing between them. 'Father is waiting.'

TWENTY-ONE: Brothers Again

York stood in the alcove, framed by the leaded windows on each side. Behind him lay the spread of sky, sea and river, framed by the drape of heavy velvet curtains, something like a man playing the part of king in a pageant. Edward closed the door.

Warwick could barely hold back, striding across the room past the tapestries and bed with its gold silk tester and cushions. 'What is this? You are to be king now? Is that it? You go to Ireland for a year and come back as king? What are you thinking?'

York looked at him levelly, at them all as they stood awkwardly in the queen's lodgings. There was a smell of damp in the air, and the acrid tang of a grate that still recalled its last fire. His eyes were steely grey. 'I don't see I had a choice. It was come back as king or don't come back at all.'

'How?' exploded Warwick. 'How so?'

Edward laid a hand on the earl's arm. 'Let father explain.'

York nodded. 'Thank you. We parted at Ludlow as traitors to the throne, stripped of our titles and lands, our children denied their inheritances. We were forced to flee from our homes under pain of death, away from our families. Our lands had been given away, our tenants abandoned after years of service. The victory you won at Northampton, yes, your mother told me of it, that victory, and the support you have won, and taking London, and being here now, all of us, at Westminster, it is not real. It is not permanent. It is only a temporary thing. It is not the answer, not the end.'

Warwick looked first to Edward and then Salisbury. 'It feels real enough to me. It was real enough for the Lancastrians we left slain in the field.'

'But don't you see? We have been here before.' York ran his hand through his hair. 'We are no further advanced than we were after St Albans. Six years later and we are again holding Henry prisoner with the queen planning ways to destroy us. Do you think this situation will last? For how long? Henry will find new advisors, and we will meet

Beaufort's men in every dark city alley. We will go round and round this wheel until we do something decisive, something different. We have to break out of this or else we are dead men.'

There was a pause in the room as this sank in.

'Yes, that was a performance, a piece of drama. I meant to make an impression.'

'Well, you did that,' Warwick admitted.

'But listen. Things were different in Ireland. The people wanted me to rule them, they rejected English dominance and King Henry, and treated me as their sovereign lord. I had my own Great Seal, new minted coins, my enemies were condemned as traitors and every householder was ready to defend me. They only stopped short of placing a crown on my head. Edmund was my chancellor. I was minded to send for my family and never return.'

Warwick was shaking his head. 'So you have had a taste of kingship and do not want to give it up?'

'I did give it up, I left Ireland.'

'Thinking you could walk into the same role here?'

'Thinking I should, yes. The Mortimer line is the legitimate line. I had to come back as king or else never come back at all.'

'Father is right,' said Edmund. 'This present situation will not last, not while Henry is king.'

'And how,' said Warwick, turning to Edmund slowly, 'how exactly are we to end Henry's rule? Have you thought about that?'

'Kings have been deposed before,' the boy answered.

'And the queen? You think she will simply accept this?'

York squared his shoulders. 'The council know that I have been a better ruler as Protector than Henry ever was as king. They will agree to sign a petition deposing him in favour of me, in the interests of the kingdom. After all, they set the precedent when Henry Bolingbroke returned from exile and claimed the throne. I am now taking it back.'

The listening earls appeared baffled. Warwick turned to his father. 'How does this sit with you?'

Salisbury sighed. 'They will not agree to it.'

'But they must,' York retorted. 'It is the best solution for the country.'

221

'But not for them,' the old man continued. 'They will see it as an act of ambition and flock to support the queen. We will have full-scale civil war.'

'We already have it!'

At last Edward spoke up. 'Father, you have returned to a peaceful realm. The capital and the countryside are quiet. Henry is the nominal king but in reality he exercises little power; the queen is defeated, her followers killed. This is the best position we have held for a long time. Why seek change?'

'Let me speak with the council, I will convince them.'

'But father, if you cannot convince us…'

York drew back his shoulders, standing at his full height. 'I have had a long journey. I will retire for the present. If you will all be so good as to leave me, that I might take some rest.'

Gradually they began to melt away. Edward was one of the last, waiting so that he might shake his father by the hand.

'It is good to have you back, my Lord. You have been much missed.'

York clapped his eldest boy on the shoulder. 'Later you must tell me everything that has happened since our parting. Until then…'

*

Cecily lingered after their sons had left, until the door was firmly shut behind them. As she crossed the room, York could see the concern in her eyes.

'And you, my love? Do you also believe this is an act of ambition?'

She ran her hands over his shoulders. 'I know you better than that.'

'I don't understand!' York sank into a chair. 'I thought they would welcome me, acclaim me as king, once I was bold enough to rise to the challenge.'

'They are afraid; they will see the error of their ways.'

'No, I am not sure. The mood here is not as I anticipated it.'

Cecily winced. 'When I left London to meet you, it was different. There was a sense of elation in the air, of our victory. It seemed like anything was possible then.'

York sighed. 'Seasons change. But I will convince them in the council. They must listen to reason.'

'Shall I call for some refreshment?'

York took both her hands in his. 'I have missed you. I see you still wear the ruby ring.'

'Of course.' She lifted her hand, bearing his parting gift. 'I have never taken it off. Would you like it back now?'

'No, keep wearing it for my sake.'

She knew him too well. 'You're not staying in London?'

'Warwick is right. Before I can become king, we must defeat the queen.'

*

Edward caught up with his brother as he was crossing the courtyard. Edmund's face was stern, his lips set in a grim line: the old softness and sensitivity of his youth was still there except it had been tempered by something harsh. The boy had been left behind in Ireland; a man now stood in his place.

'Edmund! Will you not wait? Come, we have been apart so long?'

His brother submitted stiffly to his embrace. Edward could feel the growth in his limbs. He scrutinised the hazel eyes, looking for some trace of emotion.

'What is this? I hardly know you.'

'And you, the great military leader?' Edmund had never used such a tone to him before.

'Hardly! Warwick and Salisbury were at my side.'

'Oh, I have heard the stories; your speech to the men, your intuition with Lord Grey. One of the swiftest victories ever, perhaps? You have made your mark.'

Edward put up a hand to stop him. 'I was terrified. You will be the same in your first battle. But you are so changed. Tell me what happened in Ireland.'

Edmund sighed and looked round to the double gates. The entrance to the palace was guarded by men in royal livery who were halting all comers to ask their business. Shielding his eyes against the sun, he watched as they stood aside to let a cart trundle past, laden with delicacies intended for the king's dinner table.

'You remember when we arrived here, five years ago? Father was asked back as Protector. I was so scared riding through the streets back then, seeing danger everywhere.'

'I remember, but I didn't know you were so afraid.'

'I hid it, of course. All part of being a son of York. But I was excited too. The city seemed so vast.'

Edward smiled. 'And now?'

'Now it seems, I don't know, I am tired of the danger, of the fear of what might be waiting for us. I want to leave all that behind.'

'And father's plan?'

'I tried to talk him out of it at first. But I can't see any other way. He was in a bad way when we left Ludlow. It was all I could do to get him to the coast and onto a boat.'

'How do you mean, a bad way?'

'He almost abandoned hope. He swore a great many oaths, saying he had failed, that it was better that the ship sank with him in it. You must not repeat any of this.'

'No.' Edward was stunned. 'I have never seen father like that, I can't imagine that.'

'Nor had I. I had to grow up very quickly.'

'I'm sorry I wasn't there to help you.'

'No, you made the choice to go to Calais, with Warwick.' Edmund's eyes were hard.

'But I explained why. I didn't desert you. What if we had all been on one ship that went down?'

'I know, so you said.'

Edward sensed the hostility behind his words. 'You resent my choice?'

'Perhaps. Things would have been easier for us. But it is done and can't be undone.'

A well of annoyance rose in Edward's chest. The shocks of the day, married with the terrible news which he had not yet had a chance to digest, almost took his breath away. Before he was able to speak, Edmund carried on.

'I liked it in Ireland. It was easy, simple. People respected us and our word was law. It made me realise how things should be. I was happy living in Dublin Castle. If it wasn't for mother, I could have happily stayed.'

The words hurt. 'Really?'

'It has been a long year.'

'Why didn't you write to me?'

'And say what? Would you have dropped everything and set sail for Ireland?'

'Perhaps.'

Edmund scoffed.

'When did you become so cynical?'

'When we rode away from the armies at Ludlow? When I stood on the bow of the ship and watched England disappear from sight? When I watched the execution of our enemies in Dublin?'

'Does father know how you feel?'

'All he can see is his God-given right, which he thinks was taken away from him.'

'I'm sorry to see you like this. What now?'

Edmund shrugged. 'I'm going with mother to collect the children.'

'I meant after today.'

'I'm no astrologer Edward.'

And he walked away abruptly to join Cecily who had come out of the hall and into the courtyard.

*

In the lull when the minstrels stopped playing, they could hear the wind howling outside. The hall had been built thick and solid, its walls deeper than three men, but the storm ravaging London would not be silenced by any bricks or stones. It felt strange, Edmund thought, to be sitting safe inside, feeling the warmth of the fires, with a spread of food before him, while the heavens were opening on the world.

His mother had asked to have him at her side that evening. He knew how much she had missed him, and there had been times when he had longed to hear her voice, to sit beside her and ask her advice. There had been long dark nights in Dublin Castle when he had lain awake in terror that she was suffering somewhere, or that some illness would claim her life before he returned. He had even made a vow, desperate in the midnight hour, praying on his knees to the Virgin to keep her safe. It had been her face he had most wanted to see when they landed back in England, but there had been lines about her blue eyes and fear had coloured her mouth. She had seemed somehow smaller as he had leapt from his horse and run to embrace her, sweeping her up in his arms. Her body had become frail, bird-like; he could feel her bones as he hugged her. And he would fulfil his vow, as soon as this business was over, he would make the journey to Walsingham, to the shrine of the Virgin Mary and give thanks to her for keeping his mother safe.

She was watching the hall with tired eyes, but he noticed she had not eaten much. To his left there was a plate with spiced larks, one of her favourites. He passed it along to her and she took one with a smile. On her other side, father was also eating little. Their return had not gone as planned; the lords had not fallen in line as hoped and, tomorrow, York would have to go before them to argue his case. Now he was sitting watching them all, silently chewing, as they sat and watched him in return. The wind roared outside, almost drowning out the sound of the citole and the pipe.

Edmund raised his glass for more wine. The day had worn heavily upon him and he looked forward to the time when they would all rise and climb the stairs to rest. The nurses were taking up the younger children now; little Richard came to bid his mother goodnight, leaning up with his large dark eyes and head appealingly snuggled into her neck. She gave him a long kiss on the top of his head and reached behind him to George. The older boy had grown reluctant to be kissed, but let his mother pull him close and press her lips to the back of his hand. Then there was Margaret, the slender, sharp-faced Margaret whose expression proclaimed that she missed nothing. Edmund had hardly recognised her on his return. At fourteen, she was now old enough to be married, like her sister Elizabeth had been and her shy smile, as she hung back in her grey and gold dress, was more womanly than girlish.

The king had declined to dine with them that evening. Edmund could hardly blame him for requesting that dishes be sent up to his chambers instead. The scrutiny in the hall that night was intense, with the same questions on everyone's lips. Most of the Lancastrian lords had fled to their estates or gone to join the queen, but some lingered, hedging their bets, waiting to see how things would turn out. A few of them were whispering about the death of Buckingham that summer and daring to question the new regime. Edmund caught the eye of Thomas Stanley, who was seated beside his brother William. They looked physically very alike but in character the pair were worlds apart. Edmund recalled that William had committed his armies to the Yorkists that dreadful day at Ludlow, while Thomas had hung back and refused to give answer. Now

Thomas shot him a controlled smile before turning his eyes back to the place where York sat.

And then there was Edward. He was seated opposite his brother but the pair had scarcely exchanged glances. In Ireland, they had heard little of him save for his achievements; the training he was undergoing, the skill he was developing, the glorious victory he had won. Edward had struck out in the world, dazzling and successful, proving that he did not need his father or his brother. As he sat and ate quietly, he seemed to barely taste his food, barely sense his surroundings. With a mounting annoyance, it seemed to Edmund that Edward was far removed from them, his mind elsewhere. He was the same Edward to all appearances; tall and broad shouldered, his sandy hair cropped close, his face perfectly balanced in its symmetry, its nobility, his collar open at the throat, jewels sparkling among his clothes. He was the sort of son any parent would be proud of.

Edmund sighed.

'What is it?' His mother was at his elbow. 'You don't seem yourself.'

Edmund shook his head. 'I don't feel it.'

'Everyone is on edge tonight. Things will be better once this council meeting takes place.'

'Depending on what the council say.'

'We cannot know that yet. Try to eat.'

Edmund realised he had scarcely noticed his plate.

Cecily touched his sleeve. 'Are you pleased to be home?'

'Is this home?'

'Pleased that we are all together again?'

He laid his hand over hers. 'Yes, of course.'

She smiled. 'Speak to your brother. Something troubles him.'

*

Edmund was following when Edward left the hall. He caught up with his brother just as a clap of thunder broke overhead.

'That was loud!'

Edward turned. 'Yes, it is a good night to be indoors.'

They stood looking out of a window at the rain lashing outside.

'What will the lords decide tomorrow?'

Edward did not take his eyes off the darkness. 'They will not vote to depose the king. Instead we have to worry what father can do now.'

'What do you mean?'

'He has put himself in this position. Can he remain here, as a man who has attempted to replace the king? Will England ever be safe for him?'

Edmund bit his lip. 'You said earlier that I am not myself. Neither are you.'

'Perhaps not. I am not as I appear at the present.'

'You are still my brother.'

But Edward could not reply, stilled by an intense emotion that surged through him as the rain beat against the glass. He gave a shudder. Edmund had intended to speak of other things but at once he saw that nothing was quite so pressing.

'What is it? What troubles you so deeply?'

Edward's sandy head drooped.

'Not here.'

They walked towards the chapel, the sound of their boots echoing around them.

Edward pushed open the door. 'It's so quiet at this time of night.'

The lines of the chapel were shrouded in gloom: the altar with its candles snuffed, the colourful hangings and silent pews.

'Have you ever been in love, Edmund?'

His brother's silence was all the answer he needed. Edward ran his hand along the back of a pew. 'It was in here that I first kissed her. And now she has gone, along with our child, and I never told her that I loved her.'

'I had no idea.'

'It was our secret, for various reasons.'

'You did not think of marriage.'

'It was not possible.'

'I am so sorry.'

Edward looked up to the windows, where the colours of the stained glass were darkened by the storm.

'And she has gone. Those few occasions were all we had, our entire time together, and I always took for granted there would be another meeting, another chance.'

'Did she know you loved her, even if you never said it?'

'I hope so.'

'And the child?'

'I never saw it.'

He could not prevent the tears, but broke down and wept.

Edmund was at his side at once. 'You will be reunited one day; she is in a better place, you should not mourn the fact that God has called her to his presence.'

'I cannot take consolation in that.'

'But Edward!'

'I cannot thank God for taking her away.'

Edmund's mouth gaped open.

'But that is the only consolation of it.'

'Yes, the only one, and yet not one at all.'

'Do not speak that way.' Edmund indicated the chapel around them. 'Think of where you are.'

And at once Edmund saw that his words were stretching across a gulf between them, that they could not reach his brother, that his words of comfort were just shadows beside the pain of having loved and lost. 'I'm sorry. That's all I can say.'

The thunder clapped again overhead.

'Edward, go and get some rest, tomorrow is going to be a big day.'

He left his brother outlined against the windows, in a play of light and dark, where a statue of the Virgin Mary stood with outstretched arms.

TWENTY-TWO: Nemesis

The council chamber had fallen silent. It was so still that Edward could hear his breath rising and falling, in unison with all the men ranged around the tables, conscious of the enormity of their decision. And all moments seemed to come back to this one: rivers and fields of his childhood, father sitting at the table with his head in his hands, the days of fear, triumph in the London streets, the ignominious flight from Ludlow, the blood caking his hands. All that had gone before, every summer and winter, every murmured prayer, all came together now.

Looking up, he caught Edmund's eyes upon him, wearing an air of concern and wonder; then there was Warwick, his firm round head ready to snap round and squash any doubters; Salisbury with a half-smile and, finally, York himself, standing simply, almost monastically, his face betraying no emotion.

Before them, at the head of the long table, sat King Henry. He was dressed in a robe and thick furs, his scanty dark hair covered by a cap set with a jewel, his long hands resting on the table before him, fingers open, palms turned up.

'And by this you will agree to the act,' Archbishop Bourchier said with slow caution, pronouncing each word deliberately. 'And it will be binding according to the word of the law.'

The king's head moved slightly, almost imperceptibly, in acknowledgement.

Bourchier addressed the chamber. 'It has been put before this council by the Duke of York, that his is the rightful claim to the throne of England, Ireland and France, from his due, rightful and legitimate descent from Lionel, Duke of Clarence, second son of Edward III, and thus senior in line to the Lancastrian line, descended from John of Gaunt, the fourth son. This comes to him through the bloodline of his mother, Anne Mortimer, daughter of the Earl of March, son of that same Earl of March whom the late venerated Richard II nominated as his heir, departing this life without issue. God have mercy on his soul.'

The phrase was echoed on the lips of those present.

'This council has replied to the Duke of York, that himself and those lords present, both spiritual and temporal, have sworn repeated oaths of loyalty to the anointed King Henry VI, as have our fathers, since he came to the throne almost forty years before. These cannot, and should not, be undone. Thus, by due process of debate and consultation with the law, and with our consciences, it has been decided that King Henry VI shall remain king for the duration of his life. After that time, the throne shall pass to the Duke of York and his heirs, nominally the Earls of March and Rutland, and his subsequent issue, George and Richard of York.'

A thrill ran through Edward's body to hear those words.

'By this act, the Duke of York and the legitimate heirs of his body are granted an annual income of ten thousand marks, drawn from the Earldom of Chester, formerly held by the Prince of Wales. Thus, the Duke of York is confirmed as the Prince of Wales, Earl of Chester, Duke of Cornwall and Lord Protector. To take arms against him, to speak against him or threaten or do injury to those of his blood is an act of high treason punishable by death. And this shall be made law.'

Edward thought of his mother, waiting in their chambers, while George and Richard read their Latin primers, just as he and Edmund had at Ludlow as boys.

'Then all are agreed,' concluded Bourchier. 'By signing this act, King Henry VI consents to these terms, and to their immediate effect.'

There was a pause.

'It only remains for his highness to sign the act.'

The long paper roll stretched out across the table in front of Henry. Just beside his hand, within reach, lay pens and ink.

And in that moment, poised on the verge of an unexpected victory, Edward could not help but feel a pang of compassion for the man in the chair. Henry had never seemed so old, so frail: he recalled the day at Windsor when he had crept into the sickroom with his father, to see the king prostrate in bed. But, even then, Henry had simply been waiting to reawaken: this was a sort of death-in-life, as if he was a natural fool being baited, required by his gaolers to sign away the rights of his eight-year-old son.

But Edward shrugged his conscience away. Kingdoms could not be run on pity. Henry was more suited to a life of monastic piety. England demanded a ruler who could fight to keep her strong, not this shell of a man. He stared at the top of Henry's head, willing him to sign.

The long white fingers twitched. The king lifted his chin.

'And this... I am still the king?'

'And we your loyal subjects,' replied York swiftly.

With a smooth gesture, that might be reassuring, or might be sinister, Warwick moved to place a hand upon Henry's shoulder.

The king toyed with the pen, rolling it between finger and thumb as he read the terms again, for the final time.

Then, straining in the stillness, Edward could just hear the sound of the nib scratching on parchment.

*

York turned to survey the palace. Westminster stood out proudly against the white sky, with its turrets and sloping roofs, the steeple of the abbey and carvings of the great hall. Birds circled overhead, looping through the clouds and the streams of smoke rising from the dozens of hearths burning through piles of winter fuel. In the many rooms, stacked up behind one another like a puzzle, women were pounding laundry and watching boiling pans, clerks copied letters and added lists of figures, dogs dozed on thresholds, boys swept floors and sprinkled herbs. This was the heart of England, where laws were written and justice dispensed, where kings slept and woke, where the bones of saints gently turned to dust.

He faced his wife. 'We shall not be long. The law will protect me; once the queen and Beaufort are defeated for good, no one will dare to challenge our position.'

Cecily was pale from lack of sleep. 'I don't see why you must go to them. Why not wait until they make the first move against you and then use the new law?'

'Because then I am in their hands, you know this. I will not sit tight and wait upon their fancy; I am their future king, Lord Protector of this realm and I will go to seek out my enemies and silence them. That is the way a king must be.'

'But I have only just got you back.'

He kissed her forehead, touched his fingertips against her chin tenderly.

'And I will be back soon. You will be quite safe here. Warwick remains in the capital to keep Henry safe. He will defend you against any dangers.'

'I know it.' She smiled at her nephew, standing nearby, waiting his turn to take his leave. 'I do not fear for myself.'

'We will be quite safe. Who better to look after me than your own brother?' York gestured to Salisbury. 'What can we not accomplish together?'

'We shall be back in time for Easter,' said the old man, creasing his pale eyes. 'Sister, I give you my word. Live quietly and piously, observe Christmas, fast in Lent, teach your children well and the days will fly past. We will all celebrate together when spring arrives.'

York nodded. 'This is our final battle, I give you my word. There will be no more enemies. After this, I shall hang up my spurs.'

Cecily laughed. 'Now that I cannot imagine.'

Edmund came forward, wrapped about in his great cloak.

'Mother? Give me your blessing.'

She cupped his face in her hands, feeling its new-found manly contours amid those of the boy she remembered.

'Come home safely to me. My prayers will go with you.'

He nodded. 'I will do such service in your name that you will never lack cause to be proud of me.'

'I am proud enough already.'

Servants brought round the horses, hung with the murrey and blue liveries of the house of York. The duke went round to inspect them.

Warwick appeared at his aunt's side. 'All will be well, I will be here with you. Edward will go south to meet Tudor's army and York will meet the queen. Remember they have the new law on their side: it is an act of treason even to raise arms against them, so there is a chance that not even a single blow will be exchanged. With this act, they will be forced to come to terms.'

'That is a relief,' said Cecily.

'And York will make them submit. He will be generous.'

She nodded, smiling at the realisation. 'He has always been too generous.'

'And as he says, they will be back soon.'

'But where is Edward?' asked Cecily, scanning the courtyard.

'Here he is. Dressed for the part.'

They watched as the tall figure appeared from the direction of the stables, swathed in grey with ermine around his throat.

Cecily suddenly turned to Warwick. 'But why does Edward go alone, when the three of you go north?'

'Because we go to meet the greater threat. Tudor may not even be able to raise men and Edward will halt his progress then join us in the north. Don't forget I was with him at Northampton. He has a gift for inspiring men to follow him.'

The duchess followed her eldest son with her eyes as he approached.

'All is set,' Edward announced. 'I am ready.'

'Come here.'

Cecily took him in her arms and pressed her lips to his cheek. 'My blessing and the love of God will go with you.'

'Thank you mother. I will see you again soon.'

She stood aside to let the men mount. York turned his horse around to take a last look at his wife.

'Wait!' She hurried forward, pulling the ruby ring from her finger and holding it up to him. 'Here, take this, wear it for my sake. Bring it back to me.'

York smiled and slipped it on his finger. Then, with a wave of the hand, he rode out of the gates with Edmund and Salisbury behind him. Edward watched them go, then looked over to where his mother and Warwick stood.

'For the house of York! Soon to be kings of England.'

And the courtyard resounded with the sound of his horse's hooves.

*

The days passed, in marching feet and masses sung, in long dark nights and frost-kissed mornings, until Christmas arrived. England lay grey and white in the early mists after dawn, with the church bells pealing out in steeples from parish to parish. Few birds sang in the bare branches and the roads and roofs were slippery with rime. People came out of their houses in response to the summons; women wrapping themselves up warm, children rubbing their eyes and men yawning, some side by side in silence as they passed under the porch. Inside, there were green boughs and berries, candles glowing bright and clouds of incense. They knelt and offered prayers, they sat and listened, or whispered or slept,

234

thinking of absent ones, or the cows to be moved, or the fence to be mended in the field.

Across Westminster, a hush descended as the bells rang out for Terce. Before a carved altar, hidden away inside his closet, King Henry knelt in prayer, seeking rest and peace from the stormy political currents. His tired body ached with the strain of the past few years as he pressed palm against palm and put his trust in the Almighty. A short distance away, Warwick entered the queen's apartments dressed in tawny velvet, with embroidery of gold and jewels on his hat. His wife, Anne, and his two daughters were waiting for him by the fire. Outside, the river ran past the palace into the distance, past the leaden windows and brick turrets, the stable yards and ornate gardens. The fields beyond were quiet but in the distance, the smoke and huddle of roofs marked the location of the city, of the thousands of souls lodged between St Paul's and the tower, of the waters gushing below the bridge, where the boatmen daily took their lives into their hands. At Baynard's Castle, Cecily sat with a book open in her lap, reading to her younger children about the lives and works of the saints.

On the battlements of Wigmore Castle, Edward gave the orders for food to be distributed among his men once the morning service was over. Liveried men brought out bread, pies and cold meat, flasks of ale, carried in procession across the courtyard. Towards the hills in the east, rain was gathering, pooling in great dark clouds that promised to reach them before the day's end. Somewhere, under the darkening storm, lurked the Lancastrians, tramping along narrow country lanes with the wind at their backs. Far away in the north, in a Scottish castle, overlooking a grey loch, candlelight warmed the stones of a turret room. Queen Margaret bent over the contours of a map spread out over a table, her eyes both weary and angry as she traced the route with her fingertips. Seated to her right was the dark figure of Henry Beaufort, his mind knotting with plans. Curtained off in an alcove, her son, the eight-year-old Prince Edward, lay asleep, dreaming of a world where crowns and castles did not crumble overnight. The clouds moved across the sky and drew out a feeble ray of sunshine, to brighten the spot where he lay.

*

Something was moving in the trees. York strode to the edge of the battlements and stared down into the greyish mass of woodland that

235

shaded the road to Pontefract. At first he had thought it was the flight of a bird, but no such creature appeared against the white sky; and then he had seen the second movement, solid and cumbersome, like a stray horse or deer. Sandal Castle rose high above the treetops, with its keep set on top of the ancient motte, giving views over the River Calder and the Yorkshire countryside.

It was nine days since they had arrived, riding in slow cavalcade through the county, the drawn sword before them again as a sign of the duke's new status. People had come out to cheer them along the route, bowing their heads as a sign of respect at the grey-haired man who would be their next king, at his son who grew more confident and more handsome every day, at the snowy head of Salisbury, renowned in the county for his experience. They had passed the feast of Christmas quietly, in prayer and remembrance of the dead, before sitting up late into the night, laying out their plans. They had seen quiet dawns spread mistily across the valley and the flights of birds in search of food. They had heard the silence of night in the middle of a dark nowhere, with only the stars spread overhead and the occasional bark of a fox in the undergrowth. They had prayed in the castle chapel, anticipating the moment when they met with the queen and her armies, lying just miles away to the east. Their requests for an audience had been refused, so he had letters dispatched south to Edward. A time might soon come when they were in need of his support. At least they had a few days of grace, until the feast of Epiphany, which should allow him enough time to march his armies up from Wigmore.

York turned back to the trees. He had become familiar with their lines, with the shapes made by their trunks and naked winter branches. Tuning his senses, he strained to see and hear, but all was stillness in the woods. The sun was climbing in the sky, despite the heavy veil of clouds. The gates of the castle had been locked since their arrival and supplies were running low; perhaps this was the day they might venture out across the green space to the farms and houses on the edge of the town. There might be eggs and smoked meat, or whatever was available at this time of year. Edmund certainly would welcome the change of scene. But York needed to be cautious; since the Act of Accord had named him as Henry's heir, there would be no grounds on which he would trust the queen. Slippery and twisting like an eel in a stream, she would continue to elude him before turning to bite just as soon as she had her mouth. He would watch the road for any signs of life and make a decision later in the day.

Inside the keep, Salisbury was sitting before the fire, watching the flames lick around the hearth. Here, Edmund was kneeling on the stones, disturbing the glowing logs with a poker while the earl's own youngest son, Thomas, stirred herbs into a flagon of wine. He was a tall youth, born in the same year as Edmund, and just as keen to prove himself alongside the wisdom of his own elder brother. There was some resemblance between Thomas and Warwick, with the boy's mop of dark curls, but his face was still soft and smooth, his expression as yet unresolved.

'Yes, I was in France when they burned Joan of Arc,' Salisbury was saying. 'I was with King Henry in Rouen, while the preparations were being made for his coronation.'

'You saw it?' Edmund asked, letting the poker fall.

'I wish I had not.'

'What sort of end did she make?'

Salisbury shrugged, accepting a tankard from his son. 'What sort of end does any woman make on the pyre? I have seen many things, fought in many battles and witnessed acts of brutality, but this was one I will not forget.'

'She was young?'

'Yes, not much older than you.'

'But the things they said about her, as a witch, inciting the French against the English.'

'The French did not need much inciting. She was just a girl, standing there in a white dress.'

The young men exchanged a glance.

'But she had faith, such faith. There was something of the divine about her, I could see it even then, something serene in her face, in her simplicity. She was just a peasant girl, she knew nothing, she had no military training, and yet she led the French to victory.'

'And she was put on trial, as a witch?'

'I attended her trial. I was then in the service of my uncle Beaufort.'

'Beaufort?' Edmund's eyes opened in surprise.

'My mother's brother, the cardinal. He is long dead now. Yes, my line descends from her, from John of Gaunt, from the same Lancastrian route as the king himself.'

'Was it...' Edmund hesitated. 'Was it a swift end?'

'Swift enough. She called for a cross at the end. An English soldier gave her one made from wood and she died in prayer.'

The fire between them crackled.

'They burned her again,' said Salisbury. 'After she was dead. As if they had to be certain. It was unnecessary.'

'And the French did not try to save her?'

'It was the French who betrayed her, who sold her to the English. Well, it was the Burgundians really, but the French did nothing to rescue her. She was taken by the Luxemburgs, by the uncle of that woman, the one now the wife of Baron Rivers. The Woodville upstarts.'

'Where did they bury her?' asked Thomas.

'There was not much left to bury. They threw her remains in the river.'

Thomas shook his head. 'They might treat a man like that, a dangerous enemy, but a young woman?'

'God rest her soul,' agreed Salisbury, with solemnity.

Edmund remained on his knees by the fire, his eyes blazing behind the fall of hair across his forehead. The earl could see that the story had moved him.

'She is with God now, Edmund, she was a martyr. It happened in the past, it cannot be changed now, whatever we might wish.'

Edmund picked up the poker again and raked over the embers.

*

Mounted, they formed a line facing the open gate: York and Edmund, Salisbury and Thomas, with a few dozen men behind them. The road stretched away across the open space, through the trees and towards the town. Lines of smoke rose into the distance, indicating their direction.

'We'll be back within the hour,' York stated, his eyes fixed on the horizon. 'To the town and back, then we'll be provisioned until Edward arrives. Lord Harington will hold the castle with the other men.'

Salisbury peered out into the open space. 'Where does the queen's army lie?'

'Outside Pontefract, nine miles to the east.'

'For certain?'

'As the scout reported this morning. They will not venture to strike at us yet, not during this holy season. I would hope the queen's mind is elsewhere.'

'Running on young Beaufort most like.'

York pretended not to hear Salisbury. 'Shall we part at the bridge and try different ends of the town, Edmund and I to the south and you with Thomas to the north?'

'That sounds sensible to me.'

They urged their horses forward at a walking pace. 'We'll move slowly,' said York, scanning the trees either side of the road. 'Cautiously, just in case.'

'You fear attack? They might just as easily have caught us on the road north ten days back.'

'And they will not dare strike at you now, father,' added Edmund. 'It would be an act of treason to do so. The king would have to condemn his own wife!'

York rode on in silence. A sudden movement to his left made his grey head snap round and his heart pound. In a clearing, amid tall grasses, a hare bounded away, disturbed at his play. Behind him, Edmund and Thomas were talking about their homes; the meadows and orchard around Fotheringhay and the rolling green hills that surrounded Salisbury's Middleham Castle. They spoke of the sun rising on misty summer days, filtering through treetops, of autumns with the valleys choked in brown leaves, of riding home through May lanes at dusk, as the sky lay in ribbons of pink and purple. Thomas's thoughts turned to his young wife, Maude, newly married and left behind at home, awaiting his return. Halfway through his speech, the young man's voice cracked with emotion and touched York's heart. When Thomas spoke of love, Edmund's silence was complete, and his father knew the boy had never yet experienced that emotion; not for a woman other than his mother, or sisters, or the Virgin Mary gilded and serene above the family altar. And yet he had the heart most receptive to love, most gentle and tender, than any other the duke had ever known.

They came out of the trees on both sides. York saw at once that they had walked into a trap. The handful became dozens, lining the road, dark in the Beaufort livery.

'Turn,' he shouted, pulling on his reins. 'Turn back to the castle. Edmund, turn!'

But they were already behind them, across the path where their horse had just left their print in the dust. More were pouring down out of the trees and already drawing their swords against the Yorkist troops who had followed their duke on foot.

York felt himself break out in a cold sweat. They were caught in a pincer movement on both sides, trotted like lambs to the slaughter. All he could think of was his boy, his dear boy, at his side. His eyes met Salisbury's pale ones and a silent understanding passed between them.

The enemy drew closer, with the glint of steel forming a ring around the riders. The first casualties were falling: men in murrey and blue with whom they had played dice and drank ale at Christmas tide lay blooded upon the ground. The only vulnerable spot was the direction they had been travelling, towards the bridge, towards the town. Fewer men stood there; there was a brief window of hope.

'Thomas, Edmund,' urged York. 'Ride now, break through, ride along the bridge to the town and on to York. Go now, you must go now!'

'But father!' Edmund's eyes were incredulous.

'Go!'

'No, I will stand with you.'

'Go, boys,' added Salisbury, drawing his sword to fend off the first attack. 'We will meet you in York, by and by. God speed.'

Still Edmund stalled. 'Father?'

'I command you, in your mother's name. Go now, go fast. Give her my love.'

Reaching over, York landed the flat of his hand down upon the rump of Edmund's horse, sending him speeding away, with Thomas following. The duke did not have time to see them disappear; attackers were approaching from his left, their faces intent upon death. He hacked down at them with his drawn sword, feeling the satisfaction of its cold hard blade slicing through enemy flesh. But hands were pulling at his clothing from behind: he gripped his knees tighter but could not hold on and slipped from the saddle. Salisbury was also down, landing on his feet and, back to back, they swung wildly against the enclosing circle. York's blade sliced clean through one, crumpling him to the ground in a gush of bright blood, then up through the legs of a second and down again upon some fellow's skull.

The blow came from the side. Its cold steel came as a surprise between his warm ribs. He had imagined this moment a few times, but it was never quite like this, a sudden stillness and slowness, as he realised the entire length of the foreign object inside his own body. He dropped to his knees, his head light. Some new sensation made him raise his hands, to find they were wet with someone's blood, coming in waves, as if it was being worked out of a pump. And then there was a thrusting in his back, another in the side of his neck. He could not keep upright any more. He fell onto the ground. His cheek lay in the mud and the texture of grass played against his moving lips. Then there was nothing.

*

At once he saw that the bridge into the town was guarded. Edmund's chest was beating as if to burst as he reached the bank, pulling up the reins and looking round wildly to see if there was another route for escape. But the bulrushes grew thick and dense along each side and the slope would easily break a horse's ankle. They might dismount and swim, he supposed, turning round to find Thomas. But the other boy was nowhere to be seen, just the empty road behind him, echoing with approaching horse hooves. They were following and they would soon be upon him. He gripped the reins with trembling hands. There was no time for prayer; he must take his chance and try to break through these four or five planted on the path ahead, with the river coursing beneath them.

Then he saw it. Halfway along the bridge was a little chapel, set against the side, protruding the depth of three windows into the stream. A chantry chapel, dedicated to the Virgin. If he could only reach it, he could seek sanctuary there; no one would dare violate the holiness of such a place. The men were slightly beyond it. He judged that he had a good chance.

'Go boy, go,' he urged his horse, straining forward in the saddle. But with some strange presentiment or foible, the beast was reluctant to mount the bridge. Perhaps it was the waters coursing below, or perhaps the creature had been disturbed by the sudden flight. Edmund kicked its sides in vain. It only reared its forelegs up and threatened to unseat him. Now the riders behind him came into view, their bloody swords drawn.

241

There was no choice but to dismount and run. He hit the ground hard and his knees buckled, but at once he was up and racing ahead.

Then he saw with relief, that there was a familiar face in the middle of the bridge. The grey-haired Lord Clifford, whom he had seen at Westminster, dining in the hall, jousting in the tilt yard, seated among the lords. His sympathies were Lancastrian but once, when Edmund was a small boy, he had given him a pair of silver buckles.

'Clifford!'

Edmund ran towards him, as he had placed himself before the chapel doors, perhaps to suggest he had the same idea about shelter.

'Clifford, thanks be to God! We were ambushed along the road. Father, and Salisbury and Thomas…'

Clifford was tall and broad, almost twice the weight of Edmund. The man strode towards the boy who hurried into his shadow, panting and heart pounding. His solid face was a pale mask, the eyes mere slits and the lips pressed firmly closed. Then Clifford raised his right arm. Edmund barely registered the blade. Its tip pierced his throat, sudden and brutal, taking away his breath. Warm blood poured down his chest and filled his mouth. Edmund saw it flow over Clifford's hand and up his arm, before that same arm twisted the blade and severed his windpipe. He fell just a short distance from the open chapel door, the dark liquid pooling around him between the stones.

TWENTY-THREE: Acts of Valour, February, 1461

It was still dark when they woke him. The shadows seemed to fold about the corners of the tent, about his heavy form and receding dreams, as Edward pulled himself to his feet. The air was bitterly cold and he dressed swiftly, pulling on layers for warmth, raising his arms as his servants arrived to buckle him into his armour. The recent weeks had taken a toll on his face: the lines of his features were touched by suffering, his jawline and cheeks almost gaunt. And yet his hazel eyes still burned with an all-consuming fire, a passion that might be hunger or anger, but on this morning, was no less than determination and revenge.

He stepped out into the cold air of the pre-dawn, into the camp where his men lay under the stars in makeshift tents, stretching out numb limbs and moving their lips in prayer or questions. Across the field, the army sprawled out its men, its horses and carts, with lines of smoke rising to the sky. He had chosen this place, close by Mortimer's Cross, where the main roads met and the River Lugg snaked past, swollen with winter rain. These were cruel conditions: it was not the usual season for battle and Candlemas Day was better spent indoors, before the hearth, or in the chapel. But all the rules had been broken.

He had good men on his side: here was William Herbert of Raglan, whose father had been a friend to York, and Reginald Grey of Wilton, and John Tuchet, the new Lord Audley, and Edward's distant cousin Humphrey Stafford: between them they had some five or six thousand men, drawn from these Herefordshire plains and the purple Welsh hills. He had passed the Christmas season in Shrewsbury and was still merry, with wine on his lips, when they brought him the terrible news: his father's head, dressed in a paper crown, set on top of one of the gates in York. And those of Edmund, Salisbury and his son Thomas, sitting pitifully alongside, staring over the city with unseeing eyes. It had not seemed real. Somehow those terrible days and nights had passed. He had been on the verge of returning to London, to comfort his mother, when news arrived that a Lancastrian army headed by Jasper Tudor was marching to meet that of the queen in the north. And thus he was waiting, in the pre-dawn, to hear word of their approach, his mouth dry with the desire to taste their blood. He had an almost insatiable hunger to see the life flow out of them. Like the wrath of heaven, he would strike his enemies as a lightning bolt and dispatch them straight to hell.

Through the camp, a messenger drew close. There was something familiar about the man, who was short and stocky, with dark hair and a lumpish face, wrapped in furs against the chill. Herbert had intercepted him before he reached the royal tent.

'My Lord, this man has ridden over from Croft Castle, with news.'

Edward nodded. 'Let him come forward.'

The man dismounted, approached and knelt.

Edward gestured to raise him up. 'What is your business?'

'God save you, my Lord, I am Alan Croft, the son of your father's almoner at Ludlow.'

And indeed, Edward could see traces of the child he had been; the cowed younger brother, traipsing after the taller Rick, open-mouthed at his brother's cruelties. At once he thought of that terrible night outside Ludlow when Rick had stirred trouble among the troops, telling them of the king's presence in the field.

'Well, well, Alan Croft.'

'I am at your service, my Lord. I have brought my retainers to fight on your side and news of a sighting of Tudor's army, beyond the river Lugg.'

Edward stared at the top of the man's head. 'Is this true? I have been betrayed by Crofts before.'

'I am not that which my brother is, my Lord, I am your loyal vassal. He might be of my blood but I no longer consider him to be my kin.'

'Your words commend you.'

'I was but a child at Ludlow, in his thrall. He was stronger and older than me; what you suffered at his hands, I endured threefold.'

Edward nodded. 'And so you align yourself with my cause?'

'Your father was always good to me, my Lord, and your brother was a kind and gentle boy. God rest their souls.'

Edward's throat felt thick with emotion.

'My Lord, might I make an observation? If Tudor is planning to cross the Lugg, you might consider placing a line of archers along the

Hereford road, either side of the cross itself, to pick them off as they struggle across the river.'

'It is a sound suggestion. Herbert, select a portion of our archers and set them in a line, while I rouse the men into their flanks. Croft, you will fight with me, at my side, in the middle.'

Croft bowed his head in honour.

*

They were in position as the sun began to climb through the sky. The road stretched wide and expectant from north to west, marking out their waiting divisions, the dense crowding of men, shoulder to shoulder. Before long it would be stained with blood, an eternal memorial for what was to take place there that day. Mounted on horseback, Edward made a rough assessment of their area and the route Tudor was likely to take. There was a line of trees, a field lying fallow, a piece of scrubland: they were likely to push their way through there.

'My Lord!'

The voice came from behind, along with the clatter of horse hooves. Nerves on edge, Edward spun round, his hand flying to his sword. But it was a familiar figure who rode up alongside him; a slight but wiry man, lithe in armour, his mirthful eyes serious for once and his untamed hair hidden beneath a cap.

'Hastings?'

'I came as soon as I could, with all the men I could muster. Herbert sent me forward.' Drawing his horse alongside Edward's he reached across and clapped him on the shoulder. Edward had never seen his face so resolute.

'My deepest condolences, my Lord. I thought that since you had lost so fine a brother, the least I could do was to fight with you, as a brother-in-arms.'

Edward breathed deeply, unable to find the words.

Hastings scanned the scene. 'So here I am. Where is Tudor?'

'Just beyond the river: Jasper and his father, Owen.'

'The old man too? Is he fit to fight, after all those years lying about and growing soft in the queen's lap?'

Edward nodded. Jasper's father had entered a secret marriage to King Henry's mother following the death of her husband, to the great scandal of parliament. Yet he had lived the last few years in retirement, only visiting court on occasion.

'Let us hope the years have left him feeble and unready.'

The comparison with the late York's strength did not need to be stated.

Edward looked at Hastings afresh. 'You have my gratitude and thanks.'

'It is a time to show where loyalties lie.'

Murmurings behind them caused them to turn. Herbert was on the ground, moving among the men, issuing instructions. Then he paused, lifted his hand through the cold air and pointed in the direction of the sun. Shielding his gaze, Edward followed where he indicated. And something unusual, something spine-tingling and strange caught his eye, something that filled him with a sense of wonder at the world, of heaven and earth, which he could hardly begin to understand. There, on the horizon, the sun's great white orb hung amid the misty clouds, opaque as if seen though water. There was nothing strange in this alone, but around it a sort of shattering of the light had occurred, like glass smashed in pieces, and there appeared two more spheres of glowing brightness, one on each side, making three suns in total, shining in the morning sky.

At first it took Edward's breath away.

Hastings was more vocal. 'By our Lady, what is that?'

The question spread across the ground like fire, the men asking each other what it might mean and whether this was some sort of divine sign. A few began to look afraid. Some crossed themselves. Action was needed at once. This might destroy the men's spirit, or it may be turned to their advantage.

Edward stood up in his stirrups. 'Do not fear! Behold the sign from God! Be of good comfort and dread not, for it is a good sign, a blessing. These three suns are nothing less than the Holy Trinity, symbols of the father, son and Holy Ghost, watching over us and giving us their comfort. So be of good cheer and stand firm, have good heart and in the name of Almighty God we shall defeat our enemies.'

There was a moment of stillness, then the army broke out into cheering.

'That,' said Hastings, raising his eyebrows, 'was inspired.'

*

The men scattered across the road, their faces and arms blooded, eyes wild in terror and pain.

'That's most of our right flank destroyed,' observed Edward with grim determination. 'I will advance and meet Tudor in the middle; Herbert, you wait with the left until you see which way Owen will move, and then engage him as soon as he is in place.'

'Yes, my Lord, God speed you.'

'And you. Come Hastings, and Croft, today we will fight in the name of my father, England's uncrowned king, for the honour of my mother and the memory of my brother. Forward!'

*

Wielding his sword, Edward pushed forward on foot. The waves of Lancastrian men kept on coming, to right and left, but there was fire in his belly, a burning well of justice that needed to be quenched. He slashed his sword through the belly of one and pulled it out coated in blood, then advanced towards another, who turned and fled in fear at the sight of him, before the blade of a third clashed against his steel again. Running the man through, he kicked him to the side and quickly took stock. The sun was overhead now and he had ceased noticing the cold a long time back. He could make out the form of Hastings, who had proved himself to be a skilful swordsman, avoiding blows with lithe movements, but bringing down his weapon with surprising strength. A little beyond him, Alan Croft fought steadily and methodically, as he had promised, advancing the line bit by bit. Across the other side, Owen Tudor's men were moving forward but he could not see Herbert anywhere. In a sudden rush, the left flank of the Lancastrians broke forward and Edward realised that they were planning to move around behind his position and cut them off.

'To the south!' he cried. 'Men to defend the south!'

And then there was another, a tall brute of a man, coming at him with the gleam of easy victory in his eyes, hoping to dispatch the son of York, the heir to England's throne. But Edward was not going to concede his life that readily.

*

Herbert stood and watched as the Lancastrians poured across the field. The archers were in place along the line of the road, snaking unseen behind hedgerows. At his signal, they rose with bow strings drawn, to loosen a swathe of arrows into the sky. Herbert watched them fly and fall, dropping down upon the advancing Lancastrians out of the white clouds, where the three suns had so lately shone. Some fell at once, hit in the chest or the head. Others were felled by wounds to the limbs, littering the ground with groaning bodies, trampled into the winter mud by those following, who could not avoid them. Out of the knot of men, a wave of fighters picked themselves up and urged forward.

'Ready?' Herbert cried, raising his sword. 'For the house of York!'

The swell of men behind him echoed his cry and the ground began to rumble with their feet, before the clash of metal and wood, bone and flesh.

*

Edward watched the last men retreating, scattering back through the trees in the direction they had come.

'The day is ours, Hastings, the day is ours.'

His companion wiped the sweat from his brow. 'Indeed it is, my Lord, ours for the taking, thanks be to God.'

'You fought well, you fought bravely.'

'It was nothing, my Lord, it was necessary.'

Edward lifted his chin. 'It was nothing less. Herbert comes this way!'

The figure hastened towards them, armour stained and dented. They walked to meet him, across ground littered with objects and bodies: an arm twisted out to enclose a fallen helmet, blank eyes stared up to the sky.

'The Tudors have fallen!' cried Herbert from a distance. 'Jasper has fled into the west and we have the old man in custody. Stafford and Tuchet hold the south and Grey has the north secure.'

'Thanks be to God and to you all. I shall not forget this day, there will be rewards for all those who fought loyally at the cross, and the families of those who fell. Let us advance to Hereford and give thanks in the cathedral there. Bring the prisoners and let the surgeons tend to the sick. The rose of York may have been cut down by its enemies, but with the victories of this day, it will live to bloom again.'

*

John Litlington stared at the letter. His hand trembled more than usual as he read the lines written in brown ink, from a brother of the same order in the city of York. Litlington had been Abbot of Croyland for over thirty years, guiding the prayers of the monks in the chapel, the scratching of nibs and brushes in the scriptorium, the tending of the sick

248

in the infirmary, the nurture of herbs in the garden. Now the still stone walls around him were at peace, but his mind was already running on their defences; the bolts they might pull, the keys to be turned in locks, the gates to be closed. Would it be enough?

Brother Walter wrote that the queen's army was on the march south, heading down Ermine Street to London, and hunger and lust, destruction and terror rode with them. Without wages, the men had been given licence to plunder and steal in order to feed themselves, so they were spreading out across the countryside like a plague of locusts, covering a distance of thirty miles or so, leaving little but misery in their wake. Litlington shivered. York to Peterborough was over a hundred miles and the armies would move slower than the messenger, so he estimated there were four or five days before the queen's arrival. The people must be warned: some might take flight into the countryside but he knew others would arm themselves, in an attempt to defend their property. He must begin the prayers; how could the queen allow this? How could God?

*

Warwick faced the north road. There had been enough time to set up defences in advance; lines of cannon to decimate the enemy as they approached, barbed netting strewn across the road and wooden shelters erected for bowmen. He could see the men there now, in the shadows on the verge, shifting their positions expectantly, checking their bows. They were positioned on a ridge of high ground above St Albans, where the land swept up to the sky abruptly, affording a view of a mile or more. His brother John and the Duke of Norfolk were in place and King Henry was being guarded in a tent, in the fields outside the town.

In the market square, where the old Duke of Somerset had met his end, the archers were positioned in upstairs windows, from where they might pick off the invaders in safety. No doubt young Beaufort would be there, intent on getting his revenge. But with the image of his father's head set upon the gates of York, Warwick felt the duke was evenly matched in that quarter. Perhaps it would be today, or tomorrow; perhaps even longer, but soon the Lancastrians would appear, on their march to retake the capital. He had won a victory here six years before; he must do it again.

*

John Owens the butcher stood firm, his broad red hands gripping the handle of the axe. He reckoned he had about two hundred townsmen behind him, men he knew by name and greeted in church, whose wives came to the weekly market, whose children helped gather the stray corn at harvest. They carried whatever they could, ranged around the market cross, while the houses lining the square were hidden behind hasty shutters. Dunstable was not a large town. They had not thought the armies would pass this far west, but the travellers had seen the mass of men on the move and confirmed this morning that they had taken this road.

Stories had reached them, from those in flight. Lincoln, Peterborough and Royston had been decimated, as if barbarians or savages had sailed in from the east. Owens had not dreamed of being a hero or a martyr: he had been building his business for sixteen years and had twice been mayor of the town, a guildsman and soon to be a grandfather. Like all his neighbours, waiting on that sunless afternoon, he would rather be going about his business, or tending to his own fireside.

A shout went up from the road ahead. The men steeled themselves and before long, they saw them. It seemed at first as if the horizon had come to life, teeming with unruly creatures, or swarmed over by a sea of insects. Owens gripped his axe. He knew how to handle a weapon but he could not say that for all his men. As the swell increased and headed towards them, hell bent on plundering the town, he stood firm.

'We will show them that the men of Dunstable are not prepared to be beaten and robbed. We are loyal citizens of the king and we will defend our homes and families against this lawlessness.'

The Lancastrian leaders rode into the square. Owens could not hear their words but the swift waving of hands indicated that orders had been given.

'Stand firm my brothers,' he shouted. 'Stand firm.'

But behind him, they were already slipping away. Quickly they were outnumbered, and as the hungry faces drew closer, in their tens of dozens, weapons were dropped to the cobbles with a clatter. Owens saw the blow coming and raised his axe to parry it. He was unable to stop the swordsman though, who had approached unseen from behind and cut him down with a single movement. The last thing he heard was the sound of men tearing down the shutters of the homes around him.

*

The mist was swirling. Visibility was poor. Warwick's men charged forward across the road, some heading for the field, some for the town. Somehow his scouts had missed the queen's diversion to the west. It meant her army had approached the town in the dead of night, silently moving into range, ready to launch their attack at dawn. He had been taken by surprise, hurrying to rouse the men, but now all depended upon the next hour. And this terrible fog made it impossible to see whether a man was friend or foe, until almost too late. There was nothing to be done about it, except to fight as best he could. He raised his sword and raced forward.

TWENTY-FOUR: The Race for the City

Foot by foot and inch by inch, the mist rolled away; rolled back from the green fields around St Albans, driven out by the sunlight, fading into the hollows. The white veil lifted from the town and details became clearer. The world became patterned again, with branches and knots in wood, chinks in armour and the print of a footstep in the mud. A silence descended and birds on the rooftops thought it was safe to sing again.

On the high point of the ridge, Queen Margaret sat mounted on her horse, trapped in cloth of gold embroidered with the blue fleur-de-lys of France. She held herself tall and proud, feeling the stiffness in her spine, the tension in her shoulders under their swathes of silk and fur. Yet along with her regal posture there was a curve of triumph about her lips and her eyes, those dark, slanting almond eyes that seemed to hold all under their spell, gazed out boldly across the landscape. She took in the arc of every tree, each winding lane and twist of bushes, each wisp of smoke and spread of clouds, falling somewhere between white and blue. But there was more than boldness in them: her face told of victory, of entitlement, of possession.

The day was hers and she knew it. The tide was turning and soon all England would be at her feet. The rebel Earl of Warwick had been sighted fleeing from the scene on horseback, his men scattered and defeated, in spite of all his careful planning. And she had had the satisfaction of riding through the streets into the market square, where the traitor York had once killed her loyal friend Somerset, and seeing the wounded lying there, bleeding through their liveries, pulling themselves onto their knees in hopes of saving their pitiful lives. And then had followed the moment when they had found Henry himself, awaiting her outside his tent: the king of England finally free from his captors again. Such had been his joy to see her, that he had drawn his sword and knighted their son, Prince Edward, the rightful heir to the throne. The world was righting itself again.

On this bright morning that followed, this rebirth of all their hopes, the road to London stretched out before them, snaking its way south through the valley, all the way to Westminster. She breathed in the air. The tang of woodsmoke mixed with the hair and dung of the horses. Such were the moments when decisions were made that might overturn a country.

'My Lady?'

She turned to see Beaufort approaching from the camp, with his usual air of smooth control.

'The women have arrived.'

'So it is true,' she answered breathily. 'The mayor and aldermen of London have sent a deputation of women to negotiate for them.' She paused and her eyes sought the horizon. 'I wonder. Is this an honour or a grave insult?'

'I have shown them into the royal tent. They bring the message that the mayor asks you not to attempt entry into the city. He regrets to inform you that the gates will be locked for the safety of the citizens.'

'Henry?'

He turned back, his sharp features suddenly attentive. 'What is it?'

'Who have they sent?'

'Lady Scales, the Duchess of Buckingham and Lady Rivers.'

'Lady Rivers. Jacquetta?'

Beaufort nodded his dark head.

'I had not thought it would be her. She was once Henry's aunt by marriage, you know that?'

'From her first marriage to the Duke of Bedford.'

'And now the wife of a squire. I think they do mean to insult me.'

Beaufort put his head on one side. He knew her moods, her pride and her passions.

'Don't forget that squire has just fought with us, and lost his son-in-law yesterday for our cause.'

'Is that true? Here, help me.' She held out a hand and Beaufort took it, smiling as she dismounted. 'Then I shall pour her wine with my own hands. Until we are secure in Westminster again, we shall take our friends as we find them.'

'A very wise policy my Lady.'

*

It was London: London was the answer. Edward felt the certainty of it pulsing through his veins as he galloped along the path. London, louring over the Thames with its church steeples and tall narrow houses, from the green sprawl of Moor Fields up to the gardens of the Charterhouse and over to Smith Fields; London, from the tower to the abbey, St Paul's to Cripplegate, where every street trader or leper, every swineherd and tavern owner, every alderman and silversmith could hear the bells tolling and smell the smoke of the many fires in the thousands of hearths: London was the answer. If they could only beat the queen into Westminster, Edward's victory at Mortimer's Cross would overshadow Warwick's tactical withdrawal at St Albans.

Hastings drew alongside him, driving his own horse hard. The wind blew his fair hair and gave his features a pinched look.

'The scout spotted a party ahead,' he shouted.

'Hostile?'

'Some in Neville livery, but it might be a trap.'

'How far?'

'Three or four miles on, where we planned to cross the river.'

*

They saw the men waiting by the bridge, a dozen or so wrapped in cloaks stamping their feet and hugging themselves close against the cold. The little group shifted and exchanged glances as the riders approached, Edward and Hastings flanked by Herbert, Grey and Audley, followed by a retinue of fifty.

Edward came to a halt a little way off and raised his hand. 'Wait here,' he declared. 'We know the queen's ways.'

But one of the group had broken free and was striding down the lane towards them. Edward's hand hovered above his sword, but then the figure drew back its hood to reveal a square head covered with dark curls.

'Warwick!' Edward dismounted rapidly. 'It's Warwick. All is well.'

He hurried to embrace the sturdy figure of the earl, drawing him so tight that the man winced.

'A shoulder wound, a few bruises,' he explained.

'Tell me how it went.'

'We met them at St Albans. I prepared the ground well, but at the last moment they veered off the road and approached from the west. We held our ground until dusk, but the men were demoralised and outnumbered, so I made the decision to withdraw.'

Edward nodded. 'You did right to leave. There was no point staying and sacrificing all your lives.'

'We heard about Mortimer's Cross, about the sign in the sky.'

'Indeed, a sign of approval from heaven.'

'And of the death of Owen Tudor.'

Edward breathed deeply, recalling the old man on his knees, the white head bent and the blood spilt on the mossy stones as cathedral bells tolled.

'He survived the battle and was taken prisoner. I was lenient where circumstances allowed but we took Tudor to Hereford and beheaded him in the marketplace. Since Wakefield, the rules of engagement have changed.'

'Did he make a good death?'

'At the end, but he did not quite believe it was going to happen until the axeman swung.'

Warwick spoke softly. 'So it must have been with my father. I heard that Salisbury was taken alive after Wakefield and beheaded in Pontefract castle.'

'Aye, I heard the same. Let them now taste the bitter loss of fathers.'

The earl snapped back to the moment. 'What now?'

'By killing my father they broke the Act of Accord and committed treason.'

'And King Henry has gone back on his word. He reinstated his son as his heir, the day we fled the field.'

Edward looked behind the earl to the group of men, 'The king?'

Warwick shook his head. 'It was not possible. I placed him in a tent outside the town, well guarded, but I could do no more, other than take him into fight with me.'

Edward raised his hand to signal for fresh horses, 'The loss of the king is a blow but what matters is what we do now. By the act signed in October, and by my victory in the west, I am the lawful king of England. We must ride to Westminster and make the council enforce the terms of the act.'

'They must indeed. The council themselves were responsible for setting those terms; they cannot ignore them now.'

'Come, we will ride ahead of the army and be in London by nightfall.'

'Only pray that the queen takes her time.'

'She can no longer be queen by virtue of her actions. If I am England's new king, she is merely the daughter of the Duke of Anjou, the wife of Henry Plantagenet. I will force her to accept it.'

'Then all speed,' added Hastings, drawing alongside. 'All speed to London, the day draws on.'

And the horses kicked up the dust into a cloud which did not settle until they had crossed the river.

*

The priest hesitated outside the closed door. The entire house was dark and quiet: anyone might think that Baynard's Castle had been uninhabited this past month, with its hearths cold and its kitchens so still. Within those walls, so elegantly and powerfully built, it seemed as if a permanent night had fallen. Life, such as it was, had retreated to a corner of the chapel, behind lock and key, with only communion bread and wine for sustenance. And yet, although he felt deep sympathy with the poor lady for her loss, it was his job to coax the bereaved back to the world, in order that they might continue to go about God's work.

Reluctantly, he raised his hand and knocked upon the wood.

The sound echoed hollowly within but, soon, there was the scrape of a wooden chair across the floor, followed by footsteps.

The door opened a crack. From inside, the breath of incense and sorrow escaped like a blast from a tomb. A figure in black slipped into the space made by the opening, a creature from a hinterland between this world and the next. It had been the same yesterday, and the day before that.

'Might the duchess admit me today?

Margaret pushed back her hood, her dark eyes lined and heavy, looking much older than her fourteen years. 'Not today, Friar Jerome. She is prostrate again. I fear I will never reach her.'

'Does she sleep? Eat?'

'A little of both, she takes some broth but she is waking for all the observances of the night.'

'And yourself? It is hard on you.'

'I am...' her voice faltered.

'You are a young woman, with your life ahead of you, soon to be a wife. You must take care of your health.'

'I will, Friar, thank you.'

'Is there any word from the little boys, masters George and Richard, from Burgundy?'

'We only know that they are safe and that is a blessing. But the duchess takes their absence hard.'

'I will offer my prayers for you all, and for the souls of the duke and the Earls of Rutland and Salisbury. Tomorrow I will bring a poultice that might ease her suffering. Perhaps she will be persuaded to admit me.'

'I will try my best, thank you for coming.'

As Margaret stepped back, the friar caught a brief glimpse of a woman on her knees before an altar, draped in black, her hands clasped in prayer. He had been in service to Duchess Cecily long enough to recognise her form, but also to see that she was much changed by tragedy, in a way that would never leave her. And who could blame her, with the loss of her husband and son in such terrible circumstances and the two little boys sent across the sea for their own safety.

The door clicked shut and Friar Jerome shuffled off down the corridor back into the quiet of the house. His feet padded softly across the rushes of the great hall and past the cold hearth where the family had used to feast together in the past. Pausing, he looked at the two carved chairs, empty under the canopy, where the duke and duchess used to sit, their children ranged on each side, laughing and feasting, or bowing their heads in thanks. The arms and achievements of the house of York were hung about the walls, to the east and west, and seemed to look down upon the friar now in reproach. He told them silently there was nothing more he could do. Perhaps he might find a meal in the kitchen, where the cooks and servants sat idly, from among the cold meats and winter preserves. Surely the fires must have been lit to bake bread this morning, if only to provide for the communion table?

But there was all of a sudden such a stirring in the house, such a clattering in the courtyard outside that it seemed as if the world was being rearranged. The friar stood rooted to the spot. In the last few days he had overheard people's fears in the London streets, swapped in the marketplace or outside the church porch; women who pulled their children closer, or dared not take their washing down to the stream. Stories of the queen's army had been read aloud at St Paul's Cross and ran rife along Thames Street, down to the merchants arriving at the docks, wondering whether it was safe to unload their cargoes. This noise could only mean the army had arrived, hell bent upon rape and destruction. He looked wildly about for a weapon, his heart beating fast in his chest. They would have to climb over his dead body in order to reach the women. At least he might buy them some time.

But time was not on his side. The double doors that linked the great chamber to the courtyard burst open, letting in the daylight. Jerome gasped and turned, to find that this was no marauding mob. Instead, the space was filled by Edward, Earl of March, striding into the hall as he had done during his father's time, except that now he was master of all.

Jerome dropped at once to one knee.

'My Lord! Thank God...'

'Where is my mother?'

'In the chapel, my Lord.'

He scurried behind as Edward strode across the open space and down the corridor. Pulling off his glove, the earl rapped once upon the door, turned the handle himself and entered the darkness. Jerome reached the door in time to see him raising Duchess Cecily up from the floor and holding her in his arms.

*

St John's Fields lay outside the city walls, at Clerkenwell, overlooked by the church. It was a cool morning but the turnout was good. Men came in pairs, or groups, bringing their friends and kin, or their associates. There was a particularly strong presence from the guilds and their apprentices, some still dressed in stained aprons, waiting with expectant faces to witness the city poised on a cliff of change. Warwick recognised a number of his retainers, of men in Neville and Yorkist livery, along with those summoned by Bourchier, Hastings and those who had served in Salisbury's London household. He turned to look down towards the city, a jumble of roofs emitting smoke, spires jutting up to the heavens. Still they kept coming, in defiance of the old king, the French queen and her favourites, in remembrance of kindnesses done by York and his family, or in defence against their worst fears. The queen might have done the unthinkable and turned her troops north again, back to York, but Warwick would not tell the citizens just yet.

He leaped up onto the back of a cart, Fauconberg and George Neville steady at his feet.

'Good men of London, I bid you welcome. You know right well the cause of the fear within our city at this time. There have been outbreaks of lawlessness in the country and we have heard the stories of destruction caused by the queen's army so the mayor saw fit to close the city gates against the queen and send a party to her asking her not to attempt entry.'

There was murmuring among the crowd.

'Well, I can tell you now that a saviour has come forward to protect the city from harm: a man who loves this city as his home, who would defend it to the death and has the power and might to ensure each and every one of you will sleep soundly in your beds this night and every night after.'

He scanned the men with his eyes. 'Moreover, this man is nothing less than the rightful king of this land. By assent, the Lords of Parliament swore an oath and passed an act, that the Duke of York be named as the rightful heir of Henry VI, on account of his lawful descent from a senior line of Edward III. From that moment, it was an act of treason to harm the duke or his bloodline, the Earl of March and Duke of Rutland. And yet, just weeks later this bloodthirsty queen pitifully slew the duke in the middle of a truce when he was celebrating the Christmas season.'

He paused to let this sink in.

'Thus the queen has committed an act of treason. As if that was not enough, the king, who put his signature to the act, has gone back on his word and reinstated his own son as his heir. A son whom many at court whisper was not conceived in wedlock, after eight years of unfruitful marriage, and most unlikely to be of the royal blood, but instead a bastard sired by a bastard, borne by a woman of France.'

George shot him up a glance as if to warn his brother not to go too far.

'And on these terms, can we truly say that King Henry is fit to rule this city and this land? What do you say to that?'

Those primed in the front row raised up their voices first, and the rest were swift to join in: 'Nay, nay, nay!'

'But instead, the rightful king is a young, strong man of honour, of royal and legitimate birth, elected by the lords of our land. A man who has won a great victory in defence of his father's memory, a man of generosity, charity and forgiveness. Will you consent to be ruled by Edward, Earl of March? Will you accept him as your king, as Edward IV?'

The cheer went up at once, 'Aye, aye.'

Warwick smiled in satisfaction and stared above their heads in the direction of Baynard's Castle.

*

Baynard's had come to life again. A great fire burned in the hearth, the hall had been freshly swept and cleared and the kitchen fires were baking again. Under the canopy, in the old duke's carved chair, sat Edward, Earl of March, resplendent in a pleated doublet of gold and yellow satin, hung with jewels, over a fur-trimmed tunic, every inch befitting a king; to his side sat Cecily, still dressed in deep mourning, her pale face covered by a thick grey veil. Around her neck she wore a heavy silver cross, given to her once by Edmund, and her hand held that of her youngest daughter, Margaret. Two other young women stood behind her chair. Her two elder daughters had travelled to be by their mother's side: Anne, the unhappy wife of the traitorous Duke of Exeter, who had brought her own small, wide-eyed daughter, and Elizabeth, Duchess of Suffolk, almost seventeen, and wife to John, who waited loyally at her side. It seemed that an age had passed since Cecily and York had celebrated their wedding, walking from the church with their arms full of spring blossoms.

Around the table was a crowd, summoned in haste, watching in expectation. They were men who had proved their loyalty in recent weeks; at Mortimer's Cross, or St Alban's, or who had flocked to Edward's side on hearing of his return to London. William, Lord Hastings, John, Duke of Norfolk, George Neville, William, Lord Fauconberg and others. Most of the council had been summoned, barring those who had openly backed the queen. They spoke in low tones, heads bowed to hear one another, eyes downcast unless they were seeking out the doorways and corridors, hoping to hear the approach of feet. Some still bore their wounds, bound about in cloth strips, inflicted by Lancastrian weapons, scarring over older marks received in the service of the Yorks.

Cecily's ears appeared to be sharpest. The men were approaching along Thames Street, and had not even reached the house gates before she had turned her head to listen. Sensitive to her movements, Edward followed, his straight nose and chiselled jaw turned towards the doors, as the clatter of hooves on the courtyard cobbles could plainly be heard. He raised one hand and the hall fell silent.

They all knew what was coming. It was a mere formality, but an essential one. Edward rose from his seat and stood squarely, feet apart, the jewels on his clothes catching the light.

Then there was a great knocking upon the wooden doors, echoing all around the hall, up to the rafters. The servants had been under instructions to wait, but now, upon Edward's signal, they drew back the bolts and let in the daylight. All turned to see who was standing there. The Earl of Warwick, backed by a guard that filled the courtyard outside, strode over the threshold, followed by Archbishop Bourchier.

Warwick took the centre of the room, circling with arms spread, seeking out each man for dramatic effect. 'I call upon Edward, Earl of March.'

Edward stepped forward. 'I am here.'

'Edward, Earl of March, heir of the late Richard Plantagenet, Duke of York, descendent of Edward III and heir to Henry VI by the terms of the Act of Accord, sworn in parliament this October last. It has been put to the council that Henry Plantagenet, known as Henry VI, has refuted his agreement to protect your life and those of your kin, but instead has taken arms against you, forcing you to defend yourself and resulting in loss of life and at grievous cost to this realm.'

The hall buzzed with voices.

'And thus,' Warwick continued, waiting until they had fallen quiet. 'And thus, it is my duty to inform you that according to this same act, and by your descent from the senior line of Edward III, the right to rule this country passes to you, and to your heirs. The former king, known as Henry VI, has failed in his sworn duty to his people, who now implore you to accept the throne and rule England on his behalf.'

Warwick dropped to bended knee.

'Will you do this country the great service of accepting the throne? Will you rule us all as Edward IV?'

There was a long pause. All eyes were turned upon Edward. He took a deep breath and looked about the hall, at the men assembled, at his mother and sisters, at the arms of his father over the fireplace, recalling the image of York seated before the flames, or Edmund waiting upon the stairs.

'I accept. I am the true king of England, just as my father would have been, had his life been spared. I will do my best to rule justly, to defend this realm and the people in it against enemies from afar and those within.'

'God save King Edward IV,' cried Warwick.

The words echoed through the hall as the assembly fell to their knees in honour of England's new king.

'God save the king! Long live King Edward IV.'

TWENTY-FIVE: The Last Battle, March, 1461

By dawn, the Yorkshire hills were covered in snow. The driving sleet continued to fall in needles and, even though the sun had risen, its light was so faint it seemed to be shining from under water. Between the villages of Towton and Saxton, the wind was howling through the valley, where the white waters of the river encroached upon the banks and trees bowed before the wrath of the storm. The whole earth seemed to recoil against the onslaught of the heavens. It was a day for settling scores.

This was no routine Palm Sunday. Cecily and her daughters would be on their knees in prayer, in the flickering light of the chapel, miles away in London. Friar Jerome would lean forward with the silver chalice, engraved with the arms of the house of York and let each of them in turn take a sip of the communion wine. In their name, the Yorkist army had battled their way north, planting their feet along rutted roads, through the foul-smelling mud of tracks turned into streams and between the ridge and furrow of many an Englishman's field.

Edward felt that familiar sensation of anticipation; the thrill that gripped him before any battle, the pumping of blood in his veins, the jumping in his chest which was almost enough to keep him warm in spite of this wind. They were less than a day's ride from Wakefield, less than a heartbeat away from Sandal Castle, where the blood of his father and brother had stained the ground, and he felt it keenly. They were waiting across the other side of the plateau, in the shelter of the woods: Henry Beaufort, with his dark silhouette and vulpine smile, Sir Andrew Trollope who had gone over to the king at Ludlow and Edward's own treacherous brother-in-law, the despised Earl of Exeter. Somewhere beyond them, the queen and King Henry waited with their son, awaiting the outcome. Two kings in one field. He gripped his sword. Only one of them could survive.

It had begun yesterday. The intention had been to march on York, to reclaim the city so important to his family, to ride with head held high beneath that gate that had been adorned with his family's blood. And yet the bridge before them was broken. At Ferrybridge, while they carried stones and timber to rebuild the crossing, a shower of arrows had fallen out of the sky, felling men to the ground. Amid the confusion, Warwick had pulled an arrow out of his leg and looked up to see the attack being led by the grim-faced Lord Clifford. Word of the ambush spread and Edward, scouting out the terrain a few miles to the east, had leapt upon his horse and sped to the scene. Now, watching the Lancastrians assemble in the distance, he thought in satisfaction of the way Clifford had died, staggering forward with an arrow through his neck, slipping in his own blood before collapsing upon the earth.

'That,' Edward had whispered under his breath, 'was for Edmund.'

Today, they had the better location. The wind was behind them and, as he raised his arm to the line of archers, nothing could shake his conviction of success.

The archers drew back their bows in unison. Edward brought his arm down, slicing through the freezing air. Like one creature, they responded, sending their deadly stream high up above the frozen fields and forward towards their enemies. Edward watched the arrows rise, turn and fall. Their downwards trajectory was, indeed, longer than he had anticipated: the wind took them like autumn leaves and sped them on, driving down into their targets. The distant line of men crumpled.

'Another!' He raised his arm again and let it fall. The second wave seemed to travel even further and they could see men staggering in their death-throes, clasping the wounds where blood poured from their bodies.

'Brace yourselves, they will return fire.'

He could just make out the unity of the Lancastrian archers coming forward to the front line, stepping over their fallen friends. Then, squinting through the clouds, through the arrows of sleet, he could see the tiny driving lines rising and falling. There was no resounding wind, no thud as they embedded themselves in flesh. Edward waited. His men waited. Yet the arrows did not come.

'There!' shouted a man at the front. 'They have fallen short.'

And Edward realised with a rush of joy that with the wind against them, the Lancastrians could never broach the distance with their arrows.

'Again!' he cried. 'At the ready!'

*

Across the snowy void, a forest of fallen arrows, the two armies advanced. They met with a crash, with the swing of swords, metal on metal, and the impact of the war hammer upon a shoulder blade or skull. On both sides, men shattered. They were so close to each other, so close they could hear their breath, see the warmth escaping from other mouths. As close as lovers, or mother and child, bound together in this eternal moment, this rite of passage, this struggle for life. There was no avoiding the contact of eyes, pupil to pupil, or the touch of skin. Bodies jostled against each other, armour clanged, legs kicked out. When an axe cut through an enemy's shoulder, or split his head from ear to ear, there was no escape from the spray of blood and brains, no release from the terrible howls of the dying, of the fear and anger, the despair and disbelief of those in their final moments. Others were already growing cold, trodden down into the mud, where their bodies were stumbled over, or used as a bridge through the worst of the wetness. And amid this desperate fight, Edward swung his sword, hardened against the cries of the dying, teeth ground together in determination. Taller than most, stronger than most, he cut a swathe forward through the fields of flesh and his men followed.

*

But now the Lancastrians were pouring down from the west. Horsemen were emerging from the woods on Castle Hill, sending the Yorkists' left flank into chaos. Fauconberg needed help at once. Calling for a horse, Edward looked round to see Warwick and Hastings behind him; they would have to do the best they could in the middle. Riding around the edge of the action, in and out of the savage sleet, Edward was able to reach the spot where the flank had disintegrated. He leapt down and shouted at the top of his voice, his sword held high.

'Men, gather round me. We face them together. Come back and fight.'

The Lancastrians were dismounting, forced to rely on their own two feet given the treacherous conditions of the terrain. Men in partial armour were sliding on ice and crashing down.

'Seize the moment! Stand together!' Edward cried, bringing his sword down upon the skull of one, then slicing away to the right, to fell a second with a blow to the back.

Around him, the fleeing men began to stop. Tired, frozen and wounded, they watched in awe the young giant of a man, who fought like Hercules, as if he did not even feel the wind.

Then there were three Lancastrian lords bearing down on him, intent upon cutting him down as they had his father. Edward recognised the arms of Sir Andrew Trollope, newly knighted for his bravery at St Albans, for his treachery at Ludlow, and for planning the ambush at Sandal Castle. The story went that he had led the attack on York in person. A fresh kind of fury descended upon Edward. He hurled himself at the man, trusting to his ferocity and determination, in spite of the soldiers at his side. But yet, he found that he was not fighting alone. Fauconberg's men had rallied and were closing in on each side. Repelling Edward's blade, Trollope caught him off balance and pushed him aside with a swift kick. He was just raising his axe to bring it down upon Edward's skull but the younger man was swifter, drawing his dagger and thrusting it up between the traitor's ribs. Trollope's eyes registered the blow. His arms dropped. A wave of fresh red blood ebbed from his mouth. A second blow straight to the neck brought him down. There was no time to reflect; another Lancastrian blade was aimed at Edward's side. He parried the clumsy blow and dispatched the man with his sword. As he fell forward, his helmet came loose with the force of the blow. A head of dark hair was pressed into the mud, face stained with blood and sweat. By the time Edward recognised Rick Croft, the man was already dead.

*

There was movement on the further side of the field. Over to the east, where the London road passed behind a ridge, Edward saw a sudden flood of men, silhouetted against the sky. They had been fighting almost three hours. The men were tired, their limbs frozen and they were in danger of reaching a stalemate; they might not be able to repel a fresh supply of the queen's troops. He shaded his eyes. The sleet had given way to snow but it was no less difficult to see.

'Fresh troops!' Hastings appeared at his side, his visor up to reveal the small, intelligent eyes.

Edward swung round. 'How goes it with you?'

Hastings nodded, dismissing concerns about himself. 'The Duke of Norfolk has arrived. He is putting Beaufort's flank to flight. They are shedding their armour in their desperation to retreat.'

'Is it really so? Thanks be to God!'

'He will pursue them through the valley. Some are trying to escape across the river.'

'Come, let's bring this flank round and cut them off in the west. I will have Beaufort's blood and drive Henry Plantagenet out of England!'

A terrible sight met them on the banks of the river. The woods and the valley had hemmed in the retreating Lancastrians and the steep slopes were slippery with a mixture of entrails, brains and mud. Conditions were treacherous, as those escaping quickly found, losing their footing and climbing pitifully over the bodies of others who cried out for help as their bones splintered and shattered under desperate feet. The waters were full of men, some alive and some dead, piled up against each other as they lost control in the current. Heads, limbs, backs, feet, all bobbed like corks on the surface, but the volume of bodies was too great, as men in their dozens slid down the bank, unable to halt their descent. At the crossing place, the river was dammed with them, the living trampling the dead in an attempt to float, or to cross to the far shore, the weight of the others dragging them down until their screaming lips were filled with flowing water. Around them, the currents and eddies ran red with blood.

It turned even Edward's stomach, watching them pooling together like pitiful insects.

'They are also fleeing to the north,' said Norfolk, appearing at Edward's shoulder. 'My men are still fresh. I will pursue them as far as York, if need be.'

'Thank you for your timely arrival. Your loyalty will not be forgotten.'

Norfolk nodded. 'My Lord.'

'Pay close attention to Beaufort. See where he rides. He may lead us to Henry Plantagenet and his wife. If you find them, do them no harm, but bring them south.'

'They shall be brought south, carried in chains through the streets for all to see.'

'And I will found a chapel here to say masses for the souls of the dead. Clifford was killed yesterday and Trollope lies on the field. There will be more. I hope we shall find Exeter rotting in the mud.'

'Amen to that.'

'And then to London. Following this day, here at Towton, there is only one king of England. I have a coronation to plan.'

*

Cecily stood in the gallery and looked out across the lawn. Deer grazed in the distance, and the silver line of the Thames cut between the fields.

She had seen the boat approaching and now it was drawing towards the landing steps.

The Palace of Placentia lay to the east of London, its quiet green park spreading away on all sides, rising up to a hill with a view over the little village of Greenwich. Not so long ago, these rooms had been refurbished by Queen Margaret, and her motif of the daisy, or marguerite, was carved into the woodwork and painted on the walls in yellow and white. Cecily felt the presence of the other woman, imagined her here during her husband's illness, dancing in these rooms, or sitting quietly with her ladies, sewing or reading. Perhaps this chamber was the one in which she slept, or rocked her infant son. Now the former royal family had fled into exile in Scotland, miles away from their old home.

As she watched, the barge drew closer, servants at the quayside waiting to help those on board disembark. It must be them. The fluttering arose in her chest again. She couldn't move as quickly as she used to; since the terrible news, her body had been slow to respond, as if the tragedy had suffused her bones. Yet nothing would stop her now from hastening outside as quickly as she could, to bring the meeting closer, if only by a few moments.

'Margaret?'

Her daughter appeared in the doorway, her thumb in a book to hold her place.

'They're here. Your brothers have returned.'

'George and Richard?'

'They are safe. Look.'

She pointed out the boat.

Mother and daughter exchanged a glance and, at once, they headed out of the room together, through the next chamber and down the corridor to the outer door. Their way lay through the queen's gardens, planted with the red roses and rambling blooms Margaret had favoured, the gillyflowers and lilies that were the symbols of her heritage. Through the clouds of colour, the painted rails and herb patches, Cecily and her daughter hurried. They passed through the archway in the red brick wall and onto the river walk, a railed path leading down to the Thames. Already Cecily could see the two precious small forms, who had climbed safely out onto the land, their legs shaky from so long at sea. It seemed that they had also spotted the two figures approaching; the tall, stately mother, gaunt in her grief, and the young girl with the determined cast to her face, both dressed in deepest mourning.

The boys started to run. The distance between them was not so great. George reached his mother first and flung himself into her open arms. In the intervening months, he had grown taller and broader, his sandy hair longer and his eyes had something of the cast of Edward's at that age.

'Mother, mother, we're home, we're safe at last. We sailed in a huge boat, there was a storm! Is Edward really king? Is it all over at last? Are we to stay here at Greenwich?'

'So many questions!' Cecily breathed, kissing the top of his head.

Eight-year-old Richard was soon upon them, trying to push between his mother and brother. He was more subdued, the enormity of the moment capsizing any words that might have been welling in his chest. Instead he buried his dark head in Cecily's lap and looked up at her with eyes that spoke of sensitivity, of passion and understanding beyond his years, with the same touch of melancholy that had characterised Edmund's. His mother swallowed the lump that had risen in her throat and bent down to kiss him.

'Now, my darlings, come inside. This is our new home. You must tell me all about your adventures.'

*

The sun blazed down over London out of a vivid blue sky. Through the maze of streets there was a blur of activity and colour, a blur moving as if was the lifeblood of the city's veins, snaking its way among the buildings, a blur that hummed with voices like so many bees at work in high summer. Then, above it all, louder than the mayor shouting orders or the choir singing, came the drone of trumpets. The rapport was picked up at every station and repeated, so that it ran like an echo, rippling out to every corner of the walls. The very bricks vibrated with excitement to hear those first warning notes, for the king was coming.

A procession rode out through the gates of the tower. First, there appeared the knights of the garter, dressed in their robes of midnight blue touched on the shoulder with a froth of white lace: the newly knighted Hastings and Norfolk, followed by the king's brothers, George and Richard, now made the Dukes of Clarence and Gloucester respectively, then Warwick and George Neville, Fauconberg and Herbert, all those who had stood loyally shoulder to shoulder with the house of York. As they emerged into Tower Street, the bells of All Hallows' and St Dunstan's began to peal and people lining the streets, ten deep under the streaming banners, raised their voices to cheer. After them came the figure they had assembled to see: King Edward IV, seated high in the saddle, his horse trapped in gold and tawny silk, with emeralds and diamonds at his throat and sparkling on his doublet. He held himself straight and tall, his hazel eyes fixed ahead, his profile clean and sharp with its straight nose and generous lips, the aristocratic nostrils and well-moulded chin. A ripple of crimson and ermine hung from his shoulders, draping down his back and lying across his saddle. On top of his sandy curls was fixed a gold coronet set with a single ruby, the size of a child's fist.

At St Andrew's Church, the procession turned down St Botolph's and into the wide space of Thames Street. Colourful banners, silks and carpets hung from the windows and ribbons were strewn high across the route, billowing up and down as the breeze caught them. Those flowers left over from adorning the doorways were strewn across the street to be crushed under the feet of the approaching horses. As the train moved forward, the people called to Edward by name and, in spite of himself, his face split into a brief smile. They passed by St Magnus and the entrance to London Bridge, through Bridge Ward and the Old Swan Inn, into Candlewick Ward, where the bells of All Hallows the Great threatened to deafen the singers below it. Then they were into Dowgate Ward, where Warwick's house 'The Erber' stood, and on to St Martin's Vintry and St James, Garlickhythe. Edward knew it was coming. He had not returned to the Salucci house on the corner of Trinitie Lane since he had learned of Alasia's death, haunted as it was with the memories of their stolen happiness.

As the procession approached, he could see it was much changed, freshly painted, with new shutters and a wooden sign hanging over the door, depicting a bulbous flask of liquid. A family stood in the doorway, a woman with a child in her arms and a man wearing the robe of an apothecary. Edward glanced up to the window of the room where Alasia had used to sleep, perhaps even the room where she had delivered their child, where Edward himself had once stood at the window, or crept into the darkened room and surprised her. The memory of her sleeping returned to him, her hands folded under her chin and her long dark hair loose over the pillow. It gripped his heart but he fixed his eyes ahead and rode on. Soon they would pass Baynard's Castle, Blackfriars and cross the Fleet, then it was on towards Westminster.

*

They were gathered in the abbey, where the gold hangings reached the floor. Some of the faces he had known since childhood, others had served in one of the Yorks' houses or were allies of the Nevilles or Howards, servants of Salisbury at Middleham or those who had been pardoned for their offences and sworn an oath of loyalty. A few had been known to the family since the early days, from Cecily's childhood, or those who had rocked Edward's cradle in Rouen. There was the white head of his old tutor, Peter, his eyes red and raw as he watched the young man approach. There was the Ludlow stable hand, the baker and the physician who had cured his childhood illness and the Fotheringhay cook and the wet nurse. Familiar faces were turned towards him as he walked the length of the aisle, resplendent in his robes. Halfway along he recognised the smooth head of Earl Rivers, beside his wife Jacquetta, whose silver-threaded veil caught the light. Edward recalled the moment in Calais last year, when he, Salisbury and Warwick had berated the upstarts and held them prisoner. It had been no surprise for him to learn that Rivers and his son Anthony had fought on the side of the Lancastrians at Towton. Only his royal pardon had saved them, accounting for their presence now, dazzling in the jewels brought from Jacquetta's former existence. And with them, their serene daughter Elizabeth, her lidded eyes cast down, her beauty concealed by the widow's veil she had adopted since the death of her husband at St Albans. The pardon was enough. Edward did not feel the need to acknowledge them, but kept on walking, his head held high.

Towards the altar his eyes found his mother and sisters. Cecily had drawn back her veil and the pale contours of her face in the gloom made her seem much older. But in her expression he understood everything: this was her moment, her rightful moment as the Duchess of York, descended through the line of John of Gaunt, the wife of the heir to the throne. It should have been her and York walking towards the altar now, robed in gold, ready to be anointed and crowned, had there been any justice. Briefly, the throne had been held before her, a dazzling opportunity that would have seen her become England's queen: nothing less than queen by rights. But it had passed, in bloodshed and tears. This was the next best thing, watching her son's coronation.

And what a coronation: such a day would be remembered for decades to come. England had not witnessed the crowning of a king in over thirty years and the abbey's nave, with its gothic pillars soaring away into the skies, was hung with scarlet and cloth of gold. Thousands of candles and tapers burned bright and the air filled with song and incense, crackling with anticipation. And the new king was celebrated in ballads and songs, in imagery painted on parchment rolls, likening him to Moses and Joshua, who led their people to victory, his roots spiralling back to Adam and Eve, with roses and heraldic shields and hands of God, as he sat astride the creation of the world, mounted in armour, with plumes on his horse's brow. And the poets wrote his name in gold, and called on the astrologers and astronomers to seat him in the tree of knowledge, at the centre of the earth, at King Arthur's right hand. People in the streets spoke of his victories at Northampton and Mortimer's Cross, of the omen of the three suns in the February sky and the slaughter of Towton, where the fields ran red with blood. As he walked towards the altar, he was overlooked by the tombs of dead kings and the shrines of Edward the Confessor and other saints. Each seemed to be urging him forward through the ancient stones, wishing him well, with encouragement and words of warning, to take his place in history.

Thomas Bourchier was waiting in front of the coronation chair. Fashioned from oak, lathered in gilt, it was carved with animals and birds, with curling foliate shapes and painted with the figure of Edward I, resting his feet upon a lion. But to Edward, all these details blurred into one, in a haze of red and gold, with the waving of hands and the bowing of heads, as the archbishop spoke the coronation oath. The words seemed to pass quickly and wash over him.

'All this I promise to do,' he heard himself say. 'All this I promise and more, in the name of God, Amen.'

Gentle hands removed his cloak. He was guided to the gilded seat and turned, facing the crowd, as he took his place. The weight of thousands of eyes did not oppress him. Bourchier moved slowly, stilled by the momentous occasion, to anoint him with oil upon the head, heart and hand. Then came Lord Hastings, to present him with the spurs of chivalry, the bishops to offer him the sword of state, Norfolk to hand him the orb, Herbert with the sceptre and his own young brother George to slip the gold ring upon his finger, to signify his marriage to the state. Behind him, Bourchier was holding up St Edward's crown, studded with its heavy jewels.

His hands full of all these riches, his throat choked with tears, Edward could not speak. In this holy place, he felt the press of the past, present and the future; of the boy he had been at Ludlow, impatient for the days to pass, of running through the long grass with Edmund, of riding into London with his father, of holding Alasia in his arms. And now, the sad and solemn faces of his mother and sisters, of this expectant crowd and the bodies of the recent dead eaten by worms under the Yorkshire soil. And the future, stretching before him like a mist, where no doubt he would be put to the test as a son of York, as the first Yorkist king of England.

But the abbey bells were ringing and the trumpeters were sounding a fanfare up to the rafters. And the people had risen to their feet, crying, *'Long live the king, long live King Edward IV.'*